Last Rights

Days of Drums

GATEKEEPER

GATEKEEPER

PHILIP SHELBY

SIMON & SCHUSTER

SIMON & SCHUSTER
Rockefeller Center
1230 Avenue of the Americas
New York, NY 10020

SIMON & SCHUSTER and colophon
are registered trademarks of Simon & Schuster Inc.

DESIGNED BY BARBARA M. BACHMAN

Manufactured in the United States of America
1 3 5 7 9 10 8 6 4 2

Library of Congress Cataloging-in-Publication Data
Shelby, Philip
Gatekeeper / Philip Shelby
p.   cm.
I. Title.
PS3569.H39258G38   1998   97-39934
813'.54—dc21   CIP

ISBN 0-684-84260-2

ACKNOWLEDGMENT

The author wishes to thank Regional Security Officer Jeff Pursell (Los Angeles) for his expertise and assistance.

Any deviation from strict procedure is wholly the author's responsibility.

It should also be noted that, regarding the United States Embassy in Paris, certain details, along with surrounding landmarks, have been slightly altered for security reasons.

Philip Shelby

THIS BOOK IS FOR MY WIFE,

Daphne,

WHOSE HEART IS

THE LIGHT OF MY LIFE.

LOVE ALWAYS,

P.

PROLOGUE

MAY • THE HOUSE was built from the land: river rock, black slate, western red cedar. Its angled planes and linear facades suggested a hunting lodge, yet up close the entire structure seemed to dissolve into the landscape. The knoll on which it stood was surrounded by towering firs that shielded it from view from the air. The windows had been treated to eliminate glare.

All the principal rooms had a direct line of sight onto the private dirt road that dead-ended at the driveway leading up to the house. The two-and-a-half-mile road, deliberately left rutted, and near impassable after first snowfall, connected to a two-lane county blacktop. The blacktop meandered around the shores of Coeur d'Alene Lake for three miles before reaching the town of the same name.

The host was standing on the deck, which ran the length of the house. He was in his sixties, short, barrel chested, favoring the wide stance of a mariner on a schooner's bridge. His hands were large and callused, like those of a fisherman who still used the nets. His tanned, deeply lined face had a two-day growth of whiskers, and his blue eyes, set in crinkly pouches of weathered skin, rounded out the nautical image. In point of fact, the host had an aversion to the ocean, although he had swum and canoed in Coeur d'Alene Lake so often that he could chart its shoreline from memory.

Feeling the wind stir the trees, the host raised the zipper of his down vest, beneath which he wore a red flannel shirt, the fabric tight over his forearms and biceps; below that, coarse, faded jeans and old but carefully tended hiking boots. The host knew that down at the lake, in the full brilliance of the sun, the temperature was ten degrees warmer; here in the north Idaho woods, the remnants of a cold, wet spring lingered into the first days of May.

The host could see for a half mile down the road. No sign of the vehicle yet, but he knew it was coming. There . . . a curl of dust rising above the tree line.

Over the years the host had had many visitors. All but a few were lifelong friends who shared his passion for fishing and hunting, or who came to enjoy the quiet and solitude. The exceptions were different. The one coming now was different.

Like the others, he had been instructed to fly into Spokane International Airport, forty miles away in Washington State. Better the hour's drive from there to Coeur d'Alene than to land at the town's airport, where private aircraft attracted unwanted attention.

Like the others, he was making his way without his retinue. Coming alone was the host's nonnegotiable rule. It assured privacy and gave credence to the visitor's ostensible reason for being here: a weekend of peace and quiet, perhaps an overnight horseback ride into the mountains. The breathtaking natural beauty of the area and its exclusive resort was a lure to wealthy sportsmen, who fished the lake and played golf on the spectacular waterfront course. Its name, associated with rough-hewn luxury, never aroused suspicion.

The host saw a flash of blue between the trees. Then a Jeep Cherokee came around the bend. The driver was going too fast, catching every pothole, the fat tires throwing up gouts of mud.

They're always in such a hurry.

The host knew all there was to know about his visitor, about the questions that were streaming through his mind—the where and when and, most of all, how. Because like all others who had come before him, this visitor was carrying a problem that had defied solution. The host knew how galling it was for such men to have their vast resources and influence stymied. He could chart the inevitable downward spiral of their emotions, from indignation to anger to rage. He knew how spent and desperate they were when at last they made their pilgrimage to Coeur d'Alene.

The Cherokee turned up the driveway, growling in low gear. The host watched it rock to a stop in front of his house. The door opened, and a pair of shoes stepped onto the muddy gravel drive. City shoes. The visitor must have driven directly from Spokane Airport without bothering to stop at the Coeur d'Alene resort to register and change.

The host stepped into the living room. From a crystal decanter on the heavy pine sideboard he poured two snifters of his private, very old reserve cognac. At the foot of the staircase a door opened, closed. Leather soles brushed against the stiff bristles of the doormat, then slapped softly up the peg-and-groove stairs. The visitor reached the landing and looked around. His uncertainty dissolved into a tentative smile when he saw the host, his arm outstretched, fingers cradling a snifter.

CITY SHOES. CITY CLOTHES. CITY MAN.

Three thousand dollars' worth of tailor-chalked, hand-sewn Dunhill ultralight wool. Charvet shirt. Sulka tie. Cologne blended by Armitrage of Jermyn Street. Sixty-two years old, tall, patrician, with the blood pressure and muscle tone of a man twenty years younger.

He sat in an ancient club chair in front of the stone fireplace, one long leg draped over the other, the pant crease perfect. The balloon snifter was cupped in his palm, the glass stained henna where the cognac had slid toward his lips. The long draft seemed to have steadied him.

"I've been expecting you," the host said.

The visitor frowned. "Yes. The arrangements were made a while back—"

"I don't mean today, now. Just in general."

"Really?"

The host shrugged. "The election's six months away. You've been trailing the president by a consistent seven percent in the polls." He paused. "Some people are beginning to think they chose the wrong candidate at the convention. When that kind of feeling spreads, campaign contributions start to dry up. No one invests in a lame duck."

The host laid this out in a matter-of-fact tone, implying no judgment for or against the man. Still, he was not surprised to see color rise to the visitor's cheeks.

The visitor rotated his wrist lightly, swirling the cognac in the balloon, staring into it like a Gypsy seeking to divine the future in the whorls of tea leaves.

"I've spent forty years working for this," he said. "The party *owes* me."

"But can you collect?"

"I'm trying." Both men knew that this was the first time in four attempts that he'd won the nomination. "No one's going to give me another shot. Either I go all the way to the White House or I'm history."

True enough, the host thought. His visitor had been a distinguished presence on the political landscape for more than forty years, as a representative, a governor, and finally as a long-standing senior senator. Divorced once, many years ago, he was now married to a Washington insider whose name was a staple in the media. With all that coverage there hadn't been even a hint that the senator ever stepped out on his wife. Quite the contrary—in public they made a loving, supportive couple, as they had for twenty-two years.

Nor did he abuse the power and perquisites of his office. Certainly he was conscientious enough to ship substantial amounts of pork back to his home state, and he accepted enough special interest money to keep his electoral war chest topped off. But he had a nose for the treacherous and the corrupt who could bring him down and sidestepped them even when it cost him money or votes or both.

What set him apart, the host mused, was not only his dress, speech, and bearing, but the way he wore his life. Decently.

Which was a lot more than could be said for the scandal-plagued, morally bankrupt incumbent, whose legal and ethical problems had created a leadership vacuum. The country could not afford much more of him. It wasn't just the anemic stock market, or the disastrous flip-flops on foreign policy. It was the malaise that was eating into the nation's fabric like dry rot.

The host considered himself a patriot. As such, it was his duty to come to the assistance of his country. Which was why the visitor had been allowed to come here. He never suspected it, but he and the host had a confluence of interests.

"So . . . Can you get me the seven points—maybe a few more?"

The words sounded lighthearted but beneath them the host heard the trilling of nerves.

"The price is ten million."

To his credit, the visitor laughed. "You really were expecting me. You've got this all figured out."

"You wouldn't be here otherwise."

"Price isn't the issue. It's what I get for my money."

"You get exactly what you want. But here's the thing: You have to know, right now, how badly you want this. Because if I go ahead, there will be no stopping *anything* that follows."

Always, a pause followed this declaration. The host could almost feel the visitor pull back, like a horse shying away from a snake. He would be thinking about the dark, circuitous path that had brought him here, remembering his first, tentative reach, what a trusted friend had told him about the host.

Look, if you really want to make a problem go away, there's a guy you should talk to at Coeur d'Alene. He did some work for me a while back and everything came up roses . . . No, don't ask for details. Just mention that you talked to me. You want the number or not?

In the end they all wanted the number.

The host had vetted his prospective visitors carefully. The majority of those who called were politely listened to, then firmly informed that there was nothing the host could do for them.

A lie, of course. In almost every instance there was a solution. But the host's bare-knuckle consideration was always this: Could the supplicant be trusted? Could he be compromised in such a way as to ensure his trust and silence, forever?

The one sitting before him? Yes. That their agendas happened to overlap was mere coincidence.

But now came the moment when the visitor had to commit. He had to relinquish control of his destiny—an action that went not only against his nature but against every political lesson he had ever suffered.

"There's no stopping anything that follows," the host repeated. "Ten million. Five now, deposited in a Liechtenstein bank. The other five upon completion of the contract. That's one hour after you declare victory in November."

"Ten million should buy me a few details."

"It buys you a *result*. Not the when or how or anything else. You get no reports. You don't contact me again. Ever. We do not consult or debate." The host paused. "Are we clear?"

Somewhere in the room, under the floorboards, came a tiny scratching. A field mouse had found a crevice in the foundation.

He saw the fight and the fury in the visitor, that struggle between ambition and conscience, the overwhelming belief in one's destiny set against consequences that now were only vague and distant notions.

"We can stop right here," the host said.

The visitor set down the cognac balloon and pushed it away.

"If what you intend to do involves hurting the president, we most certainly stop right here."

The host smiled. "Never crossed my mind."

The muscles of the visitor's face slackened. He nodded slightly, an unconscious gesture.

"How will I know you're working on this?"

"You'll know. Now I'm going to ask you one last time: How badly do you want this?"

The visitor glanced down at his lap. "You can't possibly imagine."

The host knew exactly what possessed the visitor at this moment: a loss of innocence, shaved off like a curl from the limb of morality that over the years had been whittled smaller and smaller.

Mies van der Rohe, perhaps the greatest architect of the century, had missed the point: It wasn't God who was in the details, but the devil.

There was a moral here: Always check the fine print.

CHAPTER ONE

I T WAS TOO early in the season for the sirocco but the wind dashing against the fortress harbor of Marseille was hot and dry. It carried a North African legacy of grit and dust, the odor of persimmons and decaying ocean catch. It glazed the eye and embedded splinters of homicidal thoughts in a population that moved like an uneasy, suspicious herd.

Rue de la Colombe in the east harbor was a shabby affair, narrow, with overflowing gutters and dog-turd-stained, slippery sidewalks. The peeling facades of the buildings gave the impression of industrial leprosy.

Most of the market stalls belonged to Algerians and Tunisians and were shuttered for the midday respite. Cutting through the stink of cat piss and rotting produce was the sweet smell of burning hashish. The high-pitched wail of Arab songs on radios drifted through the cracks of doors and windowsills warped by the sea air.

There was only one café on the street, a dark hole with a bar by the door and five tables in the back. The owner-bartender was an old *harki,* an Algerian who had fought with the French against Algerian independence. His one good eye was focused on the small television perched above the bar. Olympique de Marseille, the local soccer team, was humiliating the visiting English team.

The only customer was also watching the game. Not because he followed the team or even the sport but because the young waiter, a Kabyle, was pouring *thé de menthe.* The teapot, filled with sugar-laden boiling water and mint leaves, was held four feet above the cup. The waiter dipped its narrow spout and deftly poured a stream into a glass decorated with faded gold trim. The customer remained motionless until the ceremony was concluded.

The waiter set down the teapot, slipped the bill across the table, and took one step back, waiting. The customer made as though to look up, then hesitated, and instead dug into his coat pocket and produced a fistful of greasy coins. He set them down on the table and carefully counted out the francs, setting aside the centimes. He added up the francs, then pushed a few of the centimes into the pile.

The waiter swept the coins off the table and walked away. A few seconds later the customer heard the ring of his tip being tossed contemptuously into a glass jar.

The customer leaned forward and cupped the glass of tea like an old man would, with both hands. Hunched over, he looked even older than at first glance. His hair was long, iron gray, streaked with scalp oil. His face was the color of rotting pomegranate, a brown sheen to the skin that had worked itself into the wrinkles on his cheeks and forehead. The glass shook slightly as he brought it up to tobacco-stained teeth.

In spite of the heat he wore a coat, the frayed cloth cut long with wide lapels. Over the left breast was a tattered three-colored service bar. Only in Marseille would men of his generation and experience recognize it as the symbol of active duty in Algeria.

Except that Algeria was one of the few places on earth where he hadn't fought, because he detested it and the whole of North Africa.

The customer reached for the newspaper he had set aside while the waiter had served tea. His hands were large and fine boned, the fingers long and delicate but powerful. But all anyone ever noticed was the dirt under his cuticles.

The customer opened the conservative Parisian daily *Le Figaro*. The rustle of newsprint could not be heard over the blare of the television.

Nor could today's edition of the *International Herald Tribune*, tucked into *Le Figaro*'s centerfold, be seen.

He bought the paper every day and always kept it hidden away in a French paper because it wasn't in his interest to let people know he read or understood English. That English was, in fact, his mother tongue. Every day he came to this café for a late lunch, assured that other patrons would have come and gone. He always took this table in the corner, his back to the wall. Ordered couscous or *merguez*, a lamb dish, drank his tea, and read his paper. He'd overheard speculation between the bartender and the waiter as to what he was. The former said a vet, the latter insisted he was a clochard, a bum who panhandled enough coins for one meal a day.

The customer took no offense since both were wrong.

The *Tribune* was open to the international page. The lead—and only—story was about a U.S. foreign aid bill that was deadlocked in the House of Representatives. The rest of the page was devoted to the international real estate market and classifieds.

The subheadings in the classifieds began with *Announcements,* which included the times for upcoming Rosh Hashanah services to be held at the Mouvement Juif Libéral de France Synagogue; several prayers would be recited in English. Legal services in Huntington Beach, California, offered one-day certified divorces. Isle of Man trustees had 750 nameplate companies to shelter income. Funding problems for upstart companies would be a thing of the past if one were to contact Bancor of Asia.

After fifteen years the ads had become depressingly familiar. The names changed; the scams and false promises, never.

Employment: German native, 29, fluent English, official qualifications, seeks challenging position in export, sales . . .

....

Trades wanted: Handyman sought for special renovation. Must have 15 years experience. References essential. Call 001-1-202-555-1647.

The customer blinked, sat back slowly. He was intensely aware of everything—the crinkle of the newsprint, the crackle of his wooden chair, the nasal drone of the soccer commentator. The air was filled with fat motes of greasy lamb. The roar inside his head was an avalanche.

Handyman sought . . .

Fifteen years he had waited for this.

Fifteen years to be contacted by a man who had wished him dead.

Fifteen years to be forgiven.

Or could it be a trick to draw him out so that he could finally kill him?

He thought not. He would not call him by his name, the Handyman, or give him a contact number. There were other, more subtle ways to lure the goat.

He needs me. Again.

The Handyman's fingers trembled as he reached for the tea glass. A burst of light from a television commercial reflected off a well-worn ring on the third finger of his left hand, its signet deliberately left dirty, the figure in the seal obscured by grit.

The Handyman stared at it, contemplating how great a fool he was to wear it. Even sullied, it was much too grand a possession for one who appeared so poor. But he allowed for this single flaw in his elaborate disguise because it was his only connection to a life that had been frozen in time. It was the wellspring of his hope, the bedrock of what was left of his sanity.

THREE BLOCKS AWAY, in the Rue des Jardiniers, four Moroccan children were kicking a filthy soccer ball up and down the street. It caromed off the parked cars, rolled into the gutter, was kicked again, leaving dirty blotches where it had smacked against the vehicles' fenders.

The eldest boy was passing the ball from foot to foot, deciding which friend to kick it to, when he spotted the Handyman ambling down the street. The boy recognized him. He'd been a fixture in the neighborhood ever since he could remember. A silent, smelly old man who shuffled along like a gimp, never said a word to anybody. As a child the boy had been afraid of him. Now on the cusp of adolescence, he wondered why none of the older kids had ever beaten up the old man, or set him on fire, just for fun. Grinning, he waited for the old man to reach an open space between two parked cars.

The boy's eyes never wavered from their target. Here came the old man, his coat almost dragging on the sidewalk, head bobbing like that of an ancient turkey. The boy licked his lips and drew back his right leg. He was scrawny but strong in the way children become when they grow up on the street. His leg shot out like a piston, his foot connecting with the ball perfectly. It rocketed away on a low trajectory directly toward the old man's head.

The boy ran toward the sidewalk, thinking how fast he could go through the old man's pockets while he was down. And maybe he wouldn't stop at that. Maybe he'd hurt him a little, *for fun*.

The ball should have taken the old man's head off. There was no way he could have seen it coming. Yet suddenly the old man dipped his shoulder, spun, and threw both arms up in front of his face.

Six feet from the sidewalk, the boy froze. The old man lowered his hands, holding the ball he'd plucked in midflight, and stared at him. The boy gasped. He had never really seen the old man's eyes before. Now they would not let him go, cold, black eyes, shiny and opaque like coal.

They never wavered as the Handyman tossed the soccer ball in the air, spread his arms, and brought them together.

The boy shrieked as the soccer ball exploded between the old man's hands. What was left of it fell into the street. And still the old man's eyes were on him.

The boy backed away, skidded on the cobblestones, and fell hard on his bottom. He scrambled up, skinning his knee, and tore past his friends, who were still staring at what had happened. Then they too turned tail.

The street became quiet again save for the Arab music drifting out from the windows above. The Handyman continued along the street. What he had just done would have been foolish—even fatal—an hour ago. Now it didn't matter. Now it was a tiny payback for all the years of taunts and jeers and veiled threats.

It felt good.

THE HANDYMAN'S APARTMENT building was a nineteenth-century pile of limestone built around a central courtyard. Long ago gilded carriages and prize horseflesh had passed through the big double doors that opened onto the street. Now the courtyard was strewn with broken appliances and furniture and soiled, gutted mattresses. Above the debris that no one wanted and no one would ever come to haul away, clotheslines crisscrossed the courtyard, running from balcony to balcony.

The Handyman climbed the narrow steps easily, stopping at each of the landings to hit the time switch on the staircase light. The hallways under the rafters smelled of cumin, rosemary, and coriander. A baby was bawling somewhere in the recesses.

The Handyman lived on the sixth floor, in what had once been the servants' quarters. The rooms were cramped; the ceilings sloped so that near the windows even a child had to crouch. The Handyman's apartment was no different from the other ten on the floor: a single room with a waist-high partition that created a cooking area, consisting of a cupboard, counter, two-burner electric hot plate, and sink. There was a bed and an ancient dresser, and a scarred desk and chair by the slanted, grimy window, which was the only source of ventilation. The floorboards were buckled and worn; the walls were covered with seepage-stained wallpaper, the floral design eaten away by cockroaches and filth.

In one corner was a closet fashioned out of raw drywall slabs framed by two-by-fours. The Handyman opened it and removed a small old hard-shell suitcase and a hanger draped with dry cleaner's plastic.

He put these on the bed, then filled the kettle and set it on the hot plate to boil. He stripped and carefully went through all the pockets of his clothes, arranging coins, keys, and fake ID papers neatly on the desk. His body was surprisingly lean and muscled for one who looked so old. Now his movements were precise and economical, with none of the hesitation of age.

He poured the boiling water from the kettle into the sink, mixed it with cold water, and lathered a bar of soap. After refilling the kettle, he scrubbed his face and hands with a rough sponge, rinsed, then did it again. When he looked at himself in the small mirror above the sink, the face of the tramp had disappeared.

The Handyman washed the rest of his body, working the sponge carefully between his toes and under his groin. He drained the water, cleaned the sink, and filled it with more hot water. He dipped his head and worked a cheap shampoo into his scalp.

He dried himself with a coarse towel and opened the suitcase. He brought out clean socks and underwear, a necktie, and a pair of oxblood brogues. He pulled the plastic wrap off the hanger, removed and slipped into the shirt, pants, and tweed sports jacket. Because he was out of practice, it took him three tries to knot the tie correctly. He picked up a comb and carefully ran it through his hair, then looked in the mirror again.

The image was that of a teacher, maybe an untenured professor who could not afford to dress with the times. The sports jacket lapels were too narrow, the pants baggy at the waist and hips. The sturdy brogues were impervious to fashion swings.

It was perfect.

The Handyman kneeled and with one hand lifted the bed by one of its round steel posts. Gripping the leg with his other hand, he gave it a hard twist. The threads in the leg yielded reluctantly, sprinkling rust over his palm as it came loose, then free. He lowered the bed gently to the floor.

The Handyman turned the pipe upside down and tapped out its cache: a roll of money—French and Swiss francs, American dollars—and a phony birth certificate whose name matched the one on a genuine Canadian passport. The passport had expired but could be renewed quickly enough. The staff at the Paris consulate was predominately French-Canadian and the Handyman's birth certificate led one to believe he was Québecois.

The last two items in the bedpost were a slip of paper with a phone number on it, fifteen years old—*001-1-202-555-1647*—and a slim bundle of very old pages the texture of papyrus.

He placed the contents on the desk, rescrewed the bed-frame leg, and burned the paper in an ashtray. The ashes went into the sink, down the drain. The money, including the coins from his old coat, was pocketed along with the birth certificate and passport. The clothing he'd been wearing was stuffed into the small suitcase, which would be disposed of later.

Almost ready now, the Handyman sat down on the edge of the bed and carefully peeled back the pages, dry and yellow with age, the black ink having faded to blue. There was no title or publisher's imprint; the language was Mandarin.

He could read the text easily enough but his skills of interpreting horoscopic elements—the stars and other portents—had dulled. Horoscopy, like its sister divination geomancy, required constant practice at the feet of a master. For the last fifteen years, the Handyman's fate had been ruled by a single, overpowering factor that had denied him his studies, one that even the stars, in perfect alignment, had not been able to release him from. Now that factor had shifted. The Handyman badly needed to know why. Even though he could not help himself, he was aware of one who could.

Geomancy, the study of one's orientation to the natural world and its elements—fire, water, metal, wood, and earth—was more accessible. Focusing on interpretations written three millennia ago and passed down the ages like forever-drifting leaves, the Handyman concluded that the force oppressing him was not at all in harmony with these elements. It had been disturbed. There was discomfort and uneasiness within it. Even a hint of fear.

Which makes the oppressor vulnerable. All the more so because there is an acknowledged need for me.

The Handyman stifled the thrill his conclusion stirred in him. He knew from experience how dangerous it was to seize the answer one desired. His interpretation was sound—as far as he could take it. More and deeper meanings would have to be coaxed forth before he was absolutely certain that his intuition wasn't merely whispering what he wanted to hear.

THE HANDYMAN WAS not surprised that almost two hours had elapsed since he'd first opened the book. Long ago, when he was working, he would easily lose an entire week in this kingdom of the unseen where his were the only footprints. He took a deep breath, returned his thoughts to the present, and carefully rolled up the pages and put them in the inside pocket of his jacket.

The Handyman rose to the door and appraised the room. His eyes touched on everything, missed nothing. He knew his absence would go unnoticed. The rent was paid until the first of the month. The landlady wouldn't come by until next week. She'd see the empty closet and figure he'd left. Not a problem, since everything that belonged in the room would still be there. Renting out the garret to another pensioner would be no trouble at all.

The Handyman was not concerned about fingerprints. His had never appeared in any police file in the world. Nor was there any reason for anyone to connect him to this room.

He gripped the doorknob, then looked at the room one last time. He'd spent fifteen years in places like this—most of them worse—moving frequently at first, then settling in when he'd found this neighborhood, where he was invisible, too poor to prey upon, too weak to be a threat, too old to merit even a glance.

For the first time in a very long while, the Handyman smiled. It was an unfamiliar sensation. He thought that if the biblical Lazarus had ever existed, this was how he must have felt when his grave had been thrown open onto the world.

SHOPS WERE REOPENING and traffic filled the street when the Handyman stepped out. He had to move quickly to avoid being struck by a garment trolley wheeled by a young black.

He gave the street a cursory glance and fell in behind a group of gossiping women, all carrying empty string bags on their way to market. He never noticed the man who stepped out from under the awning of a butcher shop and watched him fade into the crowds farther down the street. The Handyman had no reason to suspect that he was under surveillance.

The watcher's name was Sam Crawford. He was in his late thirties but looked younger. He was tall and lean, with a tanned, outdoors face and a shock of white blond hair. He could have been a fading ski bum or a hand-to-mouth print model. In the right clothes, maybe a gigolo.

Until one looked a little closer, watched him as he crossed the street to the Handyman's building. His movements were fluid, as if he were skimming the surface of the road, not walking on it. And when he walked, he silently cut the air around him, instead of pushing against it. He was the kind of man who could perch on your conscience and you'd never even feel his breath.

Crawford took the steps two at a time, up the staircase the Handyman had descended just moments ago. At the top landing he paused, then moved down the hall.

The Handyman's door had an old-fashioned lock, the kind that opened with a long, double-tongued key. Crawford had no problem with this.

When the lock clicked, he moved back against the wall, slowly pressing his palm to the door, letting it swing open. He counted to five, allowing for a time-delay trigger to activate an explosives-laden booby trap. The smell of soap and shampoo drifted out into the hall.

Crawford let out his breath. The Handyman hadn't left any trip wires behind. He stepped inside and closed the door behind him. His eyes panned the room but he already knew what he was looking at: abandonment.

The bed was neatly made, the thin blanket stretched military tight at the corners. But there were rust particles on the floor by one of the legs.

The sink was still wet but the few dishes stacked in the rack were dry. The hand towel was dry but the larger bath towel was damp. The soap smell was shampoo, not dishwashing detergent.

The Handyman had cleaned himself up.

The closet was empty, but one of the wire hangers had a shred of paper attached to its neck. The remnants of a dry cleaner's logo.

Which accounted for the Handyman's atypical attire when he'd left the building . . .

Crawford would have the room combed, though he was sure that the search would prove fruitless. The Handyman had not survived this long because he overlooked details or was careless. If Crawford had known nothing about him, the room wouldn't betray the man who'd lived there.

Crawford felt a slight vibration just above his right kidney. He reached around to touch the silent beeper, then pulled back his jacket lapel, where a microtransmitter was nestled in the seam.

He pressed his finger to the flesh-colored plastic receiver in his ear.

"Talk to me, Wally."

There was static, like someone was crumpling aluminum foil. Then: *"He's at the train station. Just bought a ticket for the express to Paris."*

"And he's not coming back. Stay with him. Tell Paris to throw a full blanket over him."

"Confirm full blanket. Sam, he made a couple of phone calls."

Crawford cursed. "Was anybody close enough to hear?"

"No. He made it at the train station, from inside a booth. Even if we'd been set up, it would have been a long shot."

"How long was he on?"

"You're not going to like this. Dialing the first one took about fifteen seconds. The second took longer, and it lasted a good five minutes."

Crawford didn't like it. The time frame indicated that the Handyman had made a regional call, probably to Paris, and an international one. Those connections always took longer to complete. Staying on-line for five minutes plus meant that the Handyman could have received detailed instructions.

"I'll see you up in Paris," he said.

Crawford took one final look around the room. Its silence and poverty seemed to mock him, revealing no more than he already knew: The Handyman was on the move.

To Paris.

From there he could fly to anywhere in the world.

CHAPTER TWO

"*BONJOUR, MADEMOISELLE.*"

"*Bonjour, monsieur.*"

The newspaper vendor held out the day's edition of the *International Herald Tribune,* folded three times over, bound by a thin rubber band, and slipped into a small paper bag. He did this for his favorite customers so that the newsprint would not soil their fingers or their clothes.

As he accepted the ten-franc coin from the woman, he nodded, giving her a quick once-over.

She was American, of course. The vendor had known that at a glance the first time she had come by his kiosk in the park near the Espace Pierre Cardin. It was not the accent that had given her away. In fact, it was surprisingly good for someone who was neither French nor a day over twenty-six. Nor was it her wardrobe. The jacket and skirt were last year's Hervé Léger but they hung beautifully on her tall, slender frame. The wheat-colored fabric and green blouse picked up the highlights in her hair and the flecks in her eyes. An office girl's outfit. Someone who was conscious of what worked for her but had to shop carefully. Witness the well-used but classic leather purse and sensible Bally pumps. This was a woman who understood how harsh Parisian sidewalks could be.

It was her eyes that had betrayed her. Not covered with a tourist's glaze—the vendor saw plenty of those every day—but with a wide-eyed innocence shot through with excitement. None of the cool boredom he saw in Parisian natives who used the park for a postlunch rendezvous with their lovers. This one radiated the joy of the place and moment, as if Paris were a limitless cornucopia of delights, some already tasted, a multitude yet to be savored.

Once, the vendor had pointed her out to a friend of his, a successful con man who worked the foreign-widow contingent at the deluxe hotels on the Right Bank. The con had taken a single glance and pronounced: "She has a getaway face." A face so beautiful that no harm could ever come to the woman who possessed it. It was unthinkable.

"Is there something wrong, monsieur?" Hollis Fremont asked him.

The vendor shook his head. "I was only admiring because you are even more breathtaking than usual today."

"And you are even more gallant than usual, monsieur." She grinned, revealing a tiny gap between her two front teeth.

As she walked away, she laughed softly to herself. Hollis didn't need to buy the paper; there were plenty of them floating around the American consulate, where she worked. But she enjoyed the vendor's gentle, avuncular flirtation.

Hollis continued through the park. Three months ago, when she'd just arrived from Washington, the traffic that thundered around the obelisk at the Place de la Concorde had grated on her nerves, a constant assault of noise and noxious diesel fumes. Now it was just backdrop.

She came out of the park at Avenue Gabriel and turned toward Rue Boissy d'Anglas. She reached the curb and waited at the red light. Three businessmen, talking rapidly among themselves, came up behind her.

Across Avenue Gabriel were two police cars and a dark blue van. Six members of the quasimilitary Corps Républicain de Sécurité—dark blue uniforms, black paratrooper boots, submachine guns—slowly patrolled the sidewalk in front of the American embassy.

One of the CRS constables looked her up and down, his eyes hard and suspicious in an otherwise expressionless face. Hollis looked away.

Diagonally across the street was the Hôtel de Crillon, an eighteenth-century landmark that had been converted into one of the legendary hotels of the world. She forced the image of the CRS officer from her mind and thought instead of the quiet, delicate beauty of the Crillon's L'Obélisque restaurant, where she was going to breakfast.

If this light ever changes . . .

Which it did. But not before a Mercedes transport truck hurtled around the corner. For an instant it filled Hollis's vision, seemed to be bearing down on her. Reflexively, she jumped back. She never felt herself crashing into the men behind her because that's when the gunshot exploded. She whipped her head around toward the embassy, her mouth open to scream. But no sound emerged, and all around her, colors and sounds crumbled into oblivion.

FIFTEEN YEARS AGO.

Noon, Sunday, the Fourth of July. Only tourists were up and about on the grand boulevards. The Parisians who had no truck with foreigners had fled to the countryside to escape the heat.

The flag over the entrance to the American embassy hung limp. A pair of flics, ordinary policemen, posted in front of the embassy gates gratefully accepted paper cups of lemonade brought out to them by one of the secretaries.

There was a lot of foot traffic in and out of the embassy grounds: furniture-rental people, caterers hired to help the embassy kitchen staff, florists, wine merchants. Other than the annual Marine Corps Ball, the ambassador's July Fourth evening gala was the affair of the embassy's social calendar. The cream of the diplomatic corps, the French government, and Paris society would attend.

But the afternoon event was informal and more a reflection of the holiday's true spirit. Adjacent to the embassy's west wall, on a manicured lawn studded with ancient chestnut trees and flower beds ringed with white stones, an employees' barbecue was in full swing. The smell of exhaust from the Champs-Elysées was obliterated by the tangy scent of ribs, hamburgers, and hot dogs sizzling on an old-style grill. Picnic tables and benches had been set up, covered with red-and-white checked cloths and laden with Tupperware bowls of potato and macaroni salad, coleslaw, pickles, and condiments. There were six kegs of Miller beer, flown in courtesy of the air force attaché and set in plastic bags of shaved ice.

The children of the embassy employees and some embassy-employed French nationals had their own old-fashioned soda-and-ice-cream parlor. There was also a puppet show and a clown who juggled sticks of hard candy.

But the real treat was the small carousel that had been set up in the middle of the lawn between two towering chestnut trees. A gift from the French minister of education, it was powered by a small generator tucked in the bushes along the embassy's perimeter wall. It had eight brilliantly painted horses and a circus big-top cover. The song that pealed from the tinny speakers was a xylophonic version of the children's popular song "Frère Jacques."

Hollis Fremont, eleven years old, wearing a pink dress, white knee socks, and brand-new black patent leather shoes, tapped her foot impatiently, waiting for the merry-go-round to stop. Behind her, she heard her father laugh. She turned and looked at him sternly, as if to say, *I've been polite. I've given the younger kids their turn and now it's mine!*

Her father bent down and kissed her cheek. Hollis giggled because his soft, thick mustache tickled.

> *Sonnez les matines,*
> *Sonnez les matines,*
> *Ding dong dang*
> *Ding dong dang*

Hollis knew the song by heart. Two more *ding dong* refrains to go.

She looked up at the perfect blue sky, caught a whiff of barbecue, and realized how hungry she was. But not hungry enough to give up her place in line.

A man came over, smiled at her, and said hello in French. Hollis replied in kind, and the man leaned down and gently brushed the top of her head. Hollis saw his smile disappear as he turned to her father. They stepped away, hands in their pockets, heads bowed together. They spoke in low tones so that she couldn't hear their words. But she saw her father gesture with his hands, sweep his fingers through his hair, and look around nervously.

Hollis was puzzled. She knew that her father was a regional security officer at the embassy. It was, he'd once told her, like being a kind of policeman. She could grasp that, but she didn't understand why he looked so worried. She was too young to recognize the face of fear.

The music started to wind down. Hollis watched parents step up onto the circular platform and pluck their children from the wooden saddles.

"Daddy . . . " She tugged her father's pant leg.

His hand squeezed hers but he didn't look down as he continued talking to the Frenchman.

Hollis glanced at the children who'd been standing behind her. They were piling onto the platform, scrambling for the horses. A towheaded boy, Jimmy Dawes, whom Hollis detested, got on the horse she'd wanted, saw her frustration, and stuck his tongue out at her.

"Daddy!"

"I'm sorry, pumpkin."

Before she knew it, Hollis was being lifted onto the merry-go-round. She dashed for the last available horse—red, blue, and gold—and jumped onto the saddle. She sat up straight, gripping the horse's ears.

The paint, she noticed, was beginning to flake.

She glanced around, ready for the music to start.

"Mind if I ride along, honey?"

Hollis felt a stab of anger—she wasn't a baby who needed her daddy to ride with her. Nor did she have any idea that her feelings showed in her expression. But there was no mistaking the hurt she saw in her father's eyes.

Not conscious of having made a decision, she reached out and grabbed her father's big hand, pulling him toward her. She scooted forward in the saddle and smiled when he got on behind her, not quite sitting all the way down, his feet planted on the platform. She felt his warm breath near her ear and the slippery fabric of his seersucker jacket on her arms as he reached forward to cover her hands with his. She knew that the hard thing poking into her back when he shifted was his gun. Her father had explained to her that it was just a tool he might sometimes need in his work, like a carpenter might need a hammer. Hollis had accepted the explanation because everything her father told her was true. So, in her mind, a gun was just that—a tool.

The music started up. Somewhere beneath the platform, ancient gears and chains, coated with grease, began to move. The merry-go-round created its own breath of wind, which made Hollis's hair drift over her father's throat. One by one the horses emerged from the shade of the chestnut trees into the sunlight, then curved around past the dappled lawn where other children were waiting their turn.

Frère Jacques,
Frère Jacques,
Dormez-vous?
Dormez-vous?

As her horse drifted through the sunlight Hollis saw her mother come across the lawn. She thought Felicia Fremont was the most beautiful woman in the world. Long golden hair, slender arms, and a smile that seemed to light up the world. She was wearing a silk garden skirt that trailed behind her like a queen's train.

Hollis waved at her mother, who blew back a kiss and turned to walk toward the Frenchman who'd been talking with her father. Hollis twisted around and saw her father wave too, saw his big smile and two crooked lower teeth, which she sometimes thought made him look goofy. She felt her heart ache but didn't know the reason: that at this moment she loved both of them more than she ever had before.

Nor could she understand why it was that all at once her father let out a sharp grunt and his mouth exploded with blood.

THE BULLET THAT entered Alec Fremont's brain stem and exited through his mouth was an instant kill. It left an incredible amount of damage even though it had been fired from over six hundred yards away. At that distance, even if the shooter hadn't been using a silencer, no sound would have been heard by anyone in the embassy compound.

The shooter's vantage point was the control cab of a construction crane set in the courtyard of a building whose renovations had been going on for months. To the local police, the crane had become a fixture in the landscape of Rue du Faubourg-St.-Honoré. Even so, the security detail responsible for the safety of the French president checked the crane and its operators whenever the head of state was in residence at the Palais de l'Elysée, across from the American embassy grounds, between Avenue de Marigny and Rue de l'Elysée.

French internal security, which was responsible for the safety of diplomats and worked closely with the embassy's regional security officer, also kept tabs on the crane. As long as it remained there, it was the only structure that would allow an assassin a clear line of sight into the embassy gardens. The embassy building was protected both by a thick growth of trees and by the angle at which it stood relative to the crane.

On July 4, the president of France was at his countryside retreat in Giverny, so his detail had not bothered to check the crane. Neither had the embassy RSO or his French counterpart. Security was concerned only with the ambassador's party, to be held inside that night.

Nor was there any reason to believe that any threat existed. French security had an excellent network of informers among the nation's Arab population. If there was to be trouble, it would come from that quarter. Reports evaluated by both security teams indicated that all was well.

The shooter had climbed the crane at four o'clock that morning, wearing the dirty blue overalls of a construction worker, and had hidden himself away in the control cab. He knew that no one had seen him go up, so there was no reason to think that there was anyone up there.

The killer had slept until the cab became too warm from the sun. He opened the window a crack, drank from his water bottle, and ate field rations, the kind issued to troops in the desert. Through binocular lenses coated with nonreflective film he watched the preparations for both embassy parties. Once the merry-go-round was up and running, he assembled his weapon and mounted the scope, and positioned himself.

The shooter recalled the argument he'd made to his principal: The targets' movements would be spontaneous. They would follow no pattern or timetable. Luck would play too much of a role.

The principal had listened quietly, then said, "Just get it done."

When the merry-go-round had started up and Alec Fremont had slipped in behind his daughter on the red, blue, and gold horse, the shooter knew it could be done.

And the first bullet had flown.

The killer hadn't waited to see Alec Fremont's head explode; he was already turning to the second target—the Frenchman. And then suddenly a problem he had never considered loomed in his sights.

Fremont's wife. Her mouth formed an O as she saw her husband slam against their daughter, knocking her off the horse. Felicia Fremont should have been frozen in shock, but instead she was racing toward the merry-go-round, her long hair and skirt flying behind her. Her shoulder knocked the Frenchman, spinning him around.

Which was precisely the instant at which the shooter placed the final ounce of pressure on his delicate trigger.

HOLLIS'S FIRST REACTION was to throw her arm up against the gout of red goo erupting from her father's mouth. She had seen blood, but never so much at once. Even as the momentum of his body threw her off the horse she was thinking how warm and sticky it felt.

She cried out as first her shoulder and then her bottom hit the re-volving platform. The pain made her yelp. She twisted around to touch her knee and that's when she saw her father, slumped forward on the horse, the red stuff dripping down his back and the side of his face onto the platform. His arms had fallen forward and were draped around the horse's neck.

Hollis didn't hear the other children scream. She squirmed her way toward her father, tried to stand up, but her left knee collapsed from under her. She fell, then managed to grip a pole and pull herself up. And that's how she was able to see her mother running toward the carousel. Her feet were hidden by the grass and her skirt and it looked like she was floating.

"*Mommy!*"

Hearing Hollis over the screams and the tinkling music of the carousel, she raised her head—and at that instant ran right into the man her husband had been talking to. He spun away to the left, leav-ing her to stagger forward, her arms flailing. Then suddenly she was vi-olently thrown back.

Hollis saw that same terrible redness burst out of her mother's chest. She didn't know she was screaming, never felt the pain shooting from her knee down her leg as she clawed her way on all fours off the plat-form and tumbled onto the grass.

THE SHOOTER SAW the life streak out of the woman the instant the bullet impacted. His training told him to ignore the chaos that had erupted on the lawn; it calmly whispered that he had one more shot left.

He dropped the crosshairs on the Frenchman who had been knocked from the line of fire and sighted on his spine. He exhaled and squeezed the trigger.

The Frenchman was thrown forward and, for a second, lay still. The shooter kept his sights on him. A clean kill to the base of the spine.

People were racing toward the bodies. A woman snatched up the lit-tle girl, whose pink dress was now a bloodied rag, and held her to her breast, looking around wildly.

Within seconds, others, armed and much more competent, would also be looking. The shooter knew that if he stayed a second longer they would pinpoint his position and take him down.

Better to survive and face the cold wrath of his principal.

As he climbed out of the control cab and down the crane's skeletal frame he couldn't rid himself of that last image: the little girl straining over the shoulder of the woman who held her, reaching helplessly for her parents, who now lay in puddles of blood.

"MADEMOISELLE! MADEMOISELLE!"

Hollis blinked and whirled around, straight into the arms of a CRS constable. The men who'd been standing behind her at the curb were crossing the street, looking back at her, shaking their heads.

"Mademoiselle, is anything the matter?"

"I thought I heard a shot."

Even as the words passed her lips she realized how ridiculous they sounded.

The constable's expression indicated that he agreed. "It was a back-fire—a truck with a bad muffler." He looked at her coldly. "Your iden-tification, please."

Hollis fumbled in her purse and pulled out her wallet. Next to her American driver's license was her diplomatic ID.

The constable examined it carefully before handing it back. "Why would you think you heard a shot?"

Hollis shook her head. "Because that's what I thought it was."

"I assure you it was nothing of the kind." The constable pointed to-ward the embassy. "May I escort you to your office?"

Hollis managed a smile. "No, thank you."

The constable raised his arm in a lackluster salute and walked back across the avenue to his station. Hollis watched his partners come up. The constable shrugged, said something, and pointed his forefinger at his temple: the universal gesture used to describe a lunatic.

Hollis turned away. When the traffic light changed, she crossed Av-enue Gabriel and walked toward the hotel. All the while she felt the constable's eyes on her back.

On that day fifteen years ago, Hollis hadn't actually heard the shots. Death had flown silently and had struck without warning. Only much later had she learned what gunfire sounded like. And she heard it a hundred times a day, even in the darkest corners of her sleep.

CHAPTER THREE

THE CRILLON'S SECURITY officer, dressed by Armani, spotted the woman as soon as she stepped into the vestibule. He watched her move across the lobby and up the steps to the reception area. He noted the paper bag she carried in her left hand, a folded newspaper protruding like a baton. She was holding the bag away from her body. Her face was pale.

One of the security officer's duties was to memorize the features of everyone who was registered at the hotel. This one was not a guest. She was dressed well enough not to appear out of place in these luxurious surroundings, but . . .

What else is in the bag? What do you have inside that newspaper?

The security officer casually lifted his right arm and murmured into the wrist mike tucked under the cuff of his shirt. Now the command post knew that he was moving to intercept an individual who had aroused his suspicion. Reinforcements were on the way.

"May I be of assistance, mademoiselle?"

Hollis started. She turned so quickly that her handbag knocked the man's arm. When she looked at him, she thought he was the concierge or an assistant manager.

She didn't notice that his other hand dropped behind his back, his fingers slipping through the vent of his jacket, curling around the butt of his gun.

"I'm sorry. I don't know what's wrong with me." Hollis thought her laugh sounded strained. "I'm here to have breakfast with a guest. Mr. Dawson Wylie, from the United States."

The man smiled. "Of course. Monsieur Wylie. And you must be . . . ?"

"Hollis Fremont. I'm a . . . friend."

"Naturally. May I escort you to L'Obélisque?"

"I can find it myself . . . "

"It would be my pleasure. Please, may I take that for you?"

The man removed the newspaper from her grasp so gently that Hollis barely realized it was gone. Nor did she think anything of his cupping her elbow as they walked down the marbled hall, past ten-foot mirrors in gilded frames, toward the restaurant.

She heard the crinkle of paper but never suspected that by now the man had checked, by sight and touch, whether there was anything hidden in the newspaper.

The security man gave an infinitesimal shake of his head, a signal to the maître d' not to interfere. He spotted Mr. Wylie immediately but pretended otherwise.

"I don't see him," he said.

"There he is—over there!"

Her excited voice carried enough for the guest to sit up and turn around. When Wylie waved to her, the security man released his light grip.

"Your newspaper, mademoiselle. Good day."

The security officer nodded to the maître d' and quietly slipped out of the restaurant.

"Hollis . . . "

Dawson Wylie was out of his chair before she reached the table.

His broad smile and twinkling eyes welcomed her as he threw his arms around her.

Hollis thought Dawson Wylie could easily be a poster boy for the American Association of Retired Persons. Nattily attired in his usual blue blazer, gray cavalry twill slacks, and white shirt accented by a conservative, wine-colored tie, he appeared like a prosperous, globe-trotting retiree. But there were subtle differences between him and the other foreign guests in the dining room. Wylie was relaxed and comfortable in his surroundings, not overwhelmed by them. He treated the maître d' and waiters with a warm familiarity, as though they were old retainers. And when he ordered for Hollis, his accent was flawlessly Parisian.

Hollis thought that it was all very much in keeping with a man who'd spent almost his entire adult life in the Foreign Service, much of it in this city, his career peaking when he'd been appointed deputy chief of mission of the London embassy.

"You're in fine form this morning," Hollis said.

She thanked the waiter who was holding back her chair, adding that she wanted her orange juice and coffee immediately.

"You look a little under the weather," Wylie observed. "Fighting something?"

"Just lack of sleep."

"Oh-ho! Been up all night with that new beau of yours?"

Hollis felt her cheeks crimson and lowered her gaze. She unfolded the starched linen napkin and rearranged the heavy silver on the table-cloth. When she glanced up at Wylie, his eyes were teasing her.

"Paris is the only city in the world to be young and in love in," he said. "And you promised I'd get to meet him before I left."

"You will."

Hollis reached out and ran her fingers down the side of Wylie's cheek. "I think it's cute that you worry so much."

"I'm not worried," Wylie grumbled. "Just . . . *curious.*"

"Sure. How was the reunion? What time did *you* get to bed?"

"Probably earlier than you."

"Probably *not,*" Hollis shot back, laughing. She reached across the table and gripped his hand. "It's been wonderful to have you here, Dee."

Dawson Wylie came to Europe every spring and always spent at least a week in Paris, getting together with old friends from the Foreign Service who'd chosen to retire here. This year was special since Hollis was working at the consulate. Because of her previous posting, she hadn't seen Wylie in six months.

Hollis had been worried that her schedule at the consulate wouldn't leave much time to be with Wylie. When she'd mentioned this to him, he had grumbled good-naturedly, "Don't you think you're obliged to baby-sit me. I've got places to go, people to see."

They would get together at the end of her day, for cocktails at a Left Bank brasserie that Wylie had frequented years ago, or for dinner in tiny restaurants off the beaten track, where he was welcomed like a long-lost member of the family. In the evenings they walked the banks of the Seine, talking for hours before ending up at the Crillon for a hot chocolate and eau-de-vie.

Hollis had treasured every moment and now dreaded Wylie's inevitable departure.

Wylie picked up the bread basket and deposited a *pain au chocolat* on Hollis's plate. The waiter came by with her juice and coffee, and Wylie watched as she stirred her *café crème,* then lifted a spoonful of hot whipped milk and made it disappear over her tongue.

"Just like you used to do when you were a little girl," Wylie said softly. "But you're all grown up now. Working at the consulate, a young man hopelessly in love with you . . . "

"Dee, I've only been here three months!" This was what she had called him since childhood.

"So? I was posted here less than two weeks when I met Martha."

Hollis felt a tug at her heart at the mention of the name. Martha Wylie was the woman who'd picked her up off the carousel that terrifying July afternoon. And had never let go of her, until she died six years ago. She and Dawson Wylie, her father's best friend, had become her family long before then.

She looked at Wylie's face, the character lines etched into his freshly barbered cheeks, the silver mane swept back over the collar, and silently thanked him for the life he'd given her.

"Do you have to go back so soon, Dee?"

"Yeah. Time to do a little painting, mend some fences." He winked. "You know, you might want to come and visit, bring your friend."

"I'd love to but I'm low person on the vacation totem pole." Now it was her turn to look him over. "You okay, Dee? You didn't overindulge at your reunion?"

Wylie lathered a thick layer of marmalade on a croissant and held it up like a particularly fascinating specimen, then smiled. "Maybe a little."

Wylie bit into the croissant. Hollis went back to her coffee. She knew that Dee treasured these reunions, but they had their downside. Each year there were one or two familiar faces missing, as old friends passed away. But Dee never talked about this, and she never brought it up.

"This town was something back then," Wylie said out of the blue.

Hollis could see the memories behind his eyes, the best times and the regrets, the triumphs and losses chasing one another like shadows.

"All us dinosaurs were your age," he continued. "Full of piss and vinegar. Thought we could change the world . . . And I guess we did, for better or worse."

Wylie paused. "We ended up talking about your dad, how much we all still miss him. The things we could have done if he'd stayed with us."

He looked at her. "I'm sorry, Holly. An old man's ramblings . . . "

Hollis slid her hand across to cover his. "I miss him too, Dee. Him and Mom. Maybe that's why I put in for the Paris post, because here I might get rid of the demons. Does that sound crazy?"

"No. I only wish I could have done more to help you."

"Don't give me that. You called in some favors to get me here."

Wylie laughed. "You vastly overestimate the influence of a retired public servant."

Hollis shook her head. "No, I don't. Not his love, either."

She felt his two large hands envelop hers.

"It's been grand to see you, Hollis. We had us some times, didn't we?"

"We had us some times, Dee. And we'll have plenty more."

The other conversations in the dining room, the unobtrusive bustle of the waiters, the soft classical music in the background all dissolved into their moment. Hollis wished she could reach out and pluck it out of time, press it into her soul like a flower into a diary, so that it would always be there for her, to look at, to touch, especially in those hard, cold moments that, she knew, were still to fall through the hourglass of her life.

PAUL MCGANN'S OFFICE was in the west wing of the embassy, exactly fifteen paces from the ambassador's suite.

It was spacious, as befitted his rank, and McGann had furnished it personally. No government supply services teakwood veneer here. The Bokhara rug, Chippendale desk and cabinets, the collection of Paul Revere pewter, and the grandfather clock whose provenance traced back to Benjamin Franklin—each would have fetched six figures at Sotheby's.

The tall French doors opened onto a second-story balcony. The view of the lawn and gardens was spectacular, but McGann rarely noticed it.

As deputy chief of mission, he was responsible for the embassy's day-to-day operations, answering only to the ambassador. He had had the post for eight years. Certain coworkers had other monikers for McGann: Hatchetman, Little Hitler, the Bad Seed. McGann was aware of them all, and of the identities of those who whispered them. But the labels had no effect on him because he didn't care what people thought of him personally. His bedrock principle was that it was better to be feared than liked. A man much more powerful and ruthless than any diplomat had taught him that.

McGann was on his third ambassador, a midwestern twit who'd been a dark horse vice presidential candidate years ago. Awarded the post for years of fealty to the party as well as for his prodigious fund-raising activities, the ambassador was easy enough to steer once he understood exactly who and what McGann was. His predecessor had summed it up: "McGann's a son of a bitch, but he's *your* son of a bitch. Don't push him, don't cross him. Let him do his job and you'll come out looking like a genius."

The twit had had the good sense to take the advice.

And well he should have. Paul McGann's mother had come from one of Paris's leading families. After marrying a wealthy American software pioneer she had taken up residence in an ancestral city home that was as rich in history as it was derelict in plumbing. The software pioneer's patent checks had paid for the refurbishing of that and other family seats. They had also provided handsomely for a son who was raised as a Parisian first and an American second.

A tall fine-boned boy with dark hair and inky black eyes, Paul McGann was the same in manhood. A loner, he had gravitated toward the martial arts as much for the discipline as the ability to tear a bully apart. Prone to sudden and savage violence when confronted, he seemed not to understand the concept of compassion. McGann's fists had gotten him expelled from four universities before he finally made it through Yale. There, he discovered the arcane arena of international politics. His professors should have caught on that something was wrong when he could quote Machiavelli's works verbatim. But they hadn't.

Tant pis.

After graduation, McGann aced the Foreign Service exams, written and oral. Fluent in French, Spanish, Italian, and German, he bypassed the Virginia Language School and was sent directly to Paris.

It took him less than six months to get off the "visa line," the consulate's entry-level position. Superiors noted his quiet, hard drive, his discipline and will to succeed. But what they valued and could use was the young man's connections in French society.

Paul McGann, the fellow with the quiet eyes and enigmatic smile, was on the fast track. He made himself indispensable when all the while it looked like he was just helping. He sabotaged the careers of subordinates, peers, and superiors but made it appear they were victims of their own ineptitude. He traded in favors and shortcomings, gossip and innuendo, and used all of them with a skill and finesse that his sixteenth-century mentor would have lauded.

McGann tamed his first ambassador when he was barely thirty. Now, eight years later, *tout Paris* knew whom to call when quick, decisive—and discreet—action was needed. It was an acknowledgment of McGann's power that his phone calls to French government officials were prioritized over the ambassador's.

But none of the power he held in his palm was of any use to him at this moment.

He studied the man sitting opposite his desk. Luc Tessier reminded him of a circus bear—burly, slow moving, dressed to inflict pain upon the eye. French prisons were full of men who'd dismissed Tessier as a buffoon, only to learn that he was one of the shrewdest detectives in the country.

In all fairness, McGann admitted, the circumstances creating the slow burn in his gut were not of Tessier's making. Still, there was much to be said for killing the messenger.

"That is all I can tell you, Paul." Tessier rolled his head, adding more grime to his already soiled collar. "It was an accident, not a deliberate killing."

"Let me see the paperwork."

McGann didn't move a muscle. He always made people stand up and hand him things. In this case, an accident report with very detailed black-and-white photographs: the vintage Citroën wrapped around a lamppost on the Boulevard Montmartre; the driver still inside, his chest crushed into the steering wheel; the victim lying in the street.

McGann flipped through the pictures and pulled out only those showing the victim—the angle at which the head rested, the pool of blood, the soiled pants.

"Documents?"

"We found Beauchamp's passport and the air tickets. But not the onetime INS entry form."

McGann closed his eyes lightly in an effort to dispel his anger. Beauchamp had been very good, one of the best at moving cargo from point A to point B. His talents would be missed.

But could they be replaced?

"Tell me about the driver," McGann said.

"Emil Leclerc. Accountant with Crédit Lyonnais for twenty years. Model employee, family man, absolutely no connection to Beauchamp."

"And to French intelligence?"

"Our computers tell me no." Tessier paused. "What do *your* machines tell you, Paul?"

McGann opened his eyes. "That Beauchamp never knew anyone called Leclerc. He never had contact with any employee of Crédit Lyonnais. His account was at Banque Nationale de Paris and he preferred to fuck stockbrokers, not accountants."

"Bad luck, then." Tessier hesitated, fingered an aubergine-colored tie years out of date. "We cannot wait on the transfer. It has to take place tomorrow. You have to find a replacement for Beauchamp, someone equally—"

"I will."

"What about the missing entry form?"

"I said I'll take care of it." McGann's voice rose barely but it was enough to silence Tessier. "In the meantime, find out what happened to that form. Beauchamp should have had it with him, and it could tie him to our man."

"But the name on the form is meaningless. It has no connection to—"

"Find it anyway. You know I hate loose ends."

McGann rose to indicate that the meeting was over. He forced himself to speak kindly. "Then, go home to your wife. Wait. It's Tuesday, isn't it? I meant your mistress."

Tessier grinned and shambled toward the door.

"You know me too well, Paul," he said as he left.

The odor of Tessier's sweat and cheap cologne blanketed the office. McGann opened the French doors to let the breeze in. Beyond the embassy walls rose the perpetual hum of traffic on the Champs-Elysées.

McGann focused on the ticktock of the grandfather clock, slowly ridding himself of the lingering reminders of Tessier's visit. His thoughts turned to the man who was his real employer, a living, lethal legend.

Three years ago, when McGann's star was rising more brightly than Halley's comet, he had received a call from a very senior member of the French Foreign Ministry. McGann had done business with this official, had compiled an extensive dossier on him, and thought he knew him very well.

As things turned out, though, not that well at all.

Their meeting took place in a suite at Nice's fabled Hôtel Negresco, where it had been suggested McGann spend his vacation. After a few minutes of polite chitchat, the French official left and a middle-aged, nondescript man came out of the bedroom.

McGann had been mildly amused by this subterfuge; after assessing the man, he was bored. He looked like some shady businessman who held enough favors with the French to curry an introduction to an American diplomat. McGann idly wondered what it was he'd ask for. As it turned out, nothing. And the man was an American.

The man further startled McGann by reciting the most intimate details of McGann's professional career, ones that McGann knew for a certainty had been deleted from his personnel file. There was a superior's complaint questioning McGann's ethics in dealing with a French government official who was later indicted for bribery, and a case involving what appeared to be a valid sexual harassment complaint in the embassy. McGann had refereed the hearing and in the end had quashed the complaint. The woman was immediately transferred stateside, while the accused, who turned out to have ties to McGann's family, was promoted, becoming McGann's creature.

McGann listened to this without comment, forcing himself to stay calm. He'd already concluded that there were only two possible reasons why he was being told this: extortion or blackmail.

"I know what you're thinking," the man said. "But I don't want anything from you. In fact, I'm here to make you an offer. If you accept, *then* I'll need something from you. Or you may walk away right now and be assured that this meeting never took place."

McGann had found it impossible to walk away. Someone who knew such things about him was a force to be reckoned with. McGann, who was well versed in the delicate art of bending men to his will, had to know more.

In the course of the afternoon he learned things that even he, with all his access to information, had never dreamed of. He was told how the fates of entire nations had been decided by the actions of one man, carefully prepared, calibrated, and sent into action. He was offered specific dates, places, and names that could be cross-checked. He was asked to consider the tiny anomalies in the official stories behind these events, anomalies that could be accounted for only after the hidden elements were factored in.

McGann had the gift of patience. He was a good listener, knowing that even the most discreet of men needed to hear the sound of their own voice. But not this one. He told McGann only what was necessary to convince him, nothing that could come back to hang him.

When he finished, he asked a single question: "Do you wish to join me?"

McGann understood that unconsciously he had been waiting for this moment all his life, one that would define him forever. Like the acolyte pledging blind faith to the church, he said yes.

From that day forward, Paul McGann had only one real master. He was applauded for his understanding of power and made to accept that at his core he was driven by a greed for it. This was good, because some of the duties that would come his way would decide life and death for men he might respect, admire, even love.

The man explained that the fraternal organization he headed did not pledge allegiance to any one government, even though its members were all highly placed members of various governments. The overriding concern was the stability of the new world order. Anyone who threatened the harmony between nations, constructed on secret, ironclad protocols, was the enemy. Such individuals, no matter how powerful they might appear, were only grains of sand. Remove a single pebble and an entire pyramid—and threat—would crumble.

Paul McGann met with his mentor three times a year. Gradually he was introduced to others in the fraternity, but only when circumstances dictated its absolute necessity. He was only one part of a secret, far-flung, invisible team, one silent factor among many. Until now.

The chimes of the grandfather clock striking the hour roused McGann. He had to make his decision.

The operation that was currently running in France was approaching a critical stage. Nothing could change or be allowed to interfere if it was to proceed to the next stage.

He had planned meticulously and had sworn that nothing would go wrong. However, the unforeseen death of a drone had already threatened this first mission McGann had been given total control over. He knew it was a test, and how much was riding on its success-ful completion.

But now he was faced with a hard choice.

Procedure dictated that he contact his chief and mentor. The prob-lem was time. Tessier himself had underlined the urgency of staying on schedule. McGann knew that if he waited or even hesitated, the opera-tion would be delayed or, worse, canceled. He could not allow that to happen. His mentor was watching, measuring him.

McGann understood that his only option was to act unilaterally, to take the fallback position. He appreciated how dangerous this could be, not only because of potential failure but because of the nature of his plan. Yet he was certain that a successful result would forgive all tres-passes. In the end, results were all that mattered. His mentor had shown him, by example, how true that was.

McGann looked back at the clock, as though listening for a particu-lar sound. But that wasn't what came to him on the last toll. It was ac-ceptance of the only solution within his grasp.

THE HANDYMAN HAD paid a premium for the first-class roomette on the Marseille–Paris overnight train.

It did not matter to him that the train whistle-stopped its way north, pulling into obscure country stations and sometimes shunting off onto a siding to allow an express or freight to roar by. For years his life had been circumscribed by Marseille's North African ghetto. To be able to look out at the countryside, to marvel at the beauty of the setting sun as it touched hills and valleys and rivers, to glimpse at people going about their daily lives without fear or suspicion, all this brought him an exhilarating sense of freedom.

The Handyman sat by the window, transfixed, for hours, even after darkness had fallen. He'd been startled by the knock on his door, but it was only the porter coming by to prepare the foldout bunk.

After the porter left, he tugged out the old, stiff sheets from his jacket pocket. Turning on the reading lamp, he traced his fingertips over the vertical row of Chinese characters. He felt tiny charges of electricity prick his skin as though the characters were trying to communicate with him.

From his two brief phone calls from Marseille the Handyman knew some immediate and long-range specifics of his mission: times and places. These were essential if one was to forecast the horoscopic conditions accurately. Following a pattern he had used on every one of his previous assignments, the Handyman was able to project the possible obstacles that lay ahead and clues as to how he might circumvent them.

But two essential factors were missing: an in-depth knowledge of his ultimate goal, and the true motive of the man who had resurrected him. The Handyman accepted that there was nothing—for the moment—that he could do about the first. Later on, information would, of necessity, be made available to him. Also, as he got closer, he would be able to tap his own resources.

As for the second, discerning the motive of his employer not only was possible but could be accomplished with a high degree of success. Here, patience was called for until he reached his destination, where there was a man who could help him.

His eyes weary, the Handyman put away the pages, washed up at his private sink, and lay back in the crisp, clean sheets. He turned out the light and through the window followed the moon as it flew high above the train, leading him to some destiny he could not imagine. When he finally closed his eyes it was a dreamless sleep that stole over him, as though the horrors of the past no longer had the power to touch him.

He was dressed and ready when the train pulled into the Gare de Lyon. As he stepped onto the concrete ramp, he looked up at the crisscrossed girders and large grimy skylights of the station's roof. He picked out the surveillance cameras immediately and turned so that his back was to them.

He fell in with the crowds walking toward the exit, then suddenly veered left to a newspaper kiosk. He was looking at two things, one of which was a distant memory, the other a scrap of a nightmare that sometimes overwhelmed him.

Near the exit, below a double staircase, was a makeshift patio of large red and green umbrellas, each with Coca-Cola or Heineken logos. At the top of the staircase were tall curved windows and a handsome arched entryway. Above the entrance, in red-and-blue swirling neon, was the sign: LE TRAIN BLEU.

The Handyman stared at it, recalling every detail of its posh, clublike atmosphere. Small wonder. Le Train Bleu was where he'd had his last good meal before fading into exile.

The second image was quite the opposite. Thirty feet away were two plainclothes detectives. Between them stood a prisoner, a young man neatly dressed but with three days' beard on his face. One had to look closely to see the handcuffs, almost hidden by the young man's jacket sleeves and attached to a flexible steel tether encased in bungee fabric. One of the detectives held the tether casually as he might hold a dog's leash. His eyes were not on the prisoner but on a pretty girl in a leather miniskirt seated at the café. His partner was smoking, staring idly at the overhead arrivals and departures board.

To the Handyman, the prisoner was a creature who dwelled in the tiny crevices of sleep where the worms of fear twisted and squirmed. Capture was the only thing that terrified him. In the young prisoner's resigned slouch and darting eyes he saw a fate he himself could never surrender to. To be seized, abused, and ultimately broken was an indignity he would never permit. He would fight even when he could feel his pursuer's breath on his cheek. He would take down as many as he could. But there would always be that last bullet for himself, to cheat them.

Outside the station, beneath the imposing clock tower overlooking the circular drive, tour buses were taking on arriving tourists. The Handyman spotted what he needed—an unattended baggage cart. The driver and tour guide were taking tickets, shepherding their charges into the bus, their backs to him. He moved around the cart, piled high with luggage, and squeezed his suitcase in between two garment bags.

Eventually the suitcase would arrive at some one-star hotel. When no one claimed it the porter would put it into the storage room. Then, before going off duty, he would jimmy the suitcase lock in the hope of finding something valuable. When he didn't, the evidence of his pilferage would end up in the hotel's garbage bin.

The Handyman strolled down toward the Boulevard Diderot and into a café, where he ordered coffee. The place was crowded but he didn't mind. He pressed his back to the counter rail and watched the people on the sidewalk, listening to the conversations swirl around him. A raw wind blew in whenever the door opened and closed. The sky was the color of lead. The Handyman drank it all in, feeling very much the way he thought he appeared: like someone who'd been away for a long time and was glad to be home. His instincts remained neutral. He sensed no danger in the environment. In fact, everything was exactly as he remembered it, down to the white-and-orange Alliance Petroleum Marquage van across the street, creating another of the minor traffic jams that were the bane of Parisian drivers.

Inside the van, everything was *not* as it should have been.

A padded bench with flip-up trays ran down the center of the floor. On the left were still and video cameras mounted on tripods, focused through one-way-glass panes that had replaced three of the van's original windows.

On the right was a sophisticated communications console—a bank of TV monitors, reel-to-reel tape recorders, and controls for the laser unit built into what appeared to be a cell phone antenna.

Behind the driver's seat was a small but powerful air-conditioning unit. Beside that, a six-cubic-foot refrigerator.

The van was one in a stable of six vehicles that Crawford kept in a long-term garage out in Marne-la-Vallée–Chessy, not far from Euro-Disney. The others included a Mercedes moving van, used for transport and to haul equipment, an ambulance, and a Black Maria, or prisoner van, stolen from the Palais de Justice on the Ile de la Cité.

Crawford shifted on the bench, gently pressing his cheek against the rubber eyepiece mounted on the x400-equipped Nikon. The passing traffic and pedestrians were a blur, but the Handyman was in sharp focus. The camera, working in tandem with the laser and programmed to eliminate foreground detail, clicked automatically whenever the laser clearly sighted the target.

"Fifteen years you've been hiding in rat holes," Crawford said under his breath. "Nobody's seen you. Nobody's heard word one about you. Most of the people who would have been curious think you're dead."

He rubbed an old scar at his temple, near the hairline. *Why are you back? Who drew you out?*

"Sam, we have maybe a minute before he finishes his coffee and is on the move again. Let's take him now."

Crawford pulled back from the camera and glanced at Wally Liggett. With his moon face, snowman build, and walrus mustache, he could have been anybody's favorite uncle. Dressed in grease-stained blue overalls with a tool-laden utility belt around his waist, he looked like any other city worker dawdling on the taxpayer's dime.

"No," Crawford said.

"Sam—"

"*No*. Whoever resurrected him has a very special job in mind."

"The Handyman can enlighten us as to who and what."

Wally was of the opinion that they should have snatched the Handyman the minute Crawford had first spotted him in motion. There had been plenty of opportunities, especially on the train, but Crawford had passed on every one.

"Not him," Crawford said. "We might be able to take him alive, but we'd never get him to talk. He'd swallow his tongue first."

Wally shrugged to indicate that that was, in his opinion, an acceptable risk.

"He made those phone calls, Sam. He might not need any other contact."

"He'll still need a clean cutout," Crawford said, knowing he sounded stubborn. "Someone who'll have papers and money. More detailed instructions." He paused. "If we play this right, we get both ends: the target *and* the Handyman's control."

Wally's attention was still on the Handyman when he said, "Sometimes you want too much."

"Sometimes I'm not willing to settle for less. Go paint him, Wally."

"What about Susan?"

"I'll call her now, tell her we have a new customer in town who might be looking for our kind of papers. I want a rundown of everything her department's processed in the last month. Plus what's in the pipeline."

"What if he's not headed our way?"

"We know that for a fact, we hand him off to de Jong at Interpol."

Wally sighed. "I'm outta here."

He squeezed his way to the rear doors of the van and dropped a weatherproof orange curtain behind him. Jamming a Gitane into the corner of his mouth, he put on his best scowl, opened the door, and hopped out. When he landed on the pavement, his left ankle turned slightly, and he cursed. He'd forgotten he was wearing his old sneakers while his work boots were being resoled.

He moved past the orange-and-white traffic cones surrounding the van, found a break in the traffic, and darted across the street with surprising agility. In the café, he bellied up to the bar next to the Handyman and ordered coffee. Avoiding eye contact with the Handyman, he flirted slyly with the proprietress. He brought out a small box of wooden matches, pulled one out, and lit his cigarette. Casually his hand drifted toward the ashtray to the right of the Handyman's arm. Wally held the match in such a way that its clean end brushed the Handyman's wrist.

"*Pardon,*" he mumbled.

He dropped the match into the tray and finished his coffee. In the mirror over the bar he saw the Handyman rub the skin where the match had grazed it.

All the better, because now the colorless, slightly oily film was spread across a wider area of skin. The oil had been exposed to radioactive isotopes. In this minute quantity, it wasn't lethal. But there was enough for a laser tracker to pick it up. Soaked into the skin, the oil would not wash away, either with water or sweat. "Painted," the Handyman could be tracked for the next twenty-four hours at a distance of one hundred yards.

Wally drained his cup, slid three francs onto the counter, and with a wink at the proprietress, ambled out.

THE MAÎTRE D' AT L'OBÉLISQUE recognized Paul McGann immediately.

"A pleasure to see you again, monsieur."

"Thank you, Henri. You made the arrangements?"

The maître d' indicated with his chin a spot behind his lectern. Set in a crystal vase were a dozen perfect roses.

McGann nodded his approval, palmed the man a hundred-franc note, and entered the dining room, his carriage and gait both casual and proprietary. He was only steps from the table when Hollis turned around. He assumed it was because she sensed his presence.

"Paul!"

She started to get out of the chair but McGann pressed gently on her shoulders. He leaned down and kissed her between her cheek and neck.

"I'm sorry I'm late. A last-minute thing . . . "

Then the flowers arrived, the maître d' and a waiter fussing with the vase, clearing a space for it on the table. The scent filled the air, and Hollis gave an "Oh!" of delight.

McGann took his seat and, smiling through the roses, studied the older man, picked up the bemused curiosity in the blue eyes.

"Paul, I'd like you to meet Dawson Wylie," Hollis said. "Dee, Paul McGann. He's the deputy chief of mission."

Wylie shook the man's hand and sat back, grinning at Hollis. "So this is the fella you've been carrying on about."

Which made Hollis blush.

"Glad to meet you, son," Wylie said. "Holly hasn't told me anything about you. Guess she wanted me to see for myself."

"Hollis told me you used to be in the Foreign Service," McGann replied.

"A long time ago. Not even close to your level."

"I'm a glorified water carrier."

Wylie shot Hollis a pointed look. "Humble too. A rare thing in this business."

"Will you be in Paris much longer, sir?"

"Sad to say, no. Already checked out. My plane goes in two hours." Wylie paused. "Which means you and I will have to get acquainted another time."

"You can at least start now," Hollis said. "While I go freshen up."

She stood, leaned over to inhale the heavy scent of the roses, and left the room. At the entrance she looked back and saw Wylie and Paul chatting easily.

In the washroom Hollis took twice as long as she needed. She wanted to give Dee as much time with Paul as possible. She craved his approval.

Paul McGann was not the only man Hollis had ever loved but he was the first one she loved so fiercely and completely. The first she had allowed past her maze of defenses after knowing him for less than a month. The first who'd moved slowly and patiently toward her heart, never rushing, insisting, or overwhelming her. The first who had captured her so completely that even now there were moments when she felt afraid. She knew too well what it was like to be vulnerable. The footsteps of that long, painful journey from the orphan's shadow into the light of hope and trust were like imprints on her soul.

Yet the attraction between her and Paul had felt so natural that everything that had followed seemed preordained. Hollis was pleased that she had never so much as raised a finger to pursue him. Paul McGann was the embassy's most eligible bachelor. When she'd come on board at the consulate Hollis had heard the women's room paeans about him—charming, drop-dead gorgeous, great sense of humor. He knew how to show a girl a good time but it was seldom the same girl twice. If women found out whom he had bedded, that information came not from male scuttlebutt but from the trophy fuckers. And who could believe them?

Hollis recalled how the other women on the visa line had started looking at her when word got out that she and Paul were dating—with the critical "What does she have that I don't?" eye. The questions were desperately casual and Hollis's oblique answers only stoked envy.

The women didn't care that Hollis, the newest kid on the diplomatic block, had yet to find anyone she could call a friend. Her novitiate's shyness was interpreted as disdain; her reluctance to trade in such frail currency as confidences of the heart was taken for a diva's arrogance.

The women who desired Paul McGann turned on her like hens pecking a chick that had stumbled into their preserve.

As an only child Hollis had learned to do without the close comforts of siblings. She knew that in time some of these women would look past her affair with Paul and accept her for who she was. In her private moments she hoped that that would come soon. For all the joy Paul brought her there were things about him she could not understand, things she could never share even with Dawson Wylie but only with another woman.

When Hollis returned to the table, Dawson Wylie was counting out francs, laying them across the bill resting in a saucer.

"This was supposed to be my treat," Hollis said.

Wylie shrugged. "Not like I can use it back home." He looked at her. "Ready?"

Outside, Paul moved off to tell the doorman to flag a cab. Hollis stood facing Wylie. They were almost nose to nose. She waited until she couldn't stand it anymore.

"Well?"

Wylie feigned confusion. "Well *what?*"

"You know!"

His eyes gave him away, as they always did, to her.

"He seems like a great guy, Holly."

Hollis flung her arms around him and kissed him on both cheeks.

"*Yes!*" she whispered fiercely.

Clinging to Wylie's arm, she walked him to the waiting cab. He got in, then thrust his arm out the window and gripped her hand.

"I'll call you as soon as I'm home." He turned to McGann. "Paul, you take good care of her, hear?"

"I will, sir."

The driver either understood English or had just spotted an opening in the traffic, because suddenly the cab rocketed away. In the maze of flashing metal and glass, Hollis thought she saw Wylie waving out the window.

A tear suggested itself to her but she blinked and willed it away.

"I really am sorry for not getting here sooner," Paul said.

Hollis kept looking after the cab, though by now it was long gone. She traced a fingernail along Paul's cheek.

"It's okay. He liked you."

"Really?"

"Really. The roses helped. By the way, what happened to them?"

"They'll be sent to your apartment."

"Very considerate." She gave him a tender, shyly seductive smile.

McGann put a finger under her chin, gently lifting it.

"And what about you? Do you like me too?"

"Enough to say yes if you were to ask me to go out to dinner tonight."

CHAPTER FOUR

THE AMERICAN CONSULATE is located at the end of Rue St.-Florentin, where it empties into Rue de Rivoli. For months its stone facade had been covered by scaffolding and construction tarpaulins. The sidewalk in front of the building was cordoned off by steel crowd-control barriers. Thick, paint-spattered boards created a ceiling over the sidewalk, but most pedestrians chose to walk on the other side of the street to avoid the dirt and dust that rained through the cracks. On the first two levels of the building, the tarps were green; on the third, a dark gray. The floors above that were covered with a filmy, gauzelike netting, as though some giant spider were slowly spinning a web to mummify the victims inside.

Businesspeople, tourists who'd been pickpocketed, students down to their last few francs, and petitioning foreigners all paused in front of the building, convinced they'd gotten the address wrong. The CRS patrolmen across the street had become the unofficial receptionists. Their bored answer was always the same: "Yes, that is the American consulate."

So everyone nodded and silently presumed that the building was getting a face-lift. Which was true, if one's idea of renovation was armor-plated glass for the windows and steel-reinforced walls that could withstand the impact of a car bomb.

Hollis turned onto the narrow sidewalk on Rue St.-Florentin, with its expensive shops, and passed Toraya, a Japanese teahouse, and the Café Le Florentin, both hangouts for the consulate staff.

Ducking under the scaffolding, she quickened her pace through the open barn-size doors into the courtyard. On the left, sixty feet from the front doors, was the security post, which included an airport-style scanning machine.

"Hi, Mac."

The plainclothes security officer smiled, gave her ID a cursory glance. Hollis deposited her purse on the conveyor belt and watched it disappear through the plastic flaps for the X-ray check.

"How's Mr. Wylie?"

"Going home today."

"I hear that he and some of the embassy old-timers had themselves quite the shindig last night."

Hollis laughed. "Nothing that he'd tell me about."

At the top of the steps before the front doors, Hollis paused and looked back across the courtyard, watching the people pass by on the sidewalk without giving the consulate a second look. It was a sight that she still wasn't used to.

Before coming to Paris, Hollis had had a two-month posting in Santo Domingo. There, the line of visa applicants would start to form well before dawn. Each morning Hollis would walk past hundreds of people standing patiently, gossiping quietly with those around them. The talk would stop when they saw her. Did this young, well-scrubbed American woman hold the keys to their destinies? Could she, with a flick of a pen, send them on their way to their dreams? Their eyes and smiles reached out to her, and in them Hollis felt all the hope and desperation and uncertainty that had raised these people from their beds at dawn to stand under an already blazing sun, in the hope of getting through the golden doors of America. A whole day's labor might be lost, and at the end there might be nothing to show for it. But still they came and lined up, and would return the next day and the next, as many times as necessary.

Once, Hollis had stopped in front of a middle-aged man clutching a tattered, sweat-stained file that held the sum of his life. She asked him who he was and he said a garbage collector, married, with five children. Hollis should have stopped there, but she was so young and she cared.

"And you're willing to leave your family, just like that?" she asked.

The garbage collector stiffened; then, realizing he might have offended her, he replied in his soft island drawl. "The rich here—they have no need to go anywhere. But we who are poor, we are eating stones. I want to improve my life, to see my family live in the green."

After that, every application Hollis reviewed carried back those words: *live in the green.*

The uniformed guard in the foyer gave Hollis a brief smile, then reached beneath his desk and pressed a button. The steel-sheathed door with no nameplate on it buzzed open.

The corridor behind the door was long and so narrow that people usually had to sidestep to get by one another. On either side were cubbyhole offices, the walls so thin that the constant stream of voices carried into the hall. Hollis came to a large room that had been created by breaking up a host of smaller offices. The wood floor still bore light marks where walls had stood.

This area was an old-style bull pen, filled with forty workstations, the shoulder-high partitions covered in gray upholstery. Only the far wall had windows, and those overlooked a decaying brick wall. The overhead fluorescent tubes tended to sputter and crackle in damp weather. There had been talk of revamping the electrical system—which sometimes played havoc with the computer terminals—and of putting in a new floor to replace the bowed, creaking boards. The water-stained ceiling was in need of replastering. So far, only the heating and air-conditioning units had been redone, outfitted with powerful air scrubbers. Someone had finally determined that cleaner air would cut down on how often staffers called in sick.

On the way to her station, Hollis bumped shoulders with harried messengers, secretaries, and coworkers lugging files under their arms. She waved at the few faces that acknowledged her passing, and out the corner of her eye saw her supervisor, Susan Garcetti, at her desk, talking on the phone. The room was filled with the clicking of computer keys, reminding Hollis of a field of cicadas.

"Hi! How was breakfast with Dawson?"

Hollis turned to see Julie Tomkins's moon face staring at her over the top of her workstation wall.

"Okay. But I felt really rotten when he had to go."

"I know what you mean. I still remember my mom and dad seeing me off at the airport. I cried the whole way over."

Hollis offered what she hoped was an encouraging smile.

Julie was the newest member of the visa line, having arrived less than a month ago. She was a working-class girl from Chicago who'd joined the Foreign Service in search of romance and adventure. But nature had trapped a sunny personality and quick wit in a body that was constantly fighting weight and the dictates of fashion.

Hollis, herself an outsider, had taken Julie under her wing, helping her to learn the ropes of the visa line and taking her around Paris to alleviate some of her homesickness. A couple of times she'd suggested to Paul that he introduce Julie to some of his friends. Paul's response had been, "Yeah, sure. I'll give François or Henri a call and we'll all go out." But it had never happened.

A few weeks went by and every time Hollis raised the subject, Paul had what seemed a plausible reason to say no. Finally Hollis had realized that Paul didn't want Julie in his circle and that his string of excuses was his way of dealing with the issue. She found it a curious character trait in a man who was usually so decisive, but she thought he didn't want to come right out with it and hurt her feelings.

As if reading her thoughts, Julie asked, "Are you going out tonight?"

Hollis was a poor liar and knew it. "Yes," she said carefully. "With Dee around, Paul and I haven't had much time together."

Julie forced a smile but got the hint. She nodded in the direction of their supervisor. "You're on her radar. We'll talk later. Lunch?"

"Great."

Hollis sank into her chair, looked around her cubicle, and decided it wasn't in such bad shape. Piles of visa applications and assorted other documents were stacked two feet high on the floor. A slew of phone messages and the morning mail, in one-foot piles, nearly obliterated her desk.

Gingerly, so as not to unduly disturb this fragile ecosystem, Hollis began shifting files and papers. She found the application she'd been working on yesterday, took a deep breath, and started to earn her paycheck.

THE MORNING DISAPPEARED in a blur. The next time Hollis looked up, it was noon. She finished up the file she'd been working on, leaned over the top of the partition, and said to Julie, "Ready for some food?"

"You bet. Even if it is meat loaf day at the cafeteria."

"I meant *real* food."

Feeling guilty because she couldn't ask Julie to join her this evening, Hollis took her to lunch at a new place called Le Petit Restaurant, in the First Quarter. It had become an overnight success, but Hollis had telephoned ahead. One of the few perks of working at the consulate was that no restaurant ever turned down a reservation request from a patron in the diplomatic corps.

Hollis and Julie each ordered a glass of white wine that was the perfect complement to their main dishes, mushroom ravioli and baby scallops in vinegar sauce. They ate slowly, savoring every morsel, chatting across the table over the noontime din. They compared notes on some of the consulate's more eccentric personalities, made plans to go together to an upcoming embassy-employee event, and then over coffee mused on their futures in the Foreign Service. Both were aware of the glass ceiling for women in the State Department and of the male hierarchy that found ingenious—and insidious—ways to promote its chosen successors. But the careers of women such as Jeane Kirkpatrick, Reagan's ambassador to the U.N., and Madeleine Albright, the current secretary of state, indicated that times were certainly changing.

After lunch, Hollis joined six other visa slaves in a weekly briefing session conducted by her supervisor. Susan Garcetti, a tall, handsome blond woman in her early forties, kept her staff on a short leash. She demanded their utmost attention and professionalism on the job but was just as concerned about any problems that could interfere with the visa department's assembly-line-like functioning. Comments and suggestions from the junior officers were encouraged.

Hollis ended the day slightly later than she'd hoped. She said good night to Julie, then walked quickly through the early-evening traffic to her apartment. She barely had time to shower and dress for dinner before Paul was at the door.

"You've ruined my lipstick," she scolded him after a lingering kiss.

He laughed. "Fix it. We have plenty of time."

"Where are we going?" Hollis called over her shoulder as she disappeared into the bathroom.

"Bofinger."

"I've heard it's great."

With Paul, Hollis never had to worry about eating at the same restaurant twice—unless she wanted to. He knew all the best old haunts, as well as the hottest new spots, where tables were impossible to get.

She returned to the foyer and did a little turn, her black cocktail dress wafting around her thighs. "How do I look?"

He raised one eyebrow and grinned lecherously. "Seriously, how hungry *are* you?"

She breathed him a kiss and pushed him out the door. "Hungry enough."

One thing Hollis had had to get used to in Paris was eating late. Dinner, whether in restaurants or in private homes, rarely started before nine and, depending on the number of courses, could go on for three hours. She'd had to learn to pace herself and to order dishes that were not only light but served in small portions.

Bofinger was everything she'd heard it was: a beautiful brasserie in the ancient Bastille section of the city, with crisp white linen, Art Nouveau *verrières* that exuded soft, romantic light, and the owner's signature: white china highlighted by tiny dancing dolphins.

The restaurant was packed with upscale diners, equally split between corporate chieftains and couples with enough jewelry on their fingers and wrists to service the national debt. Hollis thought her single strand of pearls was completely lost in their mass of fire and ice. She would have preferred a less ostentatious place, but she knew that Paul preferred this kind of setting, not only for the cuisine but for networking. On the way to their table, he paused three times to press flesh with people who made a point of catching his attention.

Paul had chosen to eat upstairs, in the smoking area. The downstairs, he informed Hollis, was for rabidly health-conscious Americans. As a nonsmoker, Hollis would have preferred the downstairs, but Paul, like many Frenchmen, enjoyed a cigarette with his *fine* and espresso.

Over grilled sole with *beurre blanc* and rack of lamb, they chatted with the easy familiarity of lovers whose hunger for each other is tempered by a comfort in each other's presence. The conversation meandered from the sphinxlike quality of French politics to the question of whether they could time their vacations so as to be able to get away together, and where they should go. Paul was pushing one of the Greek islands, but Hollis was holding out for Venice and the Italian lake country.

They were still going back and forth on the issue when Paul signed the check and said, "How about a nightcap?"

It was almost midnight and Hollis had a good idea of what Paul was really saying. She'd learned the hard way that Paris nightclubs didn't start moving much before the witching hour and remained open until 5 A.M. Twice she'd shown up at the visa line looking like death warmed over after an all-nighter.

"I think you'd better drop me off," she told him. "I'm swamped at work—"

"Only for an hour. It's a new place, and I promised a couple of people I'd meet them there."

"Paul . . . "

He took her hand, his thumb moving along the inside of her wrist, stroking her skin tenderly.

"One hour," he whispered.

"You make me crazy," she murmured.

"Not yet. I'm saving that for later."

THE CLUB MINOTAUR was in the heart of Place Pigalle, a district legendary for clubs that served up naughty, Vegas-style extravaganzas to the delight of visiting Asian businessmen.

The Minotaur, however, was in a class by itself. Unlike the other clubs, it was licensed as a *boîte privée,* which allowed it to have a strict, members-only door policy, keeping out the hordes of tourists.

Inside, it was a surrealistic blend of California tech and Caribbean passion. Mounted against three walls were floor-to-ceiling backdrops depicting L.A. landmarks: the HOLLYWOOD sign, the Walk of Stars, a studio lot, and even *Jurassic Park*'s *T. rex*. On the stage—made to look like a section of Venice Beach, complete with papier-mâché palm trees, the boardwalk, and gyrating young girls wearing only thong bikinis— a reggae band pumped out hot, sensual island tunes. The floor was crowded with dancers caught in the cross fire of overhead strobes.

As Paul guided them to a row of banquettes next to the bar, Hollis took in the crowd: young, moneyed, and hip. Stockbrokers, lawyers, and bankers by day, they had transformed themselves into nighttime satyrs. The women, none over twenty-five as far as she could tell, were dressed by the most trendy and expensive designers of the Left Bank.

Paul introduced his friends, two thirty-something men from the Foreign Ministry and their dates, sloe-eyed dollies wearing black-on-black, with slicked-back hair, lipstick, eye shadow, jeans, and cutoff T-shirts that exposed health-club-molded abs.

When the waitress came by, Paul ordered a bottle of champagne, then huddled with the two men. Hollis strained to listen but couldn't hear a word over the music. She smiled uncertainly at the two girls, who were staring at the crowd on the dance floor, smoking Dunhill cigarettes fitted into six-inch holders. When the champagne arrived Paul peeled off several five-hundred-franc bills from a thick roll.

Hollis was wondering how long she'd have to stay when the two girls shifted closer to her and raised their glasses. Hesitantly, Hollis lifted hers, conscious of the girls' eyes roaming over her. She'd barely had a chance to taste the wine when she felt something brush her thigh. Once. Then a second time. She stared into her lap and was shocked to see a girl's hand stroking her leg.

"Tu veux, chérie?" the girl whispered throatily, her breath hot on Hollis's cheek.

Now the other girl was crowding close, her fingernails running along Hollis's arm.

"The three of us, *tu sais?* Your boyfriend can watch if he wants to."

Hollis jerked away. "Thanks, but no."

She squirmed around the tiny table and got to her feet, then literally bumped into Paul.

"Hey, they're finally slowing the pace," he said. "Let's dance."

Before she knew it, Hollis found herself on the dance floor, in his arms, the soft music washing over her like moonlight.

"You're shivering. What's wrong?"

She looked up at him. "Your pals' girlfriends made a pass at me."

He drew back. "What?"

"They thought we'd make a nice threesome."

"Hollis, come on! Maybe you misunderstood . . . "

"Their groping me? I don't think so."

"Shhh . . . Forget about it. They're gone."

Hollis turned. Sure enough, the dollies were slithering through the crowd, heading out. Paul's friends seemed to have disappeared as well. The tension drained from her body and she lost herself in the music and the strong arms that enveloped her. Hollis giggled. It *was* funny, in a bizarre, Parisian kind of way.

The soft songs continued, one after the other. With her head on

Paul's shoulder, her eyes closed, Hollis felt transported to a magical land where nothing existed except his lips brushing her cheek and neck, his hands moving slowly over her body, coming close but never quite reaching those places she wanted him to touch. Her tongue slid over her lips, tasting the residue of sweet champagne.

"Let's go," she whispered urgently.

The ride to Paul's apartment seemed to take forever. In the privacy of the elevator, Hollis began to devour him, clinging to him as they stumbled down the hall. The door was flung open, she kissed him hard, her tongue filling his mouth, a soft groan escaping when she finally pulled away. Hollis kicked off her shoes and went straight into the bedroom, flicking on the soft, recessed lighting.

The package, wrapped in thick, cream-colored paper, lay on the large four-poster bed. Hollis had seen similar boxes before, from the finest lingerie shops in the city. This one was from Jolya, a specialty boutique near the Place Vendôme. Others had come from Dior, Lanvin, and other top designer shops.

She looked around at Paul. He had his back to her. He had placed a snifter of cognac on the small coffee table, next to his cigarettes, and was arranging the cushions on the love seat facing the bed. Hollis knew exactly what was in the box and what he expected her to do with it. He'd bought her many such gifts. Without a word, she picked up the box and took it into the en suite bathroom.

Soft jazz was drifting across the room when she returned. The lights had been adjusted just so; a cigarette was burning in the ashtray. Paul had changed into a silk bathrobe. She knew he was naked underneath it.

She was still wearing the black cocktail dress and now pulled the zipper down all the way. With a gentle shrug, the dress slipped to the floor.

Fixing her eyes on the small Utrillo picture on the wall behind the love seat, she began to undulate to the music, her fingers reaching behind her to undo the lacy bra that barely contained her breasts. She moved closer to Paul and closed her eyes, her thumbs hooking under the elastic of the silky, transparent panties. She could never look at him when she exposed herself like this. The first time he'd asked her to strip she'd been taken aback, thinking he was joking. But when he persisted, and she relented, all she'd felt was shame. Nothing in her sexual experience—all of six men, who had shown passionate enthusiasm but little imagination—had prepared her for this. Yet, then as now, she could not deny Paul. She let him dress her up, then she took it all off in front of him. And all the while she had to avert her eyes, fearful that she might burst into tears or that he might see the painful question mirrored in her eyes: *Why isn't my naked body enough for you? Why are your gifts to me for your gratification, not mine?*

"No, leave it on."

His hoarse command froze her. She had been reaching for the snap on the garter belt, ready to roll down a black stocking.

He was on his feet, reaching for her, sweeping her up . . . and carrying her to the bed. His hands were lifting her buttocks and his tongue was tracing across her belly, moving lower and lower until she cried out, arched up to meet it.

Hollis lost herself in the pleasure he showered on her. His fingers and tongue were so busy probing, stroking, caressing so slowly that she couldn't help the tiny orgasms that erupted. When she thought she couldn't stand it anymore, she felt him slide into her, his rhythm locking with her, following her desires, coaxing her to pinnacles she never believed existed. When she climaxed again, she threw her legs around him, gripping him fiercely, crying out that she needed him, that she would do whatever he demanded, anything at all.

Paul always made certain that she was satisfied first. Then he plunged deeper and harder into her, sending jolts of pain through the waves of pleasure. She heard him moan "I love you" over and over again, then something in French, which, because of his strangled voice, she didn't understand. "*Ma petite poule . . .*" And as she felt him explode, Hollis wondered why it was that at that crucial moment, he could never look into her eyes or call her name.

A HALF HOUR later Hollis was still awake. Beside her, Paul lay on his side, his shallow breath indicating deep sleep. Hollis slid out from under the quilt. She stood in the patch of moonlight streaming through the windows, undid the garter belt, rolled down the stockings, and flung them into a dark corner. Quietly, she opened the French doors; the cool air felt good on her skin.

Ile St.-Louis was not only an island but an oasis moored in the River Seine. Perhaps because it was removed from the bustle of Rue St.-Jacques and Boulevard St.-Michel, and the traffic generated by government buildings on Ile de la Cité, the noise of Paris seemed to float around and above it.

It was also home to some of the most enduring landmarks in Paris. Paul's apartment building was almost three hundred years old. Situated on the Quai de Bourbon, at the very tip of the island, the bedroom had a view of the river all the way to the twin towers of Notre Dame.

It was a panorama Hollis loved, especially at night, when the whole universe seemed to consist only of fog and the river and the things that moved upon it. She wondered whether, if she stared at the river long enough, it might cleanse her of her doubts, carry them away forever.

Tu veux, chérie? *The three of us,* tu sais? *Your boyfriend can watch if he wants to.*

Why had the girl said that to her? Had she been intimating that Paul *wanted* to watch as women made love to her? The idea of being touched by another woman left her cold, and even the hint that Paul might have set up the situation at the club rankled.

Jeez, Hollis. Get a grip!

Maybe it was the ten-year difference between her and Paul. Hollis knew that he must have had many women, in a variety of circumstances. Maybe there were things about him that she still hadn't discovered, things that might offend or hurt her.

Yet she couldn't help but remember that in spite of Paul's coaxing and mood-enhancing suggestions, he always gave all of himself to her.

Even that first time, there had been no fumbling, no awkward moments. His fingers and lips and tongue had gone precisely where she would have guided them, had there been a need to. He had discovered all her secret places on his own and opened the treasures of her passion with only her pulse and her murmurs to encourage him.

Sometimes, when he lay beside her sleeping, she would study the creases of his face for clues, like an archaeologist who's discovered a new species of man.

With all the women you've had, could ever have, why do you love me? You never tell me, and it's something I need to know so badly . . .

When they talked and laughed and loved, Hollis could not imagine herself happier. But sometimes at night, like now, she could not still the chants of doubt, like incantations of the lost in tunnels that never led to the light.

As she slipped back into bed, Hollis knew she had no need of a psychiatrist to help her sort this out. The bullets that had killed her parents had shattered the trust that other children give so willingly. And now, when that trust was needed for the mortar of love, she was so afraid.

So she reached in the dark for her man and spooned against him, imagined her fears flying out the window, settling on the lapping waters of the river that would carry them far, far away forever.

ALL SHE COULD hear were murmurs, someone unseen talking. Hollis opened her eyes and rolled over, discovering that the other side of the bed was empty. No surprise. Paul was a morning man, up and out at first light, the hour changing only with the seasons. Once, in the predawn, she had padded sleepily through the apartment and found him in his study, whispering on the phone. He'd hung up the instant he saw her standing in the doorway.

The murmurs stopped, replaced by footsteps. Hollis pushed herself up against the pillows, pulling the quilt all the way up to her chin.

"Good morning."

He looked too good, dressed for the office in one of the tailored suits that he wore with casual elegance. In his arms was a breakfast tray: a bowl of raspberries, coffee, juice.

"Have I told you I love you?" he said, kissing her on the lips.

She grinned. "Yup."

Hollis pushed herself up against the headboard, her breasts spilling across the quilt.

"Won't you be cold?"

"Not if you take the hint." She sipped the juice and reached out to him. "You're *not* taking the hint."

He nodded toward the tray. "Maybe that will make up for my being so dense."

Hollis frowned, then saw it: a long black velvet jeweler's box. Her first thought shamed her: *It's not a ring.*

"You *will* have to open it."

What lay inside the box made her gasp: a thick antique cameo, pale white ivory, threaded on a gold chain, the figure in relief Helen of Troy.

"Read the inscription."

Hollis turned the cameo over. In gothic script were the words *This is forever.*

Hollis was laughing and crying and throwing her arms around him all at once. Her fingers were trembling so badly that she needed him to close the chain's clasp.

"Paul, it's gorgeous! Where . . . ? *Why?*"

He shrugged. "I couldn't resist. Besides, I still feel bad about yesterday, being late for breakfast with you and Dawson."

"Call the embassy," Hollis said. "Tell them you'll be late. The four-hour flu. Then get naked. Later we'll go for crepes at La Sarrasine."

"I wish I could."

The finality in his voice chilled her. She draped the quilt around her shoulders and patted the edge of the bed.

"What's going on?"

"A last-minute screwup. Want to hear about it?"

"Of course."

McGann took a breath. "Okay. There's an old man, an American called Simon Jones. In another life he was a banker who embezzled a few million from a Boston bank—good money in those days—and disappeared over here. Now he's sick and wants to go home.

"He contacted the embassy. I caught the case and talked to the Justice Department. They told me there's still a fugitive warrant out on him but they were willing to deal. I went back to Jones, laid out the terms, told him they were the best he'd get: six months in a country club prison, plus seizure of all his assets, which are considerable.

"Problem is, he doesn't have a passport or any other papers to get him back home. I needed someone to shepherd him home and hand him over to federal marshals at JFK. But the man lined up to do it was in a car wreck last night."

He paused. "So I need a favor."

Hollis sat up. "You want *me* to go?"

"You're accredited. Jones needs a onetime INS entry form, but you can do that. I sent the authorization over to the consulate last night. All you have to do is fill out the form. It'll be on your desk when you get in."

Hollis nodded. She'd heard about consulate staffers being pulled from their jobs to run last-minute errands like this. Usually it meant ferrying documents that hadn't been ready in time for the courier pick-ups. Hollis couldn't recall a real, live person ever being the object of an informal escort. As far as she knew, embassy security personnel were responsible for that.

"I wouldn't ask," Paul said, as though reading her mind, "but we're short staffed at security. If I could wait, I might be able to find a warm body . . ."

"It's okay. But I'll have to talk to Susan Garcetti and let her know I'll be gone . . ."

"I already cleared it with her."

"So?"

He hesitated. "It's schlep work, Hollis. You'd leave this afternoon, fly seven hours to New York, hand Jones off, then catch the same plane back on its turnaround. Long day."

"The things a woman does for love." She shook her head. "Something I don't get. If Jones has been on the lam for years, what's the rush in getting him back—besides his health?"

"The French government. The State Department found out that Jones had surfaced, some eighty-five took the matter up with the French Foreign Ministry—"

"What's an eighty-five?"

"Any idiot with that IQ. Anyway, now the French want to arrest Jones, to show us how tough they can be. My police contact told me that either Jones is on that plane today or they pop him."

"Well, in that case, whatever it takes to help avoid a diplomatic incident."

"Sure?"

"Yes. But only for you. And for a price."

"Name it."

"I'll give you a hint," Hollis said slyly. "Start eating oysters."

SHOWERING IN PAUL'S apartment, because the hot water there was far more plentiful than it was in her building, Hollis ticked off the things she needed to do right away.

"Jones will be traveling light," Paul had told her. "So will you. Only carry-on." So packing would take next to no time. Which was just as well because she and Jones had to be on American's flight 101 to Kennedy.

"It leaves de Gaulle at two-thirty-five, but give yourself plenty of time for traffic," he'd instructed. "Pick up the tickets at the first class counter."

Then he gave her several hundred francs and almost a thousand in American dollars, along with the rest of the details:

"You'll meet Jones in the brasserie of the Hôtel Terminus Nord at noon. There'll be a picture of him with the paperwork I send you. Bring him the onetime INS entry form. From that point on he doesn't leave your sight. The French won't hassle you because you're leaving the country. But who knows what kind of talent Customs and Immigration is hiring these days. So make sure the form is perfect."

Hollis knew exactly how to fill out entry forms.

"At Kennedy, you go to the airlines' hospitality suites. They're on the departures level. You'll see a door marked *E-twelve*. That's where the marshals will be waiting.

"Last thing: Don't talk to anyone at the consulate about this. The ambassador wants this done quietly and by the numbers. If there's a screwup, it's my butt."

There won't be a screwup, darling.

Hollis stepped out of the shower. She felt strong and confident about what she had to do. No way was she going to let Paul down.

HOLLIS TOOK A TAXI back to her apartment, in the Rue Berger. Her building faced a park that had once been part of Paris's famous outdoor market, Les Halles. Beyond its greenery and crisscrossing paths was the ancient Church of St.-Eustache. When Hollis entered her apartment the first thing she saw were the spires and tower. Through them she could make out the sculpture in front of the church entrance: a giant head resting on its side, and next to it an equally large hand, the palm curled as though to cup the head.

As Hollis changed into a comfortable travel suit she thought about how much she loved this *quartier*. Though not as posh as Paul's, its casual, friendly ambience reminded her of her days as a student in New York. Within a month of moving in, she'd gotten to know the people at the local market and brasserie, found solace in the Sunday quiet of the park. When she felt the need, she took refuge in St.-Eustache, within its damp, centuries-old stone walls.

All this was a world far removed from the frenetic pace of the consulate, and much more simple than Paul's circuit of famous restaurants, glamorous nightclubs, and weekend afternoons spent in the salons of the city's great homes. It was a place to pause, retreat, and reflect, to surround herself with people whose lives were bounded by these streets and whose kindness lay in sharing them with her.

Hollis zipped up and shouldered her carry-on garment bag. It contained a cosmetics bag, fresh underwear, and slacks and a sweater to wear on the return flight. She took a final look out at the cathedral, touched the cameo for luck, and locked up the apartment. As she hailed a cab, she smiled at the thought that, given the time difference between Paris and New York, and factoring in the flying time, she'd be home tomorrow morning, in time for breakfast with Paul. Breakfast and more.

CHAPTER FIVE

CRAWFORD'S BOLT-HOLE in Paris was the penthouse level of an apartment building on Boulevard St.-Germain, behind the Musée d'Orsay.

He had others—in Rome, Berlin, and London—but they weren't as large and elaborately equipped as this one. Paris, with its large émigré population, had always been the main stalking ground for those in Crawford's trade.

Three apartments on the top floor had been bought for cash years ago and reconfigured into one. At the time, the neighbors had complained about the length of the noisy renovations, but once these had been finished, the new owner had proved to be a model tenant. No children, no pets, no parties. On appropriate occasions Crawford had given a few of his neighbors business cards that described him as a one-man software specialty company. There were hints about frequent trips to Asia, the Indian subcontinent, and Australia.

The St.-Germain apartment suited Crawford perfectly. The boulevard was always busy, so personnel and vehicles could come and go at any time and not seem out of place. Most of the other tenants were elderly. They kept to themselves and were grateful for their privacy. The building had two exits, so Crawford's people arrived and left unseen.

The living room was comfortable, the furniture perhaps a little too stark, the modernist paintings in keeping with a bachelor's taste. There was a lot of electronic equipment, presumably for music. There were no photographs of Crawford or anyone else. The kitchen had been installed right out of a showroom; only one stove burner showed any sign of use. Crawford did his own housekeeping. Over the years he had become very quick and efficient.

The apartment had other features that were not visible upon cursory examination. All the rooms, except the bathrooms, were slightly smaller than the total square footage of the apartment would call for. This hidden space—built by Crawford from his own blueprints—created large closets and alcoves, artfully concealed by an antique floor-to-ceiling mirror, a large Chinese screen, and in the kitchen, a false back wall in the pantry.

Behind shelves stacked with canned goods was the weapons compartment: stun, flash, and smoke grenades hanging from hooks; cases of ammunition for MP-5 submachine guns and Beretta pistols; three fully loaded Remington over-under combo shotguns—rifle barrel on top, rocket launcher underneath.

Behind the full-length mirror in the bedroom was a ten-foot-by-fourteen-foot recess equipped with a medical gurney, the latest medical equipment, and enough drugs to stock a small pharmacy. The common wall between the recess and the bedroom had been specially reinforced and soundproofed so that not even an X-ray scanner could detect the hollow. Special paint had been laid down along the baseboard to throw off search dogs.

The largest recess was behind a massive Chinese screen bolted to newly installed four-foot-by-eight-foot beams hidden behind a replastered wall. A perfect sixty-four square feet, it was the nerve center of Crawford's operations. At its heart was a communications console designed by FDS Systems of Houston that provided a round-the-clock digitally encrypted link between Crawford and his sector chiefs in the three satellite cities, as well as the D.C. headquarters of the organization he worked for: Omega. Its signals were fed out and received through what appeared to be a commercial eighteen-inch television dish, mounted on the roof. In fact, on a specific frequency, the dish was also capable of pulling in television broadcasts from the European Echostar satellite, a feature that Crawford's neighbors appreciated since he provided them access free of charge.

Crawford had never bothered to inform the director of Omega of this favor to his tenants. Communications with headquarters, at 1800 G Street N.W.—two blocks from the White House—was limited only to flash emergency traffic. In all other instances, regional directors like Crawford were expected to use, and act upon, their own discretion. The director, a retired admiral who'd served in the Atlantic Fleet, hadn't heard from Crawford in almost two years.

Crawford sat in a red leather executive chair behind his desk, a slab of solid walnut that had once been a dining room table. Beyond the tall, one-way windows, yesterday's sunshine had been bullied out by a line of thick, gray clouds that portended rain. He sipped tea from an oversized mug and stared at the laptop screen. In its reflection he could see the interior of the communications chamber, still open even though he'd completed his work. Lined up along the shelves were computer disks containing every available piece of information on the subjects Crawford watched over. But not enough on the Handyman. Nowhere near enough.

The surveillance team—the "full blanket" Crawford had thrown over the Handyman since his arrival in the city—had reported that he had gone directly from the train station to a nearby hotel. He had emerged only once, an hour later, to drop a large envelope into a mailbox and wait there until the postal truck came by for the pickup, a minute later. Short of hijacking the mail van—which the team was not equipped or prepared to do—the contents of the package and its destination would remain a mystery.

But that wasn't all that troubled Crawford. If the Handyman was headed to another European destination, he would have gone immediately to another train station, or Orly Airport, or even rented a car. Instead, he was staying put—for the moment. Crawford's instinct whispered that the Handyman would be traveling far afield. But there was nothing in the files to back up his hunch, which was why Crawford had broken his silence and why, by now, the director's day had almost certainly been ruined.

The computer beeped out an alert. A decoded e-mail reply was on its way. Crawford hunched forward, peering at the sentences flashing across the screen.

The director's message was short and brusque, much like the man himself: Omega's mainframes could not supplement the information Crawford already had on the Handyman. But since he was active, Crawford was to stay on him. If he made any move for the United

States, he was to be intercepted and interrogated, and the director briefed on the outcome. However, since the Handyman had been dormant for so long and was advanced in years, Omega had downgraded his threat profile to neutral. Barring clear evidence to the contrary, Crawford was under orders not to involve any European police agencies, and certainly not any U.S. domestic law enforcement, in the Handyman's apprehension.

Crawford reread the directive and shook his head. The director was a sly, prescient individual who could tell when a subordinate was playing a hunch. And he would not risk exposing either Omega or its operatives on something as ephemeral as intuition. It was within Crawford's purview to pursue the Handyman, but he had to do so alone. For the director, it was the safe play.

Crawford tapped back an acknowledgment and shut down his system. He went inside the recess and set the incendiary charges that would, upon unauthorized entry, vaporize its contents. He was closing up the Chinese screen when the phone on his desk rang.

"Yes, Wally?"

"Our boy's still holed up at the Apollo, by the Gare du Nord."

Crawford was familiar with the Apollo, favored by backpacking students with little money and traveling salesmen who had to pinch expense account pennies.

"Has he moved since the last time?"

"Just to grab a sandwich around the corner and take it back to his room."

"Phone calls?"

"One. Local. It lasted only twenty-two seconds, not long enough to trace."

Crawford thought about that. From Marseille, the Handyman had made two calls, one within France, one international call. In Paris he *receives* a local one. That meant two handlers. But why the second call? Had there been a last-minute change in plans, something the Handyman had to be aware of in order to proceed?

"What about visitors?" Crawford asked.

"No."

"Other guests staying at the hotel?"

"Overnight surveillance went in with Deuxième Bureau credentials and scared the shit out of the night manager. They were lucky—only twenty guests. Thirteen French nationals, seven foreign tourists. So far, everyone checks out."

Crawford frowned. The Deuxième Bureau was part of French intelligence. For Frenchmen, it was like the wrath of God stepping into your life. The night manager would keep his mouth shut but still Crawford didn't like playing that card too often.

"What about staff?" he asked.

"Only ten people full-time, including the maids. Pretty transient. Average employment about six months. The computers show no connection to our boy, but we're double-checking."

Wally paused, then said: "He's waiting for something, Sam. Or someone. He's not going to stick around the Apollo very long. It's not that kind of place."

Money? Instructions? Equipment? What is it you're waiting for? What was in the package you sent out?

"You want me to paint him again?" Wally asked.

"No. It's too soon. People don't come close to someone like him. He'd be suspicious if they did."

"Then I'll sit on him."

Wally was very good at that. He had a surveillance agent's two greatest gifts: the patience of Job and the camouflage of a chameleon.

Crawford hung up and looked out the windows. This was the worst time: to wait, trying to forecast the quarry's unpredictable move. Crawford felt the slow burn of frustration, like a flame licking a piece of paper, turning the edges black. His information on the Handyman was years out of date. The Handyman's employers and contacts from that era were either dead or had never been identified. In the intervening years the Handyman had forged no new links, taken on no new contracts, had not exposed himself in any way that would allow Crawford to track anyone back to him.

Crawford was burdened by other restraints too. He was an American intelligence operative working without diplomatic immunity. No one at the embassy, except for two people he'd buried within the infrastructure, knew anything about him or his activities. If French counterintelligence ever caught on to Crawford's scent, took down him or any of his people, the repercussions would rock directly to the White House.

But in the case of the Handyman, Crawford heeded not Omega's super mainframes but his own dark gift that told him that far away certain events beyond his control had been set in motion and were now playing themselves out.

It was a measure of his self-discipline that he didn't worry the scar by his temple as the words reverberated like a ship's bell in a fog-laden sea: *Where? Involving whom?*

CHAPTER SIX

As SOON AS Hollis arrived at the consulate, she went through the mail, looking for the requisition form Paul said he'd sent over. She checked the in stack first, then the out, in case the messenger had misplaced it.

To the untrained eye it might appear a morass. But she knew exactly what each pile of folders contained, which papers, seemingly strewn about, demanded immediate attention and which could wait, what each of the open envelopes—bearing either the consulate or the embassy logo in the left-hand corner—held.

Most of this paperwork was generated because French nationals could apply for visas by mail. Junior officers like Hollis did little else but work on the infamous visa line, a purgatory that could, depending on one's luck or popularity, last as long as two years. The average time spent on any one application was measured in minutes. As long as the form was filled out correctly—with proof of citizenship, a return ticket, and a bank account—the application was recommended for approval. But if even one item on the form had been left blank or filled in incorrectly, the whole package became RTS: *Return to Sender.*

Hollis checked the wall-mounted messengers' schedule: forty minutes until the next round. There was still time.

Hollis busied herself with a stack of visa applications that had sprouted overnight like a giant mushroom. She was relieved that the work was routine because she found it difficult to concentrate. Time moved relentlessly.

Finally she caught a glimpse of the blue-uniformed messenger making his way from station to station. Watching him stop to chat made

Hollis grind her teeth, but at last he pushed the cart up to her desk—and continued past.

"Wait a second," she called out. "Don't you have anything for me?"

He gave her a perplexed look. "Nope."

"Would you check, please?"

The messenger muttered something under his breath but did as she'd asked. Hollis watched carefully as his fingers flipped back the letters and envelopes. There wasn't anything with her name on it.

"Satisfied?" he asked irritably.

"Sorry."

Hollis watched him rattle his way down the aisle. Her thoughts were racing and she started when she heard a voice behind her.

"I said, are you okay? You look upset."

Hollis swiveled her chair around to find Julie standing beside her. She collected herself and said, "Sorry. I was expecting a delivery." Then she added, "Where have you been?"

"At Garcetti's regular morning meeting. By the way, she noticed you weren't around."

Julie walked around to her station, then popped up behind the partition holding an envelope.

"I hope this isn't what you were waiting on," she said timidly.

Hollis took the envelope, saw that it was addressed to her but that it had no sender's name or designation. She tore it open just enough to see the INS logo on the requisition form. Clipped to it was a small color photograph.

"The guy put it in my box on the early run," Julie explained. "I meant to leave it on your desk but . . . "

"That's okay," Hollis replied, relieved.

"I didn't screw up, did I?"

"Not at all. But this thing is time sensitive. I have to get cracking."

As soon as Julie was out of sight, Hollis took out the requisition form. It was folded four times over, like a will. Her eyes flew down the last page, to the bottom, searching for Paul's signature. It wasn't there. All the anxiety that had just evaporated now flooded over her again.

Jeez, Paul. How could you have forgotten to sign the damn thing!

Nervously she glanced up at the wall clock behind the supervisor's desk. It was 10:47. Her meeting with the banker was set for noon. The flight was at 2:35 P.M.

If there's a screwup, it's my butt.

Paul's words. No way would she let him down. Hollis reached for the phone and dialed Paul's dedicated line.

EVERY U.S. EMBASSY has a completely secure communications chamber, usually located in a subbasement. Impervious to electronic or satellite eavesdropping, it allows the ambassador and a select staff to maintain a private chain of command with Washington. Although Hollis had no way of knowing, the number she'd dialed bypassed the normal embassy lines and, through a digital-encryption unit built into Paul McGann's telephone, was redirected straight into the Bubble.

McGann was one of six embassy officers cleared for the Bubble. It was twenty by fifteen feet, the steel-reinforced concrete walls padded with thick, noise-absorbing foam. There was a long oval table, chairs, a small refrigerator, and a powerful air scrubber unit.

At one end was a communications pod the size of a walk-in freezer, crammed with state-of-the-art electronics. Sitting in a high-backed chair inside the pod, the Plexiglas door closed, McGann was fighting to hold a secret terror in check—claustrophobia. He'd been in the pod for thirty-five minutes, fingers jabbing at the keyboard of the computer that linked him to the Space-Based Infrared System, a network of low earth-orbiting satellites whose sensors monitored enemy missile activity. The CIA had quietly added certain refinements to the satellites for its own purposes, something McGann had learned from friends seeded in the corridors of Langley. Among them was the Global Positioning System, which allowed a military command to track infantry operating behind enemy lines. The soldiers carried microtransmitters that sent out electronic signals, which were picked up by an SBIS satellite, which in turn relayed them back to the command post. The CIA had converted and refined this technology for its own purpose: to stay on top of agents who had infiltrated deep into hostile territory. McGann was booting it up for quite a different reason. He let the phone ring three times before he picked up. Hollis was right on schedule.

"McGann."

"Paul? It's me."

"You caught me at a bad time. I can't talk—"

"Paul, you forgot to sign the authorization form!"

McGann let a beat go by to make her think he was shocked.

"Damn it all," he muttered.

"There's still time for me to run over to your office and have you sign off."

"Hollis, I told you. I have a situation here. Besides, there isn't time. Just sign my name. It's just a scrawl."

"Paul, that would violate procedure."

McGann put some gravity in his voice. "Hollis, you know I'd never ask you to do anything illegal or that could harm you. But we're out of time here, and I need to get this thing done. I'll take full responsibility."

Hollis shook her head. She recalled her Foreign Service instructor's words: Always *follow procedure. Never take the initiative, no matter how justified you think it may be. If something screws up, you and the embassy will be covered. But if you play Lone Ranger and a situation blows up in your face, you'll be out on your ass.*

Absently, Hollis rubbed the cameo. But this was a different situation. For one thing, she would be acting on the direct orders of a superior. Second, she knew Paul wouldn't let her do anything dangerous or stupid.

"Hollis, are you there?"

"Still here. Okay, I'll put in your chicken scratching."

"I owe you. And I have to run. Call me from New York."

McGann cut the connection. He had no doubt that Hollis would do exactly as he'd asked.

He was still smiling to himself when he dialed another number. When he heard the voice on the other end, all he said was, "Mission is rolling."

HOLLIS STARED AT the phone, then at her watch. Time churned on inexorably: 11:06. She pulled out the authorization form, read it through one more time. Everything was in order, but no matter how hard she stared at the blank space, Paul's signature refused to materialize.

She glanced down at her scratch pad. Without realizing it, she'd been doodling Paul's name over and over again, an excellent facsimile of his illegible signature.

Her hand moved seemingly of its own accord as Paul's signature filled in the blank space.

Hollis sat back, shaken by what she'd done. She took a deep breath and peered over the top of the partition across the bull pen. Susan Garcetti wasn't at her desk.

Hollis had always gotten on well with her tall, slender supervisor, whose South Carolina accent was as thick as pecan syrup. Garcetti was queen of the visa line, had been for years. Like the best managers, she had a seemingly inexhaustible well of patience, advice, and encouragement.

Hollis had once asked a departing fellow drone why Garcetti, obviously quick and intelligent, had never been promoted.

"Hell," the young man had replied, "Susie could have been out of here years ago. Except she's the glue that holds this place together. They tried another supervisor—once. He lasted all of three weeks and had to go on emotional disability leave. So the chief of section begged and pleaded and broke the piggy bank to get Susie back."

Except now, when Hollis wanted to be absolutely sure that her supervisor was aware of her last-minute assignment, Garcetti was nowhere to be found.

And time was running out.

Go on and finish it.

Gripping this thought like a crutch, Hollis got up and maneuvered through the maze of workstations, her eyes fixed on the far wall, on the gleaming open door of the walk-in vault, where all the official paperwork—from passports to confidential memoranda—was stored. Where Bobby Franks—a young black security officer—was seated at his desk, flipping through a copy of *Stars and Stripes,* a toothpick dancing from one side of his mouth to the other. This was his way of dealing with nicotine deprivation.

"Hi, Bobby. How's it going?"

He looked up from his reading and smiled without parting his lips. The toothpick was a tiny lance lodged between two molars.

"Hey, Hollis. Doin' just fine now that vacation time's almost here."

"Where are you headed?"

"Home to San Anton'. What do you need?"

"A onetime INS entry form."

"A onetime?" Now he was standing, a good eight inches taller than she, holding out a long-fingered hand. "Paperwork?"

Hollis smiled up at him as she handed over the requisition. Franks flipped it over to the last page, looked at the signature, then opened up the form and checked it carefully.

"Okay. Come on in."

The vault's interior was much like a bank's safe-deposit-box room, the walls lined floor to ceiling with metal cabinets. Franks hauled out a key ring, knelt, and opened a bottom drawer. He reached inside and, without looking up, handed Hollis the blank form.

"It's all ready to go. You just need to fill in the name," he said. "Use my desk."

Franks was right. The form had been stamped and countersigned. All that was needed to make it legal was the bearer's name.

Carefully Hollis wrote in, in capital letters, SIMON JONES.

She looked over her shoulder. "That do it?"

"Almost."

Franks leaned over and scribbled his signature in the designated space. From a drawer in his desk he removed a seal, the kind lawyers use, slipped the form in between its jaws, and squeezed the handles.

"And this."

Franks flipped open a thick hardbound ledger, ran his finger down a column of numbers until he reached a blank space, and wrote in the serial number of the entry form.

"Your John Hancock here." He indicated a space beside the numeric entry. "And the recipient's name—and we're done."

Hollis gripped the pen too tightly and scrawled her signature.

"Thanks, Bobby."

"No problem. You take care."

Hollis walked back to her station, stopping just long enough to grab her purse. She picked up her carry-on from the porter's alcove and took one last look at the clock: 11:26. There were always cabs at the Crillon. If her luck held, she'd get a driver with a lead foot.

CHAPTER SEVEN

EVEN IF SHE'D been looking for it, Hollis would not have picked up on the surveillance. Her concentration was devoted to seeing her task through. She never had an inkling that anyone had been watching her.

SUSAN GARCETTI HAD been present in the room all along—just not where Hollis could see her. There was a door behind Garcetti's desk that opened upon a tiny surveillance cubbyhole filled with closed-circuit monitors. Six cameras embedded in strategic locations in the bull pen's ceiling constantly panned the activity below. They were a relatively new feature in terms of embassy security, designed to monitor potential theft of internal embassy documents, visas, and passports. It was well known among regional security officers that French counter-intelligence had made U.S. missions a primary espionage target. Low-level staffers—particularly those who'd recently arrived on post, who might be lonely or just naive—were especially susceptible. As for official documents, new antiforgery techniques had made it difficult, if not impossible, to reproduce them. The value of genuine visas and blank passports to terrorists, smugglers, and other criminals had skyrocketed.

Garcetti had noted Hollis's absence from the morning briefing, but that wasn't the reason she had placed her under surveillance. On the eight-inch screens she had studied the young woman's demeanor, noted her agitation and the way she'd dealt with the messenger. Then she'd seemed to settle down, only to lose her cool again when she made a phone call. That was followed by some apparent soul searching before she finally got up and went to the safe.

It was time to have a little chat with slick Bobby Franks.

Susan Garcetti locked the door to the surveillance room and walked up to the security guard's desk. She leaned forward, bracing herself with both arms.

"Hey, Bobby. Mind getting this out for me?"

She lifted one hand so he could take his eyes off her breasts and slide the requisition form out from under it.

"A one-oh-seven-two?"

"Jack over at the Liaison Office called in for it. He's all in a huff."

Bobby Franks offered her his best smile. He'd been trying to get close to Garcetti for months.

He picked up the requisition and sauntered into the vault. Garcetti heard him singing softly: "All in a huff . . . And I'll huff and I'll puff, and I'll bloooow your house down . . . "

The ledger was still on his desk. Garcetti waited until Franks had his back to her before she flipped it open. She thought it was considerate of Bobby to have marked the page with the ribbon sewn into the ledger's spine.

Garcetti recognized Hollis Fremont's signature immediately. In one glance she memorized the serial number of the onetime entry form and the bearer's name.

What are you up to, Fremont? That business at the safe, walking toward Bobby like she was carrying a bomb, looking so nervous when she'd handed over the paperwork.

Without glancing up, Garcetti knew that Bobby had returned. She felt his eyes roam over her.

"Here it is."

"Thanks, Bobby."

"Drinks later?"

Garcetti crossed her arms, causing her blouse to strain across her breasts.

"Let me make a couple of calls, see if I can unload some, uh, prior commitments. Okay?"

Bobby Franks's eyes danced like fireflies.

Garcetti returned to her desk and slipped the 1072 into her drawer. Even though her desk was elevated and well away from the bull pen she activated the voice privacy screen. It was a device similar to the ones judges used on their podiums, to ensure that juries will not overhear sidebars.

She made two calls on the internal line, then activated the scrambler unit before dialing out. Embassy and consular communications had been "hardened" in the wake of French intelligence operations against the United States, and diplomatic phone lines were constant targets of bugging. Both sides were aware of this cat-and-mouse game but recently the French had overstepped their bounds: They had burrowed recording devices into first- and business-class seats of U.S. airlines favored by American executives, in the hope of picking up talk of industrial and economic strategy. The tapes were changed by French intelligence operatives posing as airplane cleaners.

On the other end, a phone rang twice. Garcetti didn't need to give her name.

"We might have a hit."

"Tape is rolling."

"A onetime INS visa was just served for someone called Simon Jones. The authorization allegedly came from Paul McGann. Here's the kicker: I just spoke with McGann's secretary. She swears she never heard of anyone called Jones and that McGann never signed off on any requisition."

"The signature's a forgery?"

"Yes."

"Who did it?"

"A visa slave. Hollis Fremont."

There was a pause on the other end. "Any relation to *the* Fremont?"

It took a lot to surprise Crawford, but in this case Garcetti had known it would happen.

"He was her father. She started here three months ago, kind of shy except it's common knowledge she and McGann have been grinding pelvises."

"Uh-huh." There was doubt in the voice.

"You asked me to stay sharp for something that's out of whack. Think about this: Fremont has juice—more than enough to get out of this pit. Unless that's where she *wants* to stay. Where somebody put her, to have access to the paperwork." Garcetti paused, then drove it home. "Like that onetime form she tooled up and took off with."

"How long ago?"

"Ten minutes."

"What's she look like, Fremont?"

Garcetti gave him the description in thirty-two carefully selected words.

"Check her desk. Whatever isn't consulate business, I want to know about it."

The line went dead. Garcetti stared at the receiver and said aloud, "You're welcome, Sam."

Garcetti knew more than she cared to about how Crawford worked. Yet he was the kind of man who bred loyalty, could make you walk off a cliff for him. Garcetti was supervisor of the visa section because that's where Crawford needed her. She was one of his trip wires. Now someone had nudged against it.

Garcetti very much hoped that all Fremont had done was something stupid. Stupid but innocent. Nothing that would bring her up against Sam Crawford. Because if that happened, the consequences could put her off-planet.

THE ALLIANCE PETROLEUM Marquage van was parked on Rue de l'Aqueduc opposite the Hôtel Apollo.

"You really think this chick'll show?" Wally asked.

Today he wore the leaf green overalls of a city sanitation worker. On the floor lay a broom for sweeping out gutters.

Crawford, trying to make sense of what Susan Garcetti had told him, answered with a question: "Everybody have her description?"

Four agents were inside the hotel, two covering the delivery and employee entrances, one in the lobby, and one posted outside the main doors. Wally had radioed them the description of Hollis Fremont as soon as Crawford had called him from Montparnasse.

"You know it." He paused. "Sam, if she and the Handyman connect, it's our play?"

Crawford continued scanning the pedestrian traffic surging past the Apollo.

"She's carrying papers to get him into the States," he said. "Yeah, it's our play."

Wally was about to say something else, then he shifted, pressing lightly on the receiver inside his right ear.

"The Handyman's moving. Just came off the elevator . . . He's crossing the lobby. No bags. Headed outside."

"Got him," Crawford said.

The Handyman was wearing the same raincoat he'd had on in Marseille. He cinched the belt and dipped into the stream of pedestrians heading up Rue de l'Aqueduc.

"Metro station?" Wally ventured.

"I don't think so. Get us moving. Tell Simmons to toss his room. Get the rest ready to move. But I don't want anyone close to him who was inside. He's seen their faces."

The van chugged up the street. Wally had the yellow roof-mounted flashers going, so traffic swerved around them. On the other side of the street, the Handyman kept pace with the people around him, neither hurrying nor lingering. He did not pause at storefront windows to check for surveillance. He made no sudden dodges.

Behind him, Wally heard Crawford mutter, "He's going for that hotel, Terminus Nord."

Crawford must have seen something Wally had missed, because at the intersection the Handyman could go in three different directions. He waited for the light to change, then crossed over to Rue de Dunkerque, which passed in front of the Gare du Nord. The hotel took up the whole end of the block where Rue du Faubourg-St.-Denis and Rue La Fayette meet.

Wally edged the van in front of the station, close to the taxi stands and passenger loading zones. A pair of flics walked by, eyed him through the window.

Wally caught movement out of the corner of his eye.

"Sam—three o'clock."

Crawford already had her. She was standing beside a cab, thrusting a fistful of notes at the driver, not bothering to wait for change. Long hair whipped by the winds of traffic, tugging at the hem of a nicely cut blue suit. Good hard ankles, and eyes as large and nervous as a doe's.

"She's got luggage," Wally said.

"Where's the Handyman?"

"Inside the brasserie."

"Go on in, Wally. See what they're up to."

"You think it's just a pass—she gives him the entry form? Maybe the bag too?"

"Could be. Then he's on his way."

Wally nodded. "What if they split up?"

"We stay with the Handyman. We know where we can always find Fremont."

Crawford flinched when Wally opened one of the back doors and a gritty draft swept into the van. At the same moment, the computer next to him sprang to life with a message. It was Susan Garcetti, e-mailing Hollis Fremont's entire life.

Crawford stared intently at the screen. As an Omega regional director, he was one of the few executives privy to the organization's history, including its founding fathers. Which, if the security background check he was looking at was accurate, was a hell of a lot more than Hollis Fremont knew. Nowhere was there an indication that she was aware of her father's true job description. Nor of Dawson Wylie's. Of course, by the time she'd needed work-related references, her family was dead. But the recommendations that had gotten her into the Foreign Service were all from college professors, save one, from Wylie, who was listed as the retired DCM of the London embassy.

Don't you know who Alec Fremont and Dawson Wylie were? Didn't anyone ever tell you, when you were old enough to handle the truth, that the two men closest to you had been cofounders of Omega?

Like Britain's MI6—which until recently never revealed the identity of its current and former directors—Omega's top echelon, past and present, was a closely guarded secret. Given the nature of the organization's work, it had to be. Only a handful of veteran executives, like Crawford, had seen the files of legends like Fremont and Dawson, men who had divined the kind of path violence would take in the future, the threat it would pose not only to America but to the whole world, and who had designed a quiet, sometimes lethal response.

And on the face of it, Hollis Fremont never knew any of this . . . Yet here she was, about to connect with an Omega target.

Why?

Was she privy to the Handyman's secret? If not, then had she somehow become his handmaiden?

Crawford knew from bitter experience that during the golden years of terrorism, in the seventies and eighties, many young, privileged, well-educated individuals from socially and politically prominent families had given themselves over to groups like the Red Brigade, Baader-Meinhof, and the Popular Front for the Liberation of Palestine. All were either dead or rotting in European maximum-security prisons, their lives ruined, their ideological fantasies reduced to ashes by the fall of communism.

As the e-mail ran out, Crawford hit the print button. Hollis Fremont seemed to have no connection to those misguided martyrs. Yet she was about to touch a man whose only stock in trade was death.

Regardless of her pedigree, or despite it, this alone made her a possible enemy.

HOLLIS SHOULDERED HER way through the lunchtime crowd in the brasserie. She stopped at the bar to catch her breath. She'd made the rendezvous with two minutes to spare.

Pushing her garment bag against the foot rail, she scanned the tightly packed tables. Salesgirls and junior executives, tourists with dazed expressions and hollow eyes, blue-collar workers sipping *verres de rouge,* waiters shouting orders into the kitchen, slapping down crockery and utensils, scribbling orders.

She took a moment to steady herself. Encouraged by the promise of a ridiculously large tip, the taxi driver had run lights at every intersection. Hollis's wrist ached from hanging on to the hand strap. But she was okay. She would find Jones, explain to him exactly what they were going to do, then take a taxi to Charles de Gaulle. There would be plenty of time to call Paul from there.

Hollis scanned the tables, beginning with the ones closest to the windows, her eyes moving steadily over the faces. She had covered two rows when she felt someone nudge her arm. Her eyes widened but she had the presence of mind to keep her mouth shut.

"My name is Jones."

His voice was low and a little hoarse, as if he preferred silence to words. His English was heavily accented and gave Hollis no hint of what part of America he came from. His tweed sports jacket and gray pants lent him a neat, academic appearance. He wasn't wearing a watch or any jewelry save for a tarnished but expensive-looking ring. He was not a big man, no taller than she, really, and slim, almost frail. His face was sallow, especially under the eyes. Her first thought was, *Cancer.*

"I'm Hollis Fremont, a consular officer. I'll be taking you home."

She felt Jones weigh her on whatever scale he used. There was no fear in his eyes, no twitchy movements. She wondered if he was on painkillers.

"Please, we can sit for a minute," the Handyman said.

Hollis looked past him, at the tiny round table jammed between a wall and a tall rack of plastic tubs for dirty dishes. No wonder she hadn't spotted him. There was a cup of coffee on the table.

Hollis carried her bag over and squeezed into a chair. She didn't notice his lingering look, the way his eyes appraised and probed her, the tiny sparks of recognition that lit up in them and that made his heart beat fast.

She smiled as Jones waited for her to sit first, and by then there was nothing at all in his face for her to read.

"Did you bring the papers?"

"Yes."

"May I see them?"

Hollis fished out the entry form from her purse. He read it through carefully. "A photograph is not required?"

"I'll vouch for your identity."

"I see. But you have a photograph of me."

"Yes."

"May I see it please?"

Hollis brought it out and watched him nod. Then just like that, he pocketed the photograph.

"I need that back," Hollis said, more startled than puzzled.

"No, you do not, Miss Fremont."

Now she was angry. "I don't think you understand. I'm here to make sure you get back—"

"What you are making, Miss Fremont, is a scene. Kindly lower your voice."

His tone was pleasant enough but there was an undercurrent to it, a hard arrogance that raised hackles.

"You don't have anything to worry about," Hollis started to say, trying to sound calm and in control.

"On the contrary, Miss Fremont. I have many things to worry about. Things that you could not possibly be aware of or understand. Now I have one more: being seen with a beautiful woman. Women like you attract attention. And attention, Miss Fremont, is what I have spent many years avoiding."

Hollis leaned closer to him and gave him her most earnest expression. "As long as we get to that plane, nothing is going to happen to you. You have the word of the United States government on that."

"Then I would find it most reassuring if we were on our way."

Hollis was surprised at how, despite the close quarters, he managed to slip out and, in a courtly gesture, pull back the chair for her.

The brasserie was overflowing now. Hollis found herself in front of the Handyman. She didn't want to lose him in the crowd, so she kept glancing back. Which was how she bumped hard against the fat sanitation worker in the green uniform at the bar, causing him to swear.

"Pardon," she said.

The fat man stared at the fresh coffee stain on his sleeve, caused when she'd bumped his elbow. He gave her a sour look, mumbled something, and blew cigarette smoke in her face.

Hollis was moving again, the glass doors only a few feet away, using her garment bag to keep people moving out of her way. She was so intent on getting clear that she didn't look back at the Handyman, never saw his eyes slide over the fat sanitation worker like a cascade of cool, silent water. They widened only a fraction when they picked up the sneakers.

Old sneakers, but an American brand. The kind rich kids and executive joggers wore. And American tourists who dressed for comfort, not for fashion or to blend in. These sneakers were on the wrong pair of feet. The fat man was all wrong.

Something else: the curse the fat man had muttered at the girl. The accent was studied and well learned, and not at all working class.

Outside now, the Handyman saw the girl craning her neck, trying to find a taxi in the noon rush hour. He scanned the cars parked in front of the hotel but saw nothing out of place.

They wouldn't use cars. A van or truck . . .

He didn't have time to check. Nor did he want them even to suspect that they had given themselves away. If they really wanted him they could take him now. The girl had lured him out far enough for that.

She's not working for them.

Which meant that they would be careful as long as she was his shield.

The Handyman knew a great deal about Omega. The American group was very careful when operating on foreign soil, especially in

France, where relations with the United States were at best a marriage of tolerance. The girl was an amateur, a tool. She did not belong to them. The girl would see him through. If he could hold her together.

The Handyman slid on a calm, friendly expression and touched the girl lightly on the elbow. His tone was helpful.

"There is a faster way than by taxi." He nodded in the direction of the Gare du Nord. "Come, let us go to Kron."

She was bewildered. "Who's Kron?"

The Handyman smiled and gently relieved her of her garment bag.

CRAWFORD WAS WATCHING as they crossed the street, Fremont, in heels, picking her way carefully across the cobblestones, the Handyman moving as smoothly as a water moccasin.

"Talk to me, Wally."

Wally, hands stuffed in his overalls, was ambling fifteen feet behind them, squinting in the hard autumn sunlight.

"She wanted a cab, he had other ideas. Maybe he's worried about traffic." A blare of horns interrupted him. *"Problem is, why's she still with him? She made the handoff. He doesn't need her anymore."*

Crawford was trying to figure this out too. The Handyman wasn't one to travel with baggage, human or otherwise.

"They're headed into the train station but he doesn't need a onetime to go anywhere in Europe." This was Crawford talking to himself but also laying out his thoughts for Wally, in case something clicked.

"It's the rail link to de Gaulle," he said suddenly.

Wally was right with him. *"Yeah. They'll take the RER straight out."*

"One stop?"

"Aulnay-sous-Bois."

Crawford drummed his fingers on the edge of the computer keyboard. Wally was waiting, along with the rest of the team. He had to decide fast or risk losing the Handyman. The airport was the outermost perimeter of Crawford's operations. He had never allowed a target to get past it. No one had even gotten close.

Now he was out of time and options. The Handyman would have to be taken at one of the most secure airports in the world, right out from under the hard eyes and ready weapons of military-trained patrols.

The girl, too. And her presence added to the problem.

"We take the Handyman at de Gaulle," Crawford said into the mike. He heard Wally's sigh in his earpiece but hurried on. "You stay close to them in the station and on the train. I'll get the rest of the team moving. The train takes thirty-five, forty minutes. They won't make it out that quickly. I will."

"Not driving that heap."

Crawford was looking at a string of BMW motorcycles parked in front of the station; leather-jacketed buckaroos were seeing off their girlfriends.

"I was thinking of something a little faster."

"MR. JONES. NOW wait a minute. I don't think you understand . . ."

The problem was, he wouldn't stop. Not that he was walking quickly, just that his legs never stopped moving. Finally Hollis reached out and grabbed his sleeve.

The Handyman stared at her blankly. "Are you all right, Miss Fremont?"

"Yes. It's you I'm worried about."

She puffed out her cheeks and looked around her. Two blue-and-white TGV expresses—French bullet trains—rested in the sidings in front of her. Several tracks away were the more common, orange-and-gray electric versions.

A kind of cathedral light filtered through the huge curved windows set between the station's columns. Porters, conductors, and travelers drifted by, their conversations drowned out by chimes followed by the announcer's metallic voice.

"Where *exactly* are we going?" Hollis demanded.

"To the RER, Miss Fremont. It is the regional railroad but you probably think of it as the subway."

"To get to the airport?"

"Of course. Two flights down, line B, gate forty-three." The Handyman glanced up at the large digital clock suspended from the ceiling. "If we hurry, we can make the next train. We *are* in a hurry, are we not, Miss Fremont?"

It took a second for Hollis to realize she was nodding. She was angry because it was all happening too fast—rushing to the brasserie for the meeting; the professor's (Hollis couldn't think of him as a banker) condescending remark about how her appearance would draw attention; her inability to flag down a goddamn cab; and then having to run after this odd man who'd gotten hold of her garment bag.

Now she was agreeing with him, letting him set the agenda.

Well, screw you, Mr. Jones—whoever you really are. I'm carrying your ticket. Without it, you don't get on that plane. You don't go anywhere.

She thrust back her shoulders, took four quick steps, and was right beside him when he got on the escalator.

Not looking at each other, they rode in silence down two levels into a wide, white-tiled tunnel that smelled of disinfectant. Hollis realized that he knew exactly where he was going, because the tunnel was a series of twists and curves that spun off into other halls and he didn't look up once to check the directions, spelled out in small, black tiles set into the walls.

Then they were in an open area, with a ticket booth on the right, flanked by a newsstand. Hollis groaned softly when she saw the line in front of the booth, fifteen deep at least.

But that's not where Jones was headed. Set against the far wall were several ticket-vending machines.

"Here, let me . . . ," Hollis said, fumbling for her wallet.

"Thank you. No need."

He pulled out a fistful of coins and fed them into the slot. When the orange counter reached forty-six francs, he pressed a yellow button and out popped a ticket, which he handed her.

The Handyman repeated the process to get his ticket, then turned and favored this hatchling with a polite smile. He also glanced over her shoulder and saw the fat man in green overalls and sneakers loitering by the newsstand.

"Now we go this way," he said, indicating the turnstiles. "Do you know how to work them?"

"I can manage."

Hollis slipped her ticket into the slot, waited until the machine read the code and spit it out through another slot. She put it in the pocket of her suit jacket.

On French trains, conductors always come through to check the tickets, making sure that the fare paid is commensurate with one's destination.

"Who's Kron?" she asked as she stood beside the Handyman on the escalator heading for the platform.

She saw his lips move but at that instant a train pulled in, drowning out his words.

On the platform Hollis grabbed his arm. "Kron!" she shouted.

The Handyman pointed to the opposite track, where another train was pulling in. The illuminated sign on the lead car read ALIX.

"These trains have names, Miss Fremont. You did not know this."

He said it as a simple statement, like her ignorance was an immutable law of physics.

Hollis held back her retort. She was jostled by the crowd inching forward on the platform as the Kron train wheezed to a stop. She looked back at the Handyman and found him studying a backlist ad for Galeries Lafayette. She pressed back through the crowd until she reached him.

"What is it?"

"Did someone follow you, Miss Fremont?"

Said as casually as if he were asking her opinion about the advertised department store sale.

"*What?*"

"Did anyone follow you?"

His eyes never left the ad, and now he was pointing at it. Hollis looked in the same direction.

"No! What are you talking about?"

"Please wait right here."

When she turned, he was gone.

LIKE THE HANDYMAN, Wally always carried assorted change. When he saw him and the girl at one of the machines, he went to another, bought his ticket, and was ready to follow the pair through the turnstiles.

Wally chose the stairs instead of the escalator. He did not want to be trapped by people above or below him. On the stairs he could also dip into the vent cut next to the pocket of his overalls and feel the comforting warm grip of his Walther automatic. Wally favored Colt firearms custom tuned to his specifications. But Colt was as American as apple pie. If he was ever taken by the police, a popular European firearm would dovetail with the computer-legitimate Interpol ID he carried.

At the foot of the stairs Wally hung back to make sure his quarry was headed for Kron. Slipping behind a snack vending machine he relayed this information to Crawford. Then he watched the Handyman point something out to the girl.

As the train pulled in, Wally slipped into the crowd, and because he was of average height, he momentarily lost sight of the Handyman and the girl.

There she was, being engulfed by the disembarking passengers. And she was straining to look around her, which puzzled Wally. But only until he realized that he couldn't see the Handyman either.

ALTHOUGH THE HANDYMAN didn't see anyone covering the fat man, it didn't mean that he was alone. Sam Crawford would never permit that.

A scenario suggested itself: Crawford had tagged him, maybe as far back as Marseille. Crawford had left him alone when he knew he was on the train to Paris, but when the fat man had come into the café below the Gare de Lyon, he had physically touched him. The Handyman recalled the sensation of a wooden match scraping his skin. Recalled too the oily residue on his hand.

Despite all his years of hiding, the Handyman had kept up with surveillance techniques and technology. Now he knew that he'd been painted.

Which was how Crawford had followed him to the Apollo and why he'd never spotted the blanket thrown over him. Crawford wanted to see where he went, who he met. Had it not been for the American girl, Crawford would have taken him, handed him off to the French. Maybe Interpol.

Her presence told him which country the Handyman was headed for.

So Crawford could not afford to lose sight of either of them. Which was why he'd sent the fat man into the railroad station, down to the RER expresses.

Had it not been for the sneakers, the fat man's disguise might have held. Now he would serve a purpose other than the one Crawford intended.

The Handyman watched the fat man drift along the edge of the crowd waiting for the train. As it rolled into the station he seized the instant when the fat man, like most other people, looked toward the on-coming sound. And disappeared. Dropped into a slight crouch and weaved his way around the milling bodies, staying parallel to the fat man, then turning abruptly toward the row of vending machines.

Circling and coming up behind the fat man just as the train rocked to a stop.

There was the girl, looking around for him, then being caught between riders pushing to get out of the train and those surging to get on.

There was the fat man, one hand in the pocket of his green overalls, the fingers very close to the gun he must be carrying. Having to stand on tiptoe because now the girl was alone and he didn't understand why.

Until the Handyman deliberately exhaled against his neck. The fat man pivoted on the balls of his feet. He was very good, very quick, and the Handyman allowed him to see his eyes before driving a stiletto between the fat man's ribs.

The man's mouth fell open. The Handyman saw the lips and tongue working but the words were caught on the steel blade that now tickled his heart. The Handyman draped one arm around him, slipping a hand under his shoulder, a buddy propping up his drunken friend. He turned the fat man around and in the same motion whipped back the stiletto and made it disappear into his coat. Gently he sat him down on a bench, arranging him so that his head rested against a vending machine.

The Handyman was surprised by, but paid no attention to, the fat man's strangled whispers. No matter how strong he was, nothing could save him.

The Handyman heard something else—the pneumatic hiss of closing doors. He raced toward the train car, coattails flapping. He reached the doors just in time to jam three fingers between them and pry them back. His momentum caused him to stagger into the car, almost bump against the girl, who stood facing him, her back pressed against the opposite set of doors.

As the train began to move, the Handyman tracked her eyes. She was looking out at the platform, where a figure lay sprawled on the dirty tile like a broken puppet.

The Handyman took two steps to cross the space between himself and the girl. His lips grazed the down on her earlobe, and he registered her terror just as the train veered and the overhead lights went out.

In the darkness, his whispered breath sounded like a lover's endearment.

"If you want to live, Miss Fremont, do exactly as I say."

CHAPTER EIGHT

CRAWFORD WAS IN the van talking to the rest of his team over a secure radio link. But he was still patched through to Wally, whose mike was clipped under the collar of his green overalls. The sound Crawford heard through his earpiece reminded him of childhood, of pressing a conch shell against his ear, hearing the infinity of ocean roar back at him.

Then he heard something else: a long, sweet sigh, like the wind whistling around headstones, followed by a harsh cough. And Wally's ruined voice whispering, *"Sam . . . help—"* And then the ocean sound again.

Crawford fought the image that came to mind and acted on instinct. Even as he spoke Wally's name into his microphone, he pushed the red button on the communications console, sending an instantaneous alarm to every member of his team that one of their own was down.

Crawford scrambled out of the van and locked it. Across the street, his men were dodging traffic and drivers' obscenities. He radioed them the directions: line B, gate 43.

Despite the terrible urgency, he loped along like a man who's late but still has a good chance to catch his train. The cavernous hold of the station worked for him, allowed him to weave around people on his way down the steps and into the corridors that led to the ticket booths. The temptation to jump the turnstile was fleeting. He would gain precious, perhaps lifesaving seconds, but the ticket attendants would immediately call security.

Crawford fed the dispenser and cranked through the turnstile. He raced around the corner and at the foot of the stairs heard the screams.

The platform was jammed with people who'd gotten off the Alix train. Crawford glimpsed a trainman's uniform and wedged his way into the crowd. The trainman was on his knees, angrily waving the crowd back, a radio jammed against his ear. He was doing his best to shield the body from onlookers but Crawford saw it all: Wally on his back, eyes wide open, unblinking at the bright overhead lights. The stain along the side of his overalls was large but there was only a rivulet of blood seeping out onto the floor. The thick fabric of the overalls had soaked up the rest.

Crawford sensed and then heard the commotion behind him. Two more rail men had arrived and were pushing the crowd away. In their wake followed a man in plainclothes who looked like an undercover police agent from the teams that roamed the subways.

Crawford drifted back in time to see one of his men trying to push his way through. He caught his eye, shook his head, and walked slowly to the other end of the platform.

The agent's name was Reed. He was tall, with a wrestler's broad torso, and people shrank away from him when he was angry. Crawford saw that anger now, knew it was personal because Wally had been Reed's friend. He reached around and grabbed a fistful of the man's curly hair, forcing his head down.

"Wally's dead," he said softly. "The police will be here soon. They'll pull the Interpol ID off the body, find the gun."

Crawford paused, saw the tear streaks that slashed Reed's cheeks like scars.

"The ambulance never gets to the hospital—or more likely the morgue. You and the others make sure Wally goes home."

Crawford released his grip.

Reed shook his head violently. "The Handyman?" he rumbled.

Crawford looked at him. "Leave him to me."

STILL IN THE TUNNEL, the train swayed along the rails.

Like a sailboat lapping against its moorings.

Hollis blinked. The lights in the car had come back on, and she found herself sitting next to one of the doors, facing the length of the car. The nearest person was ten feet away, a woman reading a magazine. Beyond her were three workmen and a pair of teenagers, the girl's head resting on the boyfriend's shoulder. Farther down, a tourist family occupied four seats, sets of two facing each other. The kids were leaning forward to look at a map spread across their father's knees.

They didn't see anything.

Hollis turned slightly. Suddenly her view of the rest of the car was blocked by the Handyman, who had shifted in his seat opposite her. His face was angled toward the window, his hands were folded in his lap, giving the impression of an unhurried man patiently enjoying the ride to his destination.

Hollis tried to recall how she'd ended up here. She remembered the lights going out, the passengers reacting with curses and soft cries. Then she'd been thrown forward when the train lurched, but someone very strong had caught her around the waist, pushed her forward, and kept her moving until a flash of light revealed the empty seats. In that instant Simon Jones's face had glowed white-hot, his features those of a Saturday matinee bogeyman.

Now he was back to his academic self, the benign, slightly rumpled professor.

"I saw what you did."

He crinkled his eyes at her. "May I have your ticket, please?"

"What?"

"Your ticket. Please."

Then she understood. The conductors were coming through to check and punch the tickets. Hollis pulled it from her pocket and handed it to him.

She looked out the window, at the rail yards, factories, decrepit apartment buildings surrounded by industrial squalor. On the other side of this forbidden landscape, in the glass reflection, was Jones, holding up the tickets, thanking the conductor, who then opened the connecting door to the next car and disappeared. The rush of cold air was like a dead hand laid upon her cheek.

"You saw me do what, Miss Fremont?" Before she could answer, he added, "Please, speak quietly. You have shown great courage. Had you become hysterical it would have gone badly for us."

Hollis felt her heart pummeling her rib cage.

"What would you have done then—killed me too?"

He grimaced, as though she were a bright student who'd asked a dumb question. Hollis heard him register his disgust with a soft "Feh!"

She flexed her legs, scrunched her toes as much as she could. She could run all right, had there been anywhere to go. Maybe she could find one of the conductors and tell him—*what?* Her memory of what had happened on the platform was fragmented, with gaps between what had been a continuous sequence. She *knew* what she'd seen, but she could not articulate any of it, even to herself.

"Are you better?" he asked. "Are you calm?"

"Yes."

She detected a slight tremor in his voice, a minuscule crack in self-possessed armor.

"I kept us alive, you know."

"Who was he?"

"Someone following us. *Us.* I do not know his name."

"Who?"

A red spark of anger suddenly flashed in his eyes. "Your people did not tell you anything, did they? *I saved your life!* Can you keep your word to me? Am I safe with you?"

The plea in his voice snagged her conscience, her anger feeding her strength.

"You're not a banker. Who are you?"

"Someone who knows things."

"Knows things?"

"The man was a professional killer. He—and others—work for people who are concerned about information I possess. Your Mr. McGann assured me that everything had been arranged—that I would be safe. Not the case, is it?"

"We have to go to the police!" Hollis said fiercely.

He glared at her. "Do you really believe McGann would have gone to this trouble to get me out if he could have just put me in a taxi? The police are not our friends, Miss Fremont. You and I have no friends."

Then he looked away, ignoring her completely.

Jesus. Paul, what did you get me into? What am I supposed to do now?

Hollis grasped at the only comfort she knew: As soon as they arrived at the airport she would call Paul.

To the rhythm of the train wheels Hollis silently repeated Paul's name over and over again, the clicks against the rails sounding like the rosary beads of the old women she'd watched at prayer at the Church of St.-Eustache.

* * *

THE PARIS HOMICIDE unit came in fast and did its work efficiently. The detective in charge grimaced when he found Wally's Interpol ID and gun on the patdown. A murdered tourist was bad enough; a dead international cop meant competing jurisdictions and long nights of paperwork.

Ignoring the station officials' pleas to clean up the mess so the trains could start running again, the detective made sure his forensic team tagged and photographed everything.

When the body was finally released it was taken by two paramedics to a waiting ambulance. They paid no attention to the big, saturnine man in the crowd who watched them load the stretcher. Nor did they remark on the Ducati motorcycle that followed the ambulance down Boulevard de Magenta.

"They're not headed for the morgue," Reed said into his lapel mike. "It looks like St. Louis Hospital."

He was four car lengths behind the Ducati, in a powerful Mercedes, receiving continuous updates from the motorcyclist on the direction the ambulance was taking. Now its destination was clear; the ambulance was turning off Rue de Lancry.

"We take them at Quai de Valmy, just before they cross the canal," Reed said. "Stay sharp."

Once the ambulance turned off Boulevard de Magenta the driver cut his siren but kept the lights flashing. The klaxon wouldn't get them through the narrow streets that fed toward the canal any faster. Besides, there was no rush.

The ambulance driver saw Quai de Valmy coming up. There was the bridge and, beyond it, a mammoth Gothic pile of granite that was the Hôpital St.-Louis.

The driver was debating whether to stop for coffee at the hospital when a Peugeot veered into his path. Cunning and quick behind the wheel, the driver veered left, sending the rear of the ambulance in the opposite direction. He played the brakes lightly and managed to regain control just before it hit the sidewalk bordering a small park.

"Salaud!"

The driver hurled the epithet not at the motorcyclist who'd darted up in front of the still-rocking ambulance, nor at the man jumping out of a Mercedes that had just pulled up, but at the son of a bitch who'd cut him off.

"Go and make sure our load is all right," he told his partner. Then he hopped out the front door, only to find himself staring into the black faceplate of the motorcyclist's helmet.

"Get out of my way," he snarled.

The driver would have said more, except a fist was driven deep into his gut, collapsing him.

In the back of the ambulance, his partner fared no better. The rear doors were wrenched open and something rock hard smashed against the side of his head.

The two men in the Peugeot kept perimeter watch. Inside the ambulance, Reed knelt by the stretcher and quickly undid the straps. He so badly wanted to lift the white sheet and look into the face of his friend. But he was better than that.

Gently he lifted Wally's body off the stretcher and carried it out. He had to hurry but he took an extra few seconds to arrange the body across the backseat of the big Mercedes, much as he would tuck in a sleeping child.

When he was finished, he closed the door gently. From behind his sunglasses he saw people in the park staring at him. He gave a low whistle and his men scrambled back into the Peugeot.

Reed got into the Mercedes and laid ten feet of rubber as he swung in behind the Ducati. The Peugeot was steady in his rearview mirror.

They would ride this way all the way to the old airport, Le Bourget, where a modified MD-80 with long-range fuel tanks was waiting. The plane's logo was that of an international freight service, except the only cargo Reed had ever seen on board was human, people whom Sam Crawford had plucked out of life before they could carry out their plans of destruction.

Reed hadn't been back in the United States in five years. It would feel strange. Stranger still because the journey home would be so long and so silent.

THE RER STATION at Roissy–Aéroport Charles de Gaulle was a tomb of concrete slabs and pillars. A slow shudder coursed up Hollis's spine when she stepped off the train onto the smooth brick tile.

The dampness seeped through her clothing, and her ears were assaulted with echoing of voices and footsteps that sounded like an invading army. Yet there were few people around.

Without looking back, she made for the escalator. She was sure that Jones would be right behind her.

On the ground level, beneath huge skylights, were the exits. Hollis slipped her ticket into the machine and passed through the exit turnstile.

"The buses to the terminal are through those doors," she heard Jones say.

Hollis turned to him. "Yes. And the phones are over there."

She didn't give him a chance to argue. She strode to the bank of phones and dialed Paul McGann's number.

The Handyman stood a few feet away, next to a large, round trash bin. He watched her worry her lower lip with her front teeth, heard the impatient tapping of her leather sole on the tile. When she turned away from him he reached inside his coat and, shielding his movement from the overhead security cameras, dropped the stiletto into the trash.

THE GRANDFATHER CLOCK spun its gears, doing its duty like a long-standing family retainer. The French doors were open.

In the stillness of the office the ringing phone sounded shrill, like a spoiled child seeking attention.

Ten, twelve, fifteen times it rang. Then there was a new sound, the scratch of a kitchen match across emery, and the soft puffing of a cigar being stoked. Anyone stepping into the room would see the curl of smoke first. McGann was farther back, in the shadows of bookcases and armoires.

He drew gently on the cigar, savoring its flavor. He looked at the clock and nodded, as if he agreed with the time it told. Then he turned his attention back to the phone. Each new ring was a measure of Hollis's mounting desperation. He imagined the way she looked and felt right now: Fear would make her pale and wide eyed, the way she appeared when he'd taken her on the Ferris wheel at Tivoli. She would be on the edge of panic, needing a friendly voice and soothing, sensible advice. Above all, she needed to know she was not alone, that there was someone out there who loved and cared for her, who would reach out to help her no matter what.

She needed all that and McGann would give her none of it. His tame detective, Tessier, had passed along the details of the killing at the Gare du Nord shortly after Paris homicide had arrived. Having run the dead man's Interpol ID through that organization's computers, McGann now knew that the identification, while legitimate, had come from a batch issued to agents who had nothing to do with Interpol.

Which told McGann that the victim had to have been one of Sam Crawford's boys. Somewhere along the line, Omega had discovered the Handyman's resurrection. Whether through luck or skill, the Handyman had spotted his tracker and taken him out cleanly.

He had, McGann thought, thrown Crawford off balance, had caused enough confusion to ensure his exit from the country.

Tessier had also mentioned that while no one had seen the actual killing, several witnesses had reported a shocked young woman in the train car, staring at something. Her description was close enough to fit Hollis but McGann very much doubted the French police would move quickly enough to be able to use it.

Knowing all this, McGann had waited for Hollis's call. There was no question of his helping her. She would play out the role he'd written for her. He had every confidence in her. Once she accepted the fact that there would be no help, she would find the strength and will to see her task through. She would do it for him.

Because she loved him.

HOLLIS'S EYES STUNG with tears of frustration. Slowly she replaced the receiver but clung to it as though unwilling to accept its betrayal. Once again she felt the pulse of the Handyman's gaze.

"I do not know where Mr. McGann is." He paused. "You were going to ask me that, yes?"

"Yes."

"So the only question is, will you be able to get us on that plane?"

Hollis thought she'd never been so spent. It took all her self-control to even stay on her feet.

He came closer to her, his words so soft that they died almost before she heard them.

"You are asking yourself: Who is this old man? Where did he learn to kill like that? And why? Fifteen years of hiding, Miss Fremont. They force you to learn and do many things. Otherwise you do not survive.

"I am too old and too tired to run anymore. The government is my only hope. *You* are my only hope."

Something in his tone made her snap.

"That's all I'm going to get out of you—bullshit ruminations?"

The offense left him unruffled. "Call it what you wish. Your Mr. Mc-Gann owes you the explanation. Not I." He paused. "I'm sure you have your excuses prepared—how you failed your assignment, got me killed, or forced me to run away. Rest assured that whatever they are, they will not save your career.

"Yes or no, Miss Fremont? We have no more time."

Hollis looked around the concrete wasteland of the RER station. Beyond the glass doors she heard the whine of jet engines as they clawed the air. He was right: They were out of time.

Fuck you, "Simon Jones." I'll get you on the plane, strap you into the seat, and sit on you until we get to Kennedy. Then you can be somebody else's nightmare.

But all she said was, "Let's go."

CHAPTER NINE

CRAWFORD GUIDED THE BMW motorcycle into a slot at the airport's long-term parking lot. He had stolen it in front of the Gare du Nord, driven hard through the Paris maze, and opened up the machine on the highway. The trip had taken all of forty-four minutes.

He was shivering violently. He wasn't dressed for the ride, and his chest ached from the cold wind. He touched his face and discovered his fingertips were numb.

Crawford trotted out of the garage and along the circular concrete walk to the terminals. The first doors he came to opened on the Air France check-in counters. Beside them were an ATM and a bank of phones.

"Susan Garcetti."

"It's me."

"Are you all right?"

"I'm at de Gaulle."

"I'm sorry about Wally . . . "

Crawford's eyes tracked a uniformed security patrolman about to pass by. He forced himself to smile.

"Listen, Susie, I gotta start moving to catch that flight," he said loudly. "You have those numbers for me?"

"They have reservations on American's one-oh-one to Kennedy, leaving at two-thirty-five."

Crawford looked up at the digital clock on the wall behind the counters. It was 1:41. He was starting to think about options when Susan said, "The bad news is, it's going out full."

"Who made the reservations?"

"I'm still tracking that."

"Did you find anything else?"

"Nothing that would hang her. But there's a scratch pad by her phone. She seemed preoccupied with something called E-twelve. Ring any bells?"

Crawford knew the Handyman's file cold, and it contained no such reference.

E-12 . . . No connection to Marseille, probably none to Paris, either. Because the Handyman was *leaving* those places. But Fremont would know about E-12 because she was taking the Handyman to New York. She had a garment bag; the Handyman had nothing. Crawford didn't think Fremont would stay with the Handyman too long once they were off the plane. And he'd need things that she hadn't been given or couldn't provide: new ID, money, further instructions.

E-12.

"Check on those two items," Crawford said, then quickly gave Susan the details.

"Got it. Sam, what are you going to do?"

A part of Crawford had been considering his options. Fremont and the Handyman were either already at the airport or very close. He could go to the American Airlines counter; he might even spot them there. But taking the Handyman down quietly? Not a chance.

He dipped his hand into his jacket, to the warm leather of the shoulder holster strapped tight to his ribs. Under ideal circumstances, if he spotted him, he might be able to get a shot off, wing the Handyman badly enough that he couldn't run. But then security would be all over him, blowing his cover, and the Handyman would be whisked away by the French. Crawford, with no proof of anything, might never see him again.

Worse, he would never know where the Handyman was headed. So the threat would remain because there were other operators like the Handyman. Whoever needed the Handyman's services would surely replace him. The operation, whatever it was, would be delayed but not canceled.

"I'm going to follow them," he said, more to himself than to Susan. "I have to. I need transport—"

"I've already taken care of it. You're booked on the Concorde. It leaves three hours after the one-oh-one but arrives twenty minutes earlier. Gives you the edge."

Crawford touched the scar at his temple. "Thanks," he said softly.

"You'll take care of yourself?"

"Promise."

"Okay. Just one last thing."

Crawford was struck by the ferocity of Susan's words. "Bring momma the bastard's ears."

HOLLIS THANKED the American Airlines attendant and stepped back from the counter. She opened the folders and double-checked both tickets.

"Everything's fine," she told Jones. "Let's go."

He fell in step with her as they headed for the Customs and Immigration area.

"I understand you are working under duress, Miss Fremont. But please, try to smile. The security people always look closely at nervous travelers."

Hollis ignored him. She was determined not to stop moving until she and Jones were in their seats. She would think of nothing except getting there. After that . . . After that she didn't know what would come.

Hollis advanced on a young, blue-uniformed security officer, submachine gun draped across his chest. She held up her black diplomatic passport and quietly asked if there was a courtesy line.

The officer pointed to a booth at the far end and raised two fingers to his cap in a polite salute.

"Stay behind me and don't say a word," Hollis told Jones.

Stepping up to the small booth she slipped her passport into the metal trough, where the immigration officer retrieved it.

"*Et lui?*" He nodded toward Jones.

Hollis passed the onetime entry form through. The official stamped both her passport and the entry form, and waved them along.

"If you do not mind, I need to use the washroom."

"You'll have to wait," Hollis replied. "We're cutting this close."

Keep moving. Just keep moving . . .

She stepped onto one of the escalators, raised at a thirty-degree angle and covered with a plastic dome. Hollis recalled how these "test tubes" had been ridiculed as an architectural monstrosity when the airport had first opened.

At the security checkpoint she approached another officer, who directed her to a scanning machine at the end of the row. Hollis placed her garment bag and purse on the conveyor belt, stepped through, and waited for Jones. When he went through, the machine buzzed.

Hollis watched him smile apologetically, turn out his pockets, and dump some coins into a plastic holder. He stepped through again, without incident.

The concourse was long and wide, made for crowds that were absent midday, midweek. Hollis walked fast, looking straight ahead, ignoring the people around her. She kept telling herself that they were safe here.

Above the concourse, on the mezzanine with its restaurant and bars, Sam Crawford watched their progress from behind a round concrete pillar. The girl's body language revealed how nervous she was.

Behind her came the Handyman, perfect in the role of an elder trying to keep up with a younger, thoughtless relative. Unlike Fremont, the Handyman was scanning everywhere, including the mezzanine. Crawford dipped back behind the pillar until he was sure he was out of the Handyman's line of sight.

Crawford turned his attention back to Fremont. Something had changed in her, between the two of them. At the brasserie she'd acted like some breathless, inept salesclerk, rushing and stumbling because she was late. Now, the opposite: rigid, tightly wound, maybe lethal.

Why are you working with him? Who sent you to him? Who are you to him?

Fremont's pristine history still gnawed at Crawford. No arrests, not even a speeding ticket. The lone survivor of her family, who by all accounts had reclaimed her life. The file revealed only three visits to a psychiatrist, who commented that her adjustment had been remarkable. A bit of a loner in college but not one to drift into the radical fringe.

No one can reinvent herself that much. No one can hide so much, Crawford thought.

Which brought him back to the same question: Why was she working with the Handyman?

Walking along the mezzanine railing, he continued to watch as she and the Handyman reached the gate. Fremont had her passport and the tickets ready. She said something to the attendant behind the counter. He picked up a phone, spoke briefly, then motioned Fremont toward the jetway door.

Preboarding.

But not yet. Because the Handyman was talking to her, pointing at a newsstand on the other side of the concourse. Whatever it was he wanted, Fremont was not happy about it. But she relented and followed him over to the stand. Crawford watched him pluck a magazine off the rack and some candy from a tray in front of the register. He paid, and they walked back to the gate, disappeared into the jetway.

Crawford settled down at a café table next to the railing. His eyes never left the jetway, not even when the waiter came by to take his order.

For the next forty minutes Crawford watched the boarding of American Airlines flight 101 to Kennedy. He saw the last-minute stragglers hurry on and the jetway door close. He continued his vigil even after the plane was pushed back from the gate. He waited until the airline personnel had tallied up their tickets, removed the black plate indicating the flight number and destination from the announcement board, and left the gate. In all that time the jetway doors never opened.

Crawford paid for his Orangina and returned to the telephones.

"Any luck?" he asked.

"You're not going to believe this," Susan Garcetti replied. "E-twelve isn't an airport locker like you thought."

Chapter Ten

THE FIRST-CLASS flight attendant had offered Hollis the window seat but she demurred, staying on the aisle. Right across from Simon Jones, comfortably tucked into his own expanse of leather trimmed with sheepskin, headsets on, nodding to whatever music he was listening to, idly turning the pages of the magazine he'd insisted on buying.

The name was *EKO*. Judging by the celebrity photos splashed across the cover, Hollis thought it was a women's gossip magazine, something akin to *People*. She didn't recognize the language but guessed it was from one of the Scandinavian countries.

She and he hadn't exchanged a word since they'd taken their seats. She noticed how easily Jones chatted with the attendant who brought him orange juice, and how unfamiliar he was with the buttons and knobs that controlled the music selection and volume, and with how the video unit worked. What was it he'd said—that he'd been in hiding for years? Given his apparent ignorance of modern amenities, that much, at least, seemed true.

Her stomach dipped as the plane banked over the Atlantic. The flight attendant came along, reached past her, and pulled down the window shade.

"Makes it easier to watch the movie," she said, indicating the video unit.

Hollis welcomed the darkness. She did not want to look at Jones anymore. She did not want to think about him. But the phone built into the armrest presented a temptation. She could call Paul at the embassy.

But the line would not be secure, as she knew it had to be for her to say what she needed to. Besides, there was nothing Paul could do or say that would make any difference now, except that hearing his voice would probably make her cry.

Hollis shut down that thought. She made herself think ahead, to Kennedy, where federal marshals would be waiting. Her instructions were to release Jones into their custody, but given what had happened at the Gare du Nord, she would insist on talking to Paul first.

Only then would it be over.

Over. A simple word that rang pleasantly in her mind like a chime in the breeze. She kept hearing it even in her sleep.

IN THE CREPUSCULAR light of the cabin, the Handyman watched her. Tendrils of nightmares tugged at the corners of her mouth, creating frown lines across her forehead. Once, he saw her move her lips in some silent petition.

He thought he knew her completely now, all that she was and had ever been. Because he did not believe in coincidence he accepted that she was part of some elegant plan he could not yet divine. Maybe he never would. Maybe the presence of Hollis Fremont was merely the coda in an unfinished symphony.

The Handyman adjusted the volume control of his headset. The tremulous voice of Jussi Bjoerling, the Swedish Caruso, poured out the music of *La Bohème*. It had been years since he'd heard this piece, and he thought it quite marvelous that it should be offered on, of all places, an airplane.

The Handyman also thought about Sam Crawford's surveillance net in Paris. He knew about Crawford's work, his legendary efficiency and cunning, his almost inhuman instinct and ability to track prey.

Crawford could have taken him at the brasserie, plucked him and the girl right off the street. Instead, he'd opted to follow. Why?

Because he wants to know exactly where I'm going.

Which in turn told the Handyman that Crawford had nothing to work with. He had been lucky to catch the Handyman just as he resurfaced. That had been enough for Crawford to surveil and follow.

Doe she know yet where I am going?

The Handyman touched the call button. When the flight attendant appeared, he explained that a friend of his was following him to New

York on the next available flight but that he had forgotten the name of the airline.

The attendant went to check the departure schedules and returned a few moments later.

"It's the Concorde," she said softly, leaning over, her scent filling his head. "It's due to arrive twenty minutes before us. But the pilot tells me we might be there ahead of schedule. You might even catch your friend in the baggage claim area."

The Handyman doubted that but thanked her anyway.

Was it possible that Crawford would violate his operating principles and follow him to New York?

Of course.

By now Crawford would have traced the girl back to the consulate. If he'd gotten copies of the paperwork she'd brought with her, he'd have the name Simon Jones. From there, all he would have to do was check the passenger manifests.

Would Crawford call ahead to arrange a reception committee for him?

The Handyman thought not. Here Crawford's greatest strength became his ultimate weakness. Omega Group operated exclusively outside the territorial limits of the United States. It did so in secrecy, without the knowledge of either the American ambassador or the host country's police and intelligence organizations. It had no mandate within its own home.

If Crawford reached out to the FBI, Customs, or any other domestic law enforcement, he would have to explain who he was and why he was making his request. This would take time.

But say he could do it. By revealing himself he would risk compromising the whole of Omega Group. It was quite possible, given intraservice rivalries, that word of Omega Group would leak. The press would become very interested, as would congressional leaders and certain Senate subcommittee chairpersons. Intelligence Oversight, for example.

So, yes, Crawford would follow but he would come alone.

The Handyman looked across at Hollis, still sleeping. She had to have been told exactly where to take him once they were through Customs and Immigration.

Had she in any way let that slip out?

Since he couldn't be sure, he presumed she had.

The flight attendant had said that this flight might reach Kennedy just a few minutes after the Concorde. If Crawford knew the location, he would have to hurry. A man who hurried had to improvise, would be unprepared, could make mistakes.

I suppose I will just have to wait and see how resourceful you are.

That expectation pleased the Handyman so much that he signaled the flight attendant and asked her for a flute of champagne.

AMERICAN 101 WAS three hours and twenty minutes out over the Atlantic when the Air France Concorde, designation *Speedbird 001,* thundered down the runway.

In a window seat, Sam Crawford looked at but didn't really see the airport flash by, fall away as the supersonic lifted into the late afternoon sky. He was angry about flight 101, about the fact that as of thirty minutes ago, American's flight 101 was scheduled to arrive early at Kennedy. He'd been counting on those extra minutes to set up. Now, like a sly pickpocket, the Handyman was stealing them from him one by one.

The other problem was his weapon, the Sig Sauer he carried. Crawford couldn't leave it behind because there would be no replacement on the other end. He'd talked to an Air France security officer and shown him his Interpol ID. All the European airlines had hot lines into Interpol's computer center in Brussels. Crawford's ID was validated in less than a minute. The Air France officer knew better than to raise questions about Crawford's mission. He escorted him back to the Concorde lounge and wished him bon voyage.

But Crawford couldn't be certain whether word of an armed peace officer would be flashed to New York. He didn't need some overzealous Immigration officer greeting him with a couple of Port Authority cops in tow. Especially now, when the advantage he'd had over the Handyman was being whittled down with every passing mile.

Crawford declined the flight attendant's offer of a drink and the meal. He tried to picture the layout at Kennedy, but the concourses, halls, and rooms swam and collided in his mind. When he fell asleep, his dreams were filled with the sound of running feet, of him groping in darkness but never touching anything at all.

AT 3:32 P.M., the New England shoreline briefly came into view on the starboard side of the aircraft. It disappeared as American 101 dipped into a thick cloud layer. Raindrops streaked the windows, then began to hammer on the jet's aluminum skin as it descended into the foul weather.

Hollis stirred from her sleep like a diver moving cautiously up an underwater cenote. The overhead lights flickered and came on. The flight attendant moving through the cabin stopped and said quietly, "We'll be landing in twenty-five minutes."

Hollis looked across the aisle at Jones. His seat was in its upright position, the seat belt fastened, but he appeared to be dozing.

Hollis reached into the seat pocket, dug out the amenities kit, and went to the washroom. She locked the door and blinked when the harsh light came on.

The mirror told her she'd looked better. Her skirt and blouse were rumpled and her hair was flat and dull. Her face was puffy and, in the harsh light, had a waxy sheen. Hollis took the hairbrush and makeup from her purse, removed the cellophane-wrapped toothbrush and toothpaste from the amenities kit, and went to work.

The second chime, indicating that they were close to landing, sounded as Hollis stepped out of the lavatory. She felt better now that the cobwebs of sleep were gone.

As she returned to her seat she noticed that Jones's magazine had slipped to the floor, beneath his footrest. He was still dozing so she picked it up. The cover picture showed some celebrities against the backdrop of Lake Como, a place she'd always wanted to go to. Maybe there were more photographs inside. She folded it and put it in her purse.

"Good afternoon, Miss Fremont."

His voice startled her. There he was, watching her from across the aisle, his eyes unclouded by sleep or fatigue.

"Hello."

"Did you manage to sleep?"

"Yes. You?"

"A little."

The jet dipped lower. Hollis pinched her nose to clear her ears. Somewhere behind her, along the wings, came the whine of hydraulics as the flaps rolled out.

"Is there anything I should know about procedures at Customs and Immigration, Miss Fremont?"

"Just stay close."

"Of course. You have the entry form. And afterward?"

"We go to where the marshals are waiting."

She scrutinized his face for some reaction—anxiety, regret, resignation—and saw nothing.

"You don't seem worried."

"Why should I be, Miss Fremont? Custody is the safest place for me—as you can well appreciate."

He settled back in his seat as the airliner drifted down toward the golden lights. Hollis continued to look at him for a moment, then crossed her hands over her lap, closed her eyes, and pretended she was sailing in a crystal blue lake.

SPEEDBIRD 001 TOUCHED down at 4:11 P.M. and taxied immediately to its gate, and was tractor-towed to the jetway. Crawford was the fifth person out the door. By the time he reached the long corridor leading to Customs and Immigration, the rest of the pack was far behind.

Travelers standing in long lines packed the vast Immigration hall. Crawford headed for the end booth, where a young black officer, his breath smelling of coffee and sweet rolls, took one look at the State Department ID he held up, scanned the passport, and scrawled something illegible across the entry form. A minute later Crawford handed the form off to a Customs official and headed into the tunnel to the arrivals concourse.

The International Arrivals Building—IAB—is the only facility at JFK that is open twenty-four hours a day. Crawford had not been there for four years, but it was the same cacophonous bazaar that he remembered. Its concourses, shops, and kiosks teemed with women in saris, babushkas, and Christian Dior, men in robes, wearing turbans, and some whose cheeks bore shiny pink tribal scars. The scents of a hundred different countries mingled there. There were limo drivers standing around waiting for their Concorde passengers, and cleaners who were halfheartedly mopping floors whose grime was resistant to any solvent known to man.

Crawford took all this in as he crossed the concourse, heading for the escalator to the departures level. He was on the moving steps when the announcement echoed tinnily over the public address system: American Airlines' 101 from Paris had touched down.

Crawford trotted up the escalator stairs and moved swiftly past the long lines at the check-in counters. He noted blue-and-gray doors with nameplates that read *H2-743* or *47-6C8*—designations that meant nothing to air travelers—whose locks could be opened only by authorized airport personnel.

Crawford knew that the corridors behind these doors ran to off-limits areas: baggage, security, control tower, and others. As he stepped into an elevator that would whisk him away from traffic and clamor, he told himself that he was correct about where door E-12 was located and what it was. He had to be, because this would be his only chance at the Handyman.

HOLLIS DIDN'T UNDERSTAND why the plane stopped so far from the gate. Through the downpour she could see the terminal building through the window, way off to the right.

The flight attendant must have noticed her expression because when she handed Hollis her jacket, she said, "We're waiting for the Plane Mate, dear."

Hollis watched as a large bus, its headlights cutting through the gauze of fog, approached the aircraft and stopped. Hydraulics raised the bus until it was level with the aircraft. Then a short jetway was extended to the plane's door. The plane rocked slightly as the rubber seal clamped onto the airliner's aluminum skin.

Hollis glanced at the Handyman, who seemed patient enough, as if he'd been expecting this procedure. She retrieved her garment bag and moved in line behind him.

Like the baggage carousel, the Plane Mate is the great equalizer. It takes all the passengers from first and business class plus some of the sullen, red-eyed travelers from coach. Everyone swayed and bumped together as the bus drove to the terminal.

It was strictly a fluke that Hollis found herself first at the door that opened onto the jetway. She got off and set a quick clip for herself and Jones, in part to avoid being trampled. When they reached the Customs and Immigration hall she darted to an open booth where a young woman was trying, unsuccessfully, to stifle a yawn.

"Afternoon, honey."

"Good afternoon."

The woman saw the diplomatic passport, looked Hollis up and down, then spoke past her. "You . . . sir. You have to wait behind the line."

"He's with me," Hollis said, handing over the entry form.

The Immigration officer read it through slowly. When she looked up again, Hollis saw questions in the woman's frown. She spoke as if Jones were invisible.

"He's a U.S. citizen?"

"That's right."

"Fugitive?"

"He left a long time ago. I was told some money went with him. Now he's sick and wants to come home."

The officer's eyes raked Jones.

"Help me out here," Hollis said softly. "It's been a lousy flight, I'm beat, and I still have to deal with the federal marshals who are waiting for us."

"Get yourself some rest when you're done," was the woman's advice.

She stamped the passport and papers and handed them back.

Customs was no problem either, as she and Jones sailed through the NOTHING TO DECLARE counter.

"Very efficient, Miss Fremont," the Handyman said.

They were in the arrivals concourse, the light so bright that Hollis felt it throb at the back of her skull.

"Where are we going, please?"

Hollis stepped on the escalator. "Up."

She enjoyed seeing Jones scrambling to keep up with her. She watched his eyes dart around the packed counters and seating areas, scan the jammed kiosks and shops, linger over the cleaning crews, Port Authority police strolling by, the occasional uniformed airline employee hurrying along. She wished he'd stop because his paranoia was becoming infectious. When they came off the escalator at the departures level Hollis steered him into an elevator.

"Miss Fremont, what are we doing here?"

There was a touch of panic in his voice.

Hollis ignored him. When the elevator doors opened, she swept into a long, wide hall. After the din of the public areas this oasis for the select was a relief. She walked fast, keeping her eyes on the highly polished double doors of the airlines' clubs. There was Delta's Crown Room, Singapore Airlines' Silver Kris, and a slew of other doors with intricately scrolled logos in this private reserve of quiet and comfort that most travelers didn't know existed.

"Miss Fremont!"

Hollis kept moving as she recalled Paul's instructions: *At JFK you go to the airlines' hospitality suites—those private clubs. You'll see a door marked E-12 . . .*

So E-12 had to be here. Hollis checked each door as she went by. All she saw on them were logos, no letters or numbers. She was tempted to stop at one, try the bell or the doorknob. In the halogen-lit silence she longed for the face of a helpful stranger, anyone who could tell her where to go.

Because she was running out of corridor. There, beyond the last set of doors and cordoned off by waist-high yellow tape, was a mess of construction equipment—sawhorses, stepladders, buckets of paint and paint trays, sheets of drywall stacked five feet high on a forklift pallet.

Running out of corridor and hope, with Jones's eyes dancing hard on her spine.

Hollis stopped abruptly at the construction tape and dropped her garment bag. She turned to Jones, silently held up one finger, and ducked under the tape. She picked her way around the buckets and ladders and once caught her toe on the edge of a drop cloth. When she looked up, she saw that the ceiling too was being redone.

Past the pallet of drywall, half hidden, was a dust-covered door, the wood lighter where it had been covered by some plaque. A small blue nameplate had been stuck on, slightly askew. *E-12.*

"Jesus!"

Hollis wasn't sure if her soft exclamation was one of relief or disbelief. Why would federal marshals choose this place for a transfer?

Unless I got it all wrong . . .

Hollis stepped on that thought fast, gripped the door handle, and was relieved when it turned. She waved to Jones to follow.

It was an airline lounge that had obviously just been renovated. The walls were covered in blue fabric, the carpet was gold, good quality, the recessed lighting soft. There was a small receptionist's desk just past the door but no brochures or schedules on it. No airline logo on the wall behind it.

The carpet and wall finishings muffled Hollis's "Hello?" She walked down the short hall, past the horseshoe bar with its shelves stocked with glasses and trays of miniature liquor bottles, and into an L-shaped lounge, complete with soft easy chairs, sofas, and coffee tables with candy dishes filled with M&M's.

Along the far wall were two lavatories, their doors open, the interiors dark. Hollis checked them anyway, then came back into the lounge.

"Another problem in your agenda, Miss Fremont?"

She was half expecting him to take one look at the deserted lounge and jackrabbit. Instead, he laid her garment bag on the sofa and helped himself to a handful of M&M's.

"I don't understand," Hollis said slowly. "The marshals were supposed to be here."

"I see."

His words came out on the crackle of candy shells being split open.

"Maybe they didn't get our arrival time straight."

Jones lightly slapped his palms together, like a baker dusting off flour.

"Maybe."

As she reached for a courtesy phone next to the magazine rack, Hollis saw him walking around the bar. She lifted the receiver and discovered there was no dial tone. Behind her she heard a bottle cap pop, a familiar sound that did not warrant her turning around.

Not that she would have seen much if she had, because the bar was waist high and the Handyman's hands were busy below, in a drawer he'd silently rolled back. Only if Hollis had caught his reflection in the floor-to-ceiling mirror behind the bar would she have seen his fingers deftly attaching a suppressor onto a nine-millimeter Beretta.

Screw the marshals. I need a phone. Have to phone Paul. Right now.

These were her thoughts as she turned around. The first thing she registered was the old-fashioned bottle of Coke, open on the bar, its cap beside it.

Then the gun, with a thick black cylinder attached to the barrel, in Jones's right hand, pointed at her.

"And maybe not," he said.

Hollis blinked. The tableau was so outrageous that she couldn't will herself to move.

"Maybe your marshals aren't late, Miss Fremont. Maybe they were never coming."

His voice was different, not phlegmy or halting, and there was none of the arrogance or edge she'd heard in it before. It was soft, matter-of-fact in a terrible, final way. The voice of a man who understands precisely what he will do, who does not need to step over his conscience in order to do it. In that moment Hollis knew she was about to die.

Which was when the Coke bottle exploded.

She threw her arms over her face and dove to the floor. She felt something hot and fierce sing by her ear, like a wasp that just missed its mark.

SHE HADN'T SEEN Crawford come around from behind the tall, empty bookcase in the corner. He'd been watching through a splinter of an opening where the bookcase backboard was glued to the sides.

Crawford had seen the Handyman open the Coke bottle. Then his hands had disappeared, and when they came up again, there was the gun. Crawford didn't have a clean head or chest shot. And the Handyman's Beretta was blocked by the Coke bottle. Crawford knew that even a nine-millimeter slug would be deflected by that thick glass. But if he didn't fire, Fremont was dead.

The Sig Sauer bullet wasted the bottle, creating fine glass shrapnel that tore into the Handyman's wrist and palm. But his finger was already squeezing the trigger, sending round after round into the bookcase, which was falling forward as Crawford, airborne, leaped behind the sofa.

The Handyman kept firing, shattering the glass in the coffee table and in the picture frames. He did not waste bullets on the sofa. No way would they pierce the thick padding. He needed to create obstacles, sharp, dangerous, and slippery, to slow Crawford down. So that he could run.

Now.

Searing pain finally forced the Handyman to drop his gun. Crouching low, he ducked around the bar and ran down the short hall and out the door. Crawford's rounds tore chunks of wood and plaster but never connected with flesh.

Crawford leaped over the couch and skidded on the glass-strewn carpet. He regained his balance just as he saw the lounge door easing itself closed. He raced to it, primed himself, and hurled it open.

Nothing except paint cans, still rolling, that the Handyman had kicked over in his flight.

Crawford swung under the yellow construction tape but quickly pulled up. There were people farther down the hall, business types checking into the airline clubs for a quick drink and phone call before boarding, deliverymen loaded down with magazines and the afternoon-edition newspapers, club attendants arriving for the evening shift.

But no Handyman. And no way to give chase. Crawford felt a wave of sickness choke him.

"Can I help you?"

Crawford saw a club attendant about fifty feet away, taking tentative steps toward him. His gun was already out of sight, so he used both hands to point to the drywall and ceiling.

"Building inspector," he shouted. He wanted to sound rude. "Assholes left shit all over the place. Almost broke my neck."

He waved dismissively and turned away but not so much that he couldn't watch the attendant stop, pause, and finally turn around.

Crawford went back into the lounge, across bloodstained carpet and past ruined furniture.

He heard her voice but never saw her.

"Stop!"

Crawford did so, instantly. He moved his arms away from his body and slowly faced the direction of her voice. Hollis Fremont stood in front of one of the bathrooms, the Handyman's Beretta in her trembling grip. The long suppressor wavered.

"Don't shoot."

Crawford spoke as softly as he could, never taking his eyes off her. She had her finger on the trigger, could shoot him without meaning to.

Then he saw the rest of her, the blue suit stained and pitted with glass slivers, one cheek bleeding from a superficial cut, her eyes wide, terrified.

Crawford forced down the terrible need to chase the Handyman.

"Your name is Hollis Fremont. You work on the visa line at the Paris consulate. Your supervisor is Susan Garcetti. The woman who works next to you is Julie Tomkins. You're twenty-six years old. Your—"

"*Stop it!*"

Her shout silenced him.

"Who are you?"

"My name is Sam Crawford." He paused. "I believe I just saved your life."

It was the right call. He watched her shoulders sag, the arms sink a little. Now the gun barrel was wavering around his groin area.

"You can help me," he said softly.

Her smile looked like a rictus.

"Help you? You tried to kill him!"

Crawford ignored this. He had to take the initiative, get her past the shock, get her to listen to him.

A thought flashed through his mind: *She's* not *with him. Why else would he have tried to kill her? Why would I still be alive?*

"You can help me," he repeated. "Tell me who the target is."

"*What* target?"

"How does the Handyman intend to execute his contract?"

She took a step back, the gun lowered a little more. A silencer is a heavy piece of equipment, heavier still when it's on the end of the barrel, dragging down the wrist.

"The Handyman," she said. "No. His name is Jones. He's supposed to be some banker, an embezzler. We traveled together because he didn't have papers to get into the country. I'm supposed to turn him over to federal marshals."

Crawford started. The cold fingers of defeat clutched his heart. This woman wasn't who he supposed her to be.

"Embezzler?"

She nodded, and he slowly took a step. Then another, until he'd reached one of the easy chairs, leaned against its back, staring at her.

"Is that what they told you?"

She let the gun drop to her side, stood there listing slightly.

"Jones—the Handyman—is an assassin," Crawford said softly. He didn't stop talking, didn't move even when the gun slipped from her fingers and her lips parted. "He came here to do a job. But you're right: He couldn't get into the country by himself. He needed someone to walk him in." Crawford looked away as he added, "Someone who wouldn't ask questions. Someone like you."

CHAPTER ELEVEN

FLIGHTS FROM PARIS and other European cities had been joined by those from South America and Asia. The shops in the concourses did a brisk business off the new, often bewildered arrivals. The homeless who hadn't been rousted by the police lurched through the crowds, palms outstretched, or stumbled toward the newsstands, drawn by the jingling of change. The night-shift pickpockets were dropped off by their girlfriends and began trolling for unsuspecting marks.

Over the dull roar of thousands of hurrying footsteps drifted a computer-generated voice, repeating its message over and over like an unappreciated prophet: *"Do not accept solicited rides to the city. Do not allow anyone except uniformed attendants to handle your luggage."*

The Handyman was outside the International Arrivals Building. The autumn air was heavy with salt off the ocean and spent jet fuel. A solicited ride was exactly what he was seeking.

His right hand was in his coat pocket. He withdrew it and saw red, suturelike patterns crisscrossing the back of his wrist. The cuts caused by the shattered Coke bottle were only nicks, and the blood had dried. The Handyman flexed his fingers in a powerful motion. His hand throbbed but none of the bones or tendons had been damaged.

He drifted along the front doors of the IAB, disappearing behind knots of smokers puffing furiously, reemerging to watch the carnival.

Gypsy-cab drivers and limo hustlers called out to potential passengers streaming by them to the line of legitimate, yellow cabs. The few people who slowed were immediately surrounded by drivers shouting prices. It was a reverse auction, the price of the ride dropping as fast as drivers could underbid one another.

The Handyman had already picked out his driver from the pack. He waggled a finger at a sturdy young man with such heavy facial hair that his shaved cheeks appeared blue.

The driver's eyes shone greedily as he shouldered his less fortunate brethren out of the way.

"Meester! Meester! Ride to city? Private car. Cheap!"

The Handyman listened to him prattle on. He appraised the Lincoln Town Car that the driver, obviously a newly minted Russian Jew, was gesticulating at. It would do very nicely.

"How much?"

"Where you go?"

"The Plaza Hotel."

"Excellent hotel! Two hundred dollars. Tip extra."

"Naturally."

The driver smiled, offering a glittering array of Soviet steel-toothed dental work.

"No bags?"

"No."

"Okay."

The Handyman stepped into the rear seat. The interior smelled of cabbage soup and mint, the latter coming from the Christmas tree scent stick dangling from the rearview mirror.

The car rocked as the Russian jumped in behind the wheel. He had the wipers going to shave away the light drizzle and bullied his way into the traffic on the feeder road.

They'd gone all of a hundred yards before hitting gridlock.

"What's the problem?"

The driver shrugged. "Construction."

Through the rain-streaked window the Handyman saw bulldozers and earthmovers tearing up the earth. Farther along were concrete skeletal towers that might one day serve some purpose.

The Handyman considered. Although he could not wait too long, the traffic gave him a chance to put unfinished business to rest. He thought about this for a moment, then slipped a hand into his pocket.

"Please, why don't you pull into that waiting area over there? I get claustrophobic sitting too long in a car."

The driver jerked around. "*Claus* what?"

"Sick. I get sick waiting."

The idea of a $200 fare keeling over clearly worried the Russian. But to wait was also a waste of money.

The Handyman held up a crisp fifty-dollar bill. "Extra. If you wait. Okay?"

"*O-kay!*"

The Handyman sat back as the Russian eased the car out of traffic. Crawford would be very busy right now, he thought. His nine-millimeter, without a suppressor, had made a loud statement. Plus, there was the girl. Crawford would have to satisfy himself as to who she was and what role she'd played in this little scenario. Still, they should both be dead right now.

The Handyman acknowledged his fault that they weren't. He'd known Crawford would arrive ahead of him, had assumed the worst-case possibility that Crawford also knew the rendezvous point. The Handyman was certain he'd missed nothing up until the moment Crawford had sprung out at him. The approach to the lounge had been clean, the construction area covered with that fine coat of undisturbed dust. No footprints. The girl had entered the lounge first and she hadn't drawn fire or attention. She'd even obligingly checked the bathrooms for him.

So Crawford had to have found another way in, had squirreled himself away and waited. The Handyman thought it fortuitous that he hadn't hesitated in trying to shoot the girl. This had forced Crawford to fire before he was ready.

There was, however, a saving grace to this delay, one that neither Crawford nor the girl could possibly be aware of: Only half the trap had been sprung.

CRAWFORD GENTLY PRIED the Handyman's gun from Hollis's fingers. Looking at it, he tried to handle his anger. She had smeared whatever prints the Handyman had left on the weapon. They would have been helpful, since the Handyman had never been printed.

"We have to get out of here," Crawford said.

Hollis was sitting on the edge of the couch, her knees locked together. Her ears rang from the gunfire, and the stench of cordite burned her nostrils. The violence that lingered in the room clutched at her chest.

And now this quiet, lethal stranger was telling her she had to go with him.

"Who are you?" she asked, then remembered she'd already asked him that. *Sam Crawford.*

"I work for the government."

"Show me some ID."

"I don't have the kind you mean."

"Then I'm not going anywhere with you."

Hollis reached for her purse and got up, her legs a lot more unsteady than she'd expected. She took two steps and found him blocking her path. She thought that he had no right to look so good, with that tan set off by white blond hair and deep green eyes.

"You're in my way."

"And you're still in shock."

Hollis thought she detected a thread of kindness, maybe concern, in his flat tone.

"I'll live."

"Maybe."

She stepped back, to better look at him. "Listen. I don't know what's going on, who you are, he was, or anything is. Can you understand that? But I have to call Paris. I need someone to explain to me what's—"

She noticed his head shift, like a hunting dog's. Then she heard it, faint voices somewhere beyond the partially open door of the lounge.

Crawford's voice seemed filled with regret. "They're coming."

TWO YOUNG MALE flight attendants flanked the pair of Port Authority police officers as they sauntered down the hall toward the construction area.

"I'm sure it's all a mistake," one of the attendants said apologetically. "There's been so much noise around here lately, all those nail guns and power saws."

The older cop glanced at his partner, a younger but equally beefy version of himself, and rolled his eyes.

"Whatever. But the lady who called it in swore it sounded like a gunshot. We gotta check it out."

He hitched up his service belt, laden with gun, bullet pouch, and cuffs, and tried unsuccessfully to pull it over his gut.

"Well, you don't know Kiki," the other attendant chimed in. "She's as nervous as a cat. They won't let her fly because she gives off such bad *vibes*."

"Yeah, yeah. Kiki and her bad vibes."

The cops smirked at each other.

When the party trooped up to the construction site, the younger patrolman said, "Guys, you wait here. We'll check inside and—"

He didn't get any further because the door to the lounge swung open.

Crawford had been counting on catching them while they were still on the other side of the construction. He couldn't be sure who they were, but he was hoping they were PA cops called in because of the ruckus. If they were, it would be easier to bluff his way out, even with the girl in tow.

If it didn't go like that, then there was the emergency exit door, left an unpainted gray, hidden in the recesses of the *U*-shaped cul-de-sac. In the poor light it was invisible unless you knew where to look.

Crawford had not had time to coach Hollis so he nudged her out of the way, shielding her body with his.

"Hi, fellas. What's up?"

The younger cop was crawling under the yellow tape when his partner said, "Hey, mister! Why don't you and the lady hold up a sec. We'd like to ask you a few questions."

Crawford kept up his friendly smile for the cops' benefit but his attention was on the two flight attendants—on their uniforms, maroon blazers and gray pants. The logo sewed over the breast pocket carried the airline's name: Air Pacifica.

Which, Crawford knew, served the islands of the South Pacific, from Tahiti down to New Zealand.

Which was what made the attendants all wrong.

Crawford stiff-armed Hollis, sent her reeling toward the emergency exit. In the same motion he brought out his gun.

"What the hell—?"

The younger cop had ducked under the tape and was straightening up when a half dozen bullets all but cut him in half at the base of the spine.

The older cop made the mistake of whirling around first instead of going for his gun. He never even got it out of his holster before he went down in a bloody heap.

Crawford saw all this out of the corner of his eye as he dove for cover behind the pallet of drywall. The would-be flight attendants had vintage MAC-10s, very small, fully suppressed, totally inaccurate at more than a hundred feet, but spitting deadly at this range.

Buckets and cans exploded, sending gobs of paint into the air. Stepladders and lumber were reduced to kindling. Pitted and gouged drywall filled the air with fine dust.

The two triggermen were very good but they were working under a time constraint. Their job had to be finished within seconds. So, after killing the cops, they advanced a little too quickly, their suppressing fire not in sync. Crawford saw his opportunity, rolled out from behind his cover, and dispatched two nine-millimeter rounds that tore out one attendant's throat.

The other one was very well trained. He didn't waste a glance at his fallen partner but kept on coming, firing in tight, controlled bursts. Only six steps away from Crawford, he slipped in a puddle of fresh, slick paint. His foot went out from under him, his arms swinging wide. His finger was still on the trigger, sending rounds into the freshly plastered ceiling. Crawford's single shot caught him low in the sternum, spun him around, and dropped him like a cold fish.

Crawford scrambled to where Hollis was huddled at the base of the exit door, her arms covering her head. She cringed when he touched her.

"Come with me now. Please."

She responded not to his words but to his tone, soft and concerned and so incongruous with the carnage around her. As he gripped her arm and helped her stand, she managed to look back at the sprawled bodies. Then he put his shoulder to the door and pushed her into the landing.

Because Crawford never looked back, he didn't see the second flight attendant start to crawl away. He was gut shot and in as much pain as a human being could bear. But he kept on, foot by foot, until he reached the wall.

Twisting around, he gritted his teeth and poured every ounce of his strength into his legs, forcing them to push his body up the wall. He removed his bloodied hand from his wound and clawed for the wall-mounted emergency phone. His fingers managed to catch and hold on to it even as he collapsed.

The operator on the other end heard heavy breathing, then a strangled whisper: "Shooting . . . area 12. Hurry."

The attendant dropped the receiver and slipped down the wall until his splayed legs stopped him. A businesswoman strolling to one of the lounges took him for a falling-down drunk until she came closer and saw the blood pumping out of him.

"YOU SHOT THOSE POLICEMEN!"

Crawford had her on the staircase, hugging the wall, moving fast. At the next landing, when she tried to stop, he bumped her, hard.

"You weren't paying attention," he said. "The 'flight attendants' did that. They were part of the setup."

"What setup?"

Hollis shouted over the thunderous noises of their footsteps on the metal stairs.

"Think!" Crawford said harshly. "The Handyman pulled a gun on you. But he couldn't have had it on him in Paris—right? He'd never have made it past security. Someone left it for him on this end, in the lounge." He paused. "Where you were told to go."

The implication slammed into Hollis.

"No! You don't understand. The only person who knew I'd be there was Paul."

She bit her tongue, but it was too late.

"Paul McGann, DCM, Paris. Whose name you signed to get the entry form?"

"How could you know that?"

"Forgery isn't your strong suit, Miss Fremont."

They were on the bottom landing now, out of the stairwell. The door in front of them was chained and padlocked. Crawford stepped back and lifted his gun.

"The setup . . . What's the rest of it?"

Crawford hesitated until he saw her need to know.

"The killers' uniforms. But Air Pacifica doesn't hire white attendants, only South Seas Islanders. Cover your ears."

He shot away the lock.

Hollis still had her hands clamped over her ears when Crawford stripped the chain from the door handles. She couldn't believe that the noise would go unheard until Crawford grunted and pulled back one of the doors, steel over solid wood, two inches thick.

"Ready?"

She nodded, not knowing what else to do. She felt the walls closing in on her.

Crawford stepped through and she followed. They were in the main concourse, arrivals level. It was packed with travelers hurrying from their gates. A few saw her step out, saw the door close, gave her an odd look, but kept moving.

Crawford cupped her elbow and steered her into a large tour group. Hollis found herself in a sea of faces, all mumbling German, trudging to the exits.

The man ahead of her leaned over to say something to his wife, which was when Hollis saw him: a Port Authority officer hurrying in the opposite direction. He was twenty feet away and closing. She knew she could get his attention in a flash, cry out, reach out, rip open her blouse. Whatever it took.

"If you think he can protect you, go ahead."

Hollis turned her head, saw Crawford looking at her, slowing his stride.

"Or he might be part of the cleanup crew."

Hollis wavered. She felt a flash of anger because Crawford had been able to read her intentions so easily.

The cop was only steps away. She heard him breathing hard as he hurried along, toward her, abreast, and past, his handcuffs clattering against his riot baton.

Hollis swallowed the bitterness of lost opportunity. There would be others, she told herself as she stepped onto the descending escalator behind Crawford. He could never grab her fast enough if she decided to bolt.

At the exit they drifted away from the tour group and into the ground transportation area. Hollis watched Crawford study the traffic—Carey buses, gypsy cabs, and limos. She didn't think he saw whatever he was looking for.

"Do you think he's still here?" she ventured.

"Not a chance."

Hollis slumped against a pillar. The cacophony of diesel engines and the stench of their exhaust fired up a pounding headache. Now that she'd stopped moving, the blood-soaked images at the lounge rushed back.

"We have to go to the police," she said. "Those—those people will have been found by now. Maybe someone saw us."

She was surprised at how listless her voice was, as though even she didn't believe what she was saying.

"No one saw us," Crawford replied. "But someone might remember you and the Handyman going up there." He turned to face her. "I have to get us some transportation. I can't do that and watch you at the same time. So you have a choice. Give me your word that you'll wait right here, or else cut yourself loose now and take your chances with the Handyman."

Hollis took a step back. "You're letting me go?"

"I'm asking you to stay. I'm asking if your word's any good."

"My word is good."

"Then what do you want to do?"

Jones—the Handyman—is an assassin! He needed someone to walk him in . . . Someone like you.

"I want to know the truth," Hollis said steadily. "I need to know what I really did."

She felt Crawford's eyes measure her. He touched her lightly on the shoulder.

"Stay beside these doors, behind the post. There's a lot of traffic. No one coming through will be interested in you."

"What if the police—"

"If you're taken I can always find you. Believe that. Give me ten minutes, then keep an eye out on the pickup area."

"Where are you going?"

Crawford didn't think she had to know about the limousine pen, a five-minute walk from there, where drivers waited for prearranged pickups. In this weather they'd be in their cars, heaters going. It would be easy enough to separate one from the flock, take him down gently.

CHAPTER TWELVE

A T 6 P.M. Staten Island wives driving their commuter husbands home from the ferry terminal at St. George were rudely startled. An unmarked police car, dome light flashing, siren howling, tore down Bay Street, skidded on the rain-slick asphalt, and almost plowed head-on into the traffic streaming along Richmond Terrace.

Inside the standard-issue NYPD sedan were four large, competent-looking men, two wearing black leather jackets, two in trench coats. The windows were open a crack to let out some of the cigar smoke.

The driver spun the wheel, skirted the edge of a park, then booted through one of the island's tightly packed residential neighborhoods. The houses were mostly redbrick cottages, with the occasional white clapboard farmhouse for contrast. The driver cut his siren and light halfway down the block. As he pulled up into a driveway, the headlights illuminated the front of a two-story brick-and-stone home with a wraparound veranda.

The men got out in unison, in silence. A pizza delivery boy on his way out of the house next door gaped when he saw holstered guns only half-hidden by jackets and coats.

"Beat it, kid!" one of the men rasped. His voice was like coarse sandpaper on balsa.

The delivery boy ran to his car, parked at the curb.

The men marched to the wooden gate that they knew opened up on a narrow dog run along the side of the house. A low, mean growl greeted them.

The lead man, Vincent Calabrese, a nine-year veteran of the NYPD's Technical Response Unit in this life, kicked the gate with maybe two percent of his total body strength, not quite enough to knock it off its hinges. The German shepherd on the other side, tongue lolling, took one look at Calabrese and his squad of doom and wisely retreated into the backyard.

The foursome pounded along the wet grass to the small patio and barbecue area. Behind the windows of a small covered porch stood a young woman clutching a quilted housecoat around her.

"Where is he?" Calabrese bellowed.

The woman gestured toward the attached garage.

The side door was open. Calabrese stepped into the dimly lit interior, his thick fingers tracing up and down for a switch. He found it and a second later the garage door began rolling up.

There were oil and radiator fluid stains on the concrete floor but no car. Mounted along one wall was a pegboard with a home enthusiast's tools, and beneath that, a long wide worktable, the drawers scarred with drippings of old paint.

Along the back wall, next to the bicycles and skates, were an old refrigerator and a dented, run-down freezer chest. In front of the refrigerator, a man knelt over a large zinc washtub.

Calabrese and his team formed a half-moon behind him.

"Jacoby," Calabrese rumbled.

The man rocked lightly, like a devout Jew at prayer.

"You killed them, didn't you?"

Harry Jacoby turned and looked up into Calabrese's looming, pitiless expression. He was in his late thirties, rail thin, with red Brillolike hair and pale skin dotted with freckles.

"Didn't mean to," he said softly. "I took real good care, you know. Made sure they were kept nice and cold, changed the water . . . "

"You really are pathetic." Calabrese sneered. "C'mon. Let's have a look."

He stepped around Jacoby and, gripping the tub by one handle, pulled it into the light.

"Son of a bitch!" one of the team muttered.

"The stink . . . ," said another, breathing through his mouth.

Calabrese squatted and slipped a meaty hand around Jacoby's neck.

"You know what this means?" he whispered. "What it makes you?"

Jacoby hung his head. Calabrese's breath was hot and thick in his ear, like a bull's.

"A clam killer!"

"*Clam killer, clam killer, clam killer . . . *"

The rest of the team took up the chant until they saw Jacoby's pissed-off expression and couldn't hold back any longer. A neighbor arriving home across the street gaped, wondering what could be funny enough to make four grown men laugh so hard.

Jacoby stood up and looked sourly at the thirty pounds of littleneck clams in the tub. He'd brought them down from Rhode Island this morning, a special deal his father had gotten him. Kept them in iced seawater, the tub covered with burlap just the way his old man had told him. Got home and the little fuckers were dead or dying, their shells hinged open.

He looked at Calabrese and the team and wondered how to shut them up.

"They were okay when I left Providence. I spent half the goddamn day on the road and the rest in here with the fucking garden hose."

The crew stopped laughing just long enough to look at him as if he'd grown a tail, then doubled over again.

"Did you give them mouth-to-mouth too?" Calabrese wheezed.

"Oh, fuck you!"

"You should have seen him."

It was Kathy Jacoby, the woman in the housecoat. A belt was cinched around her dancer's waist, and her blond hair fell softly to her shoulders. There were flashes of thigh as she walked into the garage, the housecoat billowing around her long legs. All the men looked at her as chastely as if she were their younger sister.

She set down a pot of coffee, mugs, and fresh-baked brownies, then fondly ran her hand over her husband's head.

"It was so cute," she told the crew. "There he was with the hose, pouring in fresh water hour after hour. Adding kosher salt to boot."

"These were *Jewish* clams, Harry?" Calabrese inquired, chuckling.

"I thought that if they had, you know, saltwater, kind of . . . Aw, shit!"

"When the kosher stuff was gone, he started in on the rock salt."

Kathy took a bite of brownie and pointed to a half-empty bag of de-icing salt.

"Un-fucking-believable," Calabrese murmured, his mouth full.

"It wasn't *your* two hundred bucks that went into the toilet," Jacoby said sourly. "Now I'll have to pony up another two for that seafood supper . . . "

Calabrese poured hot coffee down his throat, then slapped Jacoby on the back.

"Supper's canceled. We're not going to be around for the next couple of nights."

"What's up, Vincent?" Kathy cut in.

She was six weeks along with Jacoby's child. They'd been trying for three years for a miracle the doctors had said would never happen. Kathy had made Jacoby try harder. Now, anything that even hinted of risk, Kathy demanded to know. She had a private understanding with Calabrese that if Jacoby had to be in on a hunt, he'd be at the back of the pack.

"Two things," Calabrese said, pulling out a cigar.

"Put that away," Kathy ordered.

Calabrese was momentarily startled. "Right. Sorry." He picked up his train of thought. "First, we got a request from the Secret Service to help out with Senator Ballantine and his wife while they're campaigning here."

"Threats?" asked Jacoby.

"The usual wacko shit. But the commish is Ballantine's pal."

"Personally, I think Claudia Ballantine's the one who should be running," Kathy said. "I'm a volunteer on her America Forward project."

"You and a coupla million chick—uh—ladies," Calabrese said. "Except she's not the candidate and everyone loves her. The same can't be said of hubby."

"What's the second?" asked Jacoby.

Calabrese shuffled from foot to foot. He didn't want to meet Kathy's eyes, so he kept his gaze on the tools hanging on the pegboard.

"There's been a shooting out at Kennedy. Two PA cops dead, two civilians—flight attendants, looks like."

Jacoby saw his wife's eyes flutter. He moved in close and held her. "Give me the short version."

"Two shooters—a man and a woman. No eyewitnesses, but PA is working hard on possible composites. Looks like a terrorist scenario."

Jacoby digested this. "That so? A guy-gal combo. Don't see much of that these days. What are the feds saying?"

Calabrese waved his finger like he was shooing away a fly. "CIA and FBI haven't rolled out of bed yet, which gives us some time before they try to horn in."

"You think they'll want to make this their own?"

"After the World Trade Center bombing, they think they own this town."

"So we're going to butt heads over turf."

"I don't think it'll come to that," Calabrese said, studying his fingernails. "Whoever this team is, they're in *our* town. So unless we find out that they've gone to Connecticut, they're our play. The feds can go spit."

Jacoby nodded. He had that glazed look in his eyes, the Mr. Spock look, some called it. No one spoke. No one wanted to break the spell.

Like the rest of them, Jacoby had once been part of the Technical Response Unit. Unfortunately, his tactics, as well as those of the team, had been deemed somewhat overzealous, not to say violent, by several federal judges. He and the others had been quietly turfed out of TRU—and told by the commissioner to form a separate strike force. The team also did baby-sitting jobs when the commissioner had a vested interest.

Every major city has a team like this. In Los Angeles they're the Ghoul Squad; in Chicago, the Hats. Their only targets are criminals no other police division could—or wants to—deal with.

Calabrese's group called themselves the Muffin Men because Kathy, who was a professional pastry chef, never let them go anywhere without a bag of homespun goodies. At first, certain elements considered the moniker a joke. In short order, Jamaican posses, Russian mobsters, and Colombian drug enforcers learned that it was best to disappear when the Muffin Men came knocking. Except they were seldom successful in doing so. Calabrese and his team never bothered with such niceties as search warrants, court-authorized wiretaps, or civil rights. They operated strictly by the laws set down by their quarries, neither giving nor asking for any quarter. Their byword was KISS: Keep it simple, stupid.

This was especially true when the commissioner had extended the team's mandate to include terrorism. With so many competing jurisdictions and agencies—federal, state, local—acting on a real or perceived terrorist threat could become a bureaucratic nightmare. There had been sad examples of that in the past, enough to convince the commissioner and the mayor that the city needed its own boys to handle the job.

Six months ago, the Muffin Men had done just that. When letter bombs were sent to the offices of propeace Arab newspapers, Jacoby, working in sync with Israeli intelligence, led the team to a nest of Palestinian fanatics. The takedown was hard and swift. The Muffin Men delivered the terrorists, along with the incriminating evidence, to the U.S. attorney's office early one morning, depositing them outside her front door like babies in baskets.

In spite of the attorney's repeated demands, no details about the operation were ever provided. How the Muffin Men worked, how they got their contacts with foreign intelligence services, was deep graveyard.

Jacoby finally stirred. From his clear, cold gaze, the team knew that he had run every conceivable option through his computerlike brain. Now for the punch line:

"Immigration didn't tag them, so they might be using diplomatic paper," Jacoby said. "Thing is, if we start running them down and they wave immunity in our faces—"

No one in the unit trucked to that concept.

"Diplomatic immunity?" Calabrese made it sound like nuclear physics. "Fuck if I know what that means."

He said the rest to Kathy, the truth. "Harry's going to tag them for us. That's all. When he does, we hand Ballantine over to somebody else and drop on this pair like the fucking wrath of God."

Kathy thought that Calabrese's smile made him look like a particularly evil jack-o'-lantern.

"Works for me." She turned to Jacoby. "Better go wash up, hon. You have to drive me to the prenatal-care class."

CHAPTER THIRTEEN

THE RUSSIAN WAS getting fidgety. The Handyman heard his fat buttocks shift on the front seat, his fingertips drum on the steering wheel.

"Meester?"

The Handyman kept watch on the headlights inching out of the arrivals area. By now he knew that the cleanup crew had not carried out the disposal. If they had, he would have seen them drive out.

So, Crawford and the girl had survived. Somehow. But Crawford still faced a problem: no ready transport. He would not risk hemming himself in by taking a taxi or bus. He would improvise. The Handyman wondered how Crawford would do that. But no matter which method Crawford chose, he'd have to use this artery to get out of the airport.

The Handyman thought it would be very helpful if he could spot Crawford, slip in behind him, follow him until the moment was right. Because there had been a minor oversight—insignificant, really, but with someone like Crawford it was best to take care of it. The Handyman felt he should deal with it now, while Crawford was still off balance, his hands full with the girl.

Except here was the Russian, bleating.

The Handyman watched two more police cruisers scream by—that made six in the last twenty minutes—and accepted that he had to move things along.

The reason he'd chosen the limo over a gypsy cab was the lack of a barrier between the front and back seats. No reinforced Plexiglas or stout wire mesh to get in his way.

"Okay," he said.

The Russian didn't quite get it. "Okay? We go?"

"We go," the Handyman said agreeably.

He leaned forward, the two $100 bills folded lengthwise between his fingers.

The Russian displayed his steel showcase again. In order to grasp the money he had to twist both his spine and neck around. When he did so, the Handyman merely helped him along, clamping his powerful hands on either side of the man's head and wrenching viciously. The Russian's neck snapped like a dry bough.

The Handyman let him fall onto the seat, then he got out and opened the front passenger door. He sat the Russian up and closed his eyelids. Then he arranged him so that he would slump against the door when it closed, giving anyone looking into the car the impression that he was napping.

The Handyman came around the front of the car, slipped in behind the wheel, and checked his work. All that was missing was the snoring.

The Handyman decided that even with all the police falling over one another, he'd give Crawford another few minutes before going on his way.

HOLLIS HAD COME to the conclusion that Crawford didn't know much about Kennedy Airport. Where he'd told her to wait turned out to be a prime stalking area. So far she'd been accosted by all the gypsy drivers, panhandled five times, and propositioned twice. She flinched at every voice that called out to her, every arm that reached for her. She was too busy fending off advances and lewd suggestions even to consider breaking her word and fleeing. By the time she noticed the large black Cadillac pull up, the passenger window rolled down, she was seething.

"Get in!" Crawford called out.

Hollis pushed past a teenage con artist offering to help her with her garment bag and darted for the car. The way she slammed the door got Crawford's attention.

"You all right?"

"No, I'm *not* all right. Just drive."

As Crawford steered into traffic, Hollis slumped into the fine leather seat. The Cadillac was elegantly appointed and had that distinctive new-car odor. It also had something else.

Hollis reached for the cellular phone, examined its make and model. It was the latest technology from Motorola, a satellite unit with worldwide reach and equally astronomical calling charges.

She glanced quickly at Crawford, who was concentrating on the road, took a deep breath, and punched in the number for the Paris embassy. When she heard ringing on the other end, she pulled as far away from Crawford as possible. In the instant before the embassy operator answered, Hollis asked herself why Crawford wasn't doing anything to stop her.

IN PARIS IT was just after one o'clock in the morning, and the embassy gala was still going strong. From comments McGann had overheard from the A-list guests, tomorrow's society columns would make the ambassador preen.

More important to McGann, the diplomatic babble and frolic had been a perfect camouflage for his meeting with certain Chinese gentlemen who, unknown to the other guests, were emissaries from Beijing. The understanding McGann had reached with them would make headlines in a few weeks, especially in the Seattle area, and the Boeing aircraft plant in particular. It would also put a shine on McGann's stock in the company.

He stood among a group that included the Thai ambassador, the DCMs from India and South Africa, and a Balinese model who'd latched on to him during the midnight supper. McGann was considering taking her home or next door to the Crillon when a marine guard came up behind him.

"Phone call, sir." After McGann had stepped back, the marine added, "The security office, priority line."

McGann excused himself and followed the marine across the ballroom.

The security room, which also served as the marines' interior command post, was off a foyer down a short hall. The marine opened the door for him, escorted him past the locked racks of assault weapons and tear gas and fragmentation grenades, and into a small, concrete-walled cubicle. In the event that a U.S. embassy was being overrun, this chamber, secure against everything except a tank shell, would be the marines' final communication link with the Pentagon.

Only after the marine had closed and locked the vaultlike door did McGann pick up the red phone.

"Yes?"

"Paul? Paul, is that you?"

McGann stiffened, his knuckles white around the receiver. It was the voice of one who should have been in the grave.

"Paul, are you there?"

Her voice was scratchy and he thought she was on a cellular. Where? Kennedy? Someplace in New York?

"Paul, if you're there, talk to me. It's important!"

Suddenly the room felt very warm to McGann. The receiver had become slippery in his palm. Incredibly, she had survived the Handyman. Had she been hurt? Wounded? Was the Handyman gliding up behind her even now, or had he, having failed, cut and run?

McGann knew the identity of the Handyman's target but nothing about his timetable except that it would be tight.

And what about Crawford? The Handyman had dropped one of his men in the Paris train station. Had Crawford exceeded his mandate and followed the Handyman to New York? If so, how close was *he* to Hollis?

McGann pushed a button that sent a burst of static into the line. Let her think it was a bad connection. When the line cleared, he listened to her voice very carefully. Anxious and frightened but not panicked. Nor was she demanding that he help her, tell her what to do or where to go.

Why not?

McGann had been watching the sweep of the second hand on the desk clock. Twenty seconds had elapsed. He shot two more bursts of static into the line, then hung up. Let her draw her own conclusions.

He sat back in the swivel chair, making it creak. Suddenly his meticulous plan was unraveling, all because a thread called Hollis Fremont had not been snipped. Right now, he had no way of contacting the Handyman. There were other numbers in case of emergency, numbers that would reach the individual who had ordered the Handyman's resurrection. But if the Handyman called that person, McGann would have far more explaining to do than he'd anticipated.

McGann forced himself to slow down. He was an expert in crisis management. Compared to other situations he'd been called upon to handle, this wasn't even a speed bump. The main thing now was to exercise caution and to organize a backup plan that would keep the pressure on Hollis—and on Crawford. A possibility was already suggesting itself.

McGann's thoughts of the lovely Balinese withered and fell like dry rose petals. He had to prepare himself for Hollis's next call. That she would reach out to him again he had no doubt. And when she did, he would set in motion the small precaution he'd already taken before he'd sent her off to die.

"NO LUCK?"

Her answer was her set expression.

Crawford steered around the last of the bottleneck and came up to an intersection light. The road to the left, leading past the airport construction to the Van Wyck Expressway, was clear.

He looked at her again, surprised that he wanted to tell her that he'd already talked to his people in Paris. They hadn't been able to get hold of McGann either.

"Who are you?" she asked suddenly.

"I already told you that."

"No, I mean, what do you do?"

"I'll tell you everything when we get out of here."

"Where are we going?"

"Somewhere safe."

Crawford's reply almost made her smile, that wan look when a woman no longer believes in her lover's fidelity but keeps up the pretense.

"I don't think anywhere you are is safe."

The light changed and Crawford made the turn, gliding past earthmoving equipment parked off to the side of the road. He was turning over Hollis's last words when he heard her shout, "Behind you!"

She had been sitting facing him. From this position she could, out of the corner of her eye, see through the back window, which had suddenly filled with something black hurtling toward them.

Crawford looked in the rearview. A Town Car was bearing down on him, so he spun the Cadillac's wheel to get out of the way.

But the Lincoln got there first, plowing sideways into the Cadillac, forcing it off the road and through the flimsy wooden construction barriers, toward the heavy equipment. The collision jarred Crawford but he managed to hold on to the wheel. He hit the gas to pull away, but the Lincoln had the advantage of momentum. With the shriek of metal grinding on metal, it plowed the Cadillac toward the gaping three-ton blade of a Caterpillar tractor.

"Get down!" he yelled.

But Hollis was transfixed by the sight of the blade, no more than fifty feet away, clumps of moist soil hanging from its teeth like torn flesh. She had never been in a car accident and didn't understand why everything seemed to slow down.

Two things were working against the Cadillac: its weight and the fact that the shoulder of the road was soft earth. Crawford realized that the Cadillac's tires were sinking into the ground. He dropped the gearshift into low and jammed the gas pedal. The transmission wailed as the engine overrevved but the car began to hold its own against the Lincoln.

Crawford whipped his head around. There was the Handyman, arms held out straight to the steering wheel, his face in perfect profile as though struck on a coin. Then he turned, and Crawford felt the full measure of his cold, deep recognition, of his unmistakable intent, devoid of any pity or mercy.

Not today. Nobody else dies today!

Crawford stood on the brakes with both feet just as the Cadillac slid into the tractor blade. It caught the tip, which shattered the rear window, then sheared the C-panel. The front passenger window exploded. Crawford threw up his hand to protect his face and in that instant saw tiny beads of safety glass shower Hollis.

Crawford's braking not only saved their lives but caught the Handyman off guard. The Lincoln howled past the Cadillac, scoring its fenders again and ripping off the front bumper. Crawford shifted into reverse and plowed back through the churned-up muck, away from the blade.

The Handyman was back on the blacktop now. Crawford shifted again and sent the Cadillac rocketing over the shoulder. He missed an oncoming utility vehicle by inches, fishtailed, and fell in behind the Lincoln.

"Let him go! Christ, let him go!"

Hollis was shaking her head wildly, safety glass flying out of her hair.

She stared at Crawford's grim expression, saw that the Cadillac was eating up the distance to the Lincoln. She heard the wail of police sirens behind them and knew that Crawford would never stop now.

It was one of those miracles that sometimes occurs in the traffic patterns around JFK. At a certain time of the evening, for no apparent reason, both the feeder road and the Van Wyck Expressway clear, and traffic flows quickly and smoothly.

When Crawford saw the Lincoln enter the on ramp and ease into the right-hand lane of the expressway, he followed, ignoring the screeching coming out from under the hood.

"There's a police car behind us," Hollis shouted.

Crawford's eyes darted to the flashing lights in the rearview. "Got him."

"And another one coming down the ramp."

Crawford gave no indication that he heard any of this. He was focused on the Lincoln, which was slowing down.

He's busted up . . .

Crawford knew exactly what he was going to do—use what was left of the Cadillac to take out the Lincoln. He would ram the driver's door and send the Handyman through the windshield.

Crawford drew closer and slowed just a little. The Lincoln was wobbling from side to side and drifting into the next lane, drawing angry honks from drivers who had to swerve around it.

Then the passenger door flew open. Crawford heard Hollis shout, "Watch out!" just as a body dropped out of the Lincoln, bounced, and rolled directly into their path. Crawford hit the brakes and tried to cut around, but the Cadillac was too big and unwieldy. The body disappeared from view and he felt two soft bumps as the tires ran over it.

Screaming, Hollis twisted around. Through the shattered back window she saw the corpse lying in the middle of the lane like a torn-up doll. Brakes shrieked as drivers tried to swerve or stop but succeeded only in creating an instant pileup.

"Oh, Jesus . . ."

"We didn't kill him," Crawford said coldly. "He was already dead. The Handyman kept that body in case it might be useful."

Hollis was thrown back against her seat as Crawford tore away from the scene.

"What are you doing?" she cried.

"We can't help him. And the police won't listen to us."

"But they'll think we hit him."

"They *already* think that!"

Hollis looked around. Crawford was right. The two patrol cars had stopped at the accident site, but a third, now only a distant speck, was continuing its pursuit—and gaining.

"*TANGO-ZULU-LIMA. Kennedy suspects spotted northbound on the Van Wyck, approaching Queens Boulevard. NYPD unit in pursuit. K?*"

Harry Jacoby snatched the microphone off his radio.

"Tango-Zulu-Lima copy. Will assist NYPD unit."

Jacoby didn't bother to tell the dispatcher that he was *southbound* on the Van Wyck. Why worry the nice lady?

Jacoby's immediate problem was the fact that the median between the north- and southbound lanes was blocked by heavy, chain-link fencing. There was a solution to this, but it meant going a little farther in the opposite direction.

Jacoby slapped the dome light onto the edge of the sedan's roof, hit the siren, and tore into the far left lane. He was nudging sixty miles an hour when he came up on a piece of blacktop that connected the two sets of lanes. It had been cut for highway maintenance crews and doubled as a speed trap. Jacoby made sure there was enough distance between him and the car behind him, tapped the brakes, then at the last second jerked up the hand brake. This caused the sedan to drift to the left. Jacoby discovered he'd miscalculated a bit and in the process demolished two signposts. He released the brake, hit the accelerator, and shot through the cut, bouncing on the steep shoulder and coming down hard in the northbound lanes. The lack of traffic puzzled him until he saw the vehicular carnage in his rearview mirror.

"Tango-Zulu-Lima proceeding north on Van Wyck. Uh, dispatch? You have anything on an accident here?"

"*Suspect vehicle involved in hit and run. One fatality, multiple collisions.*"

"Copy, dispatch."

Jacoby glanced at the speedometer and decided a little faster wouldn't hurt. His blueprinted engine could run at 120 without breaking a sweat.

Jacoby ran the body count. The victims at the airport and now the roadkill; that made five. He glanced at the shotgun mounted behind the dashboard, then at the submachine gun strapped in the passenger foot well. Both were fully loaded.

Ahead he saw the flashers on the NYPD unit; if it had a visual on the flight vehicle, then Jacoby was in play, closest to the suspects. He reached for the microphone and asked the dispatcher to put him through to Calabrese. Vincent and the crew might get here in time if they used the chopper. But by then, if Jacoby got lucky, it'd be all over.

Jacoby didn't quite see eye to eye with most of his law enforcement brethren when it came to terrorists. He didn't believe in cornering them, reading them their rights, wasting the next two years of his life testifying in court. You do a hard takedown, make sure the targets aren't moving, then go for lunch.

Jacoby had shared this philosophy with Calabrese, who'd shrugged agreeably and said that it must be an Israeli thing, right?

THE CADILLAC WAS dying. The lights on the indicator panel were flashing, telling Crawford what he already knew. Streams of oily black smoke slithered out from under the hood. One or more of the engine belts had been torn apart, flapping and smacking like strips of rawhide on flesh. The transmission was grinding, the gears stripped. When it came time to slow or stop, the brake pads would be worn down to nothing.

Crawford checked the rearview mirror and found he still had a good lead on the pursuing patrol car. He made his decision and swung right, onto the Queens Boulevard off ramp. He ran the light and headed for Long Island City.

Traffic was heavy here. Crawford twisted in and out of lanes, used the sidewalk when he had to, took a madman's chances at the traffic lights.

Squeezed against the door, her seat belt tight across her chest, Hollis wondered how much longer Crawford's luck could hold.

"Where are we going?" she demanded.

"In there." Crawford pointed with his chin as he veered off Queens

Boulevard and onto Jackson Avenue, then almost immediately turned again into a narrow, potholed street.

Hollis looked around at the industrial park wasteland that makes up most of Long Island City. The low-story buildings behind fencing topped with razor wire housed print-and-graphics plants, furniture makers, and clothing sweatshops. Others had been taken over by limo companies and converted into garages, by trucking firms that used them as maintenance depots, and by moving companies in need of cheap storage facilities.

Some, like the one Crawford was turning into, had been abandoned, most of the windows smashed, the copper plumbing and electric wires ripped out and stolen, the doors left open to the elements.

Crawford nosed the Cadillac into the cavernous, dimly lit warehouse, whose walls and pillars were covered with graffiti. Years of debris and decay crunched beneath the tires. Crawford pulled in behind a crumbling interior wall and killed the engine.

Hollis followed Crawford's gaze, which was fixed on something beyond the windshield, at the far end of the warehouse.

"What are we doing here?" she asked quietly.

She had to wait for his answer, which didn't come until she, too, heard the sound of a heavy motor echo in the gloom.

"The police?"

"No." Crawford turned to her. "Maybe we're about to get lucky. Climb out *quietly* and stay low, next to the door."

Hollis watched him slowly push open the driver's door, stop when the hinges creaked, and slip out of the car. She carefully brushed the last bits of safety glass from her lap before she got out. Following Crawford's lead, she crouched and duckwalked around to the Cadillac's ruined front end. She looked where he was staring and saw the silhouette of a big utility vehicle.

Her expression was all questions.

"Stay here. Don't move until I call or come for you."

He was gone before she could protest.

Lamplight was streaming in from the holes where the warehouse roof had rotted away. Crawford surveilled the ground in front of him for broken glass, nails, and scrap metal.

Moving from pillar to pillar, he came close enough to smell the heat coming off the squat brutal-looking Hummer, a civilian offshoot of the army's version. This one was painted shiny black and was heavily customized, with spot lamps mounted on the roof, chrome bumpers, and a winch bolted under the grille.

Crawford heard two men talking in low tones. He looked from behind the pillar and saw them standing next to the Hummer: a tall, broad-shouldered black in a leather coat and a shorter, ratty-looking white wearing a dirty nylon jacket with the Mets' logo on the back.

The black thrust a cheap gym bag at the Mets fan, who unzipped it and checked its contents before reaching behind him and handing over a Samsonite attaché case. Crawford didn't need to see what was in the case to know what was happening.

"Step away from the truck," he shouted, moving toward them.

The two turned quickly, their hands dipping toward their coats until they saw Crawford's gun. The black pulled himself together first.

"Who the fuck are you?"

Crawford held out his free hand. "The keys to the truck."

"Hey, fuck you! I got protection. You mess with me—"

The gunshot sounded more like a cannon blast, the bullet piercing the Hummer's steel wall.

The dopers cowered and stared at the ragged hole. Crawford let the echo die away.

"The keys."

"You shot my fucking truck!"

The black made it sound like Crawford had murdered his kin.

"One last time. The keys."

"Give him the fucking keys!" the Mets fan screeched.

"They're inside."

"Open the door so I can see them."

The black obliged, careful to keep his hands where Crawford could see them. The keys were there, in the ignition, a Tiffany's silver pig dangling from the key ring.

"Take ten steps to the left."

The dealers were still moving when Crawford called out, "Fremont! Get up here *now.*"

He heard her coming up fast behind him, waved her on. "Into the truck. Go!"

Hollis didn't break stride as she passed him. As she neared the Hummer she saw the two men.

"What *is* this shit?" said the Mets fan.

Crawford glanced down at the gym bag and attaché case as he walked to the truck. He was about to get behind the wheel when he heard the Mets fan whisper frantically, "The dumb fuck's not taking the money—or the powder!"

Crawford stepped back out, looked at the bags again, then at the two men. The black was glowering at the Mets fan.

"Give me your jacket."

The Mets fan peered at Crawford like he was crazy. "My jacket?"

"*Just* your jacket." Crawford kicked the gym bag. "I'm not interested in that, or the money."

The Mets fan worked his way out of his jacket, balled it up, and tossed it.

Crawford slipped it on, transferring his gun from hand to hand. Then he jumped into the driver's seat, fired up the Hummer, and made a tight turn. In the side mirror he saw the men racing for the stash he'd ignored. Over the roar of the engine he heard the black yell, "Hey! Carjacking's a federal rap, ya know?"

SERGEANT BALLESTEROS AND Officer Perkins were in a radio car, cruising their regular route in the warehouse district between Jackson Avenue and the Queensboro Bridge, when they saw the Hummer come screeching out into the street.

Perkins started to reach for the siren switch when Ballesteros clamped his fingers over his wrist.

"That's Dri-Ice's rig. He and Maloney probably finished up a score."

"The captain said we gotta stop anything that moves," Perkins said.

"Anything that looks like *terrorists,*" Ballesteros corrected him. "'Sides, the captain don't know about our arrangement with them." He paused. "And they both always pay their monthlies. *Comprende?*"

Ballesteros picked up the radio mike and pushed the loudspeaker button.

"You, in the truck. This is a restricted area. Move along. Repeat: Move along."

Ballesteros saw a blue-jacketed arm poke out of the Hummer's window and wave. Then the vehicle made a sharp left and roared out of sight.

"Told you that was Maloney. Fucker never wears anything 'cept that cruddy Mets jacket." He smiled. "I'm surprised Dri-Ice let him drive the rig. He treats it better than I do my dog."

"Sarge, we got company."

Ballesteros slowed as a gray sedan pulled up beside the cruiser. A mick-looking redhead was staring at him through the open passenger-side window, holding up a gold detective's shield.

"You guys see a beat-up Cadillac come through here?" Jacoby asked.

"No, sir," Ballesteros answered smartly. "But we caught the all-points. If he's in the area, we'll spot him."

"Did the squawk tell you what to do after that?"

"Call it in, pull back, keep the suspect vehicle in view, and wait for backup."

Jacoby nodded. "I'll be in the area awhile. Pass the word to the other patrols."

"Will do."

Ballesteros's two-finger salute became an obscene gesture as the sedan pulled away. He turned to Perkins.

"Remind me to tell Dri-Ice how we kept his butt out of the wringer. Maybe he'll sweeten the monthly so I can finally get the wife that TV she's been bitchin' about."

CHAPTER FOURTEEN

THE PÈRE-LACHAISE cemetery is one of the great landmarks of Paris. Each year thousands of American tourists make the pilgrimage to the grave of Jim Morrison, pause to pay homage to Oscar Wilde, Sarah Bernhardt, Molière, and the hundreds of other artists interred there.

The cemetery is also a reflection of the city. There are magnificent family vaults that seek to preserve the station one held in life, a Chinese and a Jewish section, and a paupers' row. A blend of estate-size garden and necropolis, it serves as an oasis of peace for pensioners, students, and tourists. But only during the day.

At night, Père-Lachaise takes on a distinctly dank character. Satanists, vampire seekers, members of bizarre occult fringe groups manage to find ways around the security and lay claim to the underbelly of this hallowed ground.

Paul McGann considered them morons. For him, the supernatural had no shape or substance and the shadows he saw winging through the cemetery were created by the wind and trees, not the devil. Nevertheless, there was a Taurus 9 mm on the table beside his glass of Cheverny Blanc, fifteen rounds in the magazine, one in the chamber. More than adequate to deliver a drugged-out devil worshipper to his master.

McGann was sitting in the far corner of a bistro, Le St.-Remy. By day it served the best wines and fare the Loire Valley had to offer. It had been shuttered an hour ago, but McGann, whose mother had a small castle in the Loire, had called up the owner. He came by, let McGann in without question, handed him the key with which to lock up, and went back home to bed.

It was now three o'clock in the morning. The embassy party was a distant memory. While he waited, McGann fine-tuned the details of his plan. His hand went for the gun when he heard the scrape of a door being opened.

The shadow paused, then entered and closed the door.

"Over here, Luc."

The detective, Tessier, jerked his head up. He moved uncertainly among the tables, bumping into chairs, cursing softly. When he reached McGann, he looked at the gun, then the glass of wine.

"Cheverny Blanc," he said.

"The bottle's behind the bar. Help yourself."

Tessier did so, smacking his lips after his first sip. He shambled back to the table and sat down. McGann's nostrils flinched at the sour smell of Tessier's clothes, his bad breath.

"This almost makes being hauled out of bed worthwhile," he said, pointing at his glass. He looked around and added, "What exactly are we doing here, Paul?"

"I need you to create a profile."

Tessier yawned theatrically, but McGann saw that his eyes were hard and alert. At heart, Tessier was a peasant, calculating how big a marker he was going to bank by obliging McGann.

"At three o'clock in the morning," he said dryly.

"This is special business," McGann replied. "We're like the post office—we never sleep."

Tessier grunted. He knew that McGann was more than just the Paris DCM, that he was linked to U.S. intelligence. But even Tessier's resources could not define the exact nature of McGann's work or the identity of his employers. But in the end, it did not matter. McGann paid handsomely, in negotiable bearer bonds deposited in a Swiss bank account that Tessier checked out once a year during a detour on his way to his August vacation on the Italian Riviera. To his credit, McGann had never tried to cheat him.

Tessier poured himself more wine. "A profile, you say."

"Earlier today an incident occurred at Kennedy Airport," McGann said. "It concerned two passengers, one on American flight one-oh-one and the other on the Concorde."

He sketched the bare bones for Tessier, who, when he got to his office, would pick up the details off the police hot sheet or CNN.

"Now, because it was an Air France Concorde, French interests may be involved. Especially since American authorities may be thinking that there are terrorist implications here."

"Terrorists? Really?"

"Really. I'm sure that any assistance the Paris prefecture, working with the Deuxième Bureau, could offer would be very much appreciated—and the source acknowledged."

Tessier nodded. He didn't need to curry favor with his pig of a boss, but a commendation in his permanent file wouldn't hurt either.

"And just how deeply are these two involved in—um—terrorist activities?"

"You might consider remaining vague on that. Cite reports from confidential informants. A search of a certain address, the discovery of certain contents that would lead to certain conclusions . . . "

"You want them under the hose."

It was an expression from the late sixties and early seventies, when water cannons were the tool of choice to quell student riots.

"That would be about right."

Tessier drained his wine. "I'll put something together. New York will have it by tomorrow."

He cocked his head. "I don't suppose it would be possible to obtain a bottle of this excellent wine? It's a very hard vintage to find. I'd pay for it, naturally."

McGann smiled. "My treat. The cooler is next to the kitchen. Take two bottles."

CHAPTER FIFTEEN

CRAWFORD'S ROUTE TOOK them to the far end of Long Island City, where Northern Boulevard meets Grand Central Parkway, which then connects to Interstate 678.

The night sky made good on its threat after they crossed the Whitestone Bridge and got onto the Hutchinson River Parkway. After a brief pause the rain returned as a fine drizzle and increased steadily as they headed north toward White Plains.

The drumbeat on the Hummer's steel cage sounded like marbles rattling around in a tin can. Hollis kept shifting in her seat because the vehicle's suspension was so tight. Every time the Hummer's wide tires hit a tar strip, she felt a jolt ratchet up her spine.

Then she caught a glimpse of something that made her look down at herself. Her jacket was ripped in at least several places and her skirt was filthy from the warehouse grime.

"Shit."

Crawford glanced at her. "What is it?"

"My garment bag. I left it in the backseat of the Cadillac."

"What was in it, besides clothes?"

"A travel kit."

"Did the bag have a tag with your name and address?"

Hollis nodded. She recalled having a hell of a time worming her embassy business card under the plastic sheath.

"The police will find it, won't they?" she said. "They'll know who I am, that I was there."

"They would have made the connection anyway," Crawford said. "Now it'll be sooner rather than later. It doesn't matter."

"You'd better pull in there," Hollis told him, indicating the lights of a mall up ahead. "I need to get some clothes."

Chiding himself for not having realized that she couldn't get by with what she had on, Crawford drove into the parking lot. Hollis pointed to a space close to J. C. Penney.

"Give me twenty minutes," she said.

"Don't use credit cards. I've got cash—"

"So do I."

Crawford watched her jump out the door and run through the pelting rain. He badly wanted a coffee, and a Starbucks beckoned, but he didn't want to leave the truck. It seemed unlikely that the doper would report its theft to the police, but Crawford didn't want to find out the hard way that the license plates were already on the computer hot sheets.

He sat there, the rain fogging out the rest of the world, and thought of what he had to do next. It all hinged on the girl—how much she would tell him, how much she really knew.

He understood that he had to be very careful here. Hollis Fremont had been hit with one shock after another. She'd reached out to someone she trusted, Paul McGann, and had come up empty. She knew that somehow she'd committed a horrendous mistake, but didn't realize all the implications or how to deal with them. Crawford had to settle her as much and as quickly as he could, had to gain enough of her trust so that she'd reveal everything she knew. Which meant working through her fear, embarrassment, and denial, and convincing her that nothing that had happened was her fault. That things had spun out of control . . .

But what were those *things?* Why had she been with the Handyman? And what was McGann's role in this?

Crawford was an expert interrogator but his skills were of no value here. Hollis Fremont wasn't guilty of anything except allowing herself to be duped and used. Had she been a professional, his would be among the bodies at JFK. If he tried to wear her down, trick her, or go the hard route, he'd end up losing her, which he could not afford to do—now that the Handyman was on the loose, with a timetable and a target.

TWENTY MINUTES LATER and she was as good as her word. Crawford had fired up the engine to run the heater and the wipers.

Through the windshield he saw her, shopping bags in both arms, running for the truck. He leaned over and opened the door, helped her with the bags.

Her face was scrubbed shiny by the rain and her hair lay in rats' tails. She looked much too young to be where she was.

Hollis gave him back his gaze. "I thought we were in a hurry," she said, reaching for her seat belt.

Crawford got onto Route 684 and drove north to the fourth exit. Taking the off ramp to the traffic light, he turned left and headed west on Route 172 to West Patent Road. They were in manor country now, the exclusive enclave of Bedford Hills. In the high beams, Hollis saw miles of stone walls lining the road, with wrought iron gates at the edges of long private drives. Sometimes she caught flashes of tall chimneys among the trees.

Crawford turned left on Broad Brook Road and followed it until it became McLain Street. The Hummer's tires chewed up the twisting country road that narrowed until Hollis thought it would disappear into the surrounding woodland. Then Crawford turned left and stopped in front of tall, imposing gates. He hopped out, unlocked a panel set into one of the stone pillars, and punched in an entry code.

They proceeded up a dirt road covered by a canopy of chestnut trees. Hollis guessed they'd gone a quarter mile before they reached a clearing. Set at the base of a hundred-foot granite outcrop was a small estate.

The main structure, a two-story farmhouse, white with dark green shutters, stood off to the right. At the end of the driveway was a three-car garage with living quarters on top. At the bottom of the sloping lawn was a fast-moving stream that flowed from somewhere deep within the outcrop and emptied into a large pond, shrouded in mist.

"What is this place?" Hollis asked.

Crawford's quiet gaze was that of a man who has been away for a very long time and now beholds something very dear and familiar.

"It's home," he said softly. He turned to her. "Why don't you get out here, wait on the porch while I park this thing?"

Hollis was careful on the slippery flagstone steps. She watched him open the garage door and ease the Hummer out of sight, then she peered through the windows but couldn't see anything through the heavy curtains.

The veranda boards creaked as Crawford joined her on the porch. He reached up and unscrewed the cover of the light fixture hanging beside the door. His fingers explored the base around the bulb and came up with a key.

He opened the door and stepped into a foyer, and Hollis saw him work the buttons on the security panel set into the wall.

"It's okay now," he said as the lights came on.

Tentatively, Hollis entered. There was a large living room on the right with a fieldstone fireplace, and on the left, a dining room with a long refectory table. The floor was all peg-and-groove, the walls a cool plaster above wainscoting. The furniture was big and comfortable looking, the kind made for curling up with large dogs.

Hearing lights snap on deeper in the house, she put down her shopping bags and made her way into the country kitchen, which had an open hearth along one wall.

"You could roast an ox in there," she observed.

Crawford was checking the larder and cupboards. There were a lot of canned foods and preserves in glass jars.

"I think someone did that once," he said.

He turned on the sink taps to flush out the rust-stained water, then went into the bathroom and did the same thing. Hollis followed along, through a large master bedroom that overlooked the backyard and the granite face, through a bookshelf-lined study, then back into the living room.

"It'll take about a half hour before we have hot water," he said. "Then you can clean up and change."

Hollis went to the fireplace, opened the flue, and put a match to the neatly stacked kindling and birch logs. As the flames caught, she opened the windows a crack to clear out the musty smell, then sat in an old easy chair.

"You have to give me a drink—brandy would be nice—and an explanation," she said. When he raised his eyebrows, she added, "You saved my life at the airport, and again on the road. And now you've brought me here, where you say it's safe." She paused. "It *feels* safe. But I still need to know."

Crawford took a bottle of brandy from the pickled oak sideboard and disappeared into the kitchen. When he came back, he was holding two jelly jars with an inch of brandy in each. He'd taken off his jacket, and she was momentarily startled by the gun strapped to the side of his chest, the way the butt dipped toward her when he handed her the drink.

"Where do you want me to start?"

"I know your name is Sam Crawford. Let's take it from there."

"You only have a Level Two security clearance."

"Right. Bottom of the barrel. But I think I've just moved up a notch or two, don't you?"

He watched her sip the brandy, never taking her eyes off him.

"This place"—he gestured at the room—"belongs to me. An inheritance. But you won't find my name on the deed. A special government service maintains it, pays the taxes, makes sure it looks lived in. The same is done with safe houses all over the world."

"Don't your neighbors get curious?"

Crawford shook his head. "Out here, people pay a premium for privacy. There's a lot of money out here—telecommunications, finance, software. These people travel for months at a time."

"Just like you do."

"No. I live in Paris."

"And you work for the government but you don't carry ID."

Crawford fished out his black diplomatic passport.

"My boss is the same as yours, more or less."

Hollis examined the passport, its pages littered with immigration stamps from every country in Europe.

"You work for the State Department."

"A small office within it. I report only to a man you've never heard of or, if he's absent or unavailable, the president."

Hollis took a large swallow of brandy.

"The secretary of state or the president. What exactly is this 'office'?"

"Omega Group."

Crawford went to the fire, poked at the logs, threw on two more. He watched the white bark curl back, turn to black.

"When a new president takes office, he's told certain things—the nuclear GO codes, the status of covert operations. And about Omega Group. If he's lucky, he never hears the name again. The same goes for the secretary of state."

"Why is he lucky?"

"Omega is a black agency. It has no budget, no personnel roster, no offices. It doesn't exist. Its agents operate strictly abroad, under deep cover. They pose as embassy staff, businessmen, academics, media people. But all they do—all *I* do—is track and hunt assassins."

Hollis set her glass down on a coffee table fashioned out of a nineteenth-century blacksmith's bellows.

"You hunt assassins."

"Omega was founded after Kennedy's assassination. One of the secret directives of the Warren Commission was that an agency be established to identify and surveil every known professional killer in the world. Each sector of the globe has its own Omega team. I'm responsible for Europe."

"But Oswald wasn't a professional."

Crawford smiled thinly. "The assassins' whereabouts are constantly monitored," he went on. "If one of them moves, we move. If it looks like he's headed for the States, we intercept."

" 'Intercept.' As in 'kill.' "

"Only as a last resort. If an assassin moves but isn't headed here, we make sure the officials of the country he's going to are informed. If his target is here we follow as closely as we can and try to pick him up at the last minute, before he can cross our borders. But getting the killer is only part of it. We also need to know who hired him and who the target is. We want to trace the original contractor because if he could hire one killer, then he could get himself a replacement. The target would still be in jeopardy."

"But if that's not possible . . . ?"

"Then we do whatever it takes to keep people like the Handyman from slipping into the country."

Hollis rose and went to the window. Leaning forward, she pressed her forehead to the cool glass pane. The night air smelled of wet, rotting leaves and pine resin.

Twilight Zone *time, Holly.*

She knew a little about security. It had been a part of her world ever since the first time she'd seen her father wear his gun. It was a vivid memory, his coming into her room to tuck her in, his jacket falling open, her small hand reaching for the cold black steel, the way he caught it and gently covered it with his own.

She knew about the background checks that had been done on her when she'd applied to the Foreign Service and recalled the lectures on embassy security. She had college acquaintances who now worked in the CIA and FBI.

But this was beyond the pale. She could grasp but not comprehend what Crawford was telling her. A man who hunted other men, assassins, killers—whatever the label. A man who could not allow anyone to get by him. But in this case had.

Hollis closed the window. Her breath misted the glass when she spoke.

"You're a gatekeeper." She turned to him. "Invisible. No one knows about you, no one reads or hears about what you do. Not even the people you protect."

She thought she saw a glimmer of acknowledgment in his eyes.

"Jones? Your Handyman?"

"He used to be one of the most lethal assassins in the world. At fifty-three—that's how old we *think* he is—he's still that." He looked at her keenly. "You know. You've seen him up close and personal."

Hollis nodded. Jones the nervous academic, always polite. Jones the wraith, disappearing into a subway crowd and flying out with bloodied hands. Jones the cool, soft-spoken killer, calmly raising his gun to shoot her.

Yeah, I've seen him up close and personal.

"Someone left the gun for him at the lounge, right?" she asked.

"Yes, they did." He paused. "The Handyman's story goes back fifteen years, when he botched a major contract. The individual who ordered that hit never forgave him—there are no excuses or mitigating circumstances at that level. Until now.

"That the Handyman has been resurrected means something very big is going to happen. Here. The target is someone whose face we all recognize."

He sipped his brandy. "I had plenty of chances to take him down in Paris, even before then. But I waited. I wanted to see who he'd contact, wanted him to reveal his principal. But somehow he knew I was after him, killed one of my men."

"I know," Hollis said softly. "I saw him fall as the train was pulling out of the station. Jones . . . the Handyman said *he* was a killer."

"The Handyman played you perfectly. He knew you'd go along. That you really had no choice."

"You keep calling him the Handyman. What's his real name?"

Crawford shook his head. "No one knows."

"But you said he's one of the best."

"Part of being the best means you keep as many secrets as you can. We think that he got his moniker when he started out in the trade, back in his mid to late twenties."

Hollis drained the last of her brandy, grimaced slightly as it burned down her throat.

"This is what I don't understand," she said. "You told me that fifteen years ago the Handyman made a mistake. He 'botched' his . . . assignment. If you knew that then, why didn't you or the local police pick him up?"

Hollis thought she'd hit a tender spot. Crawford's features seemed to sag a little, as though her question was one that haunted him, one he'd never been able to resolve.

"The Handyman's mistake wasn't that he was spotted or almost got caught," he said quietly. "The problem was that no one ever suspected this man was a target. There was no forewarning, no protection. The shots were fired. One man was killed instantly, there were other casualties . . . It wasn't until later that we learned the Handyman had been involved."

"Who was he, the man he shot?"

"I can't tell you that," Crawford said, then steered off the subject. "Tell me: How old would you say the Handyman was when you first saw him?"

Hollis thought about that. "Early sixties. But you say he's at least ten years younger."

"And he can drop another ten years or add twenty. Tomorrow you could be sitting across from him in a restaurant and you'd never recognize him. That's how good he is."

"So there's no way to really describe him. And no fingerprints?"

Crawford nodded. "I told you about Omega, where and how we work. What I didn't mention was that like the CIA we're not allowed to operate within our national borders. We're supposed to keep people out, not follow in hot pursuit."

"But if someone gets by you, there must be something you can do."

"According to the Omega charter, I'm obligated to inform the director that a threat exists against a person or persons in the United States.

I'm to supply him with all the information Omega has on the threat, suitably sanitized so that none of it can be traced back to a U.S. source. At that point, he decides which domestic law enforcement agency gets the case, most likely the FBI."

" 'Most likely' because you've never had someone like the Handyman slip by you?"

"Never."

His tone held no pride or preening. Hollis thought he said it like it wasn't an accomplishment at all, but some handicap he'd had to teach himself to live with, one day at a time.

"That's what I was getting at when I said that bringing in someone else is not an option. We've seen what the Handyman looked like a few hours ago. But by now his appearance could be totally different. A misleading composite would create confusion and an even more effective cover."

Crawford didn't think it necessary to mention how vastly Omega had underrated the threat of the Handyman.

"So the police—and the FBI—can't help because they don't know who to go after," Hollis murmured.

"By now they know about *you*," Crawford said. He gestured toward the master bedroom. "There should be hot water by now. Why don't you go ahead? I'll make us some food."

Hollis watched him disappear into the kitchen. She heard a cupboard open and cans being pulled off shelves. She looked into the fire for a moment, wondering if Crawford thought he'd lulled or satisfied her with the morsels of truth he'd offered.

THE BATHROOM WAS large, with a claw-footed tub and a shower stall. The tile seemed original and the grout was clean. The smell of disinfectant lingered, suggesting that someone had cleaned here not too long ago.

Hollis turned the faucets in the shower and let the rust-stained water shoot out while she waited for steam to warm the room, then got out of her ruined clothes. The shower was hot, stinging her skin, driving the cold ache from her bones. She stood under the spray for fifteen minutes before reaching for the soap and shampoo.

As she worked up a lather Hollis wondered how much Crawford

knew about her. His resources were vast but would he have had time to use them? Did he know of her relationship to Dawson Wylie?

The temptation to reach out to Wylie was almost overwhelming. Hollis couldn't recall a time when he hadn't been there for her. In his world, she had always been safe.

She pictured Wylie at the Crillon, recalled the way he'd teased her about Paul, invited her to come visit him, the sadness that had flickered across his features when she'd told him she couldn't. But no matter how much she wanted and needed him, she would not put him at risk by contacting him.

Stepping out of the shower, she quickly dried off and combed out her hair. Then, wrapped in a towel, she returned to the master bedroom.

Her purchases included a pair of jeans and one of wide-wale cords, two plain white blouses, two thick sweaters, underwear and sports socks, Nike cross trainers, and a waterproof faux suede car coat. Warmth and dryness had been her concerns. She'd also remembered to get a toothbrush and toothpaste.

Hollis put on the cords, one of the sweaters, slipped on a pair of thick socks and the sneakers. Then she examined the result.

She'd expected that the ordeal would have made her look different, maybe left scars. But there was nothing. Even her heart had slowed its frenetic pace, settling into a calm rhythm that steadied her.

Hollis put the rest of the clothes back in the bag and returned to the front of the house. The dining room table had two place settings, opposite each other. The overhead lights were low and a candle in a tall hurricane lamp made the pewter cutlery gleam. The smell of hot stew and fresh rolls made her ravenous.

"I was wondering how you were coming along," Crawford said.

Hollis noticed that he too had changed. He now wore thick cotton pants and a turtleneck sweater. And his gun.

Crawford gestured at the food. "Let's eat while it's hot."

Hollis tried to eat slowly but couldn't. Hungrier than she'd thought, she wolfed down the stew and used a roll to sop up the gravy. Crawford offered seconds but she shook her head. She did not offer to help when he cleared the table.

When he returned with a pot of coffee, neither of them wanted the powdered cream or sugar.

Hollis stared at the rain sluicing down the windows. She glanced at her watch. It was almost midnight.

Midnight in another dimension.

"What are we going to do?"

Crawford studied her over the rim of his earthenware mug. "I need you to tell me how and why you were sent to the Handyman."

Hollis picked up the faint suspicion in his tone. She felt the cameo pendant nestled between her breasts and immediately thought about Paul, wondered how she could explain what had happened without making it seem she was blaming him.

Crawford apparently read her thoughts. "I know McGann's involved. I need to know where he fits into all this. I'm not saying he's guilty of anything . . . "

Not yet you're not.

"When we were in the car, you let me make the phone call," Hollis said. "You knew he wouldn't be there because you'd already tried."

Crawford nodded. "You want to give it another shot?"

The offer caught her off guard. Her first instinct was to jump at it. But when she considered it, she realized that the situation had gone far beyond Paul. Only Crawford could help her now, right this minute.

Hollis sipped her coffee and cast her mind back, focusing on images. She blushed when she pictured herself in Paul's bed, naked, reaching for him.

She started with Paul telling her about his little problem, how the man who was supposed to have escorted "Simon Jones" to Kennedy had been in an accident. She took Crawford through all the instructions Paul had given her, how there had been a last-minute screwup because he hadn't signed off on the INS form, her attempts to reach him, and finally the forgery she'd committed.

"Didn't it seem strange to you that you weren't able to reach McGann?" Crawford asked.

"I suppose. But being a DCM takes him out of the embassy quite a bit."

"Not without a pager, cell phone, or contact number."

She shrugged. "I guess it was just one of those things."

"So, McGann gave you money and a picture of the man he called Jones."

"That's right."

"But didn't he also say that Jones would know what *you* looked like?"

"Yes."

"Think about that. McGann would have had to talk to Jones *before* you two met up."

Right. "What are you driving at?"

"McGann never mentioned that he was in communication with Jones?"

"No."

"All right. We'll get back to that. Tell me what the Handyman said to you from the moment you met. Try to remember his exact words, if he said them in any particular way, if anything struck you as odd or out of place."

Hollis told him about the brasserie in the Hôtel Terminus Nord, her brief introduction to Jones, how they left, and the decision to take the RER instead of a cab.

She had to stop for a minute, gather herself, before she could describe her terror on the train, the way Jones had taken control of their journey, the things he'd told her about himself in order to goad her to do what she'd promised.

"The Handyman never said he wanted you to call McGann, or that he had to?" Crawford asked.

"No. He was desperate to get on that plane. It didn't seem there was any other way out for him."

"There wasn't," he said coldly. "He knew I was behind him. You were his only option."

Hollis looked at him. "Susan Garcetti. She works for you, doesn't she?"

He nodded.

"What did *she* tell you?"

She saw Crawford hesitate, as if wanting to spare her.

"After you left the consulate, Garcetti called McGann's office. His secretary had no record—anywhere—of his authorizing the release of an INS form. No memo, no verbal request. It never happened."

"That's impossible!" Hollis cried. Then, softly: "Maybe she overlooked something."

"Garcetti tells me the secretary has been with McGann for years, knows everything that crosses his desk. Do you really think something like this would have slipped by her?"

Hollis looked away. She'd met Paul's secretary often enough. *No way.*

"And if McGann had arranged for another person to look after Jones, the paperwork would have been ready *before* the time he said he'd signed off on it. The original baby-sitter would have had it the night before so that he could go directly to the rendezvous point the next morning."

Despite the warmth from the fireplace, Hollis felt icy cold. Without being aware of it, she tugged at the gold chain and slipped the cameo out from under her sweater. Her fingers rubbed the silky relief of Helen of Troy, the touch bringing back the memories, its inscription rending her heart.

This is forever.

She felt Crawford watching her. "Are you saying that Paul knew Jones was the Handyman? That he was *helping* him?"

"Looks that way."

Her eyes flashed. "Do you even know Paul? Do you know *anything* about him?"

"I know you've been seeing him for two months and that you love him very much," Crawford said quietly.

Hollis shot him a furious look. "Susan Garcetti again?"

"Your relationship isn't exactly a secret."

Hollis shook her head. "You're wrong about Paul. About everything." She leaned forward, her elbows on the table. "Because if what you say is true, then Paul knew the Handyman would kill me once we got here!"

She bolted the room. Crawford made no attempt to stop her. He heard the bathroom door slam, followed by the sound of running water.

None of which would wash away the truth, he thought. Paul McGann *was* dirty. Crawford didn't know exactly how or why. Yet.

He walked to the back of the house and opened the door to what looked like an ordinary closet. Except, on the wall, hidden between support beams, was an electronic keypad. As he punched in the combination on the door to the communications chamber, Crawford mentally outlined the agenda for the surviving members of his Paris team.

* * *

HOLLIS WAS SURPRISED to find Crawford gone when she came out of the bathroom. She'd stayed in there for what seemed a long time, the water splashing noisily into the sink. She'd be damned if she let him hear her cry.

Hollis kept telling herself that Crawford was all wrong, that he'd twisted her words and come to a monstrous conclusion. She would set him straight, make him see how wrong he was.

But every time she replayed his words, she couldn't find a flaw in his logic. And that terrified her.

Hollis poured herself more coffee and took it into the living room. She settled on the couch in front of the fireplace, trying to slow her spinning thoughts, arrange them in such a way that they would fall together into the reality she so desperately wanted to see. But at every turn Crawford's conclusions boxed her in, and she felt like she was in some arboreal maze, unable to see over the tops of the hedges, stumbling up one path and down another.

The creak of a floorboard made her look up.

"Sorry if I startled you."

Hollis shrugged off his apology as Crawford sat beside her.

"You thought I was working with the Handyman, didn't you?" she said.

"Yes."

"So it follows that I was also working with whoever was helping him."

"You seemed to know what you were doing, getting him out to the airport the way you did. But I wasn't sure how much you really knew about the whole picture."

"When did you change your mind?"

"When I saw the Handyman pull his gun on you."

"That's what would have happened to the man whose place I took?"

Crawford nodded. "That's the way the Handyman works, cutouts all the way. The person bringing him in was a means to an end. Disposable."

"So whoever set this up also sent in those phony flight attendants."

"Independent contractors, hired to clean up after the Handyman was gone. They were never meant to see his face."

Hollis scrutinized his expression. "Something else is bothering you, something that has nothing to do with what you think Paul did."

"What I'm thinking is, why did the Handyman come after us at JFK? Ramming us like that wouldn't have guaranteed a kill—and sure kills are the only kind he believes in. Why not follow us instead, find out where we go, plan, then move in?"

It took Hollis a minute to get it. "You mean he's coming after me. And he'll keep coming."

"I think he has to. *Something* is making him do it. He went after you in the lounge, then a second time in the car. That means he's worried. About what? What is it you know that scares him so much?"

"Nothing! I told you everything."

"Did he let anything slip in Paris, maybe by mistake? A name or place?"

"No!"

Realizing how frayed her nerves were, Crawford pulled back a little.

"You know something, even if you think you don't. The Handyman knows exactly how long he needs to set up a kill. He never puts himself in a position where he has to rush. But here he is using up valuable time hunting you."

"Maybe *you* were the target," Hollis shot back.

"The Handyman had no reason to come back for me. He's free and clear. No, you were the one he was interested in."

Hollis took the measure of his somber tone. She glanced around the room, then at the windows.

"How can you be sure he won't find us here?"

"Because this place doesn't exist. And it's safer than it looks. Take my word on that."

Hollis set her cup on the coffee table. Exhaustion was seeping through her like a warm fog, gently erasing her desire to stay awake.

"I still don't believe Paul had anything to do with this," she said. "I think someone tricked him into helping the Handyman. He had no idea what was going to happen." She paused. "That means someone else out there arranged this."

"Of course."

"You know?" Hollis asked, surprised.

"I call him the broker. He's been working with assassins for a long time, setting up their assignments, getting them safely to their targets, making sure they have a safe way out when it's all over. He's been do-ing this for a long, long time."

"So if Paul was duped he must know this broker, as you call him," Hollis said. "Not as a killer's agent but maybe as a friend or profes-sional acquaintance. Someone in diplomatic circles." She paused. "Maybe even somebody in the embassy or consulate."

The prospect of eliminating Paul as a suspect elated her, but Craw-ford's skeptical expression made her quick to anger.

"You said no one knows about this place, right? So what if I use it to prove to you that Paul had no idea he was helping an assassin?"

"That would imply that McGann got his marching orders from a su-perior or someone who asked him for a favor," Crawford observed. "But okay. How would you work it?"

Hollis took a deep breath. "I'll call the embassy and leave a message with the night operator. All I'll say is where I am and that I'm all right. If Paul is working with the Handyman, then we know who to expect."

She glanced around the room. "You *did* say this place is safer than it looks."

Crawford realized that she had trapped him neatly. The idea of using his haven as bait repelled him. But the possibility of luring the Handy-man here, where Crawford had the advantage, was too tempting to pass up.

He made some quick calculations and decided that even if McGann got the message immediately and was, in turn, able to contact the Handyman without delay, the assassin would still need time to prep for his assault. Nothing would happen before tomorrow at the earliest, and probably at night.

"Make the call," Crawford said.

CHAPTER SIXTEEN

THE LINCOLN HELD together long enough to get the Handyman across the Queensboro Bridge to Fifty-ninth Street between Second and Third Avenues.

As he inched along in the evening traffic the Handyman was worried that the ruined Town Car would attract attention, but he quickly discovered that New Yorkers were oblivious to his wreck.

The Handyman had to cross Second Avenue before he spotted an open space. The red-painted curb and the contradictory parking signs meant nothing to him. He parked and left the keys in the ignition, an inducement to a passing thief.

The Handyman strolled away from the car and into the safety of the crowds along Third Avenue. Drifting toward the entrance of an Irish pub, he observed the protocol of aggression in hailing a cab. Then he stepped to the curb, picked one out with its lights on, and deftly shoved a woman competitor out of the way as he opened the back door.

The address he gave the Sikh driver was on West End Avenue between Eighty-fourth and Eighty-fifth streets. The Handyman settled back as the cab headed north on Third Avenue, turned left on East Sixty-fifth Street, drove through Central Park, and came out on West Sixty-sixth Street. His thoughts were on Crawford and the girl.

For a moment back there the Handyman thought he'd had them. Pity he hadn't been able to give that one last push that would have speared their car on the bulldozer blade. But tossing out the Russian driver when Crawford couldn't help but hit the body—that *had* been a nice touch. Effective too because it meant that in addition to their other problems, both Crawford and Fremont would have the city police after them. The term *vehicular homicide* came to mind.

All of which pleased the Handyman. True, he had not succeeded in his first objective, killing Fremont. But in the confusion and uncertainty there would be little time for her to think, even less to recall a minor detail. He would have another chance to close her eyes before she could sort it out.

The Handyman gazed out the window as the cab headed up Broadway. He had been to New York twice, more than twenty years ago. Then, he'd found it a raucous, dirty city with pretensions toward culture. Nothing he saw changed that opinion.

The cab slowed in front of a mammoth prewar apartment building that had gone co-op in the early eighties. The Handyman paid off the driver, adding a decent but unmemorable tip, and stepped out. The doorman was helping a woman with her shopping bags when the Handyman glided through the lobby and disappeared into the rickety elevator.

Unit B, on the seventh floor, was at the end of the hall. The key was under the doormat. The Handyman smiled. Sometimes the best hiding places were the most obvious. Besides, there was a trap for the unwary.

The Handyman unlocked the door, stepped inside, and immediately found the security panel. He punched in the code *E-12* and the alarm lights stopped flashing. Clever how his principal had arranged for the code and the room designation at the airport to be the same.

He locked the door behind him, turned on a light, and glanced around the apartment. It was filled with seventies Danish furniture, all teak and rosewood veneer. There were floor-to-ceiling bookshelves in every room, even in the kitchen nook, volumes that ran to history, philosophy, biography, and meditation. The walls were hung with posters depicting Vietnam War protests, Grateful Dead concerts, and jazz festivals. It was the warren of a liberal arts scholar, frozen in time like a wasp in amber.

The Handyman checked every room, to be sure of privacy. He ran his fingers around the bathroom sink, the kitchen counter, and the closet doorknob. Each time they came away with a film of gritty dust. No one had been in the apartment for a long time.

The Handyman recalled the concise instructions he'd been given when he called from Marseille. The rifle was exactly where it should have been—in the closet of the bedroom, tucked away behind three cartons of old *National Geographic* magazines.

He pulled out the canvas-backed hard-shell carrying case, which had two emblems stitched to its side. One was an internationally known symbol; the other would be instantly recognized where he would need it. He set the case on the bed and opened it. Inside was one of the finest examples of British gunsmithing, the PM bolt-action covert sniper rifle. Devastatingly accurate at distances up to three hundred meters, it weighed a mere fourteen pounds, including suppressor. The weight increased only marginally when the twelve-by-forty-two Schmidt and Bender telescope sight was in place.

In its takedown format, the pieces fitted neatly into black foam molds. There were two extra cavities, one for the ten-round detachable magazine, another for the 7.62-by-51-millimeter NATO subsonic rounds.

The only nonlethal thing in the case was a CTM brochure display map of New York. The Handyman unfolded it and glanced at the financial district, at the very tip of the island. His shooting stage wasn't on there but other necessary details were.

THE HANDYMAN CARRIED the case into the living room. There was a telephone on a tiled end table beside the couch. It looked like an ordinary unit but the Handyman knew it would be perfectly secure. He reached down for it rather than sit and disturb the dust on the sofa.

The first call was long distance but within the continental United States. In less than ninety seconds the Handyman had reported his status to his principal, explained what had occurred in Paris and at Kennedy, and was given the second and final set of instructions. The voice he listened to was electronically distorted but the Handyman pictured the face on the other end, added fifteen years to it, imagined what it might look like today.

His second call was to Paul McGann, in Paris.

"YOUR ARRANGEMENTS HAVE not proven satisfactory," the Handyman said. "You did not warn me that Crawford was so close."

McGann was locked in the Bubble pod. The digital scrambler gave a tinny quality to the Handyman's voice.

"The problem was not the arrangements," he replied sharply. "It's the fact that you failed to kill her."

The Handyman thought McGann was edgy, surprised to hear from him. Good. He'd be easier to handle.

"Crawford is very good at his trade," the Handyman replied. "Also, he was not part of the contract."

"But the girl is, and you didn't get her."

"I will visit her. Soon."

"What about Crawford?"

"He should leave the girl, but he won't. A misguided sense of chivalry, perhaps. I must go through him to get to her."

"How much?"

"An Arab gentleman once paid a half million dollars to be rid of a troublesome wife. And that was a long time ago."

"I'll double it."

"That is acceptable. I assume you have been tracking her?"

"Not yet. There are risks involved in my using the Bubble too often. It'll take time."

"There may not be enough time."

"I'll be helping you in another way," McGann said and explained what he meant. "Now tell me—wait, it's the internal line."

The Handyman timed the interval. McGann was back on the line in ten seconds, his breathing ragged.

"That was my secretary. You're not going to believe—"

"What happened?"

"Fremont just called. She said it was urgent but wouldn't wait for me to get on the line. Best thing, she left an address."

"Give it to me." The Handyman instantly memorized the number and street name McGann rattled off. "Does it mean anything to you?"

"No. She never mentioned it before. It might belong to a friend."

"How did she sound?"

"Rushed, I'm told. Said she'll call back when she can."

The Handyman considered this. "She didn't mention Crawford?"

"No. Maybe she was in a hurry because she didn't want him to know she was calling."

A likely possibility, the Handyman thought. True, Crawford had saved her life, but in all the bloodshed and terror, would she recognize him as a true ally? How far would she trust him, considering that Crawford could never tell her some of the things she would demand to know?

McGann was wrong about this: The location had nothing to do with Fremont. It had to be one of Crawford's bolt-holes. And if he didn't know she'd made the call, he would still believe that his venue was perfectly secure. That created a blind spot in his thinking and projections.

"Confirm the location," the Handyman told him softly.

"You'll get it!" McGann retorted. "Just make sure you earn your money this time."

The Handyman broke the connection, unruffled by McGann's rudeness. Amends for that would be made another time.

He picked up the rifle case and replaced it in the closet, checked to make sure he had the key to the apartment, and after resetting the alarm, let himself out.

There was one more order of business to attend to before he could be ready to move.

THE SMALL REDBRICK library on Lewis Street under the Williamsburg Bridge had been a victim of budget cuts and community apathy. Three years earlier, Vincent Calabrese and Harry Jacoby had stumbled onto it after stumbling out of O'Toole's tavern.

They had spent the afternoon getting lit to memorialize having been dumped from the Technical Response Unit. Something about undue force, illegal search and seizure, threats against suspects. Lies. All of it lies.

On the other hand, the commissioner had told them that he wasn't about to lose or break up his most effective violent-crimes unit. While he smoothed things over, Calabrese was to keep the Muffin Men intact, find new space—far away from Police Plaza—and set up shop under a different, preferably ambiguous name. The result was the Police Enforcement and Information Center.

Calabrese told the commissioner he'd found a suitable command post, the commissioner consulted with his brother-in-law at City Hall, and magically the shuttered library became the property of the NYPD.

A contractor with indictments pending sought to help his cause by volunteering a construction team, which gutted and configured the interior to Calabrese's specs. Next, the crew reached out to its contacts across the country. Assault weapons, explosives, and other SWAT essentials were trucked in from an army base in Benning, Georgia. The latest computer technology from Silicon Valley was delivered courtesy of FedEx. A Baby Bell was convinced that it would be a fine gesture in community-police relations to install a state-of-the-art communications system. General Motors was tapped for customized transport, including two utility vehicles and a decked-out surveillance van.

Within a week of moving in, Jacoby had quietly hacked his way into the data banks of the state and federal law enforcement agencies. For payback, he'd also gotten into the TRU's system.

Jacoby and Calabrese were in the conference room, glassed off from the rest of the workstations, where the crew was quartered. On the table, beside cartons of Chinese take-out, lay the garment bag Jacoby had found in the backseat of the Cadillac.

Calabrese fingered the leatherette name tag. "Nice of her to give us all the pertinent information."

"Isn't it?" Jacoby paused. "You called it, Vincent. Diplomatic."

"Yeah. But I never figured the bitch for one of our own. You have anything on her?"

Jacoby had been massaging the Foggy Bottom computers for Fremont's personnel records.

"Not yet."

"What about her pal?"

"Still mystery meat."

"Airline manifests?"

Jacoby pointed to the work area. "The crew's running them down."

Calabrese planted his rump on the edge of the table. "So what do we have?"

"A pair of dirty cops, Ballesteros and Perkins, discover two dopers they're in business with wandering around a ruined warehouse. I bust the cops, then chat with something called Dri-Ice, who claims that a Bonnie-and-Clyde duo ripped off his Hummer. That leads me to the Caddy involved in the alleged interstate hit-and-run."

Calabrese's eyebrows wiggled like hairy worms.

"Alleged?"

"The medical examiner says the victim's head was twisted all the way around, *Exorcist*-style. No accident."

Calabrese took a second to digest this morsel. "Back it up to the Caddy."

"Looked like it was in a demolition derby. The description matches a stolen vehicle report filed by a limo driver out at Kennedy an hour earlier."

"So our terrorists get off their flights, go up to a deserted airline lounge for some unknown reason. Their business—whatever it is—is interrupted by two PA cops and flight attendants. The foursome is blown away, our bad boy and girl get out of the IAB, tap a limo driver on the head, steal his ride."

Calabrese's expression was one of childlike wonder. "And?"

"And according to witnesses leaving Kennedy, some dark avenger in a Lincoln Town Car tries to paste them all over the blade of a D-nine Cat."

Calabrese nodded sagely. "This avenger—he's more mystery meat?"

"Nobody said this'd be easy, Vincent. Nobody got a plate number, never mind a description. Thing is, when the pair in the Caddy *didn't* buy the farm, they wheeled around and went after the Lincoln."

"Which was when the Lincoln tossed out his trash."

"We definitely have him on one count of felony littering," Jacoby said gravely.

"Good, Harry. That's good. I'm pissin' myself, you're so funny."

"The Caddy, a rolling wreck, stays in one piece long enough for our pair to scoot into Long Island City. There, because fortune often favors the biggest assholes, they discover a dope deal going down."

"And help themselves to new wheels."

"Forgetting this." Jacoby tapped the garment bag.

Calabrese exhaled a sigh worthy of Sisyphus.

"What was in it, Harry?"

"Gray wool slacks, blouse and sweater, underwear. Some women's stuff. Our lady travels light."

"Too light. Why bother to bring anything? A bag slows you down."

"Go figure."

Jacoby ran a hand over his curly hair as gently as a believer stroking a Buddha's tummy.

"Bullshit aside, I got a bad feeling here, Vincent," he said somberly. "We get a flash about a possible terrorist situation. Before I even get to Kennedy there's a goddamn massacre. Then I'm almost in the middle of a pileup on the Van Wyck, chasing God knows who. These are bad people. They come from places they've already leveled. It seems that now it's our turn."

"Fuck that," Calabrese muttered.

"No, fuck *them*." Jacoby's voice was cold and harsh like stone. "They don't come here and do this shit. Not without paying."

Calabrese shuddered. There was something profoundly hard in Jacoby. He didn't see it often, but it was there. Had it been possible, he would have felt sorry for the killers.

"What's your play?"

"We haven't found the Lincoln yet and there was no ID on the road-kill," Jacoby said. "Let's not worry about the dark avenger until we have more to go on."

Calabrese watched Jacoby rub the name tag gently between his fingers.

"We concentrate on Fremont, stay on the computers, and open our own lines to the Paris cops," Jacoby said. "Paris was Fremont's home base. That's gotta be where all this started."

Calabrese nodded like a grazing buffalo. In the aftermath of the World Trade Center bombing and the TWA crash, Jacoby had developed strong connections with individuals in the counterterrorism unit of French intelligence. He could also call on agents in other European countries, Interpol, and even Israel. Calabrese had made it a point never to ask Jacoby how he managed this or what he traded for information.

"Port Authority already brought in the NYPD," Jacoby continued. "And the crew just heard that the feds are galloping out to Kennedy." He looked at Calabrese carefully. "I say we hold back the ID on the girl, Vincent. If we give it over to the feds, the whole world will want in on this. Then she and her boyfriend will go to ground, and we'll never know if their plan is still ticking—if they have a backup team ready to take over. For now, let's track the Hummer as a stolen vehicle. It's like driving an elephant. Somebody must have spotted it."

Jacoby gave Calabrese a minute to chew on this. Withholding a major lead was dangerous, a move that often came back to bite you. But when they got a line on the pair, they could move fast and hard, with no bullshit about warrants or competing jurisdictions.

"I'll tell the commish we're holding back the girl's identity," Calabrese said at last. "He'll go along for now, but if we get more bodies . . . " He paused. "You think they're in the city, Harry?"

Jacoby thought carefully before replying. "No. I'll put money on it. They need time to regroup and organize. First they had the dark avenger after them; now they have us, too. They won't move until they're good and ready."

"This dark avenger. Any ideas?"

"Could be Israeli. Maybe Tel Aviv got a line on the pair and decided to help us out."

Calabrese gave him a sour look. "They could have let us in on the action. Right now we're left holding our *schwantzes*."

"I'll call Tel Aviv," Jacoby promised.

Calabrese slipped off the table. "I gotta go to the Four Seasons and check out security for the Ballantines. I'll buy what you said about the lowlifes staying put, at least for tonight, because it makes me feel better about the senator's life expectancy."

Jacoby looked up sharply. "Any recent threats against him?"

"Just the usual semi-illiterate bullshit, all of it checked out by the feds and NYPD intelligence—such as it is." He sighed. "But we know our pair's not in town for sightseeing. They've marked somebody who's here or is coming in. Tweak your pals, Harry."

Calabrese stopped at the glass door.

"Harry?"

"Yeah?"

"I promised Kathy you'd stay on the sidelines. When you tag these cretins, don't play Lone Ranger. Call us in. We'll get it done."

Jacoby was touched, which was when Calabrese sucker-punched him.

"I know you're good," he said. "But don't go puttin' all your kid's college money on your hunches. You still got clams to buy."

THE HANDYMAN HAD the cabdriver drop him off near Broadway and Canal, where Little Italy collides with Chinatown.

Accustomed to Marseille's narrow, crowded streets, the Handyman felt at ease among the throngs that jammed the sidewalks overflowing with merchandise. Hole-in-the-wall jewelry shops peddled fool's gold under garish neon lights next to ninety-nine-cent Whoppers next to "imported leather fashions" squeezed up against stores specializing in knockoff designer sunglasses. Crates and cartons, luggage samples, and display tables littered the sidewalks, almost forcing shoppers into the stalls. The last of the day's tour buses idled at the curb, the drivers watching as their clients were picked clean.

The Handyman found the address he was looking for, a narrow brick building with skeletal fire escapes attached like splints across its facade. The English sign read WOMEN'S QUALITY WEAR, but the Handyman focused on the Chinese characters, which made it to be the House of Future Delights.

He pushed open a weathered green door and went up one flight of stairs. On the landing stood a muscular Chinese guarding a steel-sheathed door. Even so, the Handyman heard the roars, squeals, and moans of the gamblers inside. He gave a name and the Chinese gestured to the next staircase.

The Fat Lee Trading Company was on the sixth, and top, floor. The Handyman rang the bell and the door was immediately opened by a delicate-looking girl, no more than sixteen, in a traditional red gown emblazoned with gold dragons. She let the Handyman pass, locked the door and reset the alarm, and beckoned him to follow her.

The hall was wide and dimly lit, the air heavy with incense. Quality pieces ranging from delicate vases to centuries-old carved armoires were arranged as though in a private home. The walls and windows had been so well soundproofed that all the Handyman heard was the soft shuffle of the girl's slippers on the polished floorboards.

The girl drew aside a curtain of stringed beads and showed him into an office. Behind a slab of ebony sat a man, old but somehow ageless. His eyes were perfectly clear, yet the long wisps of beard could have made him an octogenarian. The desk was clear except for a bottle of Canadian rye, two short glasses, a horoscopy chart, and an antique abacus. Besides a visitor's chair and a fine Chinese rug, the room was bare.

"It is good to see you again, Lee," the Handyman said.

The Chinese rose and silently extended his hand. The Handyman thought it was like gripping a falcon's talons.

The Chinese poured the whiskey into the shot glasses, gave one to the Handyman, and raised his own. They saluted each other and downed the liquor.

"And good to see you," Lee said, adjusting his gown, royal blue silk embroidered with gold thread. "It has been a long time but I knew you would come. It was foretold." He gestured at the chart.

The Handyman stared intently at the large sheets of rice paper covered with ink-drawn symbols within circles, connected to one another by thin lines. There was a vertical row of Chinese characters along the left side of each sheet.

The Handyman had not seen anything like it since the last time Lee had prepared his charts, over fifteen years ago.

"You have not had the opportunity—or the inclination—to continue your studies in my art," Lee observed.

"Regretfully, no. I will need your assistance in the translation."

Lee's skeletal fingers, with their long curved yellow nails, glided over the first sheet.

"Four times men have been sent to kill you. Each time you were ready for them. Then no more were sent."

"No one wanted to pick up the contract."

Lee inclined his head. "Understandable. And now you have been given back your life by the same man who wished you dead."

"Perhaps." The Handyman gestured at the other sheets. "There are things I still don't know."

"What details about him can you offer me?"

The Handyman gave Lee a birth date and exact time. He wet his lips with the whiskey and settled back, watching the fortune-teller draw up an astrological chart based on that information.

There was a great deal more he was tempted to tell the old Chinese but most of it Lee would divine for himself. Still, the stars could never reflect the depth of the terror he'd lived with.

The Handyman stilled his mind. The incense infused his head and a soft clicking sound, which he could not identify, became hypnotic, lulling him. Two hours passed into oblivion. He stirred only when he heard the rustle of rice paper, Lee pushing his charts across the desk.

"This man," the old Chinese said. "He has been an influence in your life since you were a young man. Not directly at first, but on the fringe, watching you, your progress."

The sheen of memory slipped over the Handyman's eyes. He saw a thin young boy dressed in tattered denim overalls and a T-shirt. Barefoot. In his hands was a BB gun; when he was twelve, a .22 rifle. He learned body-kill shots, practicing on squirrels, rabbits, other small game. Then head shots and ones meant only to maim. He never saw the creatures he hunted as living organisms, merely moving, well-camouflaged targets. He quickly dispatched the wounded animals, although he never recognized it as a residue of mercy, only an instinct he answered to.

Talent with the rifle became his ticket out of the only future waiting for him: the Kentucky coal mines and an early death from black lung. At thirteen, he won $50 in a local competition and used it to get on a Trailways bus for Bowling Green that same night. His next competition netted him $500, teaching him that he wouldn't have to sell himself in the streets to survive, that he could make money off his gift. He rented a room in the black section of town from an elderly woman whose heart went out to strays, and lived there for the next six years. The old woman was a retired schoolteacher who taught him to read and write. Her voluminous collection of *National Geographic*s became his window on the world.

The old woman passed away two days before his twentieth birthday. He bought the most expensive casket he could afford and a handsome granite headstone. Standing over her grave was the only time he could remember crying.

But her death freed him. His victories at regional competitions, along with side bets, had brought him to the attention of local mobsters, who offered contract work on human prey. Because of the old woman, he'd always refused.

Since he had not been bloodied in that way, he traveled to Georgia and practiced on vagrants. Atlanta PD files of the time showed some thirty unsolved killings of transients by a person or persons unknown.

Two contract kills later, he knew that he could not continue in the profession fate had chosen for him and remain a free man. Working as a hit man meant trusting individuals whose stock in trade was betrayal. He remembered the *National Geographic*. Those cities—so exotic, mysterious, and most important, distant—now beckoned.

For seven years he plied his trade in Europe, then expanded into the Orient, where he felt inexplicably comfortable and safe. Fascinated by Chinese culture and history, he made Hong Kong his base. He lived there for three years before meeting Fat Lee, who introduced him to the horoscopic arts. From that time on, he never accepted a job without first consulting Lee.

His reputation grew and preceded him as he traveled throughout Indochina. It was a British client, based in Singapore, who, after a contract had been successfully completed, said to him, "You're quite handy, aren't you? Actually, that's exactly what you are—a handy man."

The moniker stuck and traveled through those subterranean channels where the rich and powerful searched for men who could solve their most delicate problems discreetly and permanently.

Then there were the others who searched . . .

The Handyman vividly recalled his first meeting with the man who was to profoundly change his life. He'd been so taciturn and pleasant. So *ordinary*. Yet he held power that the Handyman had never before witnessed, and that alone should have warned him. Instead, he allowed himself to be seduced.

The first four jobs were done precisely as planned. Then came the fifth, which he took in spite of Lee's warning, and there he'd made a mistake. At the time he did not believe that a single life could have so much value. But *this* life, to *this* man, was inexplicably dear. The Handyman offered to make amends, but forgiveness was not forthcoming. Instead, his principal systematically set out to destroy him.

The Handyman thought he could afford to ignore this man, as his reputation would draw other buyers of his services. But those buyers who came to him later canceled their contracts. No reason given. No phone calls returned. One year passed with no work, then a second, and a third. The Handyman lowered his sights, making it known that he would take jobs from midlevel crime bosses and drug dealers. Still there were no takers.

The money he'd set aside began to melt away. The requirements of his profession dictated that he move around constantly. First-class travel and deluxe hotels became a thing of the past. The best forgers and gunsmiths, who also supplied him with the means to do his job, now kept their doors shuttered to him.

The principal whom he had offended ground him down relentlessly. Only after he had been shorn of everything, reduced to living like a beggar in a city he despised, had the final card been played. But this time, the Handyman had made it his business to know a great deal about his tormentor, the way he thought, how he would act. When the principal's assassins came for him, he was ready. He intercepted, killed, and mutilated all four of them, saving their ears and sending those back.

When no more executioners appeared, the Handyman knew that a kind of truce had been established. He would remain forever a prisoner, deprived of exercising his genius, condemned to poverty. But he knew too that the principal had allowed him to live for a reason. Only now, fifteen years later, would he be able to divine it.

The Handyman blinked. He looked around the room, saw Lee sitting in front of him, waiting patiently. His trance had lasted almost three hours.

"This man was an influence on your life," Lee repeated softly. "I will amplify: He is feared. With good reason."

The Handyman reached for the whiskey, draining the glass. When he spoke, his voice was raspy from the bitter drink.

"Perhaps we should dispense with our other business first," he said, wanting to steady himself.

Lee smiled obligingly. The Handyman never saw him move his hands or lips, yet here was the wisp of a girl, carrying an expensive leather sports bag. She laid it at his feet and withdrew.

Ever conscious of etiquette, the Handyman looked at the Chinese. Lee nodded, indicating that he should proceed.

Inside the bag were six small loaves of plastique, detonators, and remote control units, all neatly wrapped in a thick towel. It was exactly what the Handyman had ordered, but now he needed some other tools and wondered if Lee could provide them on such short notice. Now.

The Chinese listened to his request with equanimity. Again the girl appeared without seeming to have been summoned. Lee spoke to her softly, as he might to a favorite pet, and she left the room.

The girl returned in a few minutes carrying what looked like a wooden cigar box. When the Handyman accepted it, it was surprisingly heavy, yet she'd held it as if it were as light as a cake.

He laid it across his lap, accepted the screwdriver she held out, and carefully pried open the cover. Nestled in wood shavings were a dozen antipersonnel mines, each no bigger than a child's rubber ball.

"Payment on your Hong Kong account?" the Handyman asked.

Lee smiled regretfully. "These are uncertain days in the old colony. Singapore is preferable. The bank and account number are the same."

The Handyman closed up the box and deposited it in the athletic bag. He and the Chinese rose together, shook hands again.

"Will you tell me what the stars portend?" asked the Handyman.

Lee's fingers passed over the sheets of rice paper. He did not look down at his prognostications.

"A certain man will die."

"Someone always has to die."

"You understand the basis of horoscopy," Lee said. "Various portents predispose fate, they do not predetermine it. You can circumvent destruction through wisdom or gamble away fortune through stupidity."

"Am I to be destroyed?"

"You are to be betrayed," Lee replied. "But knowing this, destruction is not inevitable. Is it?"

CHAPTER SEVENTEEN

Aꜰᴛᴇʀ ʟᴇᴀᴠɪɴɢ Cʜɪɴᴀᴛᴏᴡɴ, the Handyman returned to the West End Avenue apartment, cached the sports bag next to the sniper's rifle case, stretched out on the couch, and slept soundly through the night.

The next morning he spent an hour performing a variety of exercises, then dialed the alternate number McGann had given him.

"Have you been tracking the girl?"

The Handyman's voice came over McGann's headset with the clarity of someone speaking from a few feet away.

It was warm in the Bubble pod, and he wiped the sheen off his forehead with a damp handkerchief. "She's still at the same location. Safe to assume Crawford's there too."

The Handyman did not believe in the safety of assumptions but allowed McGann to do so. Even if Crawford had left the location, he could not afford to leave Fremont alone for very long. By now he must have realized that she was just a dupe. He would feel a responsibility to her. He would want to protect her, keep her close because he had nowhere safe to store her. She would slow him down, distract him.

Then something suggested itself to the Handyman: If Crawford believed that Fremont was innocent, he'd have to tell her things—not many, but enough to let her make some sense of the situation. She would respond to the truth, slowly begin to trust him. She would realize that her safety lay exclusively in his hands.

So why had she called McGann and left an address? *Why call* McGann *at all?* Why would she *want* him to know where she and Crawford had gone to ground?

The Handyman turned these thoughts over gently and saw in them a very strong possibility that had obviously not occurred to McGann.

"I said, what's your next move?" McGann pressed.

"I will pay them a visit."

"Is there enough time?"

"For something like this, one makes time. I do not want Crawford dogging me—now or when I'm finished."

"Do you need any assistance?"

"As a matter of fact, yes. The local law enforcement would be tremendously helpful."

"That's already been taken care of."

JACOBY WAS PUZZLED. He had spent most of the night culling Hollis Fremont's Foreign Service personnel file and it was pristine. Absolutely nothing to indicate that she was or had ever been connected to any terrorist organization, foreign or domestic.

Another anomaly: Through discreet calls to the American consulate in Paris, Jacoby had learned that Fremont was out of town on "consular business." Jacoby, who had not identified himself as a police officer, had not dared press for more details.

Another strange thing was her connection to a retired Foreign Service officer by the name of Dawson Wylie. Given the nature of that relationship, Jacoby thought that even though Fremont had gone rogue, she might, in light of what had happened, turn to Wylie. However, a check of Wylie's phone records showed that he'd received no collect calls, nor had he made any long distance calls in the last several weeks. True, Fremont could have called him, in which case there'd be no records. But Jacoby thought this unlikely. No matter how emphatically Fremont might have demanded that Wylie not contact her, he would surely have tried to reach out to the young woman he'd raised as his own.

Jacoby had to wait until three o'clock in the afternoon until one of his many bait lines was given a sharp tug. An officer in the Deuxième Bureau, whom Jacoby had befriended in Tel Aviv during a counterterrorism conference, called to say that his inquiries into Hollis Fremont had yielded gold. During a quick but thorough search of her apartment a piece of charred paper had been found. She had either forgotten or neglected to dispose of it. The Deuxième's forensics lab had lifted the imprint of an address from the paper, a place in New York State called Bedford Hills. Did that mean anything to Jacoby?

Jacoby thanked his contact, told him to expect a very large box of toys from F. A. O. Schwarz for his newborn, and raced uptown.

THE FOUR SEASONS, on East Fifty-seventh Street, is a monument to marble and blond wood. Favored by the Hollywood crowd and local celebrities, it has some of the tightest hotel security in the city.

Jacoby raced up the lobby steps and past the concierge, only to be confronted by two muscular young men. They checked his badge and called in to authenticate it. Only then was Jacoby allowed to enter the main ballroom.

What he saw was a presidential campaign whistle-stop. Glitzier, sure, what with all the silver balloons, pictures of the candidate in red-and-blue frames, banners done up in gold foil. A fine spread, judging by what was still on the tables, and Tony Bennett crooning in front of a first-rate combo. But still a political pitch.

Looking over the round tables, which sat twelve people each, Jacoby figured five thousand a head times twelve heads times fifty tables . . . Serious money.

He scoped out the long table on the stage, divided by a podium with a mike stand and TelePrompTer. There was the presidential candidate, Robert Ballantine, flanked by the governor and the mayor. Behind the chairs was Ballantine's Secret Service contingent.

As Jacoby edged around the perimeter of the room, trying to spot Calabrese, he got close enough to check out Ballantine's wardrobe. The cut had to be Dunhill ultralight. The shirt, a Chervet. The tie, unmistakably Sulka. Four thousand dollars of needle and thread on a guy born to wear it.

The son of a tailor, Jacoby had grown up with a keen eye for garments and was a severe critic of those who wore the price tag but could never make the clothes their own.

Jacoby cursed his luck when he spotted the commissioner at a table all the way across the room. And there was Calabrese, lounging in the alcove of an emergency exit like some incipient nightmare, drawing nervous glances from guests seated closest to him.

Jacoby was threading his way through the tables when a woman on the stage rose and made her way to the podium. She would have been striking in any context, with her mass of red hair, long legs, an easy, gentle smile. But decked out in a bold, perfectly tailored Escada suit, Claudia Ballantine was a showstopper.

Jacoby made it over to Calabrese's lair just as she tapped the microphone.

"Vin—"

"Hang on."

Claudia Ballantine must have given a signal, because when she looked behind her, a giant banner unfurled, with the words AMERICA FORWARD! in red and blue against a white backdrop. The audience rose and gave her a standing ovation.

"What is it?" Calabrese rumbled.

Jacoby leaned into Calabrese but still had to shout. "We have a location for the girl."

Calabrese turned them both away from the audience. "Where?"

"Bedford Hills."

Calabrese pinched the bridge of his nose, his signal that he didn't quite believe what he was hearing.

"That's a pretty high-rent district for a pair of terrorists."

"That's the way they like to work. Stay in places where, as long as they blend, no one's going to be looking for them."

"You have a plan?"

"Does a bear—"

"*Shh!*"

Jacoby and Calabrese glanced over at an old biddy draped in heirloom jewelry, wagging a skeletal finger at them. Calabrese shot her an evil look and was stupefied to get one right back.

"Hold up," he whispered to Jacoby. "We need the commish in on this. Let's hope the lady's not a motormouth."

Claudia Ballantine was poised and relaxed on the podium. She was a gifted public speaker and felt comfortable in front of any crowd.

"Thank you . . . Thank you so much. I know what some of you must be thinking: The pollsters still have Bob trailing the president, so now he's going to trot out the wife."

The room exploded in hoots and cheers.

"But I think I'll let *him* tell you why he's here. Seriously, though, the upcoming fund-raiser has nothing to do with this election. At least not directly. America Forward is about people and issues, our common good."

Claudia Ballantine smiled through the applause, then waved for quiet.

"Five years ago, America Forward was just a dream I had. My first office was in the family room of our home. Now we have branches in all fifty states. We've raised over two hundred million dollars in the last few years from people as generous as yourselves. Every penny of that has gone to citizens of this great country who needed—and still need—a helping hand: the forgotten child; the single, working mother; the unemployed man who needs retraining, not a handout. America Forward is there for them.

"We don't ask for government assistance but for *your* help. Your donations—whether in money, time, or life experience—are what keep us going, so that we can show the world that one individual's suffering is the suffering of us all. And that one individual's triumph over adversity is a triumph for our entire nation."

The applause was deafening and followed Claudia Ballantine back to her chair. Jacoby noticed that even the cynical, stone-hearted reporters had become misty eyed.

"Hell, I haven't seen anyone like that since JFK," Calabrese said. "*She* should be running for president."

"That's exactly right, young man," the old biddy piped up. "Now aren't you glad you shut up and listened?"

Robert Ballantine was on his feet. He glanced at the prompter, appeared ready to speak, then suddenly walked over to his wife and gave her a kiss. The ovation followed him back to the podium.

"You just heard my wife say that I have to fend for myself," he opened, graciously acknowledging the laughter. "I'll be out at that fund-raiser and I hope to see all my friends and supporters. But I won't be campaigning out there. I'm putting everything on hold for the day. I'll tell you why right now, even though she made me promise I'd wait. Because I support America Forward, and my wife, with all my heart. If elected president, I pledge to further and broaden her work, to make, with her help and yours, America Forward a permanent beacon of hope in the lives of all our citizens."

That brought down the house.

Jacoby grabbed Calabrese by the elbow and pushed him deeper into the alcove, up against the alarm-wired exit doors.

"This is how I see it going down."

Jacoby outlined his plan with economy and precision. He saw the gleam in Calabrese's eyes, indicating that he was in sync with the details.

"You don't think we'll need more manpower?" Calabrese asked.

"I pulled up the tract plan from the county tax assessor's computer. We're talking about a lot of territory. If Fremont and her bud hear or see anything suspicious, they'll be out the door and gone. At night, in that terrain, not even a hundred men could track them. And a hundred make too much noise to begin with."

"No chopper? We could get a Whisperhawk."

Jacoby shook his head. The Whisperhawk was nice, as silent as baby's breath. But the only crew that could fly it belonged to the national guard. Jacoby had no intention of bringing some reserve colonel glory hound into the action and told Calabrese so.

"It's a quick in and out, Vincent," he said. "We know what to look for on the perimeter and around the house. We go in behind flash and stun grenades and haul them out like trussed *katchkes*."

Jacoby glanced at the commissioner, who had stood up and was headed backstage.

"Time, Vincent. We'll need every minute."

Calabrese made his decision. "Prep the crew," he said.

HOLLIS DRIFTED SLOWLY from the chamber of her sleep. She saw muted colors first, then heard a faint tapping sound. Her dreams were falling away into oblivion even as she tried to hold on to them.

When she awoke the words were out of her mouth before she could stop them. "Was I snoring?"

Then she realized she was still fully dressed, on the couch. She sat up quickly, looking around to see if Crawford was in the room.

He sat at the dining room table, a notepad in front of him. He smiled faintly.

"It's okay. Everything's fine. And yes, you were snoring, but only for a little while." He hesitated. "You were out for fourteen hours."

Hollis groaned and looked away, embarrassed because she'd let him peek into her privacy. When she and Paul had started dating, Hollis had thought that his getting up so early had to do with her sometimes noisy sleeping habits.

Rubbing her eyes, she stared over the back of the sofa. The tapping she'd heard was rain drumming on the windows, as heavy as when she'd fallen asleep. What was left of the afternoon light was quickly disappearing.

"Give me a minute," she mumbled.

She went into the bathroom, showered quickly, and changed into fresh clothes. When she came out, she smelled coffee in the kitchen.

"Do you want some?" she called to Crawford.

"Thanks. Just poured a cup."

Hollis made one for herself and took it to the dining room table. She glanced at the pages, covered in small, neat script, then at him. Crawford was very still, as if he had put himself in some other place and time, an archaeologist examining alien terrain. She thought he looked all right, but the shadows under his eyes seemed darker, the crow's-feet more pronounced.

"Game plan?" she asked, indicating the pages.

"I'm trying to narrow down the Handyman's potential targets. Given the high-profile traffic in town, he has his choices."

Crawford didn't think he needed to add that for most of the time she'd slept, he had been on the line to Paris. His people reported that a team from the Deuxième Bureau had quietly tossed Fremont's apartment but hadn't taken anything when they left. The Handyman's room at the Apollo had yielded no clues. And a last serving of bitter herbs: Wally Liggett's body was on the ground at Andrews Air Force Base. The secretary of state's security adviser was tending to the details but he'd made it clear that he very badly wanted to talk to Crawford.

"Are you okay?"

Her question focused him on the present. "Fine."

"It bothers you, doesn't it, sitting here like this?"

"This is the hand we chose to play."

"What if we're wrong? What if Paul is innocent and the Handyman does . . . what he came to do?"

"Then I'll feel sick for a long, long time."

Hollis picked her way through the beats of silence. "What will we do if he doesn't show up?"

"There's no need to get into that now."

She was glad he said this without sounding like he was blaming or shutting her out.

"How long have you been doing this?" she asked suddenly.

Crawford seemed puzzled, as though it were a question he couldn't comprehend.

"Years . . . A lifetime."

"Why? I mean, how did you choose it?"

"It chose me." He paused. "I was in an army sniper unit when Pan Am one-oh-three went down. My team was sent in behind Libyan lines. We did a lot of damage. Then the operation ended and we went home—and six months later one of my buddies was killed. Then another. Four in all. I was targeted but got lucky.

"By then it was clear that the Libyans had turned tables on us. An old CO of mine told me that they were paying professional assassins to come after the snipers who'd taken down their senior people. He mentioned Omega Group. The choice was simple: I could wait to be picked off, which, given the law of averages, would happen sooner than later. Or I could join up and become the hunter."

"Which is what you did . . . "

Crawford nodded.

"Did you ever find the people who killed your men?"

"All three of them."

Hollis pushed her coffee away. "Helps me to know, to understand you. A little." She looked at him. "Back at the airport, you talked like you knew a lot about me."

"I know the facts, about what happened to your family."

Hollis was surprised by her reaction—or the lack of it. Any mention of her family had always made her defensive, even quick to anger. Unless it was Dawson Wylie talking. Now, for a reason she did not understand, she took no offense.

"Do you realize that to this day I have no idea who killed my father? I know my mother was shot by accident, but my father . . .

"I remember that day so clearly. I see every detail. How he looked, what he said to me, what we were doing. I never heard the shot but in my mind I did. When I was, oh, thirteen, I guess, I made Dawson Wylie tell me everything. I learned where the killer had been hiding, how remarkable a marksman he must have been, how utterly cold . . . I imagined him sitting up in that crane, waiting, watching, preparing. But no one could tell me why my father had to die. Who had hated or feared him so much . . . "

She realized that she'd balled her hands into fists and flexed her fingers.

"Sometimes, in my dreams, I think I can see the killer's face. But when I try to focus, it just washes away. There's nothing there except a blank."

"What if you could see it?" Crawford asked softly. "If this man were still alive, what would you do?"

"I'd ask him why he had to shoot my parents."

"And if he told you?"

"Then I'd have closure. Or something like it. But it wouldn't be enough." She saw Crawford frown and realized he didn't understand. "Just knowing wouldn't be enough. I would become like you, track him and destroy him, for me and everyone else he's hurt and walked away from."

Her tone, washed clean of pity or forgiveness, chilled him.

"Do you remember when you had another life?" she asked. "Before now, doing what you do?"

"Yes."

"Wouldn't you like to go back to it someday?"

"I don't know if I could."

"I do. I could, if I knew he was dead. It would be like someone giving me a second chance."

He reached across her pain, slowly, until he was sure she would let him touch her. When his palm cupped her face, Crawford realized how long it had been since he'd touched flesh so soft and warm.

"You'll get your second chance, I promise."

She moved away from him when she said, "Maybe. If I get past the Handyman."

Crawford did not want to soil the moment. He struggled to hold on to it, to burn it into his memory so that later, from the darkness, he could reach out for and be comforted by it. He thought about everything she'd said, how she'd said it, the new truths he'd learned about her.

"You need to see this," he said.

He beckoned her into the living room, where he opened a large antique pine cabinet. Set in the recess was a home entertainment center: television, VCR, and sound system.

Crawford picked up the remote and powered up the TV. There was *Wheel of Fortune,* with its contestants squealing like piglets.

"You're kidding, right?" Hollis said.

She watched Crawford enter a numeric sequence on the remote and the television became a computer monitor. He pressed the star sign and a 3-D rendition appeared on the screen, with red dots around the farmhouse and along the perimeter.

"Intrusion sensors," Crawford said. "They can distinguish between small animals and men."

This place is safer than it looks . . .

"What else do you have?"

She felt Crawford's eyes measure her but was not offended.

He beckoned her into the kitchen and unlocked the door to the cellar. The staircase was well lit, and there were long strips of nonskid tacked into the smooth boards to prevent slipping.

The basement was long and narrow, like two bowling lanes set side by side. Where they stood was a plywood counter and a long overhead wire that disappeared in the darkness at the far end. Crawford flipped a light switch and Hollis discovered she was standing in a firing range.

The walls were covered in corkboard to absorb sound. Mounted on one of them was a gun cabinet. Set in racks behind the wire-meshed glass were handguns, submachine guns, and shotguns. On the shelves below were ugly-looking black projectiles that Hollis recognized, from counterterrorism briefs, as grenades.

"Ever use any of these?" Crawford asked.

Her aversion was clear in her expression so he said nothing more. He opened the cabinet, pulled out a submachine gun, pocketed six loaded clips, and turned to leave.

Hollis didn't understand why she hung back or why she reached into the cabinet and wrapped her fingers around a big but lightweight Sig Sauer. She hefted it in her hand, then stepped over to the counter and looked downrange. At the end was a paper target with a human silhouette, a bull's-eye where the heart should be.

"Is it loaded?" Hollis asked without looking at him.

"Just flick off the safety."

He moved to help her but Hollis already had her thumb on the catch.

"I thought you'd said you never used a gun."

"I didn't say that. I just never answered your question. I know how to use one. I spent six years growing up in Idaho. There, everybody learns to shoot. Dawson Wylie made sure I did."

Hollis put on a pair of orange ear protectors, then slid her right leg slightly ahead of her left. She flexed her knees and gripped the gun in both hands, left cupping right. She sighted downrange and lined up the target, then exhaled slowly as she squeezed the trigger.

Once. Twice. Three times, in smooth succession. The gunfire sounded like small firecrackers going off at her feet.

She placed the gun on the counter, removed the ear protectors, and looked at Crawford.

"Do you want to see how you did?"

"Not yet. What am I doing wrong?"

"You're a little quick on the trigger. You think you're squeezing it but really you're jerking it back at the last second. Think of your finger peeling back orange rind."

Hollis nodded, covered her ears again, and picked up the automatic. She took a breath and on the exhale fired another set of three rounds. Then another and another, *peeling back the rind* . . . She stopped only when she felt Crawford's hand on her shoulder, saw him reach for a switch that activated the pulley. Hollis stood very still as the paper target fluttered toward her.

Crawford stepped into the firing lane, a black Magic Marker in his hand. The dimensions of the black silhouette were slightly bigger than his.

He circled three ragged holes on the left shoulder. "The first rounds."

The pen dipped toward the lower torso, near the abdomen, where six holes had perforated the paper.

"The next two sets."

Finally he circled the upper chest cavity, the sternum and heart. "The last set. How long has it been since you shot?"

"Years."

"You have a gift."

Hollis looked at him as though he'd uttered a profanity. She wheeled around and headed for the stairs.

"You're not the only one," he called after her.

She pivoted fast. "What are you talking about?"

Crawford had had no intention of revealing this to her, until he'd seen her shoot. Now he knew that she could, if she had to, fend for herself, maybe survive. She could help him, even if it was only by her safety not weighing on his mind. But to do that she had to be focused and have a stake, a distant but reachable prize.

"Years ago there was another girl who lost her father in Paris, just like you did. He was also killed by a sniper who was never caught."

Hollis started. "No. That's not right. The embassy briefed us on American casualties in Paris. I remember five or six car accidents, heart attacks, but no killings."

"You were a visa slave. The embassy gave you the sanitized version."

Hollis took a step toward him. "Who was she?"

"She *is* Holland Tylo. She works in the Secret Service now, the presidential detail."

"The Handyman did that to her? You're sure?"

"He was using a custom-made weapon, with special ammunition. Very accurate, very lethal. But the interior of the barrel had a tiny flaw. It scarred the bullets as they came out. The scars were like fingerprints. They were found on the bullet that took out Tylo's father."

Crawford looked at her. "It's your call, but when the Handyman goes down, you might want to talk to Tylo. Tell her she doesn't have to dream about *her* faceless man anymore."

CHAPTER EIGHTEEN

THE FEDEX-TYPE step van droned northeast, its wipers beating against the rain like the wings of a trapped bird. The headlights of oncoming cars illuminated the lettering on the side: ACE ELECTRIC—RADIO DISPATCHED—24 HR SERVICE! Electricians go anywhere, anytime. No one thinks twice.

Inside, the Muffin Men sat on padded benches bolted to the floor and the panels. All were dressed in waterproof nylon bodysuits over hard-shell armor. Beneath wool caps treated with water repellent were headsets, the frequencies already tested and found true. The wafer-thin battery packs were secreted in one of the many pockets with Velcro flaps. Flash and stun grenades were neatly clipped to wide leather belts.

Weapons were an individual choice. Some of the crew preferred rapid-fire submachine guns, others swore by the shotgun, especially in close quarters. Jacoby favored the former, but that didn't matter on this run. He'd be bringing up the rear, just as Calabrese had promised Kathy.

Calabrese shifted in the driver's seat and looked over his shoulder. He thought the crew looked okay, very loose, a lot of yawning and jaw cracking. No one wanted the adrenaline to start pumping until they were in the zone.

"Anybody for some music?" he asked.

There was some debate about the selection but finally everyone agreed on the sound track from *Rent*.

Maybe if it hadn't been for the rain, passing motorists would have heard voices, off-key but enthusiastic, singing about the lost loves and lives of the dispossessed in the city that not only never slept but more often than not didn't give a damn either.

* * *

HOLLIS AND CRAWFORD had shared some reheated stew and afterward she had stretched out on the couch with the magazine the Handyman had been reading on the plane. She'd dozed off with the images of Capri, the island looking like a white diamond set in blue. She thought she could feel the warm sun and cool water in a place filled with laughter and tiny houses with ocher tile roofs.

Now the fire was banked for the night, an orange glow creeping along the wainscoting. Hollis sat up suddenly, the magazine slipping off her lap. When she retrieved it she saw, on the page it had opened to, a picture of a man and woman at a black tie event. And something else. A smudged fingerprint.

Hollis knew it wasn't hers. She hadn't gotten that far into the magazine.

She set the magazine on the coffee table, pulled her hair back, and leaned forward. There were other shots of the couple, posing with various guests, dancing. Hollis couldn't translate the captions but that didn't matter. She recognized the man and woman, and *New York* was spelled *New York* in any European language.

Given the high-profile traffic that's in this town, he has his choice.

"Crawford!"

From the way her voice carried, Hollis sensed that the house was empty. She jumped up and quickly checked all the rooms. Then as she was passing the foyer she noticed that a slicker and boots were missing. She went to the living room windows and looked out into the rainy darkness. The light inside created reflections in the glass, so she hurried from switch to switch, then let her eyes become accustomed to the dark. She pressed close enough to the window for her breath to create a circle of fog.

Her gaze swept the driveway, then fanned across the lawn to the other structures. She scouted that area three times, fighting back her panic. A tiny cry escaped when she saw him in the shadow of the garage. She'd been staring right at him and had missed him completely.

Hollis stepped back from the window as he glided back to her through the night.

This place is safer than it looks . . .

Yet there he was, huddled motionless in the rain, the barrel of the submachine gun poking through the vent in his poncho. Protecting her.

She heard the door open, snatched up the magazine, and raced back to the foyer.

"What is it?" He was through the door, his face glistening. "Are you okay? Did the perimeter alarm go off?"

Hollis shook her head.

Ripping the beeper off his belt, he went to the TV monitor and stared keenly at the security grid display. He touched a button on the remote and his beeper went off. The system was functioning perfectly.

Slowly Crawford put down his weapon and shrugged off the poncho. "What happened?"

Hollis handed him the magazine. "The Handyman bought this at de Gaulle before we boarded. He'd been reading it on the plane before he fell asleep. Somehow it slipped out of his seat pouch. I picked it up because . . . because of the story on Capri." Hollis paused. "That's his fingerprint—what's left of it—not mine. He was interested in that story. Look at the pictures."

Crawford scanned the photos and the text. He could read Danish passably. Then he focused on the print: It was fat, probably a thumbprint. Whether the Handyman had smeared it accidentally or deliberately, it was useless.

But not the pictures. They were good and true and suggested exactly what Hollis Fremont thought they did.

"It's Ballantine, isn't it?" he heard her say. "He's the Handyman's target."

The way she said this with such certainty made him think she was right.

"The Handyman bought this because someone told him to," Crawford said. "Something in here is meaningful to him but there was no risk, because he knew you didn't read Danish. He would get what he needed from the article and leave the magazine for the airplane cleaners."

"Except it fell out and he overlooked it when we were coming off the plane."

Crawford nodded. "Once he realized he'd forgotten it, he'd wonder why. Since he hadn't seen it lying close by, he had to assume that you had it. So now there was a huge risk: You'd see what he'd been reading and might be able to draw all the right conclusions. You might even tell me what they were, if I was smart enough to listen."

"That's why he came after us," Hollis said softly. "He made a tiny mistake and couldn't risk that you or I would catch it." She stepped close to him. "He *is* going to try again, isn't he?"

Crawford tapped the open page. "He has time for one more shot."

"Why only one?"

"Because the Ballantines are in New York for just a few more days. Not much time if he intends to make the wife a widow."

IT WAS MADDENING for the Handyman not to see the house. He would miss the opening ceremonies. But he would be present, front and center, for the finale.

A Range Rover had been left for him in the garage of the West End Avenue apartment building. Conveniently, there was a map in the glove compartment. The ride up to Westchester County, even in the downpour and the last of the rush hour traffic, had taken a little over an hour.

The Handyman had driven by the property twice, slowing down but never stopping. He was not about to test the front gates or Crawford's perimeter security. He was looking for something else, and that took another twenty minutes of careful searching.

The county lane, or what was left of it, was barely visible now that he'd turned off the headlights. Only the water-filled potholes gave it away. The Handyman had seen paths like these throughout Europe, cut into country estates well away from the main house, used to bring in land-clearing or farming equipment. He navigated by ambient light, the Range Rover dipping and rising like a ship in a typhoon.

Fifteen minutes later the Handyman was on the side of the granite face that backed up on the farmhouse. He guided the Rover across what had become a shallow, fast-moving stream and positioned it to face the hundred-foot-high outcrop. He turned the headlights back on and waded through the ice-cold water up to the stone face. The lights created shadows that could trick one. Here the rock was solid; a few feet away was a deep, wide fissure. And farther down, a tangle of brush and small fallen trees. Trees too small to have fallen by themselves, too green to be used for firewood. Trees and undergrowth placed there deliberately.

The Handyman carefully worked his way through the brush. When he came to an overhang, he paused to wipe his face and brought out a large flashlight. The beam revealed a wide, high cave, the walls glistening with rivulets of water. He checked the floor first, then played the light into the interior. It disappeared before touching anything, an indication of how deep the cave was.

The Handyman smiled. This was Crawford's bolt-hole, the hidden exit every safe house has. When the killing started, Crawford would think this route was still secure.

And it would be, because the Handyman had seen all the sensors planted in the fissures and crevices and had no intention of disturbing them. Nor would he risk the ones that lined the frontal perimeter of the property.

The Handyman uncovered the nylon flap of the cheap sportsman's watch he'd bought. Eight o'clock. He estimated that he had two hours to complete his work. Better to err on the side of caution and say ninety minutes.

On his way back to the Range Rover he decided to start at the front of the property. He could get there by going around the granite face, skirting the property line, and doubling back until he was just out of the sensors' range. There would be plenty of time to return and, with a touch here, a touch there, transform Crawford's last hope into his and the girl's tomb.

THE ELECTRICIAN'S VAN rolled through the town of Bedford Hills shortly before ten o'clock. Calabrese was hunched over the large steering wheel, squinting through the downpour.

In the back, Jacoby was folding up copies of the blueprint and maps of the estate, which he'd pilfered from the Westchester County registrar's computer. As quarterback of the operation, he was the one who decided when the crew was ready. Having gone over the infiltration procedure twice, he made them do it again.

Jacoby felt the truck slow and climbed into the passenger seat. They were passing the main gate, moving along the edge of a low, fieldstone wall. A rabbit darted into the road. It froze for a second, its eyes glit-

206 / PHILIP SHELBY

tering red, and vanished. Jacoby was pleased that Calabrese was loose enough that he didn't even try to hit the brakes.

"The driveways to these places are all gated," Calabrese complained. "We have to leave the rig in the street; it'll stand out like tits on a bull."

"We'll be fine, Vincent," Jacoby soothed. "Pull off to the side here."

As soon as the truck stopped Jacoby hopped out. He opened the back doors and was handed a toolbox, a spool of wire, and a small battery-powered lamp mounted on a tripod. He carried these over to an electrical pole and set them up. The rest of the crew set up orange Day-Glo cones around the truck. If anyone drove by now, they'd see an electrical crew working on a line leading to the property.

Jacoby took a last look at his handiwork. The truck was parked on the shoulder of the road; the cones would be visible to motorists but could not be seen from the house.

"Showtime!" he called out softly.

The crew was geared primarily for urban assaults. They knew all there was to know about elevators, air-conditioning ducts, and rooftop assaults. But once a month they field-trained at the New York SWAT proving grounds. Unofficial nighttime maneuvers were conducted in Central Park, which usually netted a handful of assorted predators.

They were over the fieldstone wall like wraiths, boots digging hard into the slick leaves, making for the line of trees. They flopped on the sodden ground, their bellies against the low rise of the terrain.

"Where would he set the perimeter?" Calabrese rasped.

Jacoby wriggled up the rise on elbows and knees. He could see the main house, about seventy yards dead ahead, lights burning in the windows. He raised his infrared field glasses, saw something else, and scuttled back.

"Clever boy," he said. "He doesn't set up his sensors across an open area like everyone else. No—he lets you get through that, into the trees, where you have to zigzag. And that's where he nails you."

"Can we cut a corridor?" Calabrese asked.

Jacoby fished out an aerosol can of liquid nitrogen. "One hit and the sensors are dead. Give me ten minutes."

In the pounding rain it seemed more like twenty. Then Calabrese heard Jacoby over the headset.

"I'm picking up something else."

Calabrese's heart began to pound. "What is it?"

"It's buried, whatever it is. My equipment won't give a true reading."

"These are woods, Harry," Calabrese said. "There's garbage, bear shit, Christ knows what else buried around here. Take out the sensors and get back here."

"Roger."

Jacoby gripped the can, aimed it at a sensor that resembled a tiny walkway light, and sprayed.

"Gotcha!" he whispered.

And he moved to the next one, never suspecting that it was already too late.

JACOBY HAD BEEN right: The liquid nitrogen had knocked out all the sensors, one by one. But hidden in the base of the sensors was a monitoring device whose only business was to ascertain that the sensors were active. When the first one went down, a signal was transmitted to the monitor in the house.

Hollis and Crawford whirled around. The red dots on the screen were beeping, first one, then two and three, until the entire grid covering the front of the house had been tripped.

"Son of a bitch!" Crawford said. "He found us and made it in the perimeter!"

As he spoke, he raced to douse the lights. Then he grabbed Hollis and thrust the Sig Sauer at her.

"Aim for his chest and don't hesitate," he said, switching his submachine gun on full automatic. "You know he won't."

He pressed hard on her shoulder, forcing her down against the wainscoting under the window.

Hollis glanced over at the monitor, where a semicircle of lights was now blinking and beeping. She shook her head.

"It doesn't make sense! He's just one man. He doesn't need to take out all the sensors. Two, maybe three, would be enough for him to slip through." She hesitated. "And it's too soon. You said he couldn't have tracked us this fast!"

Crawford was staring hard at the monitor, knowing she was right. The Handyman was doing too much.

"The police," Hollis said. "Could they have found us?"

"Can't be . . . "

"*Someone's* coming, Sam," he heard her say in the darkness. "What do we do?"

JACOBY CAME SLITHERING out of the darkness, his bodysuit plastered with wet leaves.

"You're clear," he said.

"And you stay put," Calabrese replied. "We'll be talking to you every step of the way."

Jacoby squeezed Calabrese's arm. "Remember, like trussed *katchkes*."

Jacoby watched as the crew worked its way over the rise and disappeared into the trees.

THE HANDYMAN WAS tracking the policemen's progress on a handheld detonation unit with a two-inch radar screen. It received signals from the explosives he'd bought from Fat Lee, which he had buried just in front of Crawford's sensors. He knew that the police would spot and neutralize the sensors and that their equipment would alert them to metal objects buried in the soil. But neutralizing the sensors would be their key concern. They would not have the time or inclination to dig for what they supposed was rusting junk.

The Handyman measured their progress while he thought about Crawford. He would be confused, wondering why so many sensors had been attacked when a lone man would need to eliminate only a few. He would be thinking about the police, estimating their firepower, realizing that to stand and fight was suicide. And he couldn't possibly know what awaited him at the end of his only escape route.

The Handyman checked his tiny screen, noted that the crawling dots were now almost on top of his charges.

Time, gentlemen.

"GET TO THE GARAGE. Use the door off the kitchen!"

"Why?" Hollis demanded.

"I think you're right: Those are cops out there."

Hollis edged away from the wall. "What do you want me to do?"

"Start up the Hummer."

"That's it? Shouldn't I back it out?"

"Just have the damn thing running when I come in. *Go!*"

Hollis jammed the Sig Sauer into her purse and scrambled into the kitchen. Her fingers searched for the doorknob, found it, pulled. A cold draft pushed diesel fumes at her. She was rising to find the light switch when the explosion hit. The concussion blew out the kitchen windows and threw her flat to the floor, sparing her from the slivers of glass that scissored through the air and disintegrated into snowflake fragments against the Hummer.

JACOBY HAD BEEN listening to the crew's progress, not their voices but the rustle of leaves and nylon, the scrape of twigs and branches being brushed aside, the occasional soft grunt.

Now he belly-crawled to the edge of the rise. Through night-vision binoculars he saw that his crew was well into the trees, maybe twenty feet from where the lawn started, forty feet from the edge of the driveway. He saw too that the lights in the house had been extinguished.

"Check lights," he whispered into his mike.

Calabrese came back instantly. *"Right. They're off. Please, God, let them be making whoopy."*

That would be nice, Jacoby thought. The Israelis liked to time their raids and abductions that way—when the target was plowing the south forty or flapping his dick over a urinal.

He was still picturing that last image when the forest exploded in a shower of fire and light. The detonations sound as one, though Jacoby's fine ears registered three. But he never heard the sharp, strangled screams, because the concussion had made him deaf.

Clamping his hands over his ears, he rolled down the incline. Even before he hit the bottom he was reaching for the radio. He punched in the emergency code for the state trooper barracks, and yelled words he himself could not hear. When he knew help was rolling he staggered to his feet and stumbled back up the incline.

The forest was an inferno now, the trees burning like giant torches in the rain. Reflexively, he picked up the submachine gun lying on the ground nearby. In the yellow light were dark clumps he could not stand to look at for very long.

Jacoby took one step, then another, like a battle-stunned infantry-man. He walked right into fire, miraculously found a path through the flames that licked at his bodysuit and singed his eyebrows and lashes.

He came out on the driveway, teetering like a drunk. Flames silhou-etted the house. Gripping the submachine gun tight against his side, he marched forward, laying down a silent, deadly fusillade through the blown-out windows.

HOLLIS WAS BEHIND the wheel of the Hummer, motor run-ning, headlights on, when Crawford raced into the garage. She watched him throw a latch, put his shoulder to the wall in front of the Hummer, and slowly push it to one side. The headlights revealed a tunnel bored into the granite outcrop.

He jerked open the driver's door. "Move over!"

Hollis braced herself as he dropped the Hummer into gear and edged it into the cavity. The side-view mirrors were the first to go, snapped off by the sharp outcrops. The uneven, rock-strewn floor made the Hum-mer bounce from side to side, the tunnel walls shearing paint and carv-ing dents in the steel cage. Crawford's safety glass window splintered but held together as a razor-sharp piece of rock tried to punch through it.

"We're almost out," he yelled.

Hollis tried to follow the Hummer's high beams but they were bouncing crazily off the rock walls. She saw nothing else in the dark-ness. Until the brilliant flash of orange.

THE HANDYMAN WAS in the Range Rover, the window low-ered. Oblivious to the wind-whipped rain lashing his face, he strained to hear the sound that he knew would come from the mouth of the cave.

The flash of headlights came first, followed by the growl of a tor-tured engine. Whatever Crawford was driving, it could not possibly save him or the girl.

The Handyman backed up the Range Rover, pointed it toward the dirt road that had brought him here, then stuck his arm out the window. His thumb found the red button on the battery-powered deto-nator. A second later, the signal reached the charges he'd planted in the cave floor.

The explosion violently rocked the Range Rover. The Handyman clung to the wheel as he steered down the road, turning his head just in time to see a gout of white flame roar out of the mouth of the cave.

CHAPTER NINETEEN

THE FLAMES THAT engulfed the Hummer would have re-
duced any other vehicle to cinder. That it survived was due to a miscal-
culation on the part of the Handyman: He had set his charges too deep
in the cave. They had detonated after the Hummer had passed and so
their force crashed against the cave walls behind the vehicle, pushing
the ensuing fire after it.

The impact and the heat would have been more than enough to destroy any conventional vehicle. But the Hummer was a steel box on
wheels, riding on the toughest tires in the world, Yokohama Maxxims
that survived the razor-sharp debris strewn on the cave floor and allowed the vehicle to come out farther than the Handyman could have
anticipated. The Hummer also had a specially reinforced, flame-
resistant gas tank.

Nor could the Handyman have foreseen that Crawford, uninjured
by the explosion, would still be in control behind the wheel, be able to
plow the burning vehicle out of the cave, where the rain quickly doused
the flames licking at the Hummer's flammable coats of paint.

Crawford felt the tires churn up the gravel bed, downshifted, and
bulled his way out of the stream onto the dirt road. There he stopped,
slumped forward on the wheel, and listened to the engine turn over,
praying it wouldn't quit. The hiss of rain on hot metal and the acrid
stink of burning paint made him wince.

He looked at Hollis, whose face was stark white against the flame-
blackened window.

"Can you hold on?" he asked. "Can you get through this?"

Hollis opened her mouth and discovered she couldn't speak. Her
survival instinct had kicked in. She was doing inventory, checking to
make sure that nothing was broken, that she wasn't bleeding. Then she

leaned toward Crawford and with her index finger traced a trickle of blood along his cheek. She followed it up to his scalp and touched something warm and wet.

Hollis looked at the bare metal roof and noticed a bolt that hadn't been clipped flush.

"You cut yourself," she said.

He searched for her finger, followed it back to the wound.

"I'll be okay."

"He almost succeeded," she said dully. "He must think we're dead."

"That's what he thinks. For now." When she looked at him, he added, "He'll know better when the news reports that the police haven't found our bodies." He gripped her hand. "We have to get out of here."

"Drive," she whispered.

NEITHER HOLLIS NOR Crawford had time to wonder what had happened on the other side of the granite outcrop. But Harry Jacoby saw it all.

He was forty feet from the house, his body shaking as though in a seizure, the submachine gun spitting out round after round at what was left of the windows. When one clip emptied, he jammed in another, and another, until the firing mechanism became so hot it jammed.

Harry threw down the submachine gun and was reaching for his automatic when the charges in the tunnel blew. He flung himself to the ground just as the garage evaporated, then the force of the explosion picked him up and tossed him toward the trees. Harry rolled with it. There was so much flying debris that all he could do was curl up and dig into the carpet of wet leaves. All around him he heard pieces of metal and wood slice into the earth. He stayed like that until there was only the sound of flames eating through timber.

I can hear.

Harry struggled to his knees and saw that the farmhouse was on fire. Then came the wail of a siren and the steady beat of an approaching helicopter. Reaching inside his bodysuit, he pulled out the chain threaded through his detective's shield. Then he tossed his handgun away. He looked more like a suspect than a police officer and didn't want to give some rookie an excuse to make a fatal mistake.

"You, on the ground. Put your hands up and stay in the light."

The helicopter hovered a couple of hundred feet above, its spotlight pinning him. Harry obeyed. The hairs on the back of his neck prickled as he looked down at his filthy jumpsuit. Wavering around the area of his heart was a small red dot, created by a laser scope attached to a sharpshooter's rifle.

Harry stayed like that until the first patrol car raced up the driveway. He saw the incredulous expressions on the faces of the state troopers who piled out, guns drawn.

"I'm a cop," he called out. "NYPD."

One of the troopers, an older man, approached cautiously and checked Harry's shield. He spoke into the mike strapped to his chest and a second later the helicopter veered away, its spotlight playing over the burning house. The trooper removed his Stetson and wiped his brow.

"What the hell happened here, son?"

"There were four in my crew," Harry said calmly. He felt as though he were watching himself talk. "They're all dead."

"What crew?" asked the trooper. "And what the hell is the NYPD doing up here in the middle of the night?"

Jacoby stumbled out of the way of an approaching fire truck. He pulled the state trooper by the sleeve.

"I need a phone."

The trooper handed him a palm-size Motorola. Jacoby walked away from the shouting firemen and leaned up against a tree. His fingers were trembling but he managed to dial the right number.

"I'm okay. I'm not hurt. Not a scratch."

These were his first words to Kathy. The day he'd asked her to marry him, he'd told her that if he ever called from the job, no matter what time it was, this is what he would say and she should believe he was all right.

Hearing her sigh of relief, the way she cleared the sleep from her voice, he listened to the questions that tumbled out.

When she was finished, he said, "They're all dead, Kathy. Vincent . . . the whole crew. Gone." He paused. "I have to go now. I have to look after them. You try to go back to sleep. I'll call again later. Kathy, I love you."

She started to sob, so he repeated his last words, soothing and reassuring her as he would a child.

The rain had tapered to a fine drizzle and now Jacoby could taste his tears. The ERU medics were among the trees, walking slowly through the carnage. He heard their choked cries and hushed profanities. The troopers and some of the firemen were staring at him.

When he dialed the commissioner's home number, his fingers were perfectly steady, and when he spoke, his tone was cool and professional. Jacoby knew this had nothing to do with his training but with rage, deadliest after it had scoured a man of his fear and pity, leaving behind only the hate.

CRAWFORD WAS HEADING south on the parkway, back to the city. The night and the soft, misty rain were their shelter, camouflaging the Hummer's scars.

"Are they looking for us?"

Crawford glanced at Hollis. She was leaning against the door, her knees drawn up, her feet on the seat. Crawford knew shock when he saw it. Better that than hysteria.

"The police?" he said. "I don't think so. No one saw the Hummer."

"I need to use a bathroom," she said quietly.

"Can you wait?"

"*No!*"

Crawford checked the exit signs and began drifting to the right through the light traffic.

"Do you have any idea what happened back there?" Hollis asked.

Crawford spoke only of things he knew. He would not give her speculation or false assurances.

"The Handyman knew where to find us. He did it quickly and got it right the first time. He also has a connection somewhere in the city that provided him with the matériel he needed."

"The explosives."

"Yes."

"And he knew what kind he would need and how much."

Smart girl. Crawford had come to the same conclusion but hadn't wanted to voice it. It made the Handyman seem omniscient, as though he knew where they were at every moment, could prepare himself and reach out at them without endangering himself.

"The Handyman couldn't have known the specifics of the property but he must have had a good idea of what the neighborhood was like. He brought along exactly the matériel he knew would be useful and effective."

"He could do that because someone told him where to find us. Paul told him that."

Hollis was surprised at how hard and flat her words were, how easily Paul's name came over her lips. She realized that from the moment Crawford had laid out his arguments, and despite her protests, she had been living with the seed of doubt about Paul. Now, suspicion had hardened into a tumor of certainty.

Hollis understood that one day, maybe very soon, the full impact of what he'd done to her would crush her. But now she could only marvel at the skill with which he had set his hook in her heart.

"I was so sure about him," she said. "I believed in him . . . "

Crawford did not want to tell her that to take a risk on trust and love could be fatal.

"How could the Handyman move so fast?" she asked. "You said he wouldn't be ready until tomorrow."

"Either McGann set it up so that he was able to move quickly, or he *had* to do so." He tapped her purse, the wet leather sticky beneath his fingertips. "According to that article, Ballantine's in town for his wife's America Forward benefit. That's in the next couple of days. I'm thinking the Handyman couldn't afford to wait on us."

"Does that mean he'll leave us the hell alone when he finds out he missed?"

"Of course not."

THE TRUCK STOP reminded Hollis of a carnival. It was a sprawling area, with hundreds of tractor-trailers parked in neat rows fanning out from a huge, garishly lit diner.

Crawford threaded his way through the semis and parked near the Dumpsters around back. Hollis reached for her purse.

"I'll get coffee," she said.

Crawford was about to tell her no: Go to the washroom and be quick about it. Then he saw her set expression.

"Black, one sugar."

"Are you going to get gas?"

Crawford shook his head. The pump islands were bathed in fluorescent lights, and traffic was heavy. Drivers would notice the Hummer and want to jaw about it. They'd stare at the fire damage and ask questions.

"Go on," he said. "I'll wait here."

Hollis walked to the washroom and locked herself in. For a few minutes all she did was run warm water over her wrists and splash her face over and over again. Then she bolted into a stall and threw up all the hurt and fear and pain.

She didn't know how long it took her to pull herself together and didn't care that Crawford was waiting. She rinsed her mouth then dug into her purse and did what she could with her hairbrush.

The diner had three counters, each fifty feet long with tall stools bolted in the terrazzo. The windows were lined with booths that could seat six and there were tables in the saloon-type back room. Every trucker gave her a once-over as she walked to the take-out counter and ordered two coffees. As far as Hollis could tell, she and the harried waitresses were the only women in the place.

The talk was about trucks and women, loads and paychecks. The jokes were X-rated and the laughter too loud, maybe the result of Dexedrine coursing through the bloodstream. From the overhead speakers a country and western singer was grinding on about his achy-breaky heart.

Mounted on the wall behind the cash register was a television, tuned to an all-news station. The volume was up just enough for Hollis to hear the anchorman's voice over the singer's laments.

Something about an explosion in the exclusive community of Bedford Hills, a police raid gone bad, at least four officers dead, a home destroyed. Two suspects at large, an unidentified man and a woman named Hollis Fremont.

The videotape rolled, showing firemen at work on the blaze. The camera panned and caught a tall man with short curly hair talking into a cell phone. Then the frame jiggled, as though someone had pushed the cameraman. When it was refocused, Hollis saw the smoldering trees and medics carrying sheet-covered stretchers. The lumps beneath the sheets did not look like anything human.

The camera pulled back to show the newscaster sharing the screen with a photo of Hollis, giving a detailed description of her and warning the public to call the police immediately if they saw her. "Armed and dangerous!" was the breathless description as a special 800 police number scrolled across the bottom of the screen.

The waitress had a paper bag on the counter and a bill in her hand. "That do it for you, sweetie?"

Hollis lowered her head. "Tic Tacs."

Amazed that the woman didn't recognize her, Hollis paid, leaving almost a dollar in change as a tip. Hollis turned up the collar of her jacket and forced herself to walk slowly to the door into the night. Only when she was well away from the diner did she break into a run.

Hollis jumped into the Hummer.

"The TV! It's all over the TV. Pictures—"

Then she realized that Crawford had the radio on. His expression was almost serene as he listened to the news report. Hollis handed him a coffee.

"McGann's a clever one, isn't he?" Crawford said. He might have been admiring the man's shoes. "Tell me what you saw."

Hollis placed her Styrofoam cup in the foot well and pried open the lid. She took a deep breath and recounted the newsman's version and the video footage as best she could.

Crawford sipped and listened, his features betraying nothing.

"Do you see what's happened here?" he asked when she was through.

"The police are after us."

"Take it back before that. What did McGann and the Handyman do to us?"

Hollis recalled the picture of her on the TV.

"The photo is the one on my embassy ID. Paul got hold of it, sent it to the New York police—no, wait. That's wrong. He wouldn't have done that himself. People would start asking all kinds of questions. He must have had *someone else* do that." She paused. "But who?"

"How much do you know about McGann, his contacts in Paris?"

"I've been with him at society functions. He's involved with charities, things like that. His mother came from aristocracy."

"If he's connected that way, maybe he has friends in the French secret service or the Paris prefecture. Maybe someone owes him, so McGann tells him about you—and what he's learned about me. This friend calls New York, says that a couple of terrorists are coming stateside. If the source was high enough up the food chain, the New York cops would bite."

"And they knew where we were because . . . Paul's source told them that, too. Because *I* let Paul know where we were."

Crawford edged her away from the shoals of guilt.

"I wonder why McGann's buddy didn't take it to the feds."

"Maybe his contacts were local, not federal."

Crawford sipped his coffee. "Do you see the rest of it?"

Hollis ran through it in a steady, unemotional tone. "Paul makes sure the police know where to come and get us. He tells the Handyman they'll be there. The Handyman already knows where to find us, so he comes out ahead of time and lays his traps. For us *and* the police. He springs the trap for the police first, killing most of them. Then we hit the second trap. Everyone should be dead by now. But still, the Handyman isn't doing badly. Now he has law enforcement throughout the northeast hunting a couple of cop killers—us. While he's free to go on about his business."

"Exactly," Crawford said. "But there's something I can't connect. You said it yourself: Why did the Handyman come after us so soon?"

"I thought that was because of Ballantine's schedule."

"That's assuming Ballantine is the target. Let's say that he is; something still sticks about how *certain* the Handyman was that we were in Bedford. I mean, everything he and McGann planned revolved around our being there. How could they be so sure we weren't moving? It's as though they tracked us."

Hollis was bringing the coffee cup to her lips and stopped. The steam wafted over her cheeks, warming them. Images and words streamed through her mind, arranging and rearranging themselves, sweeping away assumptions and misconceptions, driving forward new, hard-learned realities.

There she was on national TV, branded a terrorist by the man who had sworn his love for her. Who had told her to go to room E-12, told her about the Handyman being a sick, old banker, how bringing him home was just a last-minute drudge job . . . Would she mind doing it because the man who was supposed to go had been in an accident?

But before all this, there had been something else.

Hollis carefully placed her coffee between her feet, then put her hand down the front of her sweater. She pulled out the thin gold chain and the cameo and undid the clasp.

"Look at it," she whispered, handing him the cameo.

He turned it over in his fingers, examining the relief. His eyes narrowed when he read the inscription. McGann was some piece of work.

"I don't see," he told her.

"Cameos have a compartment."

He looked at the gold back, then at the seam. "Not this one. There's no catch."

Hollis gripped his arm. "Paul gave me this the morning I left Paris—when I was still in his bed. *But it wasn't any special occasion!* Why didn't he wait until there was something to celebrate, when I returned from New York?"

Crawford leaned into the glare from a sodium arc lamp that flooded the dash. He tried to get his thumbnail into the cameo's seam but it was too thick.

"No good. You'll have to do it."

Hollis placed her elbows on the dashboard. Gently she worked her nail into the seam and tried to pry away the back. Whatever the bonding agent was, it held.

"Can we break it open?" she asked.

"We don't want to."

Crawford started the engine and pressed down the cigarette lighter. When it popped back, he worked the glowing tip close around the seam.

"Try again."

The gold back was hot to the touch, but Hollis ignored it and dug her nail into the tiny crevice. This time the back gave, slowly, revealing the strands of epoxy that had bound it to the cameo.

She looked down at her treasure and shuddered.

"Do you know what it is?" she asked.

She felt his thumb gently wipe the fat tears from her cheek. She knew he would have done anything to spare her if he could.

"Yes, I do."

CHAPTER TWENTY

AFTER GETTING RID of the Range Rover in the theater district, the Handyman checked into the Grand Hyatt, using the false ID he'd brought with him from Marseille. In the glass and steel monolith built over Grand Central Station he was one faceless guest among hundreds. The hotel's other attraction for him was its direct access to the train station, where he stowed his rifle and the remaining explosives in one of its many lockers.

He stayed up late watching the news. The carnage at Bedford Hills was the lead story on the major networks. The video focused on medics and firemen searching for body parts among the trees at the front of the property. Only one enterprising news crew had gone around back to photograph the remains of the tunnel, now blocked solid by rubble.

The Handyman helped himself to a snack from the mini fridge while he watched a bulldozer clear the debris. Any minute he expected that more bodies would quickly be discovered, charred bones fused into blackened steel.

That didn't happen. The bulldozer and rescue workers finally cleared the tunnel but found no vehicle, no corpses. The young female reporter who gave the world the good news looked disappointed.

Lying in bed, listening to the thin wail of sirens in the street below, the Handyman considered how Crawford and the girl might have cheated him. Ultimately, it was futile speculation. He'd had his chance at them. Now time demanded that he turn his full attention to the real business he had come here for. The Handyman drifted off to sleep, thinking that if Crawford and the girl had survived the police dragnet, they were now someone else's problem.

222 / PHILIP SHELBY

* * *

A MORNING MIST threaded over and around the skyscrapers of lower Manhattan. The Handyman felt it on his face when he stepped out of the cab at Battery Park.

He walked past the restored Hudson River Pier A toward Castle Clinton, which today serves as a glorified ticket office for the Ellis Island ferries. At water's edge he paused in front of the Merchant Marine Memorial. It depicted three men on the bow of a sinking vessel, one scouring the horizon with binoculars, a second on his knees, resigned to his fate, the third on his stomach, his outstretched arm in water as he reached for the hand of a drowning comrade.

The Handyman wondered how the sculptor would have depicted the face of the man beneath the waves.

He waited for passersby to move, then took a picture of the memorial with a cardboard throwaway camera that had come complete with film. Among the hundreds of tourists who had doggedly ignored the inclement weather, a camera was all the camouflage he needed.

The Handyman meandered into the fort, purchased his ticket, and joined the line stretching along the waterfront to the ferry dock. He accepted a jovial Australian couple's invitation to share their umbrella and spent the next twenty minutes exchanging tourist horror stories about the south of France.

The ferry was a three-decker workhorse with MISS NEW YORK scrolled in red lettering along the bow. The Handyman left the Australians at the concession stand in the main cabin and walked up two flights to the open deck. By the railing stood a crew member, smoking—exactly the person the Handyman had hoped to find. He asked the sailor about tomorrow's ferry schedule.

"Tomorrow? Man, ain't nothin' happen' tomorrow. The island's closed and this here boat's all booked up for some private party."

The Handyman feigned surprise, murmured his thanks, and retreated. He'd read about the party in the Metro section of the *Times*. Conveniently included was a timetable of the party's highlights. That the ferry was chartered had been mentioned, but the Handyman had thought it best to double-check.

He walked back down into the main cabin and found the men's washroom, a tangle of pipes painted bright yellow, with barely enough room for a urinal, toilet, and sink. He examined the pipes thoroughly, especially the bolts, then got down on his knees and checked the pipes behind the grille next to the toilet. He measured the size of the screws that held the grille in place.

Someone was knocking hard on the door. The Handyman slipped the latch, brushed by a fat, wheezing man, and headed for the concession stand. He feigned interest in the T-shirts pinned to corkboard in the sample case, then slipped through a door marked CREW ONLY, down the dimly lit stairwell to the engine compartment.

It took the Handyman less than thirty seconds to locate the door to the engine room itself. The lock would present no problem. Nor would the skeletal crew. The important thing to remember was that down here the pipes were painted red.

The Handyman retraced his steps to the main cabin and on up to the open. He breathed deeply to clear his lungs of the oily fumes of the engine room. The Manhattan skyline was a blur. Off to the left was Ellis Island, its century-old brick structures looking much as they must have to the millions of immigrants who had traversed these waters. Coming up was the pier.

After *Miss New York* bumped and settled against the dock, the Handyman hung back, letting the crowds pile out. He followed them along the pier, where a National Parks Service vessel and a fire-fighting boat were moored. Drifting past the Parks Service administration building, he went into the gift shop and browsed through the tacky statuettes, sweatshirts, books, and other souvenirs until he found something that would suit his purpose perfectly. He asked a sales clerk how long the shop stayed open, then went next door into the cafeteria.

The tea tasted like dishwater. The Handyman took two sips and threw the rest into a trash can. Outside, he proceeded along the interlocking brick path to the enormous flagpole set in the circular courtyard. He stopped and lifted his face to the breeze coming off the waters and saw her, the New Colossus.

The words of Emma Lazarus, recalled from his research, came back to him:

Here at our sea-washed, sunset gates shall stand a mighty woman with a torch ... and her name Mother of Exiles ... "Give me your tired, your poor ... Send these, the homeless, tempest-tost to me ... "

The Handyman, an exile as cursed as Ulysses, gazed upon this piece of windswept rock, the throne of the Lady, the Statue of Liberty.

CHAPTER TWENTY-ONE

Harry Jacoby sat in the kitchen of his Staten Island house, holding his wife's hand across the table. Kathy was still wearing the bathrobe she'd had on when Calabrese and the crew had descended to "arrest" him for killing the clams. She'd later told him that she had known they were coming and had played along. Jacoby could still hear their laughter as they'd watched him fret—good honest laughter that now made his chest ache.

Jacoby rubbed his wife's fingers. He could tell that she hadn't gone back to sleep after his call. When he'd come home, smelling of the morgue, she was waiting in the living room, the television on. He had gone straight into the shower and scrubbed himself hard before touching her.

"You want to tell me what happened?" Kathy said.

Jacoby didn't. He was worried about the baby, superstitious that somehow words about evil and violence would slither into the womb.

Kathy tightened her fingers around his. "Tell me what you can."

He began with the call from the Paris police that led to the planning of the raid.

"They were waiting for us," he finished softly. "They knew—or at least suspected—that we were coming."

"I have to call Jeanne," Kathy said. "Go over . . . "

Jacoby pictured Calabrese's petite, dark-haired wife and looked away.

Kathy brushed a stray lock from her cheek. Her face was puffy, her eyes red and swollen, and Jacoby knew that she needed to stay busy.

"Do you know where they are, Harry? Do you know anything about them?"

"They could be anywhere, and I know very little."

That made her smile, faintly. "Liar. You know a whole bunch."

Jacoby leaned toward her. "This thing has gone ballistic," he said. "NYPD, state police, the feds—everybody wants a piece. This pair *is* going down, Kathy. Tell Jeanne I promise her that."

"You, Harry? You're going to put them down?"

"I'm damaged goods. The feds won't let me anywhere near the take-down."

"Liar," she said again. "I know you. You'll find a way."

Jacoby rose. Through the curtained window he saw the plain-Jane sedan waiting at the curb.

"I gotta go."

They walked to the door, their arms around each other.

"I love you," Kathy said.

"I love you too. And I'm coming home to you."

Jacoby kneeled, parted her robe, and kissed her belly. They embraced, and then she watched him go down the walkway to the car. Her heart fluttered as the driver slapped a bubble light on the roof. When it came on, the misty air was shot through with red, as though sprayed with blood.

THE DRIVER WAS a headquarters whelp who kept darting his eyes at Jacoby.

"The chopper's on the pad at the ferry landing. The commissioner is waiting for you downtown."

"Updates," Jacoby said.

The driver handed him two faxes that had come in while he'd waited for Jacoby to come out of the house.

The first was a search bulletin indicating that no trace of Fremont or her accomplice had been found. Jacoby grunted. Big surprise. With so many agencies involved, dreaming up and arguing over schemes took precedence over hunting.

He sat hard on his frustration and turned to the second page. The information there was even less promising. The FBI had tried to contact Dawson Wylie, the man who'd raised Fremont in Idaho. Except, when federal agents had arrived in Coeur d'Alene, they found no sign of him. No one in town knew where he'd gone.

"Shit," Jacoby muttered.

"Excuse me, sir?"

"Nothing."

The helicopter was waiting, rotors spinning. The pilot clearly had orders to move it and the ride over to the South Street Seaport took less than fifteen minutes. From there, a patrol car took Jacoby to One Police Plaza.

The commissioner was a short, dapper man in his mid-fifties who seemed dwarfed by the grand trappings of his office. His name was Lawrence Barnes and Jacoby knew firsthand that he preferred to meet his detectives in the smoky taverns that dotted the area around Police Plaza. Barnes liked his malts and his ladies, and the force loved him because he always stood behind his men.

"Commissioner."

"Harry . . . "

Barnes shook Jacoby's hand briefly and sat down on the sofa. He wore a three-piece "press suit" and kept tugging at his shirt collar.

"The media hounds are baying, Harry, and I've got squat to throw them." He tapped a sheaf of printouts. "I read your report. Anything you want to add?"

Jacoby had drafted his report very carefully. He wasn't holding out on the essentials but had left out things he didn't want others to paw over.

"No sir."

"Okay. So, for the record, the feds, who are hogging the investigation, know everything. Now what say you and I chat?"

Jacoby had been here before. A "chat" with Barnes was more confidential than a visit to a rabbi.

"Before we start, can I see the file on Wylie?"

Barnes buzzed his secretary to bring in the paperwork, watched as Jacoby scanned it, heard him grunt when he found something that seemed to interest him.

"We were looking at *three* chumps, not just Fremont and her buddy," Jacoby said, putting Wylie's file aside.

"You mentioned a third unknown in the report. What about him?"

"Given how this guy tried to take out the pair at Kennedy, I thought maybe he was on the side of the angels. An Israeli sent over on the sly to waste Fremont and her pal, spare us *tsuris*. Thing is, I checked with Tel Aviv earlier this morning. When they heard what had happened, they stopped playing shy and said, way off the record, that there was no Israeli incursion agent in the United States. At this time . . . But, they were more than willing to send us an adviser or two."

"I'll bet," Barnes said dryly. "What did you trade?"

"The girl. I think they came up empty, else I would have heard something by now."

"What're you saying?"

Jacoby bit his lip. "That most likely I was wrong. The unknown avenger *isn't* a good guy. He's part of the private war those two brought over here." He paused. "Maybe Fremont and the mystery meat are wearing the white hats."

The commissioner slumped against the sofa cushions. "Shit, Harry. Every cop east of the Mississippi is looking for a pair of terrorist cop killers. Now you're telling me they might be okay? What about what happened up at Bedford?"

"I've been thinking about that," Jacoby said quietly. "Follow me here. Fremont and her bud manage to escape ending up on the business end of a tractor blade. Do they head for cover? No. They try to chase the attacker. Then they head for Bedford Hills, to a place that's wired better than Langley. I go in, spot the sensors, take them out. I miss the charges."

Here, Jacoby had to take a few seconds to collect himself.

"I miss the charges. Vincent and the crew get wasted. I'm thinking—we were *all* thinking—that it's got to be them. What doesn't make sense is this: Why were there explosions around the *back* of the place, in a tunnel that sure as shit was an escape hatch? Why would they have booby-trapped that, then driven right into it?"

"Could have been a mistake," Barnes said. "They could have panicked, set the charges off by mistake."

Jacoby shook his head. "Fremont may not be a pro, but whoever she's with is. Guys like that don't screw up on small stuff. I think the third party, our bad boy, got to Bedford *ahead* of us. He set it up so that when Fremont and company had to get out in a hurry, they'd run right into his trap. He was there, waiting for them."

Jacoby rose. "He also had to know we were coming. Otherwise, why seed the frontal approach? He used us to flush Fremont, knowing there was only one way out for her and her pal."

Barnes walked to the wet bar and held up a bottle of whiskey. Jacoby declined and watched Barnes throw down a shot.

"You got the Bedford location from a Paris cop, Harry," he said softly. "What does that tell you?"

"That the cop could be dirty. And that this thing is bigger than anyone, including me, thought."

"You said Fremont's pal is a pro. CIA, Defense Intelligence, who?"

"Fremont works at the consulate. Maybe he's embassy CIA."

"Something Langley's not about to tell *me*."

"There may be another way."

Jacoby flipped through his file on Hollis Fremont, pilfered from the State Department computers. When he came to the places Fremont had lived, one detail was missing. He pointed it out to Barnes.

"Here, when she was going to Columbia: The feds have her listed as living in New York."

"They're probably chasing it down now. Maybe she was in a dorm or sharing an apartment."

"No, she wasn't."

Then Jacoby told him what his search into Fremont's New York days had yielded.

"And you didn't put this into any report?" Barnes demanded.

"It wasn't relevant," Jacoby said coolly.

"Maybe not then, Harry, but—"

"Not now either. Commissioner, we know something no one else does, things the feds aren't even close to finding. If you share this, they'll do a stakeout. If anyone shows, they'll drop the hammer. Then it's bye-bye, Fremont. Before they even stop to think, they'll make her disappear."

Barnes eyed the whiskey bottle and sighed. "What do you want from me, Harry?"

"Let me check this out. Let me do this one thing."

"And if you're right?"

"I'll give Fremont a chance to talk."

Barnes understood perfectly what that meant.

"Go," he said. "But call the cavalry if you have to. I want you around when your kid is born."

CRAWFORD DUMPED THE HUMMER in front of a leather bar in the meatpacking district on the fringe of the West Village. He thought it'd have a life span of no more than ten minutes. Then he and Hollis walked through the light drizzle into SoHo.

The coffee shops were opening for the day. The idea of a few minutes' rest and something warm in the belly was tempting, but Crawford had seen copies of the morning editions. The *Times* had run too early to include the story, but there, on page four of the *Post,* was a tabloid-style account of the "Bedford Hills Massacre," along with a startlingly clear photo of Hollis.

Hollis had taken one look at it and tossed the paper into the gutter.

SoHo was quiet this early in the morning, the art galleries shuttered tight, their trash bins overflowing with the detritus of last night's post-exhibit parties. A blue-and-white rolled by and Crawford draped his arm around Hollis, hiding her face against his chest. The cop gave him a stony look and continued his patrol. Hollis remained close to him for the next block, trying to concentrate on what he was saying, fighting the exhaustion creeping over her.

On West Broadway, between Broome and Spring Streets, was a vacant, unrenovated building—exactly what Crawford had been hoping to find. The nine-story warehouse was squeezed between an eclectic furniture store and an interior design studio. Most of its second-floor windows were smashed, the corrugated steel shutters over the doors and delivery bays splattered with graffiti. Next to the garbage chute, over what used to be the main entrance, was a billboard: ELECTRICAL BROTHERHOOD UNIT 657 ON STRIKE!

"Now we know why it's still an eyesore," Hollis said.

"It's perfect," Crawford replied.

"If we can get in."

Crawford looked thoughtfully at the strikers' board. "Sometimes these guys do more than picket, just for spite."

She followed him across the street and watched as he carefully checked the steel shutters.

"Shouldn't we try around back?"

"That's where security would be best—to keep out the homeless and the addicts."

Crawford peered into the squalid, shoulder-width alley that separated the building from its neighbor. He squatted to examine something, then beckoned to Hollis.

"Here we go," he said.

Hollis saw a boarded-up window flush with the ground, with mounted bars set into the foundation. They looked solid enough until Crawford gripped one of the bars and twisted it out. The concrete was so old it had turned to paste.

Inside, the only light came through the windows but it was enough to reveal that the entire ground floor had been gutted. Hollis and Crawford picked their way through the debris and up a free-standing staircase. They had to climb to the fourth floor before they saw the renovations: freshly painted walls, a smooth concrete floor with pallets of wood flooring ready to be put down, large, new windows whose exteriors were still covered by sheets of thick plastic stapled to the frames. There was no furniture except for a forgotten, paint-spattered chair in the corner.

"They're done here," Crawford said. "No one's coming back."

He walked across the room, pulled the cameo out of his pocket, and hung it over the back of the chair.

FIFTEEN MINUTES LATER they were at a pay phone at the back of a busy coffee shop by the subway exit at Houston Street. It was risky, but so far, no one paid them any attention.

Crawford dropped a quarter into the slot. Panic surged up her throat as she watched him press the buttons. She remembered what she'd said to him as they'd driven through the night back to Manhattan:

If we find out who hired the Handyman, maybe we'll know if Ballantine really is the target.

Okay. How?

Bait. We use me as bait . . .

At first Crawford had dismissed the idea. The risks would be too great; there were too many variables beyond their control. But when

Hollis had challenged him to come up with an alternative, he couldn't. She'd prodded him to help her, and somewhere between the Fifty-ninth Street Bridge and the West Village they'd hammered out their plan.

Now he was handing her the receiver, watching her carefully. "You're on."

Hollis heard the familiar double ring on the other end. For an instant she thought she might black out. Then she heard Paul's voice. She knew him now. She could do this.

"Paul?"

"Hollis? Is that you? Thank God! I was worried sick. Are you all right?"

"Someone was waiting, Paul. For me and Jones. At the airport. They tried to kill us—"

The hysterical edge to her voice was not all acting. In the cool confines of the Bubble pod, Paul McGann leaned forward in his chair.

"Hollis, slow down. I heard about the shooting, but the reports are garbled. *Who* tried to kill you?"

She recalled Crawford's words: *You know exactly what McGann knows. He would have heard it all from the Handyman. Stick with the sequence, the truth, until the last minute.*

"Jones! He found a gun in that airline lounge. Then someone else was there. Crawford. He was after Jones. When he didn't get him, he took me."

"Jesus Christ! Is he still with you?"

"No! Paul, I . . . Somehow the police found out where he'd taken me. There was shooting, explosions. That's when I managed to get away."

"Okay, slow down. Let me think."

McGann had been following the Bedford Hills massacre story on CNN, his rage growing with each successive news cycle. The first part of his plan had worked perfectly: Tessier had seeded the "terrorist threat" in the mind of his colleague at the Deuxième Bureau. The bureau had reacted predictably by raiding Hollis's apartment and discovering the charred piece of paper with the Bedford Hills address that Tessier had planted earlier. That detail had been the highlight of the report flashed to a special unit within the NYPD, which had subsequently organized and conducted the raid.

But from that point on, what should have been a clean execution had turned into a bloody fiasco. Four cops were dead; Hollis and Crawford were still loose.

Analyzing the news reports and intelligence digests, McGann knew what had gone wrong: The Handyman had set up a trap for Hollis and Crawford and had been relying on the NYPD to either flush them into his sights or kill them as they tried to escape. On paper, it may have looked great. The results indicated otherwise.

Now McGann was out of time and patience. He would have to take care of this pair himself.

And he knew exactly how he'd do it.

"Hollis, are you still there?"

"Yes."

"Where are you?"

"In Manhattan. Chelsea."

"Give me the exact location."

Hollis rattled off an address.

"Now listen to me," Paul said. "Can you stay there for another five hours—six, tops? Will you be safe?"

"I . . . I guess so."

"Because I'm coming for you. There's a Concorde going out in two hours. I'll be on it."

Hollis lowered her voice. "Paul, what's going on?"

She heard him try to sound frantic. No good. Frantic was not something he could pull off.

"I don't know! This was supposed to be a simple transfer. I had no idea that Jones was dangerous or that some wacko was out to get him. Hollis, listen to me. I'm going to pull you out of this. Believe me. Six hours. Stay out of sight for that long and it'll all be over." A pause, then: "Hollis, are you there?"

"I'm here."

"I love you. I'm coming for you."

The words threatened to choke her but she knew she had to say them: "I love you too."

Shaking, Hollis slammed down the receiver. A husky delivery man walked by, eyeing her curiously.

"She's okay," Hollis heard Crawford say.

"Whatever, buddy."

Then she felt him pry her fingers off the receiver.

"It's done. We have to go now."

She knew he'd tried, but nothing could soften the cruel finality of his words. Hollis, who had never betrayed anyone in her life, felt this first cut slide deep into her conscience. She wondered what it would take to heal it. If anything, if ever.

PAUL MCGANN LOOKED at the silent phone, then turned his attention to the large screen above the communications console. It showed a street grid of Manhattan between the Empire State Building and the Battery.

He clicked the mouse and eliminated everything between West Thirty-fourth Street and West Twenty-third Street. The pulsating orange dot on the screen was located on West Broadway between Broome and Spring, not on West Twentieth, where Hollis had told him she was waiting. And the technology that surrounded him was never wrong. It was Hollis who had lied to him.

McGann lifted the phone and told his secretary to book him a seat on the Concorde and have an embassy driver standing by. His second call went to New York, to a room at the Grand Hyatt.

CHAPTER TWENTY-TWO

JACOBY PARKED HALF a block down from the building on West End Avenue. Before getting out of the car, he called a friend at Tri-State Security Systems to confirm that he would have a fifteen-minute window.

Jacoby walked up the block and saw a lunch truck pull up in front of the building. There was the doorman, hurrying out to buy his coffee and doughnuts. Jacoby slipped through the lobby and took the stairs two at a time.

He found apartment 7B, checked his watch, and went to work on the lock with a set of picks he'd lifted off a B&E man. Eleven seconds later he was inside. The lights on the alarm panel were flashing green. The bypass he'd been promised by Tri-State Security was working. By the time he had his coat off the lights were red again, the system having rearmed itself.

Jacoby smelled nothing in the air, no hint of cologne, soap, or food. Still, he searched the apartment carefully. The rooms and closets yielded nothing. The kitchen counter and bathroom sink were a different story. Both showed faint streaks in the film of dust.

Jacoby went through the entire apartment again, opening cabinets, dresser drawers, digging through closets. There was no food, no clothes, nothing on the shelves or in the closets except books and cartons of old magazines. Nothing to suggest that anyone was living here.

But the dust had been disturbed. Someone had been in the apartment recently. To scope the place—or had they come to get something? Jacoby knew that fugitives tended to run for the most familiar ground, especially if it seemed to have no connection to them—as was the case with this apartment and Hollis Fremont.

The feds hadn't found it yet because they thought that Dawson

Wylie was their best shot to help them find Fremont. They had over-looked Wylie's wife, maybe because she'd been dead for six years. But by ignoring her, they'd missed the fact that this co-op was registered in her *maiden* name and so didn't appear in any of Wylie's or Fremont's records.

Jacoby, however, had gone the extra mile when searching property ti-tles. He'd run the wife's maiden name and come up sevens. He was willing to bet anything that Fremont had stayed here while living in New York but had never left any paper trail, like a lease or phone records. She wouldn't have had to.

Jacoby was also sure that the girl had already been here, at least once, to see if it was safe. With her face plastered all over the tube and newspapers, she and her pal couldn't risk even the cheapest hotels, nor could they keep moving around in the streets. They needed temporary refuge, and the apartment would be safe until the feds unearthed Wylie.

Jacoby went into the living room and moved a comfortable chair into the corner behind the front door. From this vantage point he could watch them come in and put two rounds into their spines if they so much as coughed.

He double-checked his weapon and laid it in his lap. Then he closed his eyes, bowed his head, and became very still. Only his lips moved as he began to recite Kaddish for the Muffin Men.

THE HANDYMAN RETRIEVED the gun case and the sports bag containing the explosives before returning to his room at the Hyatt. Several additional items had been left for him in the locker at Grand Central: a box wrapped in plain brown paper, a cardboard packing tube, and a video. He put these on the bed, cleared the lamp, hotel di-rectory, and other clutter off the small desk, and went to work.

On his way back from the ferry landing the Handyman had stopped first at a sporting goods store, then at a hardware store on lower Broadway. He had bought two pieces of two-inch pipe, each one cut to a specific length, two small cans of yellow and red enamel, and a paint-brush. He set one pipe on the table and began stuffing it with explo-sives. He left enough room for the detonator, then set the timer and finished wiring the connectors. He threaded a cap onto each end and gently set the finished pipe on the carpet.

The Handyman repeated the process with the second pipe, then spread newspaper over the desk and opened the cans. He painted one pipe yellow, the other red.

While he was waiting for the paint to dry he made a telephone call. He was not worried about taps or intercepts. It was a local number and the conversation would be brief.

He was given his instructions so clearly and concisely that he could visualize each sequence as it would unfold.

Then he said, "I've heard from McGann. There is something he wants me to do." The Handyman went on to explain, then adding, "I'm afraid it is necessary for you to intervene. I still have arrangements to make and no time to deal with matters that were none of my concern to begin with. Yes. I'm sure you will take care of it. Good-bye."

The Handyman sniffed the paint. It was drying nicely. He flipped the exhaust fan switch on the thermostat to get rid of the mild fumes, then brought out a small, white cigarillo box he'd purchased at Nat Sherman, Tobacconist, on Fifth Avenue. By the time he'd finished his third bomb, the paint was dry.

The Handyman wrapped the pipes and cigarillo box in hotel towels and packed them into the gym bag. Then he slipped the cassette into the VCR and opened the cardboard tube. For the next two hours he carefully studied the blueprints of the 1984 Statue of Liberty renovations and watched the video twice. When he had committed all the details to memory, he opened the brown box.

Inside was a tan National Parks Service uniform, complete with an expertly forged ID. The Handyman checked it carefully. The picture, which he'd taken in a Fast-Foto machine at Grand Central and had left in the locker for pickup, had been clipped just below the jaw. Usually these photographs included the uniform's shirt collar and sometimes the knot of the tie. But this one would pass casual inspection, which was all the Handyman expected it would get.

He tried on the uniform. The pants were a little loose at the waist and the jacket didn't fall exactly right at the shoulders. These imperfections were deliberate. The Handyman had insisted that for his purposes, the clothes be roomy.

He repackaged the uniform and put the box on the top shelf of the closet. Fifteen minutes later he was in a cab, the gym bag on the floor between his feet, heading back down to the Battery. He arrived at three o'clock, a half hour before *Miss New York* made her final trip out to *Liberty*.

The ferry was filled to capacity and the Handyman had to wait in line to use the bathroom. He closed the door to the stall and quickly unscrewed the grille behind the toilet bowl. He removed the yellow pipe from the gym bag and wedged it in among the cluster of others that looked just like it.

A few minutes later he was in the engine room. The red pipe went into a dark recess behind drums of engine lubricant.

After the ferry docked, the Handyman followed the crowds to the gift shop. Inside, he noted how harried the salesclerks were, and eased his way over to white bins stacked six feet high, each one crammed with souvenir sweatshirts. He already had the white cigarillo box in his hand when he reached into the top bin and pulled out a sweatshirt of the same color. In the same motion he snuggled the cigarillo box behind the sweatshirts, where it was invisible.

With the shirt draped over his arm, he wandered through the shop, feigning interest in souvenirs until a chime sounded and a weary sales-clerk announced closing time. The Handyman paid for his purchase and hung back, making sure that no last-minute impulse buyer decided to remove anything from that particular sweatshirt bin.

Outside, the tourists were trooping back to the ferry. The Handyman paused to look at *Liberty* one more time. He also noticed a sign advising visitors that the statue and the island would be closed to the public tomorrow. No reason was given.

Tomorrow, security would be tight, but nowhere near as strict as it would have been for the president. New York police would be responsible for Battery Park; the Secret Service, assisted by the National Parks Service rangers, would scour the statue itself, its base, and its support buildings, including the gift shop and cafeteria. They would not expect to find anything, nor would they.

No security would be stationed inside the statue since it would be closed off after this last ferry had departed. Tomorrow, *Liberty* would serve only as a backdrop. The Secret Service would have a helicopter in the air as well as agents on board the National Parks vessels that would keep the gawkers on pleasure boats at a safe distance. Neither of these elements presented any problems for the Handyman.

The guests would all be screened by the police at the Battery Park dock prior to boarding the ferry. Once they had been vetted and on their way, the alert level would slacken.

The Handyman climbed to the top deck of *Miss New York* and glanced back at *Liberty*. After tomorrow, she would never look the same to him. She would never look the same to anyone.

CRAWFORD AND HOLLIS walked the fifteen-odd blocks from SoHo to the Village. They stayed on the crowded sidewalks of Sixth Avenue, where, in the morning rush hour, no one paid them any attention.

After passing Balducci's food emporium they turned right on West Tenth, a pleasant, tree-lined street of hundred-year-old town houses. They had walked up about a third of the block when Crawford slowed, scanned the street, and quickly ushered Hollis up the flagstone steps to the door of a redbrick town house.

The lock was an electronic pad set below the mailbox. Crawford punched in a sequence and got them inside quickly. Hollis found herself in a tiny foyer, in front of a staircase that curved up to the second floor. She realized that the town house must have been broken up into two apartments, each one running from the front of the building to the back.

Crawford went to work on another keypad, then opened the apartment door. Hollis smelled the same odor of emptiness and disuse that she remembered from the Bedford Hills farmhouse.

In the living room Crawford opened the doors of a stereo cabinet. Using the remote control, he turned on the television and entered a security code. On the screen, a grid of green flashing dots turned red.

"The perimeter's armed," he said.

"What about the apartment upstairs?" Hollis asked.

Crawford worked the remote again. This time the monitor showed only glowing red dots.

"It's secure. Nobody's up there."

Hollis followed him down a narrow hall and into the galley-style kitchen. He flipped the switch on the thermostat. She shrugged off her coat and draped it over a chair. "Whose place is this, Sam?"

Crawford looked away from her, out the kitchen window, at the kind of tiny patio that passes for backyard in Manhattan.

"Wally's."

The way he said the name, Hollis knew exactly whom he was referring to. Images of the train station in Paris, the body sprawled on the platform, flashed through her mind.

She touched his arm. "I'm sorry."

Crawford tilted his head back, the way some people do to hold back tears.

"Wally was born and raised here. Later he and his sister divided the place up—the upstairs apartment is hers. She's a pilot for Federal Express."

"She doesn't know?"

Crawford shook his head. "I'll come back and tell her, when it's over."

The silence grew thick with Crawford's grief and fury until finally he looked at her intensely and said, "You don't have to be there. Not the way it's set up."

She looked straight back at him. "Yes, I do. He's expecting me."

"You can't make this personal. McGann's important only because he can lead us to the Handyman or confirm his target."

"That's why *you* want to take him alive, to ask him things. Well, I want him that way too. And it *is* personal."

THE IMMIGRATION OFFICER looked up from the black passport in his hand.

"Welcome home, Mr. McGann."

"Good to be home."

McGann smiled as he retrieved his passport, then walked briskly to a Customs official, who cleared him without comment. Just as well, because McGann didn't want to create an incident by pulling rank on some hapless pencil pusher in order to prevent his briefcase from being searched.

Outside the International Arrivals Building, McGann walked to the line of yellow cabs. He was lucky enough to draw a driver who not only spoke English but seemed to know where West Broadway was.

As the cab moved into traffic, McGann set the large, legal-size briefcase between his feet and opened it. There was the .357 Magnum that, as a senior diplomatic official, he was authorized to carry. Security officials at de Gaulle had taken one glance at his weapons permit, issued by the French government, and had waved him through. Now, with his hands deep inside the briefcase, McGann fed bullets into the cylinder.

The way the operation was set up, he hadn't thought he'd need the gun. But given that Hollis had lied to him about her location, he was glad to have it. She might have lied about other things, too.

Next, McGann brought out a laptop computer, his connection to the Bubble, and inserted a disk. A street map of SoHo, Tribeca, and the Village blossomed on the screen. As did a tiny, pulsating orange dot on West Broadway between Broome Street and Spring Street. Hollis was still at the same location she'd been at six hours ago, not on West Twentieth Street in Chelsea as she had wanted him to believe.

Smiling, McGann imagined her expression when he burst in on her and tore apart her pitiful little refuge.

Stepping out of the cab on West Broadway, McGann held the briefcase in his gloved left hand. The right side of his overcoat sagged a little from the weight of the gun. In his right hand was a locator device, smaller than a pager, a companion to the laptop in his briefcase. The locator could read a signal fifty yards away. It was functioning perfectly.

McGann looked up and down the street. It was crowded with large trucks, deliverymen struggling with designer furniture wrapped in thick plastic or trying to balance enormous canvases and avant-garde sculptures up narrow stairs under the fretful eyes of gallery owners. The pavement and stairs, still slick from the rain, made everything difficult. No one paid any attention to the well-dressed man who crossed the street and leaped nimbly over an overflowing gutter onto the sidewalk.

McGann walked by the warehouse, examining the graffiti-fouled steel shutters and smashed windows. He read the strikers' billboard, then checked the loading dock doors. Everything was buttoned up. But the locator could not lie: Hollis was inside the building.

McGann retraced his steps, looking carefully at all the padlocks. Then he noticed a small door, behind the Dumpster filled with construction waste, positioned under the garbage chute. A door with no lock.

McGann squeezed his way past the Dumpster and put his shoulder to the door. It moved only a few inches, so he pushed harder, this time creating enough of an opening to slip through. His eyes swept the gutted interior and settled on the staircase. As he moved toward it, the locator signal grew stronger.

McGann climbed four flights before he saw the renovations. Now he understood why Hollis would want to hide here: It was clean, dry, and warm. And as long as the electricians were on strike, no one would disturb her.

He scanned the newly plastered walls and pillars, the floorboards stacked on pallets, the puffed-out plastic covers on the outside of the windows . . . the paint-dappled chair with something hanging from its back.

"Hollis?"

His voice caromed off the walls and ceiling. He glanced quickly at the locator in his palm. It was registering the strongest possible reading.

"Hollis. It's me, Paul. Where are you?"

He dipped his hand into his overcoat pocket and wrapped his fingers around the gun. Slowly, he crossed the concrete floor toward the chair, having seen something dangling from it. Then a draft caused the object to twirl on its chain, and McGann realized that it was the cameo. With its back pried open.

"Hello, Paul. You kept your word. You came for me."

Her voice startled him. McGann whirled around just in time to see Hollis step out from behind a pillar. His hand was coming out of his pocket when he heard her say, "Stay very still, Paul. Don't move. Not even now."

The concrete at McGann's feet splintered as two bullets dug into it an inch away from his shoes. McGann stared down at his feet, then back at Hollis.

"You wouldn't have believed me if I'd told you there was a gun pointed at you," Hollis said. "Now you know. Take the gun out of your pocket. Carefully. Drop it on the floor."

Never taking his eyes off her, he pulled out the weapon using two fingers, held it away from his body, and let it fall. McGann was struck by how different Hollis looked now, her skin pale and her face thinner, her eyes hard and alert. The soft, warm woman he'd known and used had been thrown into some crucible, refashioned into someone he did not recognize or know how to deal with.

"Sit down in the chair. Put your hands flat on your knees."

McGann glanced over his shoulder and backed up to the chair. As he sat down he asked quietly, "Who's out there with you? Crawford? Did you buy into his bullshit about Omega? Is that why you're here?"

Hollis moved slowly toward him, careful never to step into Crawford's line of fire. She stopped ten feet from McGann. He couldn't reach her even if he lunged.

"You've got this all wrong, Holly," McGann said, shaking his head. "I don't know what Crawford told you, but I'm not your enemy. The thing with Jones, it was a monumental screwup. I should never have involved you in the first place. Now I need to make it right." He paused. "That's why I came here . . . to make it right with you."

His voice was so soothing, the intonation exactly as she'd known it would be. Back at the town house, sitting in the waning afternoon light until it was time to leave, she had fought the images that could weaken her: her first date with Paul, when he took her for a boat ride on the Seine; the first present he gave her, a simple gold bracelet hidden in a bouquet of roses; the first time they made love, in his apartment, the French doors open so that their cries mingled with the sounds of the city around them. All of it had been so good, so real—exactly what Paul would be hoping that she'd remember.

"Why, Paul?"

Had he been susceptible, her question would have shamed him. In her tone McGann heard a terrible finality that told him she had broken his spell forever. But maybe he could use even that against her.

"Because I needed a last-minute replacement and you were the closest thing at hand. I knew you'd follow instructions, Hollis." He glanced beyond her and shouted, "Just like she's doing for you, Crawford!"

Crawford stepped around the pallet, his gun held waist high.

"Move back, Hollis," he called out.

Hollis heard him but her body refused to respond.

As much as she had prepared for this moment, the cruelty of McGann's words had stunned her. She felt an overwhelming desire to savage him.

McGann had been counting on that, measuring the pain and anger in her eyes, tensing his muscles so that he could spring on her when at last she gave in to her fury. He could grab her lightning quick, jam his forearm against the soft bones of her throat, and use her to lure Crawford forward.

She took one step, then another. *Just one more, please.*

"Stop, Hollis!"

She froze, just a few feet from McGann, her arm raised, ready to hit him. She saw the anticipation in his eyes and the tension in his splayed fingers, ready to seize her. Very carefully she stepped back.

McGann watched Crawford come to Hollis and gently pull her back. He measured Crawford's concern for her and thought that as long as she was present he might get another chance. If he could get them to move in front of the windows . . .

He shifted in the chair so that Crawford would have to come forward to face him.

McGann indicated the cameo with his chin. "Clever of you to have found that. How did you do it?"

"You sent too many people to Bedford Hills."

McGann raised an eyebrow.

"You had someone in the French police tip off NYPD," Crawford continued. "Then you sent in the Handyman to set up the massacre. The police were to be taken out first, Hollis and me next. When reinforcements arrived, all they'd see was an antiterrorist operation gone bad. Problem was, there was no way you could have known we'd be up at Bedford . . . unless you were tracking."

"That still doesn't explain how you settled on the cameo," McGann said, crossing one leg over the other.

"Nothing else made sense," Hollis said, her voice faint and far away. "No one followed us. No one planted anything on Sam. I had packed that morning. The only thing that I was wearing that I hadn't put on myself was the cameo."

McGann slowly put one arm around the back of the chair and turned to Crawford.

"You bought into that?"

"I know about the Space-Based Infrared System," Crawford replied softly. "We've used that technology to track our snipers behind enemy lines. As Paris DCM, with access to the Bubble, you would have had clearance to use SBIS. That's the only way you could have tracked us to Bedford. Or here, instead of Chelsea."

"Yes, I suppose," McGann mused. "Careless of me, wasn't it?"

"You want to tell me the Handyman's agenda?" Crawford asked.

"I have no idea what you're talking about."

"Your phone records will prove differently. The Handyman made two calls from Marseille before getting on the train to Paris, one international, the second—long distance—to you. And once he was in Paris, you called him, at the Hôtel Apollo. Otherwise how would he have recognized Hollis as the person who was to get him out of the country?"

Hollis watched McGann struggle to keep his composure. At the town house she and Crawford had gone over the interrogation carefully. He would ask specific questions in a specific sequence. Her job was to gauge McGann's responses and reactions, to identify the truth, catch him on the lies. It was something only she, who had been close to McGann, could do.

Hollis knew that McGann had lied to Crawford's first question. Then Crawford had given him a little rope, told McGann things that might worry him, set him up for this:

"Ballantine's the target. We know that."

Hollis focused intently on McGann, caught the way his nostrils flared when he exhaled, the way his lower lip quivered slightly just before he spoke.

"You're so far off base . . . "

Caught the lie lurking in the crevices of his confidence. A lie that McGann tried to conceal in a torrent of angry words.

"Let me tell you how this'll come down. I came here to help Hollis. But I'm not so stupid that I didn't cover myself. If I don't make a call in about fifteen minutes, the police will be all over this place."

McGann paused. Both Crawford and Hollis had moved in front of the window. All he had to do was keep them there.

"They'll be coming for a pair of terrorists who murdered four of their own. What do *you* think they'll be inclined to do—ask questions, or shoot?"

Hollis glanced at Crawford, but he didn't seem disturbed by McGann's words.

"Where is the Handyman?" he asked quietly.

McGann looked away.

"Who benefits?" Crawford pressed. "Not the president—he's way ahead of Ballantine in the polls. Not Ballantine's rivals, because the party would be thrown into chaos. An outside factor? Payback from Tripoli or Baghdad because Ballantine always voted for retaliatory strikes?"

Hollis noticed a faint smirk on McGann's lips. *We're not even warm,* she thought. *He's enjoying this.*

She caught Crawford's attention, shook her head slightly.

"The broker—your boss—he must be close by," Crawford said, maintaining his soft, patient tone. "He brought the Handyman out of exile. He'd want to be near the action, watch him perform." Crawford paused. "He's not going to be very happy when he sees your face on the eleven o'clock news."

That got McGann's attention. "What are you talking about?"

"You mentioned the police. Personally, I don't think they're coming. But they might, if *I* call them. And the networks. Parade your gun and bag of tricks in front of the cameras. The Paris DCM in New York hunting down a consulate employee. 'Informed sources' reveal connection to a known assassin. The media will eat it up. Your boss—and I don't mean the ambassador—will be none too happy about that."

Hollis saw the flash of panic in McGann's eyes. Crawford had hit a sore spot. McGann was squirming in the chair, looking over his shoulder, at the windows . . .

She heard him say, "You do that and you'll blow Omega's cover."

"But Ballantine will be alive," Crawford replied.

Hollis saw McGann relax, as if Crawford had somehow let him off the hook. *Ballantine will be alive.* Wouldn't the failure to kill Ballantine matter to McGann? Wasn't that what the whole nightmare was about?

Hollis was still staring at the windows when she heard a *pop!* A corner of the exterior plastic cover tore free and flapped in the wind. Then another came loose, the wind pulling it across the glass, revealing the roof of the building across the street.

Two more *pop*s and the entire sheet was whipped away.

Hollis saw Crawford look up once, then turn his attention back to McGann . . . who tensed, as though expecting something. Hollis, still focused on the window, glimpsed movement on the roof—a figure, crouched, holding something in his arms, shifting . . .

"Sam, get down!"

Crawford whirled. Hollis heard glass breaking, followed by Crawford's startled cry. She watched as he was spun around, blood spraying from his upper arm.

Then McGann leaped at her, arms outstretched, fingers curled like claws. Hollis brought her hands up to defend herself, then suddenly McGann screamed and flew past her, crashing to the floor. Spinning around, she saw the blood pouring across his face, seeping from the base of his scalp.

Somewhere off to her right she heard Crawford groan, "Get down . . ."

She didn't. She turned to the window and picked out the shooter on the roof across the street. She couldn't make out his face because of the distance and the dusty glass, but she knew that she could never move fast enough if he wanted her to die.

She faced him across this piece of eternity, watched his blurred movements as he lowered his rifle, turned away from her, and disappeared behind the large air-conditioning units.

"Hollis . . ."

Crawford was on his feet, leaning against the pallet, clutching his shoulder. She glanced down at McGann, unmoving, his blood pooling on the concrete, then stepped over to Crawford and examined his wound.

"A through-and-through," he whispered. "The shooter?"

"Gone. Stay still."

Gently she removed his jacket and realized he was right: The bullet had caused no more than a flesh wound. There was a pile of painters' rags in the corner; she picked out the cleanest one and fashioned a tourniquet.

"We've got to get out of here," she said.

"McGann?"

She draped Crawford's jacket over his shoulders, looked at him, and shook her head.

McGANN WAS STILL conscious when Hollis and Crawford left the room. His pain was excruciating but he'd fought it hard, vanquished it, made himself so still that not even his eyelids fluttered. He'd listened to Crawford's questions and Hollis's replies, had envisioned her fingers tending to Crawford's wound while he lay helpless only a few feet away.

He heard the wind whistling through the broken glass. It was very cold. On the bare concrete floor, his cheek and the palms of his hands felt like they were lying on ice. His side burned as though a branding iron were being held to it. He felt nothing at all along the left side of his face. The bullet had creased his scalp, creating intense bleeding. It was the amount of blood that had made Hollis and Crawford think he was dead.

Then he heard something on the wind. Footsteps. Approaching. He twisted his head, scraping his chin along the concrete, so that he could see a little more of the room. The footsteps were coming on a pair of dark brown, oiled hunting boots. A low, terrible voice touched him through his pain.

"She was not for you. I told you that from the beginning. You were to leave her alone."

McGann groaned as he pushed himself up against the pallet. He raised his arm to wipe the blood from his eyes. He got some of it, but when he looked up, there was still a red veil drawn across Dawson Wylie, standing before him, holding a sniper's rifle.

"She wanted me," McGann gasped.

"She didn't know what she wanted," Wylie replied coldly. "To you, she was a trinket. Then you decided to use her."

"No choice!" McGann said weakly. "Beauchamp was dead. There was no time . . . Please, you have to help me."

Wylie ignored his plea. "No time to find another stooge? What did I teach you, Paul? Always have a backup. Instead, you were sloppy. Then you panicked. You thought you could use her and as long as everything turned out all right, there wouldn't be any consequences."

McGann heard the wind again, the plastic flapping like the wings of some giant raven. Then: "I'm here to tell you that it doesn't work that way."

McGann's anger pushed back his pain. "You mean it only works for you! If she knew what you'd done—"

"That's why she was untouchable." Wylie moved closer. "You were very good, Paul. I had great hopes for you. I even envisioned you as my successor. But now you've become a liability. You jeopardized the Handyman's operation. Worse, you've stirred up Omega. You can be sure that Crawford won't let go of this. He'll stay on the Handyman's trail, and if he's successful in tagging him, the Handyman will give me up. What do you think Omega will do when it discovers that I, its co-founder, have been employing assassins whom Omega was watching to prevent them from operating?"

Wylie sighed. "Maybe you never fully appreciated my work, Paul. How important it was to have access to the very best personnel, to be able to show them how to slip out from under Omega's surveillance, do the job, and return, all without their watchers being any the wiser. You've ruined so much, I can't begin to tell you. I really can't."

A shadow crossed McGann's vision. It was the tubelike suppressor on the end of a rifle barrel. McGann saw it swing before his eyes and disappear somewhere above his head. His chin fell to his chest and he closed his eyes. For all his desperate hope, he'd known this was how it would end, had known it from the moment he'd seen those boots marching toward him, had heard it in the wretched moaning of the wind.

CHAPTER TWENTY-THREE

DESPITE HIS PROTESTS Hollis squeezed Crawford into the first taxi that came down the street. She told the driver to stop two blocks away from West Tenth Street. She and Crawford walked the rest of the way, his good arm around her shoulder.

"Give me the combination," Hollis said when they were at the door.

She got them inside and settled him on the sofa in the living room. Under the bathroom counter Hollis found a first aid kit that had everything she needed. Using scissors to cut away the sleeve of his shirt, she went to work with antiseptics and swabs.

"You've done this before?" Crawford asked.

She thought his complexion was a little pasty, probably from shock.

"Growing up in Idaho, remember?" She bit her lip as he winced. "Sorry. I'm almost done. You were lucky."

"Let me see."

Crawford brought his arm under his chin. Just below the shoulder was an ugly red groove of raw flesh hollowed out by the bullet. It hurt like hell, but the bone and the big arteries hadn't been touched.

Gently Hollis pulled his arm back to her. The bleeding was mostly stemmed. She dabbed the wound with ointment and put a gauze bandage over it, careful not to tape it too tightly. She fished around in the kit and came up with a plastic vial of white pills that had no brand name on them.

"What are these?"

"Painkillers. The kind that haven't hit the market yet."

Hollis shook out two into her palm.

"Oh, no—"

"Planning on going somewhere?" she demanded.

She went into the kitchen and returned with a glass of water, watched him as he swallowed the pills. Slipping her shoulder under his good arm, she helped him down the hall into the bedroom. She found pillows and a blanket and made him lie down on the bed.

"Give me four hours," Crawford muttered.

"What's the rush? The Handyman's had his fun. He's not going to kill anyone else today."

The bitterness in her voice startled her. Then she realized that it wasn't disgust or outrage that had brought it up, but rank fear. Hollis remembered the sound of breaking glass, Crawford's stunned look when the bullet spun him around, how Paul had launched himself at her, and then a plume of blood, like he'd thrown a glass of red wine over his shoulder. She'd been the only one left standing. Fifty feet away, the man who had been trying to destroy her was caching his weapon, retreating.

She felt Crawford's hand on hers. "What happened out there?"

Crawford's voice was thick from the medication. "I didn't think Mc-Gann would be covered. He'd come armed, but I never thought the Handyman would be his long gun. McGann set us up from Paris . . . But it doesn't make sense. The Handyman wouldn't expose himself like that, not so late in the game."

His grip weakened. When his eyes closed, she laid his hand across his chest. After checking the bandage, she went to the kitchen. Standing in front of the windows, she gazed out at the shrubs and the single, lonely tree in the garden.

Why, Paul?

McGann had cut her to the quick with his words. Yet as terrible as they had been, Hollis sensed a lie. All the while McGann had been hurting her he'd never answered the most important question of all: Why had he deceived her, used her, and in the end sent her off to be killed?

Maybe because it wasn't so late in the game.

HOLLIS MADE A CUP of tea and managed to drink half of it before the tears came. She sat at the tiny round table by the windows, walking through the ruined rooms in the palace of her illusions. When her tears were spent she knew she was ready.

Hollis checked on Crawford, heard him breathing steadily, then went to the living room and using the remote control, turned on the television. She channel-surfed until she found CNN, waited for the next news cycle, then for the segment she wanted. She kept the volume very low, listening intently as the correspondent described Robert Ballantine's New York itinerary. She paid attention to the background shots and wished there were more.

When the segment ended, Hollis pressed the mute button. She closed her eyes and imagined herself back in the living room of the Bedford Hills house, Crawford showing her how the perimeter security system worked. He'd been holding a TV remote, punching in a numeric sequence . . .

Hollis mimicked the movement of his fingers.

"*Wheel . . . of . . . Fortune . . .*"

Hollis stared at the screen. It couldn't be. She must have entered the wrong sequence.

Then something caught her attention. The contestants. She'd seen them before. Maybe this was a rerun. Or else . . .

Hollis continued to watch. Two minutes into the antics of Pat Sajak and the contestants, the picture suddenly disappeared as the videotape ran out and the screen turned blue. Then MENU flashed on the screen and below that, headings under the title CODE NAMES.

PREACHER (DECEASED)

THE ENGINEER (DECEASED)

WARLOCK (DORMANT)

THE POSTMAN (DORMANT)

THE HANDYMAN (ACTIVE)

Hollis moved the cursor down to the last name and pressed *Enter.* Instantly a card like a film credit appeared.

DEPARTMENT OF STATE—CLEARANCE: COSMIC

Then the life of the Handyman—what little was known about it— scrolled down the screen. Grainy still photos of a young man in jungle fatigues, framed by rain forest, his face averted. The same man— maybe—older, the hair close cropped, in a desert setting. In a suit, sitting in a café on the busy boulevard of some European capital. Walking through Customs at an airport, a large-billed cap obscuring his face. Standing in a phone booth in a city that had streetcars.

Summaries, written in dry bureaucratese, covered the Handyman's exploits over the years. He was credited with seventeen confirmed kills—the second-highest toll for all assassins. Omega thought the number was higher but lacked proof. His primary market was Europe, although he moved easily in the Spanish-speaking Latin American countries. He was consistently a long-gun shooter, no close-in work at all. He had never taken on an assignment in North America.

Omega had been after him for years but, ironically, had run him to ground only after the Paris operation fifteen years ago . . .

Hollis stopped there. Crawford had mentioned that the Handyman had worked in Paris. What was the victim's name? Tylo. Whose daughter was in the Secret Service.

Hollis brought up the Paris file. She told herself it was all right, that she wasn't feeding some morbid curiosity. She had to learn as much about the Handyman as possible. If that meant tracking him among the bones of his victims to find things she could use, that's where she would go.

Paris, fifteen years ago.

Hollis was startled. The time frame was wrong. It wasn't Tylo who'd been killed in Paris fifteen years ago.

Now the screen showed poor-quality black-and-white footage. Hollis sat up, trying to understand what she was looking at. The camera panned a pie-shaped area of roughly thirty degrees. Hollis recognized the street as being in Paris. When the camera moved across a storefront on the opposite side of the street, she had the exact location: Faubourg-St.-Honoré. Very close to the Elysée Palace. And the American embassy.

Given the light in the footage, Hollis gauged the time as midafternoon, summer.

Now the camera swung back the other way, catching the bottom portion of a building crane.

The remote fell from Hollis's hand, clattering to the floor.

A figure, his head turned away, stepped out of the elevator cage at the foot of the crane. As the camera continued to pan, he disappeared. But only for a second. The camera caught up with him, standing about fifty feet away: a laborer wearing construction overalls and a hard hat walking swiftly down an empty street. The shot was too fuzzy to capture the details of his face.

This is all wrong, Hollis thought. *There aren't any trucks, no workers. It's the middle of the day, but nothing's going on!*

Had it not been for her concentration on the footage, it wouldn't have taken so long to come to her. The film slowed, catching the worker in quarter profile as he raised his hand to his cheek, almost as if he knew he was being photographed and was shielding himself. Next came a series of blowups, each grainier than its predecessor, focusing on what became less and less recognizable as a face. But the zoom caught what Hollis knew would have to be there: the ring on the third finger of the left hand. Poorly defined but definitely the same one she'd seen on the Handyman's finger from the first time she'd met him, in the brasserie of the Hôtel Terminus Nord.

CRAWFORD AWOKE IN darkness. He moved his arm and winced, then remembered why it was throbbing. He had been in a deep sleep, far below memories and pain. Now the events at the warehouse rushed back at him.

He sat up slowly, shaking off the sleep. Beyond the bedroom windows he saw the lighted street lamps. He cursed softly. He had told Hollis four hours; she had let him sleep at least twice that long.

In careful, measured steps, Crawford made it down the hall. He saw a light and assumed Hollis was in the living room. He went into the bathroom and washed himself with his good hand. Then he examined the bandage. No blood spots, meaning that the wound was dry. His arm was stiff but healing.

"Hollis?"

He heard a faint hum coming from the living room. The first thing he saw was the television, playing the black-and-white video footage of the Handyman leaving the crane. Hollis was in the shadows.

"Why didn't you tell me?"

Her accusation was cold, razor sharp. Crawford couldn't stand to look at her.

"In Bedford, you told me that the Handyman had botched a job. One man was killed, you said. There were other 'casualties.' One of them being my mother, right?"

Slowly Crawford went to her.

"I asked you," Hollis continued. "I said, 'Who was that man he shot?' You said you couldn't tell me."

"You never needed to know," Crawford said softly.

" 'Never' needed to know, or didn't need to know *then?*" she challenged him. "Because you were afraid I'd fall apart on you and you couldn't afford that?"

"Did you really need the pain . . . ?"

"I already live with the pain!" she cried. "Closure. That's what I wanted . . . needed."

He picked up the remote and killed the image on the screen.

"Sit down. Please."

Hollis backed away and settled on the edge of the couch, but her eyes never left his. She watched him hesitate, as though he were searching for the right words.

"Just *tell* me," she said.

Crawford nodded. "Okay. What do you think your father did at the Paris embassy?"

"He was regional security officer. You know that."

She stopped when he shook his head.

"That was his cover. He had *my* job. He was part of Omega." He paused. "Hollis, he was one of Omega's cofounders."

She flinched as though he'd struck her. Her denial and anger silently lashed out at him.

"It's true," Crawford said. "Alec Fremont led a double life. The reason he never told you—and probably not your mother either—was to protect you."

"Because if we knew, we might accidentally let it slip," Hollis said bitterly.

"Your father was on the first line of defense for his country. There were risks he just couldn't take." Crawford hesitated. "Maybe you won't believe me, and maybe it's not my place to say it, but your father loved you no less, did no less for you, was not a different man because of what he had to do. The man you loved, the life you had with him . . . none of that changes."

Hollis looked away, in her mind's eye saw herself with her father that last day, how he had played with her the way he'd *always* played and made time for her. When she tapped those memories they pealed in the perfect clarity of a wand striking a triangle. Maybe it was true, what Crawford was trying to get her to believe.

"You said he was a cofounder. Who was the other individual?"

"Dawson Wylie."

Crawford expected this blow to devastate her, yet Hollis accepted the words without any visible reaction.

"When you were following the Handyman in Paris," Hollis said, "and saw me with him, you thought I knew about my father and Omega. That I had become rotten and worked for the Handyman."

"Yes. I suspected that. Up until the moment at JFK lounge, when you had the opportunity to kill me and didn't."

Her next question took him by surprise.

"Where did you get the tape? When did you know it was the Handyman?"

"French security was pretty inept," he said. "They panicked, ran around sealing off the embassy, useless things like that. They got in the way of our people, the FBI and CIA liaisons. Me. By the time things settled down, it was night. We had a general idea of where the shots had come from, but it wasn't until the next morning that we could triangulate the exact location. It took another twenty-four hours to scour the crane and the neighborhood for any clues, another day to lean on the banks in the area. We got their surveillance tapes, enhanced them as best we could."

"That's when you knew it was the Handyman?"

"That's when we *suspected*. The proof we needed came from ballistics. The bullets the Handyman used had the same grooves as the ones used in the Tylo assassination." He paused. "How did *you* recognize him? You can't see his features on the tape."

"The ring," Hollis whispered. "You can see it on the tape. It's the same one the Handyman was wearing when I first met him in Paris."

Crawford closed his eyes and shook his head. "No one's ever gotten close enough to him to pick up on that."

"You could have." Her accusation stung him. "You had him in Marseille. You knew then that he was responsible for the deaths of at least four people—Tylo, my mother and father, and the Frenchman. But you didn't do a thing to stop him."

"I told you, I had to know why the Handyman had been reactivated. That's never happened before. It meant that something very big was in the works. I know I had all the chances, all the reasons to stop him, but I couldn't, no matter how much I wanted to."

Hollis looked at him sadly. "I wonder if my father or Dawson ever said the same thing. They probably did, didn't they? Not good enough, Sam."

Again she faded out on him, as though searching for something in a place and time that had nothing to do with him.

"Dee loves me," she said at last. "He and Martha took care of me. But he never told me why my parents died, and I always thought that was because he didn't know . . ."

Suddenly she jumped to a non sequitur. "I've been monitoring the news. Nothing's happened to Ballantine."

Crawford followed her lead. "Is he still in the city?"

"The Four Seasons Hotel."

"We have to get to him."

"Or the Handyman."

That stopped him. "What do you mean?"

"I think I know where he's hiding."

"How could you?"

She got out of the chair and stood very close to him. "Do you remember what happened at the warehouse?"

"Of course."

"No, I mean *really* remember. After you were shot, where was I standing?"

"In front of McGann. He was still in the chair."

"And then?"

"He came at you, the bullet took him out. He fell past you and you were just standing there—"

"Facing the killer. He had a clear shot at me. Couldn't have missed."

"What are you getting at?"

"Why didn't he take the shot?"

"I don't know. Maybe the Handyman was distracted, or his rifle jammed. It could have been anything."

"And maybe it wasn't the Handyman, Sam."

Crawford was stunned. "What are you talking about?"

"You said that McGann set us up from Paris. He had the Handyman covering him the minute he stepped into that warehouse. We thought the cameo was bait. But McGann was using *himself* as the real bait, to lure us out where the Handyman could kill us." She paused. "So why didn't he, Sam? I can see him missing you. But me, dead in his sights? No."

"If not he, then who?"

"The man you've been chasing for years but know nothing about— the one you call the broker. The one who protected me in that warehouse by taking the Handyman's place. Someone to whom I mean something." She looked away from him. "There's only one person in the world who feels like that about me, Sam."

AT EIGHT O'CLOCK that night Crawford left the apartment. Forty-five minutes later Hollis got his call.

"I'm on West End Avenue, on the roof of the building across the street from your old apartment. No lights are on, but you have a visitor."

"The Handyman?"

"Not this time."

"You're sure?"

"These night-vision glasses are pretty good."

"Could it be Dawson?" She'd described Wylie to Crawford, just in case.

"I can't tell but I think we should check it out. You're right so far: The place is being used."

Hollis listened as Crawford laid out his plan. "It's risky but worth it," he concluded. "Otherwise I bundle him up. Your call."

"We need to get hard information. Let's do it."

"You'll be covered all the way."

"I took that as a given."

It was the tail end of the rush hour, with enough people in the streets that she wouldn't stand out. Hollis found a subway stop two blocks away and headed to the Upper West Side. She got out near the American Museum of Natural History, crossed Columbus and Amsterdam Avenues, and walked up West End Avenue.

When she saw the building she stopped and drew back under the awning of a Korean grocery store. She looked down at the key ring in her hand. There were only three keys on it: a shiny one to her apartment in Paris, and two that were burnished with age. Hollis remembered the day Martha Wylie had given them to her, when she'd just started her undergraduate classes at Columbia.

The West Side apartment had been Martha's home long before she met Dawson Wylie. During the sixties and seventies it was the center of spirited debates and all-night bull sessions between Martha, her colleagues at the university, their students, and anyone else who wanted to participate. To Hollis, it had been both a new home and a living piece of history. Which was why she had always kept the keys—because of their connection to an extraordinary woman and to one of the happiest times in her life.

Now a stranger had intruded on that refuge. Someone who had discovered its link to her. Someone who had to be working in league with the Handyman.

Someone in for one hell of a surprise.

Crawford had told her that the doorman wouldn't be a problem. Hollis looked through the glass panels set in the tall front doors and saw him behind the counter, leaning back in his chair, hands folded over his paunch, fast asleep. She slipped one of the keys into the lock and let herself into the lobby.

The building smelled of old potpourri, just as it always had. The elevator still lurched and rattled as it made its way up.

Hollis walked down the hall to the apartment and stopped in front of the polished wooden door. She slid her hand into her coat pocket, touched the butt of the gun. Then just as quickly she withdrew it. Crawford had said she should keep both hands free and visible. The object here was to talk, if possible.

Hollis inserted the second key. It went in smoothly and the lock turned with a familiar resistance. As she opened the door, she pressed the two buttons on the lock plate. Now the door would close but not lock.

Hollis had taken two steps into the small foyer before she noticed the alarm system on the wall. This was new, and its lights were flashing red. Not knowing what else to do, she plunged ahead into the living room.

"Dee!" she called out softly.

That's when the lights came on.

Hollis whirled around to face a tall, thin man sitting in an armchair. In his hand was a pistol, leveled at her.

"Who's Dee?" Jacoby asked.

She didn't look anything like the woman in the passport photo. Jacoby thought her fresh-faced glow had been scrubbed away forever.

"Keep your hands away from your body. Sit down on the piano bench, hands under your butt."

Hollis noticed that the bench had been moved away from the ancient

Lieberman upright, where Martha and her friends had occasionally pounded out folk songs and antiwar anthems.

She sat down as he instructed, facing him.

"Who's Dee?" he repeated.

"Who are *you*?"

He smiled, but his eyes were slits. "Detective Harry Jacoby, NYPD. I specialize in people like you."

"Police?" Hollis felt her heart pound. This wasn't anything like Crawford had expected. "What do you mean, 'specialize'?"

"Terrorists. Like you and your boyfriend. Tell me, that night out in Bedford when you murdered four police officers—was that a personal best for you?"

"How could you even say something like that!" Hollis whispered.

"Because those four guys were my team."

Hollis shook her head. "You don't understand . . . "

"Sure I do," Jacoby said. "I understand that you're Hollis Fremont, that you worked in the Paris consulate. And this place belongs to . . . ?"

"Dawson Wylie. He and his wife raised me. I lived here when I was at Columbia, before Martha died."

"A regular *Leave It to Beaver* scenario. I suppose you kept the keys for sentimental reasons."

Hollis said nothing.

"Maybe you're wondering why the alarm didn't go off," Jacoby said. "I made a few adjustments."

"There was no alarm the last time I was here."

"Really? Well, someone was in here before me. If it wasn't you, it must have been your boyfriend. Want to tell me about him?"

Hollis never heard the door open but out of the corner of her eye saw a shadow cross the foyer. She looked steadily at Jacoby.

"Detective," she said, "I'm very sorry about what happened to your men, but neither I nor the man you're talking about had anything to do with that. We're not the people you're after."

Jacoby opened his mouth, but it wasn't his voice that said, "She's right."

And he knew that the cold ring against his temple was the barrel of a gun.

"You know what to do, Detective."

Jacoby lowered his weapon and let it fall beside the chair.

Crawford leaned down and took it. "Would you stand up, please?"

He frisked Jacoby, relieving him of his handcuffs, ID, a cell phone, and a small .32 backup gun in an ankle holster. He gestured for the detective to sit, then tossed him his passport.

"Crawford? You're embassy too?"

"State Department security."

Jacoby shook his head. "Doesn't say that here."

"Would you expect it to?"

Jacoby studied the pair. Nothing like he'd expected.

"How long have you been waiting here?" Crawford asked.

"Most of the day."

"You're a patient man. You must have known someone would come, otherwise you'd just be wasting your time."

"You'd show. One or both of you."

"But you came alone. That means you're shutting out your own people and the federal agencies. Why?"

"Because when this is all over I have to look at four widows and tell them that their husbands have gone down. If I'd let the feds or anyone else in, you'd be on the eleven o'clock news surrounded by Bob Shapiro and Gerry Spence. Not going to happen."

Crawford thought about that for a minute, then holstered his gun and said to Hollis, "Tell him. Everything."

Jacoby saw his opening, knew that if he moved on Crawford now he'd have a better than even chance of punching his ticket. But there was something about the way Crawford had put away his gun, like he was signaling a truce when he could just as easily have blown Jacoby's brains out. Jacoby thought he should listen.

Hollis began her story in Paris, telling him what she'd done there. Jacoby noted her embarrassment when she mentioned a guy called McGann. A few minutes later he understood why.

Jacoby listened to her intonation as much as to her words. He also watched for coaching, but all the while Crawford remained by the fireplace, his back to them. If he and the woman had rehearsed this, she'd learned her lines perfectly.

And the more Hollis spoke, the more Jacoby believed that what he was hearing wasn't being staged for his benefit. Details about the airport shoot-out, the chase out of Kennedy, the Bedford Hills killings— all of it made sense if looked at from her point of view.

And something else: how the two looked, like they'd been put through a meat grinder. From the way the big guy favored his right shoulder, Jacoby knew he'd been winged.

Jacoby held back his questions and kept his poker face even when she got into the grisliest details. When she was through, Jacoby thought he recognized the pair for what they were—survivors. But not home free.

"That's it?" he said, raising an eyebrow. "You sure there's no more? I mean, is there anything this Handyguy *hasn't* done?"

Crawford turned from the fireplace. "No, not much."

"It's all fascinating stuff," Jacoby said. "But where's your proof?"

"In the warehouse on West Broadway," Crawford replied shortly.

Jacoby blinked. "Excuse me?"

"Why are you even asking that?" Hollis broke in. "You believe us. I could tell as soon as I mentioned the Handyman. You already knew there was another player."

"I *might* believe you," Jacoby corrected her. "Have you listened to yourself lately? How you sound?"

"What was your take on the third man?" Crawford asked.

Jacoby told him his theory of an Israeli incursion agent. "Guess I was wrong." He looked at Hollis and Crawford. "How can you be positive that Ballantine's the target?"

Crawford tossed him the early edition of tomorrow's *Times*. Jacoby looked at the big spread on the Ballantines. The headline read AMERICA FORWARD FUND-RAISER AT LIBERTY ISLAND. Inset was a box with a schedule of events.

"Positive, no," Crawford said. "But the process of elimination points to Ballantine. He's the highest profile in the city. A political target—"

"Motive," Jacoby cut in. "Who'd want to nail him?"

"I don't know his history well enough to say," Crawford replied. "Ask him."

Jacoby snorted. "Not likely. Let me spell this out for you. You're looking at a class-A fuck-up, a guy who led his team into an ambush. Officially, I'm nowhere near this case. So while I have a line into the commissioner, I can't just walk in on him and say, 'You gotta ask Ballantine why someone's gunning for him.' "

"What about going to the Secret Service?"

"With my reputation and without evidence, they'd blow me off." Jacoby paused. "What about you? Can't you pick up the phone and call the secretary of state?"

"But I have the same problem as you: no proof. Even if I had it, it would take time to get hold of Ballantine and convince him that a danger exists. Do you think a presidential candidate who's trailing in the polls is going to walk out on an event that'll get him favorable coverage for days? He won't, no matter how much we emphasize the threat."

"And there's another problem," Crawford continued. "Right now the Handyman knows exactly how much security he's dealing with. Everything he's planned is based on that calculation. If the Secret Service lays on more protection, the Handyman will change tack, burrow deeper into the staging ground, making it more difficult, if not impossible, for us to get to him."

" 'Us'?" Jacoby asked.

"We're all that's left," Crawford said quietly.

Jacoby looked at him, at the woman, and realized Crawford wasn't fooling. "What if I don't go?"

"You'll be missing for a couple of days," Crawford replied. "We'll leave you here, handcuffed."

"Right. For the Handyguy to find."

"No. He's done with this place. He'll spend the night at a new roost, start early tomorrow."

Crawford pulled out the handcuffs.

"I was just kidding about not going along," Jacoby said hastily. "You knew that, right?"

Crawford looked at Hollis.

"He was kidding," she said.

"You understand that working with us might not advance your career," Crawford said dryly.

"That possibility crossed my mind."

"Harry, maybe there's something you can tell us," Hollis said softly. "Was the name Dawson Wylie ever mentioned in any of the information your unit got?"

"No. But I saw it on some FBI traffic. Seems they were trying to hook up with him at Coeur d'Alene but couldn't find him. As far as I can tell, no one knows where he's at."

Jacoby saw the look between Hollis and Crawford. "Why? What's the connection?"

"There's something else you have to know." Hollis told him about the killing ground on West Broadway.

Jacoby shook his head and sighed. "Okay. You people are a two-man wrecking crew. Is there anyone out there who's not after you?" He paused. "I have a question for you. We get the Handyguy, it's not a case of reading him his rights. I mean, we're way beyond that, am I right?"

"We need him alive," Hollis said flatly. "He has a lot to tell us. After that . . . " She shrugged.

CHAPTER TWENTY-FOUR

FROM THE TERRACE of his hotel suite, Robert Ballantine surveyed New York under a blue sky and brilliant sun. The rain had washed the city of its crime and fumes; even the din of traffic seemed abated. It was a day filled with promise.

"Sir . . . "

Ballantine glanced at the two Secret Service agents. "I know, I know."

They were so damn nervous when he came out here. Yet their presence was his possible future, the cocoon of security that awaited the winning candidate. He thought back, as he often had, to his visit to Coeur d'Alene in May. A spring and summer had passed, he had narrowed the president's lead by a couple of points, but he was still behind. Five million dollars had disappeared into the electronic void but nothing dramatic had happened. And the election was less than sixty days away.

More than once Ballantine had been tempted to call the man who'd quietly assured him victory. But each time he reached for a phone, he wondered just how secure it really was. Who would answer on the other end? Would a tape recorder be activated? Would his voiceprint be captured and identified and, sometime in the future, be used to ruin him? There was no choice but to wait.

Ballantine stepped inside, walked through the living room and into the master bedroom. He heard a light humming, slightly off-key, coming from the bathroom. Quietly, he made his way to the bed, sat down, and watched.

His wife sat naked on a bench in front of the vanity, tending to her makeup. Her light, deft movements, devoid of artifice, made his heart ache. He loved to watch her like this, when she wore only powder and

266 / PHILIP SHELBY

creams, because that was how he had seen her the morning after they had made love for the first time.

If anything, he loved her more now than he had twenty years ago, when she'd been a bright, outspoken campaign assistant. Her body still excited him but it was her soul and tenderness and companionship that he craved. She had started out as a helpmate and had become a partner in everything that touched his life. Well, almost everything. He did not think that she needed to know about Coeur d'Alene. Ever.

That she had become such a powerful, popular figure in her own right made him proud. Ballantine was experienced enough not to be seduced by envy. His achievements had always been hard won. He did not hold it against Claudia that she belonged to that select group who can turn whatever they touch into gold. It was an alchemy that was inherited or bestowed, not learned.

"You're turning into a regular Peeping Tom," Claudia Ballantine observed, keeping her eyes on the mirror.

Ballantine chuckled. "Imagine if the Capital Gang got hold of that."

"Come give me a kiss."

Ballantine entered the bathroom, stepped behind her, and brushed his lips along the back of her neck.

Claudia quivered. "You still have that old magic . . . "

"And we have time before—"

The phone mounted next to the toilet rang.

"I do *not* believe this," Ballantine muttered.

He went into the alcove, sat down on the toilet seat. "Yes?"

Claudia listened long enough to determine that it was the campaign manager on the line and went back to her makeup. Then she slipped into her bra and panties and peeked around the corner. There was her husband, possibly the next most powerful man in the world, plunked on a toilet seat, trying to get out of a last-minute appointment with a major campaign contributor. Giggling, she waved her fingers at him and went to the walk-in closet.

As she examined her wardrobe, Claudia thought that her husband could seldom say no to anyone. He was too much a negotiator and arbitrator, not a decision maker. His patience and dogged determination to do the right thing—instead of the most expedient—was one of the things that had attracted her to him. Privately, she had always believed that he didn't have the single-minded callousness to handle political infighting.

She, on the other hand, knew firsthand what that was all about. Most people, including her husband, thought that America Forward was a successful campaign created out of thin air. Only Claudia and her select group of advisers knew the truth: It had taken a lot of arm twisting, subtle blackmail, and political hardball to get her where she was now. It would take all of that and more for America Forward to reach the potential she believed it had. And reach it, it would.

Claudia slipped into a beige wool suit and fished through her jewelry for a simple yet elegant Elsa Perretti pin. She was focused on the breakfast meeting with her staff when Ballantine emerged from the bathroom. His hangdog expression told her everything.

"Couldn't shake him, sweetie?" she asked sympathetically.

"The guy fed a quarter mil into the campaign. Paulie tells me that's got to be worth thirty minutes of my time."

"But?"

"But we won't be able to leave together."

Claudia patted his hand. "Not a problem."

Actually she preferred it this way. She was a hands-on person. Alone, she could give her undivided attention to all the arrangements, making sure that everything was just as it should be.

"You sure you're okay with that?" he asked.

"Absolutely. Just make sure you're there for the speech."

"Promise." Ballantine pecked his wife on the cheek. "You know how proud I am of you."

Claudia adjusted his tie. "It's going to be all right, Robert," she said softly. "My intuition tells me that come next January, there'll be a Ballantine in the White House. And you know I'm never wrong."

A LINE OF police stood behind the sawhorses that closed off the entrance to the ferry landing at Battery Park. Dressed in a National Parks Service ranger uniform, the Handyman watched a busload of tourists approach the officers. He waited until the police had their hands full trying to explain that the statue was closed for the day before making his move.

Slipping around the edge of the crowd, he caught the attention of a young patrolman, flashed his Parks Service ID, and was waved through. Not a word about the case he was carrying. The Parks Service emblem and the prominent red cross spoke for themselves.

The Handyman strolled along the dock toward the A-list crowd getting ready to board *Miss New York*. The risk of being challenged by a city cop was remote. Had the Secret Service been in charge, there would have been metal detectors and X-ray machines. Now that he was inside the perimeter he would be taken for someone who'd been vetted and belonged here.

Loitering by the closed ticket booth, the Handyman observed a couple of NYPD officers checking the guests' names against those on the master list. For the guests, the party had already started. From their lively chatter, the Handyman learned that they were expecting a champagne brunch following Claudia Ballantine's speech. There were pitying comments about her husband being stuck in the polls and his fading chances of ever overtaking the president. The gossip held that Robert Ballantine would ride off into the sunset after November, relegated to a footnote in the annals of American politics. The Handyman marveled at how certain this well-heeled, well-connected crowd was about that. The idea of tearing apart their vain self-assurance appealed to him.

The Handyman chose his moment carefully, cutting in at the head of the line in front of a young platinum-haired woman whose makeup and laughter were too thick.

"Hey!" she cried.

The Handyman ignored her and her beefy middle-aged escort. He held up his pass for the police officer.

"Sorry," he mumbled. "I missed the Service boat."

"Whatever." The cop shrugged and thumbed him along.

Behind him, the Handyman heard the woman's indignant protests.

He put on the smile of an official as he moved through the guests milling on the main deck and climbed the stairs to the stern. It was a perfect day, but the wind was brisk. None of the partygoers would come up here. There were hairdos to consider.

The Handyman heard a door open behind him. A minute later he was joined by a burly seaman who introduced himself as the ship's captain. Together they gazed at *Liberty* in the distance.

"Never get tired of her," the captain said.

"Never," the Handyman agreed.

"You working this shindig?"

"Overtime."

The captain nodded. "Easy money. What's in the case?"

The Handyman swung the case around so that the captain could see the official insignia. He made a tippling gesture. "Plus a little something to help pass the time."

HARRY JACOBY PARKED in the yellow zone in front of the West Tenth Street town house, trotted up the stairs carrying a backpack by its straps, and peered at the discreet video camera above the door. The locks snapped open and he let himself into the foyer.

"Good morning," Hollis said.

Jacoby checked her out as he stepped into the apartment. Okay, except for the dark smudges under her eyes. He hadn't gotten much sleep either, had drifted off listening to the police radio bulletins.

Crawford was in the living room, sipping coffee, watching CNN.

"Morning. Anything on the radio traffic?"

"Zip," Jacoby replied. "Big day for our boy. He needed his sleep, too."

Jacoby set the backpack on the sofa and pulled out the weapons Crawford had asked him to bring: a pair of Sig Sauers, shoulder holsters, and four spare clips.

"If you need more than sixty rounds apiece, he's the fucking Antichrist," he said as Crawford and Hollis strapped on the guns.

"What will you have?" Hollis asked him.

"A machine gun," he said matter-of-factly. "Here's a little something extra for you."

He handed her what looked like a lipstick.

Hollis read the label. "Orgasm red? Not really my color."

"Who said anything about wearing it?" Jacoby replied, and explained exactly what it was she was holding.

He fished out wafer-thin headsets with earpieces, throat mikes, and small battery packs, then helped Hollis fix the battery pack to her belt. When the pack was connected to the headset, she pulled down her sweater. The bulge was barely noticeable.

"The frequencies are set," Jacoby told them. "The range is two miles."

"Won't the headsets seem a little conspicuous?" Hollis asked.

"Not with these." Jacoby held up a pair of laminated press passes. "You're reporters for the *Police Bulletin*." When Hollis looked at him blankly, he added, "The union rag? It comes out every two weeks. Hang these around your necks. Believe me, you'll blend."

"What's the latest on security?" Crawford asked quietly.

As Jacoby launched into the details he'd gathered earlier in the morning, Hollis turned her attention to Crawford. He insisted that his wound wasn't bothering him, but she'd heard him cry out in his sleep. This morning he seemed distant, as though he'd retreated and did not want her to follow.

Hollis realized that the last forty-eight hours were taking their toll on him. Last night, the three of them had stayed up late piecing together a plan of attack. Hollis believed they had covered as many contingencies as they could, but she also remembered Crawford's haunted expression. In Paris, the Handyman had bested him and Crawford had paid for his mistakes with the blood of a friend. Now the quarry was loose in New York, working on a schedule they could narrow down but not pinpoint. Not knowing exactly when or where the Handyman would strike was eating Crawford up.

Jacoby had finished talking and still Crawford had not stirred. Hollis touched his hand, found his skin hot under her fingertips.

"Sam?"

A shudder rolled through him. "Let's finish it," he said.

JACOBY DROVE EFFICIENTLY through the crosstown traffic, past the Empire State Building, and up to the Thirty-fourth Street commercial heliport that serviced private choppers and the shuttles from Kennedy. Beyond a converted double trailer that served as a ticket office and lounge was the landing pad, with an NYPD helicopter spooling up.

Jacoby parked next to the trailer and locked it. He motioned Hollis and Crawford to follow him to the Bell Jet Ranger. The pilot opened his door and removed his headphones as they approached. Hollis thought he was no older than she, but his face was lined and weathered, his eyes hidden behind sunglasses. Jacoby had assured her and

Crawford that the pilot would do exactly what they asked, without question. Vincent Calabrese had been his rabbi.

What Hollis didn't expect was for the pilot to get out of the helicopter and pass Jacoby the headphones.

"Get in the back!" Jacoby shouted over the rotor wash.

"You're flying this thing?" Hollis demanded.

Jacoby's smile revealed his teeth. "Surprised, are we?"

CHAPTER TWENTY-FIVE

STANDING ON THE BOW of the launch ferrying her from Battery Park to Liberty Island, Claudia Ballantine stared head-on at the statue.

Beyond the seawall and promenade was Fort Wood, the star-shaped masonry construction built in the early nineteenth century. Most people mistook it for the base of the statue, when in fact it was the frame *Liberty's* sculptor, Bartholdi, had chosen for the foundation of the pedestal.

On the lawn in front of the fort was the speaker's platform, rising twenty feet off the ground. It was festooned with balloons, streamers, and America Forward banners large enough for Claudia to read even at this distance. In front of the platform were rows of white folding chairs and striped canvas tents that would serve as hospitality suites and refreshment areas.

Claudia shivered as she gazed at the statue. Getting this venue for her fund-raiser had been nerve-racking. The whole thing had almost fallen through at the last minute until she'd strong-armed New York's governor into believing that he could score big political points by giving her what she wanted. Now, Claudia was convinced that the time and political capital spent had been more than worthwhile. She would have a captive audience with very deep pockets and the kind of media exposure she could never buy.

The bellow of a ship's horn startled her. Turning, she saw a ferry a hundred yards off starboard, plowing its way to the public piers. The railings were lined with people cheering her.

Claudia waved back until her launch slipped around the tip of the island, out of sight. It slowed and bumped gently against the pilings of the Parks Service dock. She thanked the captain for a smooth ride, straightened her suit jacket, and walked down the gangplank into the crush of her adoring staff.

THE HANDYMAN WAITED until most of Claudia Ballantine's guests had disembarked from *Miss New York*. He fell in with the last group, stepped onto the pier, and quickly made his way past the shuttered cafeteria and gift shop.

The Handyman wasn't bothered by the presence of police. They would accept him for what he appeared to be. It was the other Parks Service rangers he had to watch out for.

Coming to the immense flagpole, he cut across the lawn to the circular promenade. He walked around until he came to the bandstand, where a jazz quintet was setting up; farther along were the hospitality tents. In one, he saw caterers preparing the postspeech brunch; in another, three bars were being set up, the bartenders and waiters arranging trays of glasses and bottles of champagne set in crushed ice. He got an inquiring look from a young staff woman and a police officer when he poked his head inside a third tent. There, six tables, laid with linen and vases of fresh flowers, had been arranged. The presence of the cop gave it away: This was where the fund-raiser checks would be written out and collected.

The Handyman smiled. "Just checking," he said, and withdrew.

The guests were milling on the grass in front of the fort, some already taking seats, others strolling around, talking to friends. The gentle swell of motion and voices created a lull that pleased the Handyman. The herd was comfortable and relaxed. It sensed no danger.

He took a step back and gazed up at *Liberty*'s crown, whose seven rays represented the earth's seas and continents. The herd would realize its mistake soon enough.

The Handyman cut across the lawn, skirting the edge of the raised platform. He was careful not to appear to study it. His quick glances told him everything he needed to know: The platform was open-air, without a backdrop or any other shelter. There was a simple lectern, several chairs, and a public address system that sound engineers were testing. On both sides of the platform were roll-away wooden stairs.

The Handyman scanned the first three rows of seats. Taped cards indicated that these were reserved for the media. Glancing to the ends of the rows, he saw a small press tent but no mounts for camera operators, which meant that the event would not be televised live. A pity, but there would be enough video cams running to ensure that the consequences of his act were faithfully recorded for posterity.

The Handyman made his way back to the promenade and the shelter of the leafy trees. Coming his way was a pair of rangers chatting about tomorrow's football game. One looked up briefly and said "Hi," but both kept on moving. The Handyman failed to understand but was grateful for the American preoccupation with sports.

The main entrance to the statue faces the plaza and the flagpole. It is the largest open area and thus the most convenient place to line up visitors waiting to get inside.

Standing on a walkway just off the plaza, the Handyman saw that the area immediately in front of the doors had been roped off. Inside the perimeter were a pair of rangers and a civilian whom he took to be a Secret Service agent. He'd expected that. The doors would have been sealed last night after the Service had checked the interior of the statue and pronounced it empty.

But there were other entryways, hidden from public view, that would not merit such attention: a maintenance door on the other side of the base; another that led to the electrical guts of the statue. The latter, only a few feet from where he was standing, was concealed by a tarp-covered chain-link fence.

The Handyman was certain that both the rangers and Secret Service had tested the locks and that ranger patrols double-checked them on their regular rounds. But no one knew that between the last inspection, fifteen minutes ago, and the next one, fifteen minutes away, the lock on the engineering room door had been opened. The Handyman did not know how or by whom. He'd been told only that at this interval the door would be accessible and that once inside, he had to reset the bolts.

The Handyman hefted the bag in his grip. He had endured years of privation, traveled thousands of miles, and killed those who had tried to stop him, in order to arrive here. In less than an hour he would reclaim his life.

He reached for the door handle.

It yielded.

* * *

As the Handyman slipped inside and closed the door, he heard but did not see the helicopter skimming the treetops on its way in for landing.

Jacoby set down the helicopter on the pad next to the Parks Service dock. He pulled off his radio headset and twisted around in his seat to face Hollis and Crawford.

"You're on. I'll be your eye in the sky. You spot him and have a clear takedown, great. Otherwise, call me and I'll bring in the troops."

"Where's Ballantine?" Crawford asked.

"According to the radio chatter, still hung up at the hotel. There's a chopper waiting for him on the pad at Thirty-fourth Street. Figure you have forty minutes before he's airborne."

Crawford and Hollis scrambled out of the helicopter, crouched to avoid the spinning blades, and ran for the walkway adjoining the dock. They turned in time to see Jacoby lift off.

"Sunglasses," Crawford said.

Hollis slipped hers on. The sunglasses and baseball cap were not much of a disguise, but along with the press ID they should be enough.

They walked quickly past the administration building and the closed gift shop, out onto the promenade, which afforded them an overview of the setting. There they scanned the various tents, the seats, the platform with its loudspeakers and podium. Drifting on the fringes of the well-dressed crowd were uniformed police and rangers.

Hollis followed Crawford's gaze up to the wide terraces of the pedestal, set above the foundation of the fort. Visitors descending the statue often stopped there to take pictures of the grounds or of the Manhattan skyline. Today, the terraces were empty except for green-jacketed rangers surveying the crowds below.

"This isn't the way the Handyman works," Crawford murmured. "He always favors the long gun. Close-in work isn't his style."

Hollis realized what Crawford meant. According to Jacoby, the statue had been searched and sealed late yesterday afternoon. Rangers were patrolling the terraces. She was sure there'd be more of them around the base, by the front doors. The Handyman was a marksman who worked from high ground. If not the statue, where *was* his vantage point?

"I don't see any Secret Service around," Hollis said.

"A small advance team is already on the ground," Crawford told her. "There'll be more when Ballantine arrives."

"Maybe the Handyman will try when the helicopter lands."

Crawford shook his head. "The only other high ground around is the administration building. He'd have to get past the rangers inside and onto the roof. Problematic. Then say he takes his shot. What's his exit? He'd be boxed in between the building and the chopper pad. Private boats aren't allowed even close to the island; he doesn't have a chopper . . . "

That was the problem she, Jacoby, and Crawford had spent half the night trying to solve: the Handyman's escape route. They had pored over maps of the island and blueprints of the buildings. Every possible egress had been examined and ultimately rejected as unfeasible.

At one point Jacoby had wondered whether they hadn't made a mistake in concentrating their attention on the island. But only a madman would try to rush Ballantine and get off a lucky shot. An experienced assassin would never commit himself to a kill until he had a high-percentage chance not only of succeeding but of getting out alive. On the face of it, it seemed that the Handyman would be forced to break that cardinal rule.

"We're wasting time," Crawford said. "Let's split up. You work the area around the stage. See if you spot anything strange about the people in the front rows. I'll check the tents, then tag along with cops and rangers, check their patrol areas and schedules."

He paused. "Remember, he can recognize our faces. *You* have to spot him first."

DURING THE 1984 renovations, the Statue of Liberty's exterior was completely restored. There were also a number of improvements inside.

The old torch was taken down and placed on display in the two-story lobby. A ventilation upgrade and a glass-walled double-decker elevator were installed. Other enhancements, designed to facilitate public access, turned the statue into a lethal sniper's nest: The 168 steps of the helical staircase had been treated with nonskid coating; the windows in the viewing platform in the crown could be pushed open two inches to cool the area in summer; most important, there was a new emergency elevator that ran from the base of the helical staircase straight down the pedestal into the engineering room.

The Handyman knew that the statue's major electrical systems would be shut down to conserve energy. But the auxiliary generator had been left on, leaving him enough light to navigate through the engineering room. It took him less than a minute to find the switches that activated the emergency elevator.

Slipping out of the electrical room, the Handyman headed down a low, dim corridor lit by naked bulbs protected by wire mesh, like in ships' engine rooms. He turned right at the end of the hall and saw the emergency elevator door. He was not worried about the noise of elevator machinery because there was no one inside the statue. Even if someone chanced to check the engineering room, all they'd hear was the auxiliary generator.

Like the public one, the emergency elevator was glass walled. It glided smoothly to the foot of the helical staircase in less than a minute.

The Handyman got out, crossed the catwalk, and began climbing. He did not suffer from vertigo, nor did it bother him to look over the railing where the staircase fell away into cold darkness.

This part of the statue, roughly knee high if viewed from the outside, was wide. Beyond the high railings were stout suicide nets strung across the girders and beams. There were also security cameras, but today the telltale winking lights on top of their housings were dark.

The Handyman's legs moved like pistons, though he was careful to keep an even pace until he reached the narrowest part of the structure, just below *Liberty*'s chin.

The steps ended at a ramp that swung around the crown. Here it was possible to come right up to the slanted windows, whose bottoms could be pushed open. The Handyman set down his case, crouched low, and came up to the windows, making sure to stay beneath the sill. He checked the angle of the sun, then popped the latches and slowly turned the handles that opened the windows. Cool, damp air ruffled his hair.

Turning his attention to the case, he removed the radio detonator and set it to a side. Next he assembled the rifle, attached the suppressor, and inserted the ten-shot magazine. One bullet was all he would need, but the rifle was so finely tooled that the magazine was an integral part of its overall balance.

He set down the rifle and pushed himself up the wall below the window. Placing his fingertips on the ledge, he very slowly raised his head just enough to see the area below.

The line of sight was perfect. There was the grassy area with its tents and chairs; the platform, where technicians were running cables to the microphones and speakers; and the lectern with no obstacle between it and the bullet, which would be traveling at 314 meters per second at a steep angle of thirty-eight degrees. It would take out the back of the target's head in less than the blink of an eye.

Just before he slid back under the ledge, the Handyman heard the blast of a ship's horn. A fireboat was steaming toward the short pier on this side of the island. He presumed that it would join the postspeech celebration by creating a spectacle with its water cannons.

Unfortunately, no one would get to see it.

HOLLIS WORKED THE AREA around the platform, scrutinizing the men's faces but being careful not to stare. She eliminated women from consideration. Tall men, short men, and fat men were also ignored. The Handyman could not change his height to any effective degree or add too much weight to his frame. He could use disguises—a wig, a limp, makeup, props such as a cane—and she was alert for those.

The platform stood on crisscrossed scaffolding with no sheet or tarpaulin draped across the front of it. The denim-dressed, ponytailed crew of technicians was laying the cables and checking the sound system. The television and print reporters stood in clusters off to the side, gossiping, sipping bottled water, turning their faces to the sun.

Hollis threaded her way through the knots of partygoers who hadn't yet taken their seats. Possibly because of her casual dress she drew the attention of women rather than men. Their eyes would flit over her face, catch the reporter's ID dangling around her neck, and sweep away to something else. The men who looked scoped out her breasts. Hollis used the duration of their stares to check them out.

She examined people who had already taken their seats and drifted into the rows when she needed a closer look. She did not tarry there, not wanting to be caught in a sea of chairs.

All the while, static crackled softly in the earpiece of her headset. She listened to Crawford and Jacoby exchange the occasional clipped phrase, then there would be nothing at all. Once, she had glanced up and seen a blue-and-white helicopter make a figure-eight pattern over the island.

Hollis checked her watch. Twenty-five of the forty minutes had elapsed. Soon Ballantine would be on his way.

Hollis was working her way through the aisle and up a path that led back to the platform when she noticed people gravitating toward the press area. She fell in with them, staying on the edges as the crowd came her way. She heard shouts of congratulations and encouragement; then, as the couple in front of her stepped away, she found herself looking at the candidate's wife walking toward her.

Claudia Ballantine's tailored business suit somehow accented her femininity. She appeared as glowing and vivacious in person as she did in video clips. Yet Hollis couldn't help noticing how she worked the crowd like a seasoned politician, enthusiastically shaking hands, calling people by their first names, waving to those she recognized but could not reach.

As Claudia Ballantine came closer, Hollis remembered the photographs she'd seen of her in the Danish magazine, *EKO*. There too she'd exhibited that ability to embrace people, to make them feel special, even if it was only for a few seconds. It was a gift only natural politicians had—

A gasp caught in Hollis's throat. Something very bright, very tiny, something she almost dared not reach for, circled on the periphery of her consciousness. She drove everything else from her mind, coaxing and willing the revelation to come to her.

It did—the instant Claudia Ballantine stood face-to-face with her, smiling but clearly not recognizing her, then quickly moving on.

Her legs shaking, Hollis stared after her. She remembered she was miked and fought back the panicky words. She had to get away from the crowd so that Crawford and Jacoby would hear her clearly. *Listen* to what she had to tell them.

Hollis shouldered her way past the guests following Claudia Ballantine. She came out on the edge of the promenade and stood facing *Liberty*. Off to the side the jazz band struck up. People were hurrying past her to get to their seats. Hollis turned away, trying to block out the noise, and that's when she saw him. Just a glimpse, more a fleeting reflection in a mirror than the man himself.

But it was him.

CHAPTER TWENTY-SIX

WITH AN ARM draped around his contributor's shoulder, Robert Ballantine steered the Iowa meatpacking millionaire out of the suite. The one-on-one had run longer than he had intended, mainly because the meat packer wouldn't budge until he'd said his piece.

Ballantine thought the big contributors were like virgins: They all needed to be mollycoddled after the fact.

Ballantine handed the meat packer off to his aide and hurried into the bathroom. He splashed water on his face, combed his hair, and made sure his tie was perfect.

His aide was waiting for him in the bedroom.

"Time?" Ballantine demanded.

"You're about twenty minutes behind schedule," the aide replied. "I called your wife's people to let them know you'd be late." He paused. "They sounded pissed."

"Lucky you didn't speak to Claudia herself. What's the route?"

"From here to the heliport. The chopper's warming up. I leaned on the precinct commander to give us a motorcycle escort. He said he'd do it if you promised that he and his wife could spend a night in the Lincoln Bedroom."

"If I don't get out to the island, Claudia will have *me* sleeping there," Ballantine said shortly. "Let's go."

A SMART DOVE gray suit and shiny black boots. That's what he was wearing.

Hollis could not remember the last time she'd seen Dawson Wylie in a suit. Yet there he went, his shoulders rolling as he deftly wended his way through the crowd, the sun hard on his broad back, making the fabric of his suit coat shine.

Hollis stumbled after him, bumping into people, her eyes fixed on the back of his head. She never heard the guests' sharp exclamations and huffy remarks. Dawson Wylie was an irresistible magnet. But why was he headed *away* from the platform?

Hollis looked around. The crowds had thinned, leaving only stragglers hurrying to the festivities. Any second now, Wylie could turn around and spot her. She had to stop, contact Crawford and Jacoby.

But her feet wouldn't quit moving and her lips refused to release the words tumbling through her mind. She walked on, marveling at Wylie's casual gait, his confidence and self-control.

Who are you, Dee?

He stayed on the grass until he came to an asphalt path, then turned left. When Hollis caught up, she saw him going around behind the statue. For a second she lost him in the shadows cast by the trees but picked him up when he left the path and headed for the foundation of the old fort.

Hollis moved in as close as she dared. Ten feet in front of her was a section of tarpaulin-covered chain-link fence. She heard the click of metal on metal coming from behind it, then a scrape, like a pebble caught under a shoe. Hollis had to see what he was doing but was paralyzed by fear.

What are you going to do, Dee? Shoot me?

She covered the distance in a few quick strides and darted around the edge of the fence. Wylie had disappeared.

In front of her was a door with a yellow sign, ENGINEERING, screwed to its face. Hollis reached out and gripped the handle. It didn't turn.

Then she realized that the door hadn't closed all the way.

ONE THOUSAND FEET above the island, Jacoby was still flying figure eights. Occasionally he would dip the helicopter and skim the treetops, checking the pools of shadows. From the little bit of chatter that came over his headset he knew that Crawford and Hollis were not having any luck. Now they were running out of time.

"Crawford, you read me?"

The reply came back instantly. *"Go."*

"Ballantine's chopper is in the air. ETA, ten minutes. What do you want me to do?"

Jacoby knew there were only two choices: They could let Ballantine enter the killing ground, or he could hit the panic button and warn off the incoming helicopter. Of course, without proof that a killer was lying in wait, Jacoby's career, and probably Crawford's, would go down the toilet. No amount of circumstantial evidence would make anyone believe that Ballantine had ever been a target. Including Ballantine himself. Which meant that in a few weeks or months, whoever wanted Ballantine dead would line him up all over again.

"Crawford?"

"*We stay tight. Make sure the Service throws a blanket over him when he's on the—*"

Jacoby winced as static crackled in his ear. Through it he heard snatches of Hollis's voice.

"Hollis," he said. "Hollis, you're breaking up. Say again. Say again."

THE WEAK OVERHEAD light revealed large gray electrical boxes and thick black cables running through brackets bolted into the concrete walls. Blue and yellow pipes, the width of a man's torso, ran below the ceiling and disappeared into the gloom. The dank air was filled with the hum of the auxiliary generator.

"*Hollis . . . Can you hear me?*"

She didn't dare speak. Every sound in the chamber was magnified and she had no idea how close Wylie was.

She took a few steps, checking the names on the electrical boxes. The switches on all the boxes—except one—were in the off position.

The soft whine of machinery startled her. She got hold of herself and looked closely at that one box. It controlled the emergency elevator. Someone was using it.

"*. . . hear me, Hollis?*"

Static tore up Crawford's voice. Hollis realized that the concrete in this tomblike place was interfering with transmission. There was nothing she could do except pray that he heard her.

"Sam . . . do you read me?"

A hiss, like aluminum being crumpled up, came back at her. Then, a fragment of his voice: "*. . . are you?*"

"I hear you," she said urgently. "Sam, listen to me—"

" . . . *you okay?*"

"*Listen!* You said that the Handyman never waits on his kills. But Ballantine isn't here. And the Handyman was reading *EKO,* a *women's* magazine! And remember how you told McGann that you could blow his whole operation? Remember how he didn't care? *Why not?*"

" . . . *are you, Hollis?*"

Hollis ignored him, caught up in the desperate need to say it all.

"Because Ballantine isn't the target! Nothing about that ever made sense. It's his wife. I don't know why, but the Handyman's after Claudia Ballantine. Sam . . . oh Jesus—you've got to hear this. Wylie's here too. He's in the statue, in the emergency elevator. I'm going after him. Please tell me you can hear me!"

CRAWFORD STOOD NEXT to one of the hospitality tents, deserted now that everyone was seated. He looked over at the platform. Claudia Ballantine's assistants were making last-minute adjustments at the lectern. There was a screech of electrical feedback and a technician trotted up to check the wiring.

Hollis's garbled words reverberated in Crawford's mind as he moved closer to the stage. He picked out Claudia Ballantine in a knot of reporters, saw her raise her eyebrows at an assistant.

She wants to get on with it.

Crawford saw it all. Claudia Ballantine would mount the steps to the platform, walk across to the podium, turn to her audience . . .

He shifted his gaze to the majestic statue, looked directly at its crown, then back at the stage. There was no obstacle between the Handyman and—if Hollis was right—his intended victim. At this range, under these conditions, he wouldn't miss.

Crawford tuned out Jacoby's frantic questions streaming over his headset. He imagined Hollis inside the statue, going after Wylie. He looked at the stage. A deep, bitter anguish seized him. He could not save both of them. Claudia Ballantine was closest. He knew he could get to her . . .

No! He wasn't going to abandon Hollis.

"*Goddamn it, talk to me!*" he heard Jacoby roar.

Crawford pulled the microphone closer to his lips. "Jacoby?"

"*Right here.*"

"Wave off Ballantine's chopper. Tell them we have a situation."

"*From what I heard of Hollis's transmission I figured that would be our play. I keep trying to raise her, but with all that cement—*"

"I know. We can't wait. Get down here and pick me up."

"*What are you talking about?*"

"It's a surprise." Crawford paused. "But first I need you to do something."

THE HELICOPTER CARRYING Robert Ballantine and his Secret Service escort was five hundred yards off Liberty Island when the lead agent suddenly shouted to the pilot, "Break! Break! Get us the fuck out of here!"

The pilot was a combat veteran. He reacted instantly, throwing the machine into a gut-wrenching turn that slammed those in the back against one another.

"What the hell is going on?" Ballantine demanded, pushing a burly agent off him.

"NYPD says there's a shooter on the island, sir!" the lead agent replied. "We can't go down."

The agent pointed at the ground below. Ballantine leaned close to the Plexiglas and saw another helicopter on the pad near the ferry. A man broke into the clearing, raced under the spinning rotors, and jumped inside.

Ballantine turned to the lead agent. "But I'm *here*. I'm not in danger—"

For an instant the agent thought that Ballantine was having a heart attack. Blood drained from his face and his hands trembled.

"Sir? Sir, are you all right?"

"Get this thing on the island right now!" Ballantine whispered hoarsely.

"I can't do that, sir."

Ballantine didn't really hear him. He was violently tossed back in time, to the silent, beautiful setting of Coeur d'Alene and the lodge where he sat listening to his host, Dawson Wylie. He remembered Wylie's asking him how badly he wanted the presidency. He remembered his reply. *You don't know . . .*

Then Wylie asking if he was absolutely prepared for what was to come, because once the process started, nothing could be undone or changed, ever. There would be no contact, no discussion, no debate. He would never be told how or when Wylie would act. But whatever happened would guarantee him victory in November.

So he had gone along. With everything.

Robert Ballantine could not have said how he knew that his wife was in danger. He had no idea how she factored into Wylie's scheme. But he understood that under the circumstances, no pleas or explanations would persuade his guardians to take him to the island. And there was no time left for anything but this: In one motion Robert Ballantine seized the gun from the agent's holster and jammed it against the pilot's head.

"The island. Now!"

HOLLIS RACED THROUGH the engineering room in search of an exit. At the end was a staircase leading to a landing. She took the steps two at a time and saw the door. She wrenched it open and found herself in the lobby that had been cut into the base of the old fort, and soared close to the foot of the pedestal.

Dominated by the old flame, the chamber housed a collection of *Liberty* memorabilia. Here, the sound of the emergency elevator machinery was more pronounced.

Hollis ran up the first flight of stairs and reached the shaft in time to see the cables moving. Then they stopped. Wylie had reached the top floor. From there he would have to climb the helical staircase to the crown.

Hollis saw the red button on the girder. Taking the emergency elevator would save her precious minutes, but bringing it down would instantly alert Wylie. She couldn't risk it.

Hollis looked up at the staircases and landings that stretched into the dim recess of the statue, and felt dizzy. She took a deep breath and willed the light-headedness to go away.

There was nothing left to do but climb.

SMILING AT THE REPORTER'S inane question, Claudia Ballantine leaned forward and touched his arm. "Give me a sec, okay?"

She maneuvered her way through the media scrum, grabbed her secretary, and whispered, "What are we waiting for?"

"Your husband," the secretary replied helplessly.

Claudia rolled her eyes. "Not anymore. Let's get this show on the road."

"But—"

Claudia Ballantine was gone, cutting a swath through the reporters as she headed for the platform. Robert knew how important this rally was to his campaign—even if not a word about the November election would be mentioned. Goddamn it, the least he could do was be on time.

She was halfway up the platform steps when her secretary called out breathlessly, "Up there!"

Claudia saw a helicopter drifting down for a landing next to the ferry dock. Shaking her head, she continued up the steps, then walked across the stage to the lectern. A burst of applause greeted her.

"Thank you, but it's a little premature," she said into the microphone. "As maybe some of you saw, my tardy husband is on his way. We'll be set to go in a few minutes. Thank you."

As she walked off, Claudia waved at the crowd. Behind her smile was a grim promise to sit Robert down and tell him to get with the program.

TWO HUNDRED SEVENTY-FIVE feet away, the Handyman pulled back from the telescopic sight and took his finger off the trigger.

"HOW MUCH DID you hear of Hollis's transmission?" Crawford demanded as he strapped himself into the copilot's seat.

"Enough," Jacoby replied. "Listen. As long as she hunkers down she'll be all right. It's our play now. So what's the surprise?"

Crawford didn't think Hollis would "hunker" anywhere. He knew of nothing that could stop her.

"Did you get the list?"

Jacoby handed him Claudia Ballantine's guest list, faxed courtesy of the NYPD command post at Battery Park. Since the names were in alphabetical order, Crawford flipped to the last page.

"There he is," he said, pointing to Dawson Wylie's name, second-to-last on the list.

"The feds are trying to run him down and he's out here partying?" Jacoby shook his head. "The guy has balls. How did he wrangle an invitation?"

"A big contribution, probably. Or Ballantine finessed it."

"Finessed what?" Jacoby demanded. "Why would Ballantine want to take out his own wife? What would he gain?"

Crawford reached for the submachine gun mounted on brackets by the door. "I don't know. Maybe Ballantine will tell us. Or Wylie, if we take him alive."

The helicopter rocked lightly as Jacoby applied power. A few seconds later they were climbing over the dock.

"You didn't mention the Handyman," Jacoby said.

Crawford looked at him and flipped off the safety on the submachine gun. "He's up there too. Has to be."

The helicopter swooped around the back of the statue and began to climb. That's when Jacoby saw it.

"I do not fucking believe this!" he yelled. "Two o'clock!"

Crawford stared down at a helicopter settling on the pad they'd just left. He turned to Jacoby, who waved him off and tapped his headset. He was listening intently.

"It's Ballantine," he said. "The idiot pulled a gun off one of the Service agents and forced the chopper to land." He stared at Crawford. "The cavalry's rolling, partner. FBI SWAT teams. We got fifteen minutes, max, to get your lady out of there before she's in the cross fire."

THE MUSCLES IN her thighs and calves were burning but Hollis dared not stop. A cramp or spasm would cripple her.

She brushed the sweat off her face and wiped her hands on her pants. Gripping the railing, she continued to pull herself arm over arm. She was in the helical staircase, in the narrowest point of the statue, the neck. Her head was spinning from climbing around and around. Two flights below the crown, she finally stopped.

Hollis leaned over and massaged her calves. To stay quiet, she breathed through her mouth, taking huge gulps of air until slowly her heart stopped hammering against her chest. Flicking away a strand of wet hair, she looked up at the crown and resumed her climb.

The hollow metal statue creaked and groaned in the wind. She was grateful for the noise because it would muffle her footsteps, and for the light streaming through the windows because it might be in the Handyman's eyes. Even a split-second advantage could mean all the difference.

Hollis made sure her hands were dry before she brought out her gun. She tested each metal step before placing her full weight on it. On the last flight of stairs she pressed her back against the railing for support so that she could hold her gun out in front of her.

Hollis still had four stairs to go when her head came level with the narrow walk that curved under and around the windows. She saw the Handyman over the barrel of her gun, in his ranger uniform, crouching by the partially open window, his rifle snug against his shoulder. She felt the warmth of the trigger against her finger, the energy coursing through her arm that would add the last few pounds of pressure—

"Miss Fremont. Very resourceful of you to have found me. But what precisely do you intend to do? Shoot me? Like that?"

The Handyman said this quietly, without ever turning to face her.

Hollis climbed the last steps to the landing. "Drop the rifle!"

The Handyman's eyes darted over her. "No."

Hollis couldn't believe that he wouldn't obey her. Her arm dropped slowly, the barrel tracking along his ribs, hip, settling on the upper part of his thigh. She could shoot him there and he'd drop like a stone.

"You know, don't you?" the Handyman said. "About Paris."

The reference startled her. "Yes."

"Then you should know something else: After the incident at the farmhouse, you became untouchable. I could very easily have disposed of you and Mr. Crawford in that warehouse had I been the one behind the rifle. Now, please show me the same courtesy and let me finish my work."

Hollis was stunned. "You sick bastard . . . "

"Let him finish, Holly."

She'd known he would be there, had steeled herself for this moment.

She thought that as long as she kept the gun on the Handyman, there'd be nothing Dawson Wylie could do.

But his voice still carried into her heart, forced her to look at him standing a few feet away in his gray suit and hand-tooled boots. She never saw his arm snake out, his fingers pluck the gun from her hand, just like that.

CHAPTER TWENTY-SEVEN

A HUNDRED FEET ABOVE the pad, the helicopter lurched as a downdraft slammed into it. Robert Ballantine was thrown forward, the gun in his hand raking the pilot's cheek.

The lead Secret Service agent thought he saw an opening in which to disarm Ballantine but instead found a gun barrel wavering in front of his face.

"Get back!" Ballantine shouted.

"Sir, we can control whatever the situation—"

"Shut up!"

The agent had been talking quietly but constantly, trying to find out why the candidate had suddenly gone psychotic. None of his words seemed to register.

The agent couldn't have imagined the horror, fear, and guilt that were tearing his charge apart. Ballantine knew that the best-trained protection agents in the world were useless to him. Even if he told them what was going to happen, they would not believe him. Instead, they would do everything in their power to prevent what only he could do.

The chopper's skids hit the ground hard. Twisting the handle, Ballantine violently kicked open the door and stumbled out onto the pad. Glancing back wild eyed at the men poised to spring out of the helicopter, he waved the gun at them and began running toward the promenade.

The lead agent waited until Ballantine's back was turned, then jumped out, followed by his team. Pointing to two of his men, he said, "You're the decoys. Circle around and make sure he sees you coming. Keep him focused on you. The rest, move in from behind and take him down."

He hesitated. "We don't know what set him off, but if he starts shooting, do *not* return fire. He may be sick, a threat, but he's still our boy."

As his team piled out of the helicopter, the lead agent leaned into the pilot's window and grabbed the radio mike. Because the communications link had stayed open, the Secret Service command center in New York had heard every word that had been said in the chopper.

The agent listened to the instructions streaming in, then relayed the most pertinent fact to his men: FBI SWAT was airborne.

CLAUDIA BALLANTINE WATCHED the helicopter settle behind the trees, checked the crowd, and turned to her secretary.

"They're starting to fidget. I'm going to get things moving. Bring Bob up when he gets here."

Then she began to climb the stairs to the platform.

"DEE . . . "

"Step away from him, Holly."

"It's no good, Dee. Crawford told me about you and Dad, cofounders of Omega. We figured out the target too. Crawford's not going to let Claudia Ballantine get on that stage."

Hollis forced herself to stay focused on Wylie. She saw the loss and regret in his eyes and knew that he would never be Dee to her again. Maybe one day she would find out who he really was. But for now, all she could do was try to save his life.

Her eyes flickered over the Handyman, immobile in his firing position. Could Wylie still control him? Hollis remembered how swiftly and savagely the Handyman had killed in Paris. He marched to orders. *Do those include killing me, Dee?*

Hollis forced that thought away. Time. It was all she had. The longer she kept the Handyman from pulling the trigger, the closer Crawford might get to him. Crawford was the only hope she and Claudia Ballantine had.

Hollis slipped her hand into her pocket. Wylie still held her gun pointed at her.

"You don't know how sorry I am," he said softly. "In all the years we spent together, Martha never knew about my other . . . job. I did everything I could to make it the same for you."

"But in the end, you let McGann use me," she said. "How could you do that?"

"He panicked, Holly. When the Handyman's baby-sitter was killed at the last minute, McGann chose you as the replacement. That should never have happened."

"And he paid for it, didn't he? You were the rifleman on the rooftop in SoHo."

She saw surprise flicker in his eyes.

"McGann paid," Wylie said. "But I trusted him too much and that almost cost you your life." He strained to reach out to her. "I know how all this must look—"

"No, you don't. You don't have the faintest idea." Hollis nodded toward the Handyman. "You work with the man who murdered my father. And my mother. Your best friends. Now you've set up Claudia Ballantine. Why? Who could possibly hate—"

"It's never hate, Holly," Wylie interrupted gently. "Expediency, yes. Not hate. In this case, it's the Jackie Kennedy scenario."

"Jackie Kennedy?"

Wylie's voice had a faraway quality to it. "Remember the film clips of her after Jack was shot—in the hospital, next to Johnson on *Air Force One,* next to her kids in front of the flame at Arlington? She was the most loved person in the country. America was ready to crawl over a mile of broken glass for her." He nodded to himself. "And they'll do the same for Robert Ballantine when he becomes a widower. Because his wife is the most loved and respected citizen in the nation. Imagine the country's horror and outrage when she's killed. Imagine the groundswell of sympathy for Ballantine as he struggles with his grief. Then it's the first Tuesday in November and the groundswell becomes a tidal wave. The country's tears carry Ballantine all the way to the Oval Office."

Hollis was both fascinated and repelled by Wylie's words, so calm and smooth, yet so indifferent to human life that he might have been talking about insects.

She felt sick but knew that now, while he was talking, was the moment to dig even deeper, to reach down into his corrupt soul and rip out the last of the hidden truths.

"...COUNTRY'S TEARS CARRY Ballantine all the way to the Oval Office."

Both Crawford and Jacoby heard the words picked up by Hollis's throat mike. Jacoby had the helicopter eight hundred feet up, behind the statue, on Wylie's blind side.

"I don't care if Wylie was her patron saint," he said. "Once a killer starts talking, he's not going to leave witnesses around."

For a moment Crawford didn't move. Then he punched up a wire frame image of the statue on the chopper's dashboard-mounted laptop. He focused on the crown, enlarged it, studied it intently. Pushing open the window, he raised his submachine gun.

"We give Hollis the best chance we can," he said, and explained what he meant by that.

HOLLIS TOOK A STEP toward the Handyman. She knew Wylie wouldn't shoot, but he would move to stop her. His free hand shot out and clamped down on her wrist, and she felt his breath on her cheek.

"No, Holly," Wylie said. "He has to make amends."

"Amends, Dee? I thought you were talking about murder."

"Remove a single grain of sand and the pyramid collapses. That's what selective assassinations are all about: the removal of underpinnings. Ballantine would make an infinitely better president than the incumbent. Problem is, he can't quite reach his goal unless I remove that grain of sand."

"By killing an innocent woman."

"Sacrifices, Holly. We all make them."

"You know all about sacrifices, don't you? You should, since you murdered your best friend."

Wylie shook his head. "This may be cold comfort to you, but your father and I worked together to keep this country safe."

Hollis started but forced herself to stay on the offensive. She couldn't let Wylie distract her. Not even with dark truths.

"Until he discovered you were *using* the same assassins you were watching," she said. "Acting as their broker on killings my father knew nothing about."

It was a leap of logic, but Wylie's expression revealed that she was right.

"I tried to explain to him that we *had* to use every resource at our disposal," Wylie said. "It was a mistake. Your father's life was ruled by his conscience. To stay true to it, he was willing to betray me. I know you can't understand, but I didn't have any choice except to stop him."

"Not just him!" Hollis said. "You murdered my mother and another man that day."

"He was your father's contact in the French government, a close friend in whom Alec had decided to confide. Your mother . . . that was his mistake." Wylie gestured at the Handyman. "And I've made him pay for it with fifteen years of his life."

"You made me pay, too, Dee," Hollis told him. "You made my life a lie."

"I had no choice," Wylie replied. "I used Alec's death as an excuse to retire from Omega. But I left with a lot of secrets, Holly, and from them I fashioned my own version of Omega. Much smaller—just me at first—but no less potent. Through the years I discovered men in high positions who shared my worldview, who were willing to take the same risks as I did for the sake of world order. Part of the reason my Omega was so effective was because we were willing to *use* the resources at our disposal, not merely sit and watch them. Assassins, by their very definition, *must* kill. It was up to us to choose the targets and send them on their way."

He paused. "Only the dead have seen an end to war, Holly. The living must always continue to take up arms."

ROBERT BALLANTINE WAS in fair shape for a man his age but he was out of breath by the time he reached the area where the tents were set up.

He whirled around and caught a glimpse of the Secret Service agents pounding after him. Young and athletic, they'd be on him in seconds.

Ballantine looked around desperately and discovered one possible way out. His lungs burning, he ran for the wide expanse of lawn where the guests were seated. As he charged down the center aisle between the chairs, he heard people calling out to him, saw them stand and start to applaud. Then someone screamed.

Gasping, Ballantine suddenly glanced down; he was still holding the gun. The guests must have seen it too, because those seated closest to the aisle were scrambling away from him.

And there was his wife, walking across the stage, turning to see what all the commotion was about.

A terrible, grief-stricken cry clawed its way up his throat.

"Claudia!"

"BALLANTINE IS INTERFERING," the Handyman said.

"Is that a problem?" Wylie demanded.

"Of course not."

Hollis watched the Handyman curl himself against the metal framework like a cat against a windowpane. He was absolutely steady, his finger coming off the trigger guard.

She heard the beating first. It sounded like an enormous, prehistoric bird descending on the statue. Then a helicopter blasted into her line of sight, blocking out the sky beyond the windows. There was Crawford, standing on the skids, a harness strapped around his waist, a submachine gun in his hands.

The windows in *Liberty*'s crown exploded. As Hollis dove to the floor she saw the Handyman duck down. Next to her, Wylie leaped for cover on the step below the landing.

Then suddenly, the helicopter disappeared. Hollis saw the Handyman rise, poke his rifle out the shattered window, and fire twice at what she guessed was the helicopter. He reached for a small metal box and held it tightly against his chest. He never stopped smiling, even when he pressed the two buttons.

JACOBY WORKED THE PEDALS and stick to bring it around for another pass at the crown. As he straightened out the chopper he noticed the bullet hole in the Plexiglas, just to the right of his forehead. Kathy's image flashed in his mind.

"I thought you knew how to shoot!" he yelled at Crawford.

Still out on the skids, battered by the wind, Crawford held the gun rock steady against his hip. His eyes were fixed on the statue. He pointed at the crown. Jacoby delicately maneuvered the controls. With the windows gone, Crawford would have a clear view of the crown's interior. The Handyman was good, but in terms of sheer firepower a sniper rifle was no match for a submachine gun.

Jacoby was feeding power to the engine when he heard the boom. He looked down just in time to see the docked ferry vaporize in a volcanic eruption of fire and smoke.

He was wrenching the stick to steer the helicopter clear of the ensuing concussion when, four hundred feet below, one of the buildings exploded.

"What the hell is going on?" he shouted as Crawford climbed back into the cockpit.

"Diversions," Crawford gasped. "Don't think that the Handyman's finished. It's all part of his plan. Get us back up!"

THE EXPLOSIONS STUNNED the already panicked guests. Some were knocked to the ground by the blast; others kicked over their chairs and used them as protection. As soon as the shock waves died away, the screams erupted. People trampled one another in their attempts to flee.

Robert Ballantine had never stopped running. He was only a few yards from the stage when he was swept up in a horde of journalists clawing their way in the other direction. He struck out with his fists, desperate to reach his wife, who was huddled behind the lectern.

"Claudia!"

He saw her search the crowd, saw her relief when their eyes locked. Then she started to get up.

"No! Stay down!"

But his words never reached her.

Ballantine thrashed his way toward the stage. Suddenly he was knocked heavily against the staircase. For a second, the wind went out of him. He groaned and rolled over and began clawing his way up the steps.

"SHOOT HER. DO IT NOW."

At the sound of Wylie's voice, Hollis looked up.

Wylie stood a few feet from her. The wind shrieked through the gaping spaces where the windows had been shot out, blowing back his hair, giving him the appearance of a ship's captain confronting a typhoon.

"Shoot her!"

And there was the Handyman, back in his firing position, trying to steady his rifle barrel against the wind.

Hollis moved, then cried out as slivers of glass cut into her hands and through her pants.

Wylie pointed his gun at her. "Don't move, Holly. Please."

Enraged at her helplessness, Hollis shrank back. Then she stared at her closed fist and remembered. She glanced up at the two men, Wylie concentrating on the Handyman, the Handyman on his target, and slowly began to pull back the cover of the lipstick hidden in her hand.

Her gaze was still fixed on them when two things happened almost simultaneously: Dawson Wylie turned away from her, the barrel of his gun now pointing at the Handyman; and the Handyman fired.

AT THE TOP of the steps, Robert Ballantine staggered to his feet. Throwing his arms open, he lurched toward his wife. He was only a few feet away, certain that he could save her. All he had to do was grab her, jump off the stage, and drag her under it. This one act could never buy him forgiveness, but it might in some small measure redeem him.

"Robert . . ."

Even in panic and fear her voice sounded so sweet. Ballantine stared at the face that had brought him so much joy and comfort. His fingers actually grazed her cheek as he reached for her. Her breath was warm on his neck as he wrapped his arms around her, shielding her body with his. But he never heard her cry out to him, or knew how hard she tried to hold him up as he sagged in her arms. In the last instant of his life, as the unseen, unheard bullet tore through his skull, Robert Ballantine prayed that the woman he loved would never learn that he had unwittingly betrayed her.

THE HANDYMAN FIRED twice, so rapidly that Hollis almost missed hearing the first shot. But not the second.

The Handyman swung his rifle away from the window and, while the barrel was still in motion, squeezed off the second shot.

Dawson Wylie's throat was torn away in a gout of blood, the force of the bullet propelling him over the edge of the landing, his body crashing down the helical staircase until it jammed at the first turn.

The Handyman didn't bother to check his work. He scrambled away from the window, his rifle aimed at Hollis. He saw the shock in her face and shook his head.

"Do you think Wylie was here to help me?" he demanded. "Or to see to it that I escaped? No. He was going to kill me after I executed the contract."

"Kill you?" Hollis said weakly.

"Do you believe in horoscopy?" He studied her blank expression. "You don't even know what it is. It doesn't matter. You should know that Wylie had *never* forgiven me for my mistake in killing your mother. He only wanted me to believe he had but . . . you see, he was using all of us—you, me, McGann. Even Ballantine. His plan was to shoot me after I had fired. Then he could make up any story he wanted to, with him as the hero who managed to kill the assassin, but tragically not before the fatal shot had been fired."

"And me?"

The Handyman shrugged. "I do not believe that Wylie thought you would get this far. But since you did, you became an impediment—a contradiction to his story. What do *you* think he would have done?"

"The same thing you're going to do."

"You have been very brave, Miss Fremont, very resourceful. For those qualities, I salute you. But now, regretfully—"

The Handyman stopped when he caught a wink of light. It was coming off the gold cover of a lipstick rolling toward him.

His eyes flashed back to Hollis, who was staring at him.

"Go straight to hell, Mr. Jones," she said softly, as Jacoby's tiny flash grenade exploded in the Handyman's face.

CHAPTER TWENTY-EIGHT

SMOKE POURED OUT of *Liberty*'s crown as Jacoby maneuvered the helicopter for a second run.

"She must have used the grenade!" Crawford shouted. "Get us in as close as you can!"

Jacoby pointed to the seven rays sticking out of the crown like daggers. "Don't even think that we can get near enough to pull her out."

The gusts of wind created by the chopper's blades helped to dispel the smoke. Once again Crawford was on the skids, the submachine gun braced against his hip. Straining to catch a glimpse of movement through the smoke, he saw a figure lean out one of the shattered windows, gasping for air.

"It's her!" he yelled. "Give me the mike and flip on the loudspeaker."

Crawford's voice exploded over the whine of turbines.

"Hollis, are you okay? Are you hurt?"

He watched her raise her head, stare at him.

"Is the Handyman there? Is he still alive?"

She pointed behind her, to the staircase.

"Wylie?"

She was on her feet now, tears streaming down her cheeks from the smoke. She shook her head.

"Stay put. I'm coming for you."

Crawford climbed back inside the chopper. "Land as close to the entrance as you can."

Jacoby pointed. "God in heaven, would you look at that . . . "

By the pier, *Miss New York* was burning fiercely. The fireboat that was supposed to have taken part in the festivities was steaming toward the stricken ferry, its water cannons sending tons of water onto the flames.

On the island itself, the souvenir shop continued to burn as the fire spread to the adjoining cafeteria. Crawford saw tiny figures of park rangers racing around the edges of the inferno, dragging hoses and linking them together. They might be able to hold the flames in check, but putting them out meant waiting for another fireboat or a water-dumping helicopter.

The guests were standing along the water's edge, staring at the spectacle. Crawford imagined how terrified they were, stranded on the island with flames crawling toward them. Then in the distance he saw another ferry plowing through the waters. It gave two blasts of its horn, which immediately drew cheers from the people below.

Jacoby banked the helicopter, leveled off, and began his descent toward the open area near the flagpole.

"What a goddamn mess."

"That's exactly what the Handyman wants," Crawford said. "It's part of his ticket out of here."

MOST OF THE SMOKE had dissipated. Hollis's sneakers crunched over broken glass as she made her way down the helical staircase. She paused when she came upon Wylie's crumpled body, forced herself to look away from his wide-eyed, frozen gaze. Carefully, she stepped over him, looking for the emergency elevator.

It was gone, but she could hear the whir of its machinery somewhere far below.

Hollis looked down into the stairwell, fixed the image of the Handyman in her mind, and started down.

She had no idea how far she'd gone or how much time had elapsed when she heard the elevator again. Except this time it sounded louder. It was coming back *up*.

She glanced around wildly. There was nowhere to run. If she returned to the crown, she'd box herself in; if she stayed in the stairwell, she was an open target. Since the elevator car was a glass cube, the Handyman could see exactly where she was. He could fire through the glass, destroy the sides of the cage, but not harm the operating machinery that would bring him back down.

The thick, black elevator cables coiled like serpents. Hollis watched the car glide up the shaft, its roof looking larger and larger as it drew near. She cursed herself for not having picked up her gun—for believing that the Handyman had had only escape on his mind.

What was it Crawford had said about him? *He never leaves unfinished business behind . . .*

Hollis pressed herself against the staircase railing when she saw the figure in the car. The elevator shaft was a good five feet from the staircase, separated by thin air. There was only one way out: to jump that distance and—with luck—land on the ascending elevator's roof with enough force to crash through and land on top of the Handyman.

Climbing onto the second bar of the railing, Hollis leaned over the edge. She would have to use the top, fourth, bar as her jumping-off point, but only at the last minute. To stand on the top bar would be impossible.

The elevator was twenty feet below her and rising. Hollis gripped the top bar of the railing and placed both feet on the third one. The glass-walled car was dark, with only streaks of light moving across the interior as it passed the lamps in the shaft.

Ten feet now . . .

She put one foot on the top bar, tensed her leg muscles, ready to push off, when he turned and suddenly looked up at her.

JACOBY LANDED THE HELICOPTER, then raced across the empty plaza up to the statue's front doors. The Parks Service rangers were busy fighting the fire and controlling the crowd. No one saw or heard him shoot away the locks.

Now he was prowling the two-story lobby, shotgun ready.

He tapped his throat mike. "Crawford, can you hear me?"

Silence.

"Come on, I don't need this shit right now. Talk to—"

His earpiece vibrated. *"Jacoby . . . I've got her."*

"Wylie?"

"Dead."

"Handyman?"

"Missing. He's got about a fifteen-minute head start."

Jacoby cursed, then cocked his head. "Wait one."

He ran to the doors and opened them a crack, in time to see a large black helicopter setting down on the pad.

"The feds have landed," he said. "More are probably on the way. We have to get to him first. Otherwise he'll grab hostages. It's his only way out."

Crawford's reply chilled him: "*No, it isn't. The Handyman never carries baggage.*"

ONE FLOOR BELOW the lobby, on the engineering level, the Handyman was moving quickly through the warren of dark corridors.

His face burned as though it had been seared by a blowtorch, and white spots continued to dance in front of his burned eyes. Touching his eyebrows and eyelashes, he discovered only scorched stubs. He had been looking straight at the flash grenade when it exploded. Fortunately the device had been very small, otherwise it would have knocked him unconscious.

The corridors narrowed as he staggered deeper into the maze, past the heating, water, and sewer pipes. Wylie had provided detailed blueprints and the Handyman had committed them to memory. Wylie, he thought, had been a true professional, arranging what appeared to be a foolproof escape route but was intended to lull the Handyman into a false sense of security. If it hadn't been for the horoscoper's predictions and his own instinct about Wylie, the ruse would have worked.

As he plunged deeper into the belly of the restored fort, the Handyman asked himself if Wylie had thought to sabotage the escape route, just in case. He'd find out soon because just ahead, the corridor ended in front of an old, steel-faced door. The overhead pipes disappeared through ancient brick walls green with algae, part of the fort's original foundation.

The Handyman reached for the door handle and bore down on it. It turned.

He pulled back the door and stepped onto a steel mesh platform bolted to the walls. Beneath the mesh was a wide, shallow, concrete trough into which the pipes emptied their wastewater. It was about two inches deep in the trough, whose sides were smooth and covered with slime. But there were no handholds, nothing against which to brace himself.

The Handyman stripped off his ranger uniform. Underneath, he

wore a black, skintight diver's suit called a "skinny," designed to protect against jellyfish and anemones. It would provide some warmth, but
not for long.

He sat on the platform, pulled the wet suit's hood over his head, and
pushed himself to the edge so that his feet were just above the fast-
moving water. He glanced back when he heard voices echoing faintly in
the corridor, then flexed his arms and pushed off. The water cushioned
his fall into the trough, plucked and carried him away into the roaring
darkness.

JACOBY WAS IN the museum level of the statue, surrounded by
exhibits of *Liberty*'s memorabilia, when the emergency elevator glided
to a stop. Crawford had his arm around Hollis, who appeared stunned.
There were small bloody cuts on her hands and face, the result of the
flash grenade explosion.

"You didn't spot him," Crawford said.

Jacoby shook his head. "He must have made it through before I got
here. And by the way, I think you're wrong: He's not in the statue anymore. The place is a trap. He'd panic and try to use the crowds to get
out of here."

"No, he won't," Hollis said. "He was wearing a ranger's uniform.
That's no good to him now because I've seen it. He didn't bring a
change of clothes, so how is he going to mingle with the crowds?"

"This isn't *Jeopardy,* lady," Jacoby snapped irritably.

"There's only one place he could go," Hollis said. "I don't know
how he can get out that way, but he thinks he can."

She told Jacoby about the engineering area of the statue. His eyes lit
up when she described the network of pipes.

"The sewers! The son of a bitch is going to come out in the sewers!"

"Can you raise SWAT on these radios?" Crawford demanded.

"The feds are monitoring. They'll pick up our transmission."

"Then deputize us and tell them there are plainclothes officers in the
engineering section."

Jacoby muttered some incoherent incantation. "Consider yourselves
deputized." As he reached for his transmitter, Crawford pulled Hollis
to the side. "Help Jacoby. You've been down in engineering."

"What about you?"

"I saw a sewer opening in the seawall when we were in the chopper. If the Handyman is still in the pipe, that's where he'll come out."

Hollis gripped his arm. "Sam, did he . . . did he get to Claudia Ballantine? My receiver got knocked out."

Crawford hesitated, then shook his head. "Reports indicate that it was Ballantine who took the bullet."

Hollis closed her eyes. "That doesn't make sense. He had a clear shot."

"We'll find out later. There were a lot of cameras around. Someone must have gotten footage."

He reached out to touch her face, then realized how red her skin was, as if she'd been sunburned. He felt her fingers curl around his.

"Let's finish it," she whispered.

THE ALGAE ON the bottom of the trough saved him, preventing the rough concrete from shredding his wet suit and his flesh.

The Handyman lay on his back, his legs straight out in front of him, his arms close to his sides, his head raised slightly. He resembled an athlete strapped into a luge sled. The water moved just quickly enough to keep him skimming over the slippery growth in the trough. He kept his mouth shut and tried to ignore the hideously foul stench around him.

The most terrifying thing was not the headlong rush or the smell but the absolute darkness. The Handyman was blind. If there was something waiting to spear or tear or impale him out there, he'd never see it coming.

Then, very slightly at first, he felt himself moving faster. The sound of rushing water increased. Somewhere below he saw a pinpoint of light that grew larger until he could discern the shadows it cast. Shadows in a crisscross pattern. The Handyman lifted and pulled back his legs so that they would act like a battering ram.

The impact sent a jolt of searing pain up his spine, but the momentum and the strength of his legs prevailed, tearing away the grille over the open mouth of the pipe. It spun away and hit the cold blue-black water of New York Harbor only seconds before the Handyman did. Both sank out of sight immediately.

JACOBY REALIZED THAT Hollis Fremont, unarmed, was a fast study: She let him and the shotgun go through the closed doors first.

The layout of the engineering section was the kind Jacoby hated, studded with shadowy ambush nests. It drove him crazy to have to check out every nook and cranny but he couldn't do it any other way. He tried not to think about the Handyman moving smoothly and quickly far, far ahead of them.

As they neared the end of the last corridor, Hollis pointed to the slightly ajar door, beyond which was the sound of rushing water. Jacoby burst through it onto the empty platform. There was nowhere to hide and only one way to go. Jacoby stared at the water sluicing down the trough and cursed.

Hollis stepped beside him. "Maybe Crawford will spot him on the other end."

THE SEAWALL AROUND Liberty Island was thirty feet high, built of cut stone. There was no ramp or any footholds to access the water's edge.

Crawford climbed over the four-foot spiked metal bars set on top of the wall. He crouched down on the narrow ledge, then lay on his stomach, peering over the side. Below, wastewater from sinks, fountains, drains, and kitchens gushed into the harbor, creating a brown froth that the waves whipped up and the wind blew away.

The landfill that had been brought in to support the seawall was a mass of rocks and boulders, worn smooth and shiny by the waves. There was no body lodged in between them. If the Handyman had come out this way, he had cleared the rocks and disappeared into deep water below.

Getting to his feet, Crawford scanned the chop. The water was cold, no more than fifty degrees. Without protection, a man would freeze to death in minutes. To try to swim across to Manhattan would be suicide.

Would the Handyman try to swim around to another side of the island? Crawford couldn't think why. In the water, he was vulnerable. And if he intended to get back on the island, why leave it in the first place?

Crawford looked out at the fireboats, coast guard vessels, and harbor-police craft streaming toward the island. There were other things out there too, but he didn't make the connection.

CHAPTER TWENTY-NINE

FLOYD BARNETT, a gym-trim, mid-thirties stockbroker, loved his vessel even more than his favorite girlfriend, Lainie. The forty-eight-foot sports fisherman had been custom built for a Miami real estate developer who'd subsequently been convicted of tax evasion. Barnett had gotten the boat for thirty cents on the dollar, renamed her *Port Folio,* and brought her up to his home club of Bright's Point, New York.

Today, after a particularly stressful week on the Street, he'd picked up a Dean and Deluca picnic basket, and Lainie, and headed out toward *Liberty* for a little sun 'n' sex. He'd also read about the party on the island, and like dozens of other weekend sailors thought it might be nice to watch the festivities while munching on foie gras. He'd barely had time to take a bite of the Strasbourg delicacy when Liberty Island erupted.

Barnett was a seasoned, conscientious sailor, well versed in the laws of the seas. The *Port Folio* was three hundred yards off the island when the explosions hit, well beyond the perimeter set by two harbor-police vessels and a Secret Service chase boat. The three took off toward *Liberty* seconds after the blast, which allowed Barnett and a handful of other enthusiasts to move in closer.

At first the soaring flames from the ferry and the island buildings held Barnett spellbound. Then he snatched up his binoculars and scanned the shoreline, where people were lined up against the seawall. A second ferry was racing toward the island, headed for the small pier directly in front of the statue. He reckoned there'd be enough space on all the vessels to evacuate everyone. As far as he could tell, no one had panicked and jumped in the water. Or so he thought.

"Floyd, over there!"

Lainie's shriek damn near gave him a heart attack. Following her direction, he swept the binoculars across the waves. Thirty yards away, barely visible in the swells, was a black-clad figure swimming strongly for his boat.

"Grab the life preserver!" he told her.

He picked up the boat gaff and pushed it out over the transom.

Barnett shouted as the figure drew closer, then felt a tug as the swimmer's hand clamped over the gaff. He began pulling it end over end, dragging the swimmer toward the boat. Lainie threw over the life preserver, even though there was no need for it now.

"Get the ladder!" Barnett yelled at her.

He winced as she jammed the hooks over the polished wood, splintering the grain. Reaching down, he gripped the swimmer's forearm and hauled him over the side.

Gasping from the exertion, Barnett staggered back and took his first good look at the stranger in a black, dripping wet suit.

"Lainie—blankets and towels!"

After she disappeared, he asked, "What the hell are you doing, friend? That water's freezing. Were you near one of the fires?"

The Handyman pulled back the wet-suit hood and shook himself. He was a lot older than Barnett had thought, and scrawny, like an underfed stray.

"Thank you," he said.

"You're welcome. But—"

That was as far as Barnett got before the knuckles of the Handyman's right hand drove into his throat, crushing his larynx. He dropped to his knees, trying to breathe through crushed bones, his eyes rolling up into their sockets as he toppled over, curling up like a fetus.

Grabbing the collar of Barnett's windbreaker, the Handyman dragged the dying sailor into the saloon. No point in taking a chance that a reporter in a low-flying helicopter might spot a body sprawled on the open deck.

From down below, probably in the stateroom, came the sounds of drawers being pulled open and slammed shut. The Handyman decided it was time to help Lainie find those blankets. He was getting chilly.

* * *

THE *PORT FOLIO* had drifted a little too close to the island. An officer on one of the police boats gave a warning blast of his siren, then saw a yellow-jacketed figure emerge on deck and wave. Seconds later the engines were fired up and the cruiser made a lazy turn, heading for the New Jersey side of the Hudson River.

Preoccupied with the fires and the evacuation, the officer didn't even bother to log the incident.

CHAPTER THIRTY

THE CLOUDS HAD rolled back in, erasing the late afternoon sun until it was only a cold, bleak smudge. The wind had picked up too, raising the swells. The searchlights mounted on the police and recovery vessels bobbed and weaved along the patrol grid like trembling fingers. The belly-mounted lamps on the helicopters continued to probe the shoreline.

Hollis and Crawford watched from behind the sawhorses set up by NYPD. Battery Park was shut down tight. Uniformed patrols, detective teams, any and all warm bodies that could be turned out were scouring the piers and docks and slips from the seaport all the way up to the Seventy-ninth Street Basin.

"I don't feel good about this," Hollis said.

Crawford didn't reply, his gaze fixed on the cops crowding around the lunch wagons, buying coffee and sandwiches.

"Neither do I," he said at last. "They're looking for the wrong thing."

He didn't elaborate, and Hollis didn't get a chance to press him, because Jacoby came slouching out of the darkness.

"You two okay? Nobody hassling you?"

He had told them to keep their police press passes in plain sight, call him if someone started to give them a hard time. Hollis told him they were fine.

"The island's been picked clean," Jacoby said. "All that's left is the water. He's got to be in there." He noted Hollis's skeptical expression. "You think he drowned?"

She shook her head.

"You never know," Jacoby countered. "If we don't find him up top, we'll start dragging, do it as long as it takes."

Hollis and Crawford already knew that that was part of the plan.

They had been among the last to come off Liberty Island, sticking close to Jacoby as he briefed FBI SWAT on what had happened in the statue. The details of his account had been carefully selective.

Later, he had led SWAT through the engineering level and shown them the pipe that the assassin had most likely used in his escape. The feds had turned off the water and sent down their tunnel rats, just to be sure the line was empty.

"Wylie?" Crawford asked.

"He wasn't wearing gloves and the rifle had no prints on it," Jacoby replied. "There was ID on the body and the feds matched his name to the guest list. I'd say they're still a little confused about what he was doing up there. One of life's smaller mysteries."

He looked at Hollis. "We can spin this any way you like."

She knew Jacoby was being kind, but she had to think this through. If the truth about Dawson Wylie became public, scandals would erupt throughout the government. The fallout would go international because nations would demand an accounting of Wylie's possible activities on their territory, against high-ranking national figures. Hundreds of deaths that had been ascribed to natural causes would become the subjects of investigations.

At home, Omega would be exposed, tarred and feathered, and disbanded. Dawson Wylie would still continue to wreak havoc even from the grave.

Hollis turned to Crawford. "You'll have to talk to the secretary of state. He, and maybe the president, will have to know what really happened."

"The president will want in, but at the end of the day he might choose to do nothing."

"Even if the Handyman's caught?" Jacoby cut in.

"I doubt anyone would want him caught."

Hollis stepped away and looked out over the dark water. Images of springtime at Coeur d'Alene came back to her, all the good and wonderful times she'd shared with Martha and Dee—safe, caring times that had molded her and that she would cherish forever. The rest of it, the darkness in which her family had perished, belonged in another universe. Nothing she could change.

"Dee always said he was just a simple, midlevel career officer. That's the way I'll bury him, back in Idaho."

Jacoby sighed. "That still leaves the problem of who shot Ballantine. And if anyone cottons onto the possibility that he wasn't the target . . . "

"They won't," Crawford said. "The FBI and the press will turn his life inside out. But what will they find? A few political skeletons, but nothing that would make him sniper food for the homegrown crazies, the IRA, or the letter-bomb pen pals out of the Middle East."

Hollis remembered that Crawford had disappeared into the NYPD tractor-trailer. Jacoby must have set him up with a computer background search on Ballantine.

"So Ballantine was just . . . killed," she said. "By a person or persons unknown, for reasons unknown. You think his widow will buy that?"

"Widows don't usually have much choice. When James Earl Ray was dying, everyone begged him to finally spill what he knew about the King assassination conspiracy. He never did. Now people think he was just one lunatic working alone."

He paused. "We don't *like* to think that, because it offends when a nobody can strike down a great man. We need to believe that the execution plan befitted the man—that it was something intricate, costly, diabolical."

Hollis thought she had it now. "That's why you said the police are looking for the wrong thing."

When Crawford nodded, Jacoby broke in. "Excuse me, but what am I missing here?"

"I think you'll know very soon," Crawford said softly.

ACTUALLY, THE BREAK didn't occur until Crawford, Hollis, and Jacoby were back at the West Tenth Street town house.

Around ten o'clock that night, a watchman on New Jersey's derelict Franklin docks discovered a forty-eight-foot sports fisherman banging against the pilings. When no one answered his hail, he made the mistake of satisfying his curiosity.

Jacoby caught the New Jersey police squawk minutes after the officers had boarded the vessel. They thought it was a dope deal gone bad: a stockbroker itchy to make some fast, easy money; a young girlfriend; a killer who'd worked quickly, cleanly, and who had vanished. No drugs or money were found, but that fact didn't tarnish the law enforcement mind-set. Had the vessel and victims been found off the coast, piracy might have been a consideration. But no one would kill two people in a protected harbor and then leave an expensive boat—unless what was truly valuable had already been removed.

"You see how it happened," Crawford said to Jacoby as the three of them sat in the living room.

"Sure," Jacoby replied bitterly. "The Handyman goes into the water like he was on some fucking water slide at Disney World. All the cop boats are busy with the evacuation, so no one notices him. Except this Wall Streeter who makes like the Good Samaritan and gets his throat crushed for his trouble. The girl's downstairs, probably heating up soup, when the son of a bitch drops in and does her." He paused. "Had this whole thing figured out, didn't he?"

"He knew there would be gawkers out on their boats. He came prepared."

Jacoby glanced at Crawford and Hollis. "He's on the loose. You two have to stay smart."

"He's not coming after us," Hollis said.

"Really?"

"Really. This isn't his territory. He doesn't have help anymore. He'll want to get back to somewhere familiar."

"You might start checking the flights out of Newark," Crawford said. "Unofficially."

Hollis caught the look that passed between the two men. She knew that Crawford and Omega and the State Department would massage the story of Ballantine's death to suit the reality that politics demanded. Jacoby, though . . .

"Back in the apartment, you told me that you'd have to tell the wives of your men why their husbands died," she said.

Jacoby jammed his hands in his pants pockets and looked up at the sky. After a moment, he turned to Crawford.

"Sometimes the truth sucks," he said flatly. "If I give a different story, yours gets blown out of the water. You lose, and I don't have any partners to help me run down the Handyman. Which, by the way, is now my life's ambition.

"So I walk back the cat. I told the commissioner that maybe the third guy *was* the bad guy. Now I take it all back, say the tips from the

Paris cops were righteous: There were terrorists up in Bedford that night. And now, who knows where they've gone?"

"Will the commissioner buy that?" Hollis asked.

"It's a tidy package. My people will get the inspector's funeral they deserve. The rest of us go on." He hesitated. "That's the deal, as long as I have your word that you'll keep me in the loop."

Crawford nodded. "Newark, Harry. Get the boarding gate surveillance tapes. We don't have a name for him but we've seen enough to make him."

Crawford and Jacoby were still talking when Hollis left the room. She was cold, tired, and dirty. Bitter, too, because the Handyman had waded through so much blood and had slipped on none of it. She very much doubted that having succeeded this far, he'd surprise them by making a mistake now.

Hollis closed the door to the bathroom, turned on the shower to create steam, and peeled off her clothes. The hot water got rid of her shivers; soap and shampoo washed away the grime. But nothing could dispel the images that kept searing her: Dawson Wylie holding a gun on her; his cold, grim reasoning about the shadow Omega and the need to murder her father; that final twist when the Handyman had turned on him, somehow knowing that Wylie would kill him. She shuddered as she recalled the workmanlike way in which the Handyman had been prepared to deal with her.

There was a knock on the door, followed by Crawford's muffled voice over the drumming of the shower.

"Come in," Hollis called out.

She heard the door open and close. Through a crack in the shower curtain, she saw Crawford in front of the sink, taps running, staring vacantly into the steamed up mirror. He splashed water on his face and dabbed his eyes, but didn't dry himself. He seemed to teeter, then stepped back unsteadily and sat on the toilet, his shoulders slumped, his head in his hands.

He sat motionless for a time, then pulled his hands away. His blank, sterile expression belonged to a man who had suffered a loss that could never be recouped, who had seen something precious to him destroyed that could never be made whole again.

Hollis thought of Wally in the Paris subway station, lying on that cold cement; the television pictures of Jacoby's men being carried out of the smoldering woods at Bedford Hills. The agony the images brought on were all too familiar. Maybe it was this understanding, coupled with a need to comfort, that made her pull back the shower curtain.

She did not think about being naked. She did not hesitate or pull back when he looked up at her. Instead, she reached for him in a way she'd wished so often that a man would reach for her. She made him stand and slowly undid his clothes. Then she led him into the shower and stood him under the water, gently lathering his body, working her fingers over every inch of his hard flesh. She made him turn around under the spray, then stood on tiptoes as she scrubbed his hair and face, exploring his features like a blind woman would.

When he was cleansed, she stepped back and looked into his eyes, wondering if he knew, as she did, that they had unintentionally, yet perhaps inevitably, reached a place in time and space that was meant only for themselves. That they could seize and make it their own if they chose to, or walk away from it, but never deny that it could have been theirs.

His arms rose to encircle her, his hands moving up her back, drawing her close. He shifted so that the water beat down on the back of his neck, so that he could kiss and taste her. Their lips fell upon each other's skin, feathery touches meant to soothe and heal, caresses and whispers that pushed away the darkness and death that had surrounded them.

She felt his hands glide to the small of her back, lift her effortlessly as she opened her legs for him and cried out as he entered her. For a moment they remained locked like that—her arms around his shoulders, her face buried in his neck—until slowly, gently, they began to move in unison to a pulse only they could feel.

CRAWFORD REACHED FOR the phone in the darkness, catching it after half a ring.

"Yes?"

It was Harry. He had the airport surveillance tapes from Newark International, La Guardia, and JFK. They were being prepped for review.

Crawford looked over his shoulder at Hollis, lying beside him. She was still, her chest rising and falling rhythmically. He thought she was asleep until her eyelids fluttered and the moonlight winked off her eyes.

"It's Harry. He has the tapes."

He felt her fingertips on his chest. "Tell him we're coming."

BUT IT WAS too little too late.

By the time Harry Jacoby had copies of the airlines' passenger tapes for that night, Carnival Air's flight 3754 had landed in Fort Lauderdale on schedule at 9:15 P.M. The Handyman trooped off the jetway with a crowd of tipsy vacationers headed for buses that would take them to the pier and the start of a seven-day Caribbean cruise.

At the exit he drifted away from the crowds and caught a shuttle to the Hilton.

Riding in the overly chilly bus, the Handyman reflected on what a marvelous country America was. So much room to move around, so many ways to travel, laughable security precautions.

In the *Port Folio*'s master stateroom the Handyman had found not only an expensive casual wardrobe but a cache of several thousand dollars. He'd also taken the dead man's diamond-studded Rolex and the girl's jewelry, items that could be easily pawned if necessary.

The cash got him a taxi out to Newark Airport and a ticket on the next plane out. His new Canadian passport, which had been sent to Fat Lee's New York address, was accepted without question as identification. The flight itself, with its caterwauling revelers, was the hardest part of the journey.

The Handyman got out of the shuttle in front of the Hilton's main entrance and went into the lobby, where he asked a bellboy for directions to a bar. A few minutes later he was in the rooftop lounge, seated at a tiny table by floor-to-ceiling windows. A young waitress came by to take his order and gave him a saucy smile as she walked away.

Life was good. And it would get better. Wylie, the stone in his shoe for fifteen years, was dead. Finally, he was safe. Could start again, just as Wylie had promised him.

Nor was there any need to rush. The Fort Lauderdale shoreline looked quite spectacular at night. By day, there would be hot sun and cool waters to heal him. Farther up the coast was a long-standing French-Canadian community, so familiar that it no longer drew any attention from the natives. Nor would one more face belonging to a middle-aged man who spoke English with a soft but distinct French accent.

The waitress returned with his cognac. The Handyman flirted with her briefly but doubted he'd honor his promise to visit again the next night. It behooved him to remember that Crawford was still out there.

Crawford, busy now cutting all the ties that could link Ballantine's killing to Omega. Save Omega, that was the key.

Busy with Fremont too, explaining away her presence and Wylie's. Keeping her safe, because she had been so close to an assassin. Witnesses always needed protection.

Sipping his cognac, the Handyman was quite certain that one day soon he would cross paths with Crawford. The work he intended to return to made that inevitable. Yes, he would see Crawford again. And who knew, maybe Hollis Fremont too. He would have to make plans . . . carefully.

From across the room the waitress watched the expensively dressed older man. She found him attractive and admitted that with the right moves, he could seduce her.

Until she glimpsed his smile. It was one of fond memory, spiced with a touch of longing or regret.

The waitress had seen that particular look too often, knew it came only when a man was thinking about a certain woman, someone who was absent but who still possessed him, who had given him something dear, yet whose gift now brought sadness.

She envied this unknown woman, wished that, if only for a moment, she could be like her, away from these smoky lights and canned music, in an exotic place, in arms so strong that she would never want to come back.

SPRING CAME UNSEASONABLY early to Paris that year. The sun was still weak, but its warmth felt good on Hollis's face.

It was pleasant to sit in the small garden she'd created on the roof of Crawford's apartment building on Boulevard St.-Germain. The smell of loam and budding flower was sweet; the high, ivy-covered walls ensured privacy and reduced the city noise to a faint hum.

Pleasant too was the company of the young woman, in her mid-thirties, sitting beside her at the patio table. Holland Tylo was dressed in a navy blue business suit. Her blond hair was cut in a wedge, and her eyes had gold flecks strewn in a sea of green. Eyes that were watchful, missing nothing. Crawford's eyes.

Faint lines and creases made Tylo look older than she was. Her close-clipped, unmanicured fingernails and absence of makeup added to the effect. But Hollis understood: It was the appearance of someone who had been carelessly cuffed by life, sent spinning to the brink, but who had battled back, endured, survived.

Before calling Tylo, Hollis had asked Crawford for some background on the Secret Service agent. What she'd learned made her feel a kinship with this woman. Tylo's appearance reminded Hollis that she saw some of those same lines and creases in the mirror every morning.

"It's good for you here," Tylo said.

"As good as it gets," Hollis replied.

"No, it'll get better," Tylo said. "Trust me on that. One day it really will be over. I thought I'd come to terms with everything I had to. Then you call and everything that I'd never resolved about my father, that I'd shut away in my dark little corner, could finally be dealt with." She paused. "I owe you for that."

Hollis smiled and looked away. She too had started to come to terms and knew exactly what still lay in her dark corner.

After leaving New York she and Crawford had spent two days in Washington while he huddled with the director of Omega, the secretary of state, and the president. The conclusions they had arrived at were ones Hollis had expected: Robert Ballantine had been the victim of a lone assassin, still unidentified and at large. Omega's involvement in the matter would be sanitized. The official accounts of the assassinations of Alec Fremont, his wife, and the French security officer would remain undisturbed. Dawson Wylie's presence in the Statue of Liberty at the time of the shooting would be explained away this way: Wylie, a veteran Foreign Service officer, had noticed a suspicious-looking man enter the statue. He'd followed, tried to stop the assassin, and was shot in the struggle. A valorous coda to an otherwise undistinguished life of public service.

Afterward, Hollis had accompanied Wylie's body to Coeur d'Alene, where it was cremated and the ashes scattered on the lake. She hired a local realtor, put the house on the market at a very attractive price, and when it sold, she distributed the proceeds among the wives of Jacoby's fallen team.

She had then returned to New York in time to be with Crawford when he buried Wally.

"Did you know then that you would stay with Sam?" Tylo asked.

"I knew I wanted to," Hollis replied. "Somewhere in all that death I fell in love with him. He's the only man who could ever know who I really am and what I went through. No one else could even begin to understand."

She smiled. "But to choose him meant choosing Omega. It's what Sam is, what he believes in, what he does."

"And what about you? What do you believe in?"

"That you can never give back knowledge you have, even if you want to."

Tylo looked around. "Will you stay in Paris?"

Hollis nodded. "It's our base of operations."

"And you're okay with that?"

Hollis understood where Tylo was going with this. She'd told Tylo about her relationship with Paul, how so much of her feelings about Paris were wrapped up with him.

"A few months ago—around Christmas, I guess—Sam and I were

walking near the opera," she said. "It was early evening, and I noticed these young women driving around in sports cars. They'd go around the block, come back, go around again. Finally one of them stopped at the curb where an executive type was standing. They talked through the open passenger's window, then he got in and they drove off. I had no clue as to what was going on until Sam laughed and said the woman was a high-class prostitute. Apparently, the opera is a favorite hunting ground for pricey call girls."

Hollis paused. "Sam said that they're called *les petites poules. Poule* means 'chicken' in French, but it's also slang for 'hooker.' "

She looked up at Tylo. "With Paul, when I did—things for him— that was what he called me, *ma petite poule*. That's all I really was to him, a fantasy hooker."

Tylo reached across and gripped Hollis's hand.

"No, it's okay. Because now I don't have any illusions about him. He's gone for good, forever."

"What about your job at the consulate?"

"The secretary of state put the fix in. Officially, I'm on compassionate leave because of Dawson Wylie's death. Unofficially, no one expects me to return. As for Paul, his murder will be filed as an unsolved homicide."

"All nice and neat," Tylo said. "Believe me, I know when I see a fix being put in. But sometimes it's for the best."

She looked at her watch. "I have to get going. My shift's coming up."

They went inside, through the kitchen and into the foyer, where she had left her coat. Tylo nodded at the sophisticated security panel on the wall.

"I haven't seen one like that."

Hollis motioned her back to the kitchen. She opened the pantry door and pressed a button tucked away behind the light switch. The cupboard of half-moon shelves, filled with canned goods and bottles, turned on a hidden axis, revealing a pegboard hung with automatic weapons, ammunition clips, and grenades.

Tylo pursed her lips. "Haven't seen one of those either. Although we do have a few interesting closets in the White House."

"What's it like, working for the president?" Hollis asked as they walked back to the foyer.

When Tylo reached for her coat, her suit jacket swung away to reveal a .357 Magnum in a holster tucked against her ribs.

She grinned. "It has its moments. Like sometimes you just know that people still can't believe it's Claudia Ballantine, *Madam* President."

She shook her head and added softly, "If I were ever to reveal what you told me, nobody'd believe me. But Dawson Wylie was absolutely right: She won the election on the Jackie Kennedy factor."

"I never thought the party would turn to her," Hollis admitted.

"Who else did it have? The election was less than sixty days away. Ballantine had been transformed into a national martyr. There wasn't another pale male around to fill his shoes. It must have been gut wrenching for the party bosses to turn to a woman, and I'm sure that most of them thought she wouldn't stand a snowball's chance. But Claudia stepped into the campaign without missing a beat. She already had the grassroots network—her America Forward supporters. As soon as she hit the national campaign trail, the rest of the country fell in love with her. The incumbent didn't have a prayer."

Hollis watched Tylo slip into her coat. "What about the assassination? She's the president. She can stay on top of the investigation, take it in whatever direction she wants. If she digs deep enough, she might hit the truth."

Tylo jammed her hands in her coat pockets. "Claudia never knew that her husband had had any contact with Wylie. Or that he even knew him. Wylie's name was on the list of big contributors, but so were hundreds of others she'd never met. And since Wylie's dead . . .

"There's also the grieving, and the pressure of the job. I was next to Claudia throughout the campaign. I heard her crying at night. But every next morning she'd pick up that fallen standard all over again. She fought this election for her husband, for his ideas and beliefs. To heal, she intends to do everything he intended—and more.

"Sure, she wants to know who the killer was, to find him and bring him to trial. But she's also aware of the percentages. Terrorists can still prick us, but they've learned not to crow about it. We're learning to live with things we may never know."

"So as long as the secretary of state and the former president, and you, me, and Sam all keep quiet—"

"We'll all get on with our lives," Tylo finished.

She reached out and embraced Hollis. "Thank you for telling me about the Handyman. At least now I know *who* killed my father."

"You'll know the rest when we get him," Hollis promised.

"You think? It's been eight months. No one's seen him or heard a thing about him."

Hollis opened the door and stepped out into the hall with her.

"He thought it was safe to come out of his rat hole once. He'll come out again. Sam and I never stop looking. We never will."

Tylo took a few steps then turned. "If there's anything you need. Anything at all . . ."

"Just for him to make a mistake."

CRAWFORD DIDN'T RETURN for another half hour. He'd left shortly after Tylo arrived, giving the two women the privacy they needed.

"You went to some bistro," Hollis said, taking him into her arms. "I can smell beer on your breath."

He kissed her. "It was a cop bar. Never know what you'll hear."

Arms around each other's waists, they went into the kitchen.

"Did you have lunch?" Hollis asked.

"I thought you might want to go out."

"Very gallant of you. Yes, I think I'd like that."

Hollis ran into the bedroom, pulled out a leather bomber jacket.

Crawford was sitting at the kitchen table, flipping through a newspaper.

"Let's go."

And the phone rang. The secure line. The Omega line.

The blood drained from Hollis's face as she snatched up the receiver. "Hello?"

She listened, then looked over her shoulder at Crawford. "Sam's here. Let me put you on the speaker."

Harry Jacoby's voice filled the kitchen. In the background, a baby gurgled.

"Kathy's gone shopping so I'm holding Vinnie here," he explained. "I think he just took a dump on my shoulder."

Hollis felt the tension drain out of her. Jacoby was just calling to chat and had dialed the wrong line.

"Sorry to hear that," she said. "I think they tend to do that a lot at first."

"Yeah, yeah. But that's not what I'm calling about." There was a pause, then. "I have a hit on our boy."

Hollis's smile crumbled. "Say again, Harry."

"You know I put out his description to a select clientele across the country. No details about who he is or why I was interested. Well, a French-Canadian doper who used to run Colombian product north of the border was looking for a little bargaining chip. Seems he knows about this middle-aged guy who's been hanging out in the expatriate community. Quiet, keeps to himself. Curious thing is, he doesn't talk with a French-Canadian accent. And the description jibes."

"Do you have a picture?" Crawford cut in.

"Came in ten minutes ago. It's the Handyman."

"We'll be on the next flight to Miami," Hollis said. "I think there's one—"

"Don't bother. I've been tagging him on the computers. Calls himself Jean-Luc Savard. He's headed your way, Air France flight twenty-six, Miami to Paris nonstop." A beat. "I figured you didn't want him popped over here, what with the jurisdictional problems, his civil rights, red tape. Besides, don't the French still do it the medieval way, with the ax or the guillotine or whatever the hell it is they use?"

"Whatever . . . ," Hollis whispered.

She turned away, barely heard Crawford going over the flight number and arrival one more time, getting the rest of the details from Jacoby.

She was remembering the last time she'd been at Charles de Gaulle Airport. All the fear and panic and uncertainty flooded back, made her shiver. She shook them off. This time it would be different.

"How much time do we have?" Hollis demanded after Crawford had hung up.

"Flight twenty-six touches down in forty-two minutes."

"It's got to be a jumbo jet," Hollis murmured. "Say the Handyman is traveling first class—a stretch, because he won't want to attract attention, but he might be. He's one of the first off the plane. He won't have checked baggage, but that still leaves Customs and Immigration." She glanced at Crawford. "We can make it, Sam."

They ran to Crawford's office, where he punched up the incoming flights on the computer. Four other international carriers were coming in at about the same time as Miami-Paris 26.

"That will slow him up at Immigration," Crawford said softly.

"Unless he's gotten himself a French passport," Hollis said. "Unlikely, but we can't rule that out."

Crawford nodded as he picked up the secure phone. Seconds later he was talking to Reed, who had taken Wally's place as second in command of the Paris team. He outlined the developments and the game plan and ordered Reed to scramble the team to de Gaulle.

"Weapons?" Hollis asked as they hurried out of the apartment.

"Too risky. We'll use this on him." He sidestepped into the bathroom and came out holding a plastic syringe filled with a colorless fluid. "This, and the decoy move."

He explained the rest in the elevator as they descended to the garage.

Hollis ran past the Mercedes, ducked into the next stall, and tossed Crawford a motorcycle helmet. "The Ducati will get us through traffic a lot faster. You drive."

LUNCH-HOUR GRIDLOCK was in full force in central Paris. Crawford called on all of his skills to guide the Ducati through the congested streets, running red lights, cutting off cars. Behind him, Hollis clung tightly to his waist.

As soon as they were on the highway, Crawford opened up the motorcycle. He slipped behind a speeding BMW and used it as cover, hoping that if there were speed traps along the way, the Beemer would be the first blip on a cop's radar.

Fifty-one minutes after receiving the call from Jacoby, they roared into the parking lot nearest the Air France international terminal. Hollis imagined the Handyman standing somewhere in a line of hundreds of people, inching his way toward an Immigration booth.

"Why is he back, Sam?" she asked, staying close to him as they jogged across the pedestrian walkway and stepped onto an escalator to the arrivals level.

"I've been trying to figure that out," he said in a low voice, hurrying her along to the arrivals waiting area. "I don't understand it. He made it out of New Jersey free and clear. Safe to assume he's been hiding out in Florida since then—smart choice on his part, what with all the tourists and that French-Canadian community. He's had enough time to reactivate old contacts, get money, new papers—whatever he needs." Crawford paused. "Then he should have hightailed it to the other side of the world, to Southeast Asia, a place he knows, where he can find work. There's nothing for him here."

"There must be!" Hollis said fiercely over the din of the crowded arrivals hall.

More than two hundred people of different nationalities were milling around in the hall. Behind the barriers that separated the hall from the Customs area, hidden by frosted-glass doors, were lines ten deep. Every time the doors opened, one or two shouts could be heard above the din.

Security wasn't as tight here as in the departures area, but Hollis caught a glimpse of machine-gun-toting paramilitary guards. Crawford had been right: Using weapons would have been insane. But if they could spot the Handyman, throw him the lure, and get him to snap at it, they'd get close enough for Crawford to do his work with the syringe.

Hollis scanned the perimeter of the hall. She spotted Reed and the other members of the team already in position. Through the glass exit doors she saw the van that would be used to transport the Handyman out of the airport to a safe house in the suburbs.

Hollis looked at Crawford, who nodded, then moved away. She edged her way through the crowd, closer to the Customs doors, positioning herself so that the Handyman couldn't help but spot her when he came through.

I'm the bait, you son of a bitch. Irresistible. You'll see me even though I won't be looking right at you. You'll know that I'm here for you, that this isn't a coincidence. That if I'm here, so are others. You'll know you can't run. Your best bet is to get close to me, take me and use me as a shield . . .

That was the decoy move.

And there came the Handyman.

There was a deep Florida tan on his face and hands. His appearance was different: He'd visited a hair stylist and a good men's clothing store. The blazer, chocolate brown slacks, and polished black loafers made him look like a prosperous retiree.

The mustache and goatee were nice touches but not enough to disguise his face.

Even if they had been enough, the Handyman's tiny concession to vanity would have given him away: the ring on the third finger of his left hand. Hollis glanced at Crawford and was about to signal him when she realized that he'd already picked out the target. She moved from behind a pair of Arab women wearing the veil and showed herself.

He was scanning the anxious, welcoming faces and saw her immediately. Hollis was already turning away from him when she felt his eyes bore into her. *Blue tinted contacts.* With her peripheral vision, she saw him shoulder his way through the crowd toward her.

Keep coming, Hollis thought, slipping around frantic lovers, mothers carrying babies on the hip, bored children teasing one another underfoot. She was headed for the exit door, casually glancing about the crowd as though looking for someone. The Handyman was following, closing the distance.

She was almost through the crowd when the thought struck her: *Why didn't you have plastic surgery before coming back here?*

The Handyman had gone to ground for over seven months—plenty of time to recuperate from multiple facial operations. And in Miami, with its drug economy, he could easily have found a surgeon who would have done the work and kept quiet about it. Or been silenced forever.

Why *not* do it?

Hollis had cleared the crowd. She walked casually through the relatively open area between the people behind her and the doors ahead. She saw the van pull forward. Reed drifted in from the right. In a glass-encased ad, she saw the Handyman's reflection. And Crawford closing in. All she had to do was continue to the doors. Crawford, Reed, and the others would do the rest.

Instead, she whirled around.

The Handyman should have started, maybe broken and run. At the very least, there should have been some recognition of this woman who'd suddenly confronted him, a woman he'd been ready to kill without the slightest compunction.

Instead, after the initial surprise at her sudden move, he smiled and approached her as though he recognized her.

Because he wasn't the Handyman. Not up close.

Fighting the sick feeling in her stomach, Hollis gestured to Crawford, who was within three feet of the stranger. In his hand Hollis saw the plastic sheathed syringe.

"Miss Fremont?"

He's American . . .

"It's not him!" Hollis called to Crawford. "*Goddamn it, it's not him!* He decoyed *us!*"

She saw Crawford step over to Reed, whisper, and send him on his way. She knew the rest of the team would now scatter across the arrivals level in the hope of spotting the Handyman.

The vain hope.

"You *are* Hollis Fremont, aren't you?"

The man held a business card. "Bill Press, Worldwide Courier Services."

"Courier . . ."

Hollis turned to Crawford, who never took his eyes off the man.

"Just what are you delivering, Mr. Press?"

He removed a small package from his pocket and was about to hand it to her when Crawford stepped between them. "I'll take that."

"Who exactly are you, Mr. Press?" Hollis demanded.

"I work for WCS," he explained easily. "You know, one of those courier services—you see their ads in the travel section of weekend newspapers."

"And you carry . . . ?"

"Usually business documents that have to be at a certain place by a certain time. The client calls WCS, gives them the details, the company calls me, and I'm on my way. The client picks up the airfare and the standard charge, and I get a free trip to wherever."

Hollis did her best to hold back her frustration. "Are you from Miami, Mr. Press?"

"Good heavens, no. L.A. born and raised. I'm a retired aerospace engineer, a widower, so I have plenty of time on my hands."

"But this flight originated in Miami."

"It's a strange run," Press admitted. "I always get the Asian jobs—Hong Kong, Singapore, Bangkok. Apparently this was a special request. The client asked for me specifically."

"Really?" Hollis said softly. "Why would he do that?" Though she already knew.

"No idea. The company said he picked me, paid a premium, too. Mind you, I do have a reputation in the business . . . "

"Do you know the client?" Hollis cut in. "Have you ever met him?"

"Nope."

"Then how could he have picked you?"

"WCS has my record in their computers."

Hollis nodded. She saw it all now: The Handyman availing himself of WCS's Web site, hacking its computers, scanning its personnel records, which would include a photograph of each courier. Searching, searching, searching until he found someone who could be mistaken for him, if only for a few seconds.

Hollis wondered how many courier companies the Handyman had gone through. *As many as necessary.*

"That ring, Mr. Press," she said quietly. "It doesn't belong to you."

Press shifted uncomfortably. "I told you this was an unusual deal. The ring was sent to me Federal Express. The note said I was to wear it because you'd recognize it."

"The mustache and goatee?"

"I was to grow those. Apparently to help you identify me."

"And you didn't think that strange?"

"Ma'am, I was getting a triple fee, plus a first-class ticket good for a year. I'd have worn a dress if that's what the guy wanted." Press hesitated. "Well, maybe not a dress."

Hollis looked at Press carefully. He bore a striking resemblance to the Handyman, but without the mustache and goatee she would have spotted the difference. As it was, she'd seen what the Handyman had wanted her to see. The ring had been the final touch.

"Look, I don't know what's going on," Press said. "I don't carry contraband or drugs—"

"I'm sure you don't." Crawford spoke up.

Hollis glanced at him, saw that he had opened the package.

"What is it, Sam?"

He handed her a slim, black velvet jewelry box. "It's safe. You can open it."

Hollis's fingers trembled as she pulled open the lid. She knew what it was.

Nestled in satin was the cameo Paul McGann had given her the day she'd left Paris with the Handyman. She turned it over, saw that the back had been sealed. The inscription was still there: *This is forever.*

The Handyman was cleaning up after Wylie and the warehouse shooting, keeping a memento for just the right occasion.

"Looks real pretty," Press offered. "Old, expensive."

Hollis looked at Crawford. "He's back, and we've missed him. He wants us to know it."

OUTSIDE THE TERMINAL, in the melee of families hauling suitcases and shouldering boxes, there walked an elderly cleric, dressed in black pants and shirt with a Roman collar. A simple stainless steel crucifix moved side to side across his chest in keeping with his short, measured steps.

He moved past the taxi stand to a private car, a Citroën, idling at the curb. When he opened the passenger door, Tessier said, "Bless me, Father, for I have sinned."

"Be careful what you mock, my son," the Handyman advised him.

Tessier laughed. "It went exactly as you thought it would."

"Didn't it though?" the Handyman murmured.

The Handyman had watched the entire interception operation as it had taken place in the arrivals area. Crawford had positioned his team just so; Hollis Fremont had played the role he'd expected she'd get perfectly. Right up to the point where she zeroed in on the courier and stayed with him. Allowing the Handyman to glide right past her.

His only regret was not being able to see her expression when she opened his gift to her.

"We should go now," he said. "People are waiting."

Tessier grunted, jammed a cigarette into the corner of his mouth, and slipped the car into gear.

People *were* waiting: his boss, the French representative of Wylie's shadow Omega, along with peers from across Europe and Asia. Though Wylie was dead, the organization he had founded would continue. Like the U.S. presidency, it was an institution that transcended any one individual.

Tessier smiled as he inched into traffic. In a way, he wished McGann were still alive, just to see how far Tessier had come. Tessier might even have bought him a drink because it was his association with McGann that had brought him into the dead man's secret world.

Now Tessier worked for the same masters. It was he who had run the ad in the *International Herald Tribune* in December—"Handyman wanted"—and then flown to Miami with instructions. The face-to-face meeting had been necessary, not only to accurately convey details, but to establish a working rapport. The Handyman's next job would be in France, and Tessier had been assigned as point man. He had been reminded of McGann's failure in that role and vowed to himself that such a thing would never happen on his watch.

"There she is," Tessier said.

The Handyman glanced out the window, saw Hollis Fremont standing on the crowded sidewalk. He could almost taste her frustration and loss.

"You could take her—or both of them—when you've finished," Tessier suggested.

"When I finish, it will mean that they failed to stop me," the Handyman replied. "No need to press."

Tessier shrugged. *He* wouldn't leave loose ends like that.

The Handyman appreciated that Tessier did not understand him. Fine. The detective was not privy to Fat Lee's horoscopes. The warnings were very clear: Stay clear of the girl and the man, and success in a future undertaking is assured.

Later, there would be time to recast the forces and seize the stars, time to ponder and, if necessary, deal with this remarkable young woman whose destiny seemed to cleave to his.

CRAWFORD FOUND HER outside on the observation deck, watching the planes take off and land. There were only a few other people around, fathers with young sons, pointing out different aircraft.

Downstairs, he had let her go. Searching the terminal, let alone the airport, for the Handyman would have been a waste of time. He was gone, leaving nothing behind. They would pick up the trail at Miami airport, starting with the passenger manifest. Crawford had already spoken with Jacoby and gotten him started. Long days and nights lay ahead.

He thought she looked all right, the wind blowing through her hair, her eyes clear, fixed on some invisible point in the distance. When she spoke, her voice was steady.

"He has a job here, Sam."

"Yes."

"Probably not in Paris, but somewhere in France."

"We're getting a schedule of all the political conferences and meetings. It'll take a while."

She turned to him. "Do you think he *wants* us to catch him? Is that why he sent me the cameo?"

"He wants you to know he's still thinking about you. You're the closest anyone's ever come to bringing him down."

"When Paul gave me the cameo, he betrayed me," Hollis said.

She pulled it out of her pocket, pried open the sealed back with the blade of a Swiss army knife, and held it up for Crawford to see.

"Empty," she said. "He's telling me it can be over between us. He's offering a truce."

Crawford watched her press the cameo back together, saw the memories of that long-ago summer afternoon spill across her eyes.

"I can't accept what he's offering. It's something I won't ever give him."

She looked at her husband. "Let's go find him."